GREEN
&
DEADLY
THINGS

BY JENN LYONS

The Sky on Fire
Green & Deadly Things

A CHORUS OF DRAGONS

The Ruin of Kings

The Name of All Things

The Memory of Souls

The House of Always

The Discord of Gods

JENN LYONS

GREEN & DEADLY THINGS

TOR

First published 2026 by Tom Doherty Associates / Tor Publishing Group

First published in the UK 2026 by Tor
an imprint of Pan Macmillan
The Smithson, 6 Briset Street, London EC1M 5NR
EU representative: Macmillan Publishers Ireland Ltd, 1st Floor,
The Liffey Trust Centre, 117–126 Sheriff Street Upper,
Dublin 1 D01 YC43
Associated companies throughout the world

ISBN 978-1-0350-4862-5 HB
ISBN 978-1-0350-4863-2 TPB

Copyright © Jenn Lyons 2026

The right of Jenn Lyons to be identified as the
author of this work has been asserted in accordance
with the Copyright, Designs and Patents Act 1988.

All rights reserved. No part of this publication may be reproduced,
stored in a retrieval system, or transmitted, in any form, or by any means
(including, without limitation, electronic, mechanical, photocopying, recording
or otherwise) without the prior written permission of the publisher.

Pan Macmillan does not have any control over, or any responsibility for,
any author or third-party websites (including, without limitation, URLs,
emails and QR codes) referred to in or on this book.

1 3 5 7 9 8 6 4 2

A CIP catalogue record for this book is available from the British Library.

Map by Jenn Lyons

Printed and bound in the UK using 100% Renewable Electricity by CPI Group (UK) Ltd

This book is sold subject to the condition that it shall not, by way of
trade or otherwise, be lent, hired out, or otherwise circulated without
the publisher's prior consent in any form of binding or cover other than
that in which it is published and without a similar condition including this
condition being imposed on the subsequent purchaser. The publisher does not
authorize the use or reproduction of any part of this book in any manner
for the purpose of training artificial intelligence technologies or systems.
The publisher expressly reserves this book from the Text and Data Mining
exception in accordance with Article 4(3) of the European Union
Digital Single Market Directive 2019/790.

Visit www.panmacmillan.com to read more about all our books
and to buy them.

*For Chris.
I don't know
what I would've done
without you.*

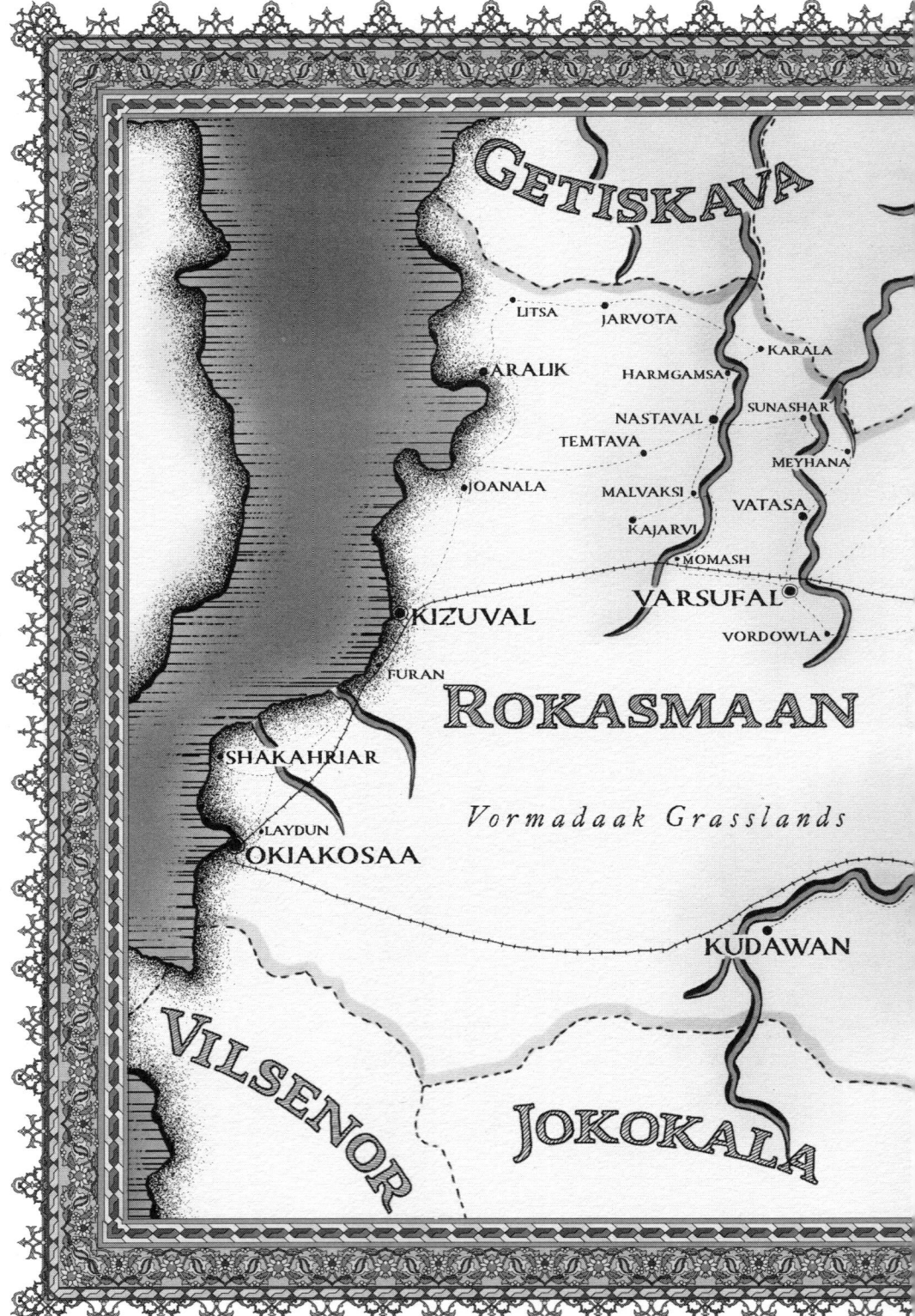

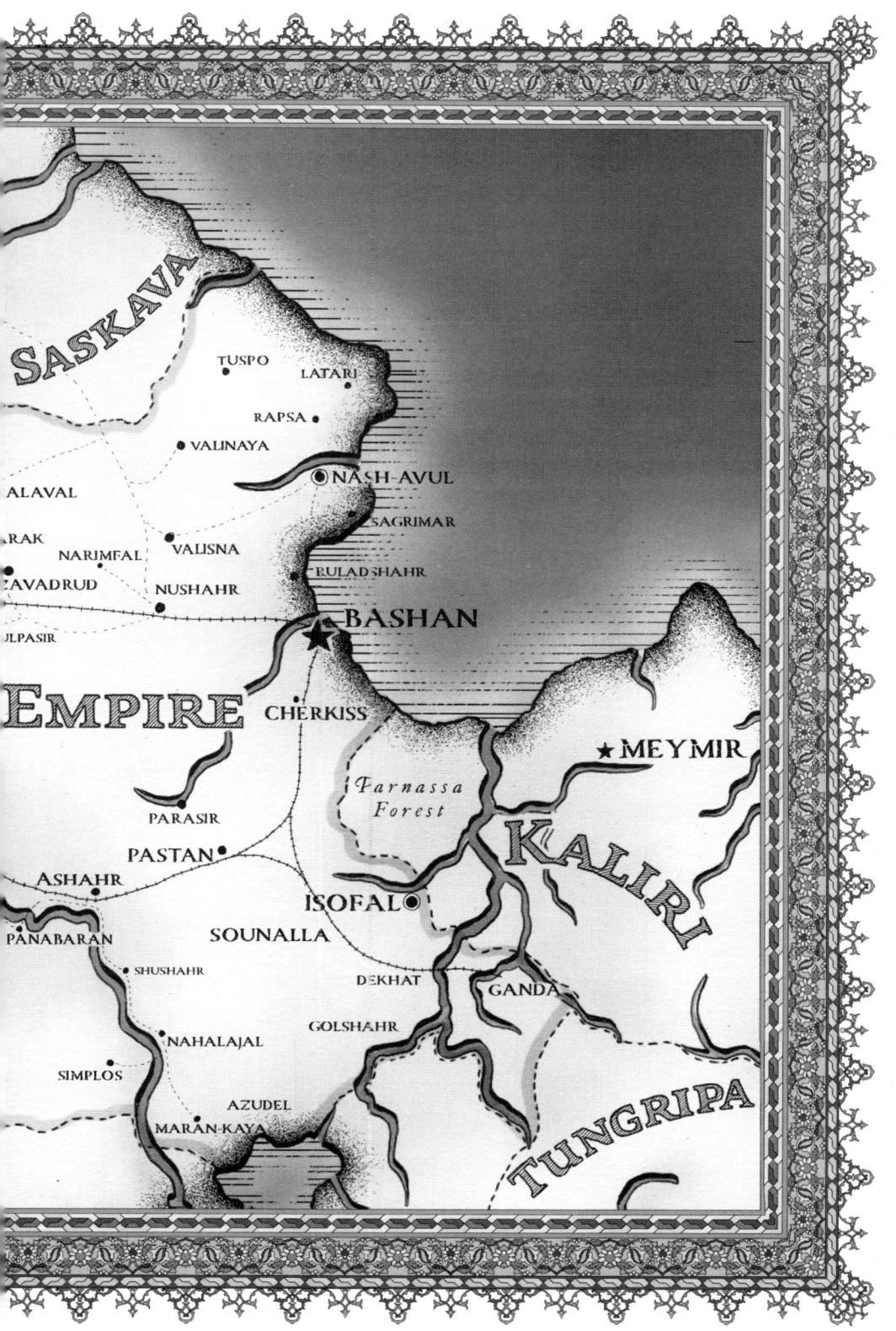

GREEN & DEADLY THINGS

PROLOGUE

We know who woke the Queens.
His name was Catimus Abhigan. He was neither knight nor king, wizard nor priest, but rather, an unremarkable manager of middling talent and minor ability, assigned to Kegomar Lumber Company's most remote logging camp in the Parnassa Forest.

He likely believed he'd do some good there, for a definition of "good" that included words like "efficiency," "quotas," and "profits." Some have claimed he was blameless, a hapless man in the wrong place at the wrong time, with no role in later events.

This is untrue.

Claims that it took him but a single day to ignite the catastrophe that followed are also untrue.

He accomplished *that* in under thirty minutes.

From the moment Catimus Abhigan stepped down from the carriage, gazing at the Parnassa Logging Camp's primary work site, he knew he would make great changes.

The base camp, for one thing—it was too far away. The crew had to walk a mile every morning to reach this work site from their camp. And that logging camp! Practically a permanent residence, wasting valuable timber on a thick palisade around the camp's perimeter. The extravagance continued with a bombard field around those same walls, only safely navigable by a narrow corridor.

Honestly.

Little wonder they lagged on fulfilling their quota. All quite ridiculous. He read the papers, littered with stories of grimmocks and black magic. One would think the country was all but overrun!

Abhigan was too smart to be fooled by such sensationalism.

How had these people ever managed without him? Abhigan studied the work site, noting inefficiency, indolence, sluggishness. So much to whip into shape.

His stare stopped at the ragged, uneven tree line. Three pristine trees rested atop a gently sloped hill. Magnificent specimens. Each one towered over the trees they'd already felled.

So why . . . ?

"Why are those trees still standing?" Abhigan pointed the trees out to the first lumberjack unfortunate enough to catch his eye.

The crew knew Kegomar had sent Abhigan to ensure they met their deadlines. They knew he was the kind of hatchet man who had nothing to do with lumber.

He expected an answer, but instead he was met with open disbelief.

"Those are the Three Queens," the logger explained—and then said nothing more.

Abhigan couldn't guess the old lumberjack's age. The man had been left outside too long, his dry, brittle skin weathered to the texture of autumn leaves. Deep folds of skin cloaked the man's eyes in shadows.

Those eyes judged him. Abhigan didn't like it.

"Pft," Abhigan scoffed. "I don't care if they're three grim lords. You doughheads named them? Like they're pets? Did you make them crowns and throw tea parties for them, too?" He flapped one arm toward the trees. "I want those trees down and loaded on a wagon by the end of the day. Do you have any idea what's going to happen if we don't have enough wood to satisfy this commission?"

Nothing good. Maybe these men didn't think it mattered if Kegomar couldn't provide enough wood for the empire's quincentenary. They damn well would if Kegomar lost its license because the governor felt embarrassed by his inability to keep up with the regent's demands.

The old lumberjack ran his tongue over his teeth like he was hunting for the last scraps from lunch. His eyes remained fixed on Abhigan's face, his expression blank. He might've been thinking about anything.

"Did you hear me?" Abhigan demanded.

"Ganner . . ." Another lumberjack, younger and more cautious, put a hand on the older man's arm. Ganner shrugged it off.

"I heard ya." Ganner crossed his arms over his chest. "And I won't do it." His gaze swept over the crowd, a warning or a dare.

"They're trees," Abhigan told him. "It's not like they're grimmocks. I checked with the Idallik Knights before I arrived. There's no 'necromancy' here." He didn't hide his contempt at the idea of "black magic" and "curses."

A grimmock had terrorized Catimus Abhigan's neighborhood once, when he was a child. He never saw it himself, but he heard the stories, each worse than the last. How the twisted mockery with two heads and four sets of jaws and scales must have been a dog before it succumbed to a curse. He always thought the stories were exaggerated. Dogs attacked children all the time—because they turned rabid.

Anyway, he'd never heard of tree grimmocks.

Ganner leaned over and spit a glob of pomuv juice, which landed close enough to Abhigan's polished leather boots to seem purposeful. "I won't touch a leaf on the Queens. If you've got even a lick of sense, you won't, either."

"You're fired! Do you hear me? You're fired! I want you off this land right now. And don't expect to be paid!" Abhigan was angrier than he could ever remember. How dare he? The look Ganner spared him wasn't hatred or anger, but a sad, weary contempt.

"Figured as much." Ganner began walking. He wasn't even walking back to the logging camp, just . . . away.

Good riddance.

Abhigan turned to the gathered crowd. He drew himself up, and bellowed, "Back to work. I want those three damn trees cut down! Grab your saws and go!"

Matters didn't resolve themselves so quickly, naturally. Tree cutting was a slow business. He paced and waited and cast angry glares in the direction of the camp. He might have been safely sequestered with a nice cup of tea, if only that lazy bastard hadn't made such a fuss. If only the camp itself were closer. He finally tracked down a folding table, complete with several pots of stale coffee.

Honestly, the trees were strange. He poured himself a cup of coffee as he contemplated the tree line. This section of the Parnassa Forest hadn't been considered old growth for over a century. And yet, those three trees had been left alone—not just by superstitious villagers, but by Kegomar Lumber.

Abhigan checked his papers again for any declarations, proclamations, or writs of protection. That would've been a hell of a thing to have missed. He had no desire to deal with angry Triunist priests, upset because he desecrated some holy landmark where one of the Tri-Mother's sainted children had carved their initials into the bark.

He chuckled and was taking another sip of terrible coffee when he heard the first scream.

Abhigan startled, scanned the area. He hadn't heard a tree fall, just the steady grind of saws drawn across wood. Perhaps someone had slipped? Accidents happened.

"What's going on?" he shouted. "Who's been—?"

Something red and wet crashed into the folding table, smashing it to the ground. At first, Abhigan didn't understand what he was seeing. Viscera? A wild-animal carcass? Then he noticed the glint of a silver buckle, the ragged, twisted strips of sturdy twill, the creased leather.

Deer didn't wear boots.

Recognition lanced through him, painful and bowel-clenching. These were the remains of a lumberjack.

Something had ... something had ripped the man open, face to feet, and then tossed him aside.

The screaming hadn't stopped.

Abhigan stared up, wide-eyed. Why hadn't the screaming stopped? He glanced toward the Three Queens ...

They were gone.

Not even a stump marked where trees had once stood. There was blood, though. Enough blood to coat the hillside slick with crimson, streams of it flowing around twisted, misshapen bundles of white, yellow, and—

"Run!" someone screamed. "Grimmocks! Run!"

The grimmocks came out of the forest.

No. The grimmocks *were* the forest.

"Grimmocks can't ... can't be ..." The trees were alive. Moving. Attacking. The wind didn't blow through the branches; the branches moved of their own volition. No eyes. No faces. They still looked like trees, but trees uprooted, now gliding downhill toward the lumberjacks on roots turned sinuous and tentacular.

"Back to camp!" he screamed out. "Retreat to camp!"

Catimus Abhigan ran to the carriage, praying his driver had been too lazy to unhitch the horse.

"Sir? What's going—" The driver sounded groggy, as if he'd woken from a nap.

"Drive, you fool!" Abhigan screamed, pulling himself into the carriage's open back. "Back to the camp! Grimmocks are attacking!"

The man needed no further explanation, although the sound of screams and men running for their lives added to Abhigan's delivery. His driver cracked the whip and set the nervous horse to a gallop so quickly Abhigan fell backward into his seat. The horses were still tired, however, so the gallop reverted to a trot after a few hundred feet.

Halfway to the logging camp, Abhigan jumped forward and grabbed his driver's arm. "The flags, you fool! Pay attention to the warning flags! There's a bombard field!"

"Thank the Tri-Mother," his driver yelled, and began searching for the safety flags.

The man was right. Thank the Tri-Mother, indeed. The palisade, the bombard field—all designed to stop grimmock attacks. He prayed the camp had messenger birds too; Isofal wasn't so far distant. As long as they could lock the gates, they could hold out until the knights arrived.

When they reached the camp, Abhigan shouted, "Grimmocks are attacking! Get ready to shut the gate."

A camp guard gaped at him. "Wh-where? Where's everyone else?"

"Running," Abhigan snapped. "They'll arrive soon."

Hopefully. Assuming they ran faster than the trees.

Should he have tried to bring any lumberjacks with him on the carriage? He dismissed the idea. A one-horse carriage couldn't hold more than the driver and one or two passengers. If he'd waited, too many would've wanted to ride. They would've overwhelmed its weight tolerance. No one would have escaped.

For an eternity of seconds, they waited. Then a thin trail of dust billowed as lumberjacks retreated from the logging site. They weren't making any noise beyond their ragged breathing and the heavy stomp of their boots. They had no breath for shouting.

Beyond them, other things moved in the distance. Things that weren't human.

"Run!" one guard screamed. "Hurry!"

When the largest group made it through the gates, the guards began to shut the doors. "Barig's still out there!" someone screamed.

"Close it now," Abhigan ordered. "They won't make it in time!"

There was no other option. Abhigan found himself almost glad when the trees caught the men before they'd reached the safe passage through the field. Had it been otherwise, they might've revealed the safe route, would've . . .

Wait. What was he saying? These were grimmocks. They weren't intelligent. Grimmocks were cursed creations of black sorcery. They couldn't *think*.

He flinched and looked away when the men screamed. He tried to stop his ears to the sound of tearing flesh and breaking limbs. A sharp thunk sounded as the lumberjacks finally closed the gate.

They'd left it open, even when he'd ordered otherwise.

He wanted to yell at them, but at least the gate was shut. The grimmocks hadn't made it inside. They were safe.

Except he didn't feel safe. He peered over the palisade and saw the monsters, really saw them, for the first time.

They were trees. Regular trees. Just trees that somehow could move the way trees never moved and couldn't move and this couldn't be happening . . .

The sun shone, a light breeze blew. There wasn't a cloud anywhere in the sky.

Thunder echoed, though. Oh yes, thunder sounded the first time a monster staggered into the bombard field. The men, Abhigan included, covered their ears against the strength of that boom. An enormous pile of dirt and splintered wood flew into the air. When the ringing subsided, the men were cheering.

Then they stopped. There had been exactly one explosion, and no more after.

Abhigan turned back to see what the trees were doing.

Nothing. Nothing at all. It was as though the forest had always started just beyond the bombard field. Then the branches moved. There was a sense of . . . undulation. But nothing entered the field; the trees slid to the side.

Another tree moved into that open space.

Only, not any tree. From its size and shape, Abhigan felt certain this was one of the big trees he'd ordered cut down—one of the "Three Queens." It was an oak tree, albeit an oak tree strangely red along its lower trunk and roots.

Oh. No, that was blood.

No one made a sound. Then one man said, loudly, "Is that . . . is that a woman?"

It was. And it wasn't. It felt like someone had set multiple paintings in front of Abhigan's eyes, again and again. Tree. Woman. Tree. Woman. Tree. Woman—

The Queen of Oaks was a woman and yet still a tree. She had no hair but branches that sprouted from her head like antlers, and no clothing save for the suggestion of different thicknesses of bark and leaves and vegetal matter. Her skin, too, seemed less skin than smooth bark, and if she had legs at all, he couldn't see them. There was just the trunk and roots, joined smoothly to her hips. More branches that seemed like arms, raised up.

She had a face and lips and, most terrifyingly, eyes.

Those eyes focused on the palisades, the camp, on the bombard field encircling it. Intelligent, aware eyes.

She turned her face to the sky; the wind pulling at her leaves strengthened. A second thunderclap rocked through the air, but farther away.

Clouds scuttled across the sky, faster than any Abhigan had ever seen before. Dark gray storm clouds moved to cover the sun like a curtain drawn over a window. That fast, that unnatural.

Grimmocks couldn't think. Grimmocks couldn't cast spells.

It began to rain.

Abhigan shouted: "Have we sent out the messenger birds? We must send word to the knights!"

The tree woman could summon rain. But, so what? The palisade walls protected them. The camp had a lightning rod. If she tried to overrun their position, she'd run into the bombard traps, wouldn't she? Everyone would shelter in the permanent buildings—the kitchen or the woodshed—and wait until the knights arrived.

Everything would be fine.

Abhigan was so busy reassuring himself that everything would be fine, he missed whether anyone had answered his question about the birds.

Maybe they didn't have birds. He hadn't checked, had he?

No. They must have birds. The company was paying the knights for a location sign. They had to be. Kegomar ... the company hadn't canceled that to save costs, had they?

Had he decried that as an unnecessary expense?

Someone whimpered. He whipped around in case that heralded some fresh horror, but it was just ... it was just everything that had already happened. The men were catching their breaths. That was all the opportunity fear needed to sink in its claws. For himself, he was ...

It all seemed distant. Unreal. Like a dream.

He wanted to wake up.

It began to hail.

Small at first, but the hailstones grew larger by the second.

Abhigan dashed for cover even as a lumberjack screamed for everyone else to do the same. Ice the size of cherries, of plums, hit him on the arms, on the side of his head, before he reached shelter. The wood roof overhead shuddered, the ice a barrage, like cannon fire ...

Catimus Abhigan turned white when the first boom echoed, when he realized what it meant.

He'd been wrong. Again, he'd been wrong: the trees had summoned hail to clear the bombard field.

Once every explosive had triggered, once the field was scoured clean, only the wooden palisades would separate the men from the Queens and their monster forest.

It would be no protection.

Maybe if he begged. Maybe if he sank to his knees and begged for forgiveness ...

He could beg. He could do that.

Thunderous booms echoed all around them, so tightly spaced it all merged into one enormous, deafening roar.

Then nothing, except for the fading patter of hail and then ...

Silence.

No one moved as they listened to the sound of—no, it wasn't silence. It was the gentle sound of a forest in the wind, the susurrus of rustling leaves and shaking branches. Abhigan had always found that sound soothing, but not that day. Now the sound meant something else.

"What was that?" someone whispered.

Catimus Abhigan didn't listen for an answer. He already knew what that sound meant.

Death.

PENANCE

The plants choked Mathaiik awake.

Technically, it wasn't the first time the flora had dragged him out of a trance. It wasn't even the fifth, although Tri-Mother knew he tried to keep himself out of these situations. Still, it had happened: that time he'd camped too close to a grimmock den. Another when someone torched the barn he'd taken shelter in.

But this—this was worse.

It wasn't a subtle shift or ambient pressure tugging at his awareness. This was a violent yank on his hair, followed by the tightening grip of something cold and coiled around his neck. He couldn't breathe.

For half a second, he wondered if one of the children was playing a prank.

Then the vine pulled tighter.

He twisted, swearing, clawing at the pressure across his throat. It resisted. Broke. Fibers snapped like hair yanked by the root. His limbs felt heavy, sluggish—weighted down by thick foliage shackling him.

This wasn't a handful of vines. It was hundreds.

Whenever he moved more than a few inches, something pinched—sharp enough to make him hesitate. He must've looked like some grotesque offering, strung up on hooks. The pressure was invasive, horrifying—but it didn't hurt.

The pain would come when he broke free.

The oil lamps had burned out. His light spell had petered out, too. The only light came from the feeble rays of yellow-green flickering through a vine-choked window. The antechamber's damp air tasted green on Math's tongue.

This shouldn't have happened. Commander Talu should have woken him. Someone should have checked on him days ago, long before the plants staged a "rescue."

Math shuddered. This would hurt.

He braced himself, then pushed off against the stone ground, standing upright. Pain ripped through him from his scalp to his toes. He clenched his teeth.

He'd never been certain if the plants grew into his body or out of it. Neither idea held much appeal.

Standing disconnected braids of foliage that had slipped under his shirt, up his trouser legs, wrapped around wrists and ankles, arms and legs.

He both felt and heard ugly popping noises as younger, more sensitive sprouts wrenched free from the points where they rooted under his skin. He panted for breath, smelling green sap and red blood, both seeping from fresh wounds.

Then someone opened the door.

There was no time to hide, no place to hide. The maze itself was hidden away behind an old, sturdy, and (most of all) locked wrought-iron gate. A safeguard against the curious and foolish wandering inside, never to be seen again.

Mathaiik shielded his eyes as sunlight poured down the stone steps. The glare felt like an accusation, like being exposed.

"Mathaiik Kaven, are you down here? Do you have any idea how many of the library sections I've looked through—" Math's sister Tanxi paused just inside the doorway, her glowing Sun sword held out like an especially lethal lamp. "Tri-Mother protect me. What have you done?"

The knight slammed the ancient door shut behind her.

Math winced at what her light revealed. Plants were everywhere: on the floor, climbing up the walls, creeping across the ceiling. More plants than any of his previous "episodes." Vines covered every surface except one: they had scrupulously avoided all contact with the engraved labyrinth map etched into the largest wall.

Every vine ended at Math's feet, fallen where he'd wrenched them from his skin.

Tanxi stared at him, open-mouthed.

"I didn't do it on purpose."

"No?" Anger blazed in her dark eyes. "You realize that makes it worse, don't you? What's the difference between an Idallik Knight and a grim witch, Math?"

Some might think the question rhetorical. Math knew it wasn't.

He answered with a stubborn set to his jaw. "One masters the magic. The other lets it master them."

"And then what is the difference, dear brother, between a grim witch and a grimmock?"

Math rubbed at his arms, where he felt blood seeping into his shirt. "The grim witch curses. The grimmock is cursed."

Usually that curse took the shape of horrible fang and claw, but not always.

"Yes!" She swept the room with her sword arm, harsh light sending shadows skittering across the dying vines. "At least if you'd done it on purpose, it would mean you were in control. But this? Tell me this doesn't look like a man turning into a monster."

"I've been like this since I was five, Tan! If I'm becoming a grimmock, it's sure as bones taking its own sweet time about it, don't you think?"

"But it's never been this bad before!" She frowned, studying him. "Has it?"

He glanced up at the window, then over to the stone bas-relief map. At least he could console himself, knowing that he'd been right. "No, I couldn't wake up."

"Couldn't wake up? It's been *four days*."

That made him pause. Four days? He'd been locked in that trance for *four days*?

Why hadn't anyone checked on him?

"My mind was trapped, Tan. The plants must've . . ." His voice trailed off. He couldn't make himself say the words. *Saved him*. There were so many vines, though . . . far more than should've been necessary to wake him.

Except it hadn't been normal sleep, had it?

"Anyway, what's important right now is that I've made a discovery." He kneeled down and yanked away handfuls of plants until he found his satchel. He retrieved a small journal and a string-wrapped charcoal stick, flipped open the book, and compared his sketch with the map on the wall.

Tanxi frowned. "Why were you even down here? I thought you'd be in one of the libraries."

"Oh, come on, Tan. Putting me in front of the Order's library collections would hardly be a punishment, would it?"

She sighed. "No. Not for you."

"So Commander Talu stuck me down here. I guess he thought it would be so boring I'd have no choice but to 'meditate on my mistakes.' Except he was wrong about this room being *boring*." He pointed a triumphant finger at his book, then the wall. "It's changed. Tanxi, the map on the wall has changed—and I'm pretty sure it's because of me."

"What are you on about?" Tanxi's temper was close to combustion.

"We've been wrong about the purpose of this map! I couldn't—" He shook his pencil at the engraving. Permanently enchanted magical effects were so rare, the secret long lost. Nobody really knew how the Illuminated had crafted their repositories. The Order just protected what they'd left behind. "The bas relief looks like the solution to the maze, but it's a trap. A nasty magical trap. It's like the maze itself, except instead of being physically lost, I was mentally lost. *That* is why I couldn't wake up."

Math turned back to Tanxi. "You know, I think this might be *why* we're forbidden from coming down to the antechamber? I never understood why the antechamber was off-limits when the maze entrance was already locked. There's nothing here. Nothing but that carving. Except . . . that carving's enough, isn't it? People could die."

"People could die? *You* could die," Tanxi said through gritted teeth. "If the wrong person had walked through that door—"

"I'm not a grimmock," he protested.

"I *know* that." His sister dismissed her sword in a warm flash, instead circling a light spell. "But you must be more mindful of how this *looks*. You're too old to be excused as someone still growing into their powers."

Math raised a finger and grinned. "Ah! But I *am* still too weird. Remember Sir Oleriatt's helmet in the armory? The one no one else can wear because it had to be custom-fitted to make room for his *actual* bunny ears? Nobody called him a grimmock: he was too adorable. These are just little vines. They're not going to hurt anyone." He paused. "Except me, I suppose."

She scoffed. "Yesterday, everyone might have believed you."

He straightened. "What do you mean by that?"

"I mean it's plants," Tanxi hissed.

"Yes, I'm aware of that—"

"No. Not your plants." She waved off his retort with an edge of urgency. "Grimmock plants."

Math blinked. "That's not—" He didn't finish the sentence. The bottom dropped out of his stomach.

"That's why I came to fetch you," Tanxi said grimly. "There's been a grimmock attack. But this time . . . it took the form of vines. Living plants. Just like—" She gestured at the room, at the remnants still twitching in the aftermath of his escape. "Just like this."

His breath caught.

"The commander wants to see you. Immediately."

All expression drained from Math's face, his thoughts retreating behind a shutter of discipline. "You could have led with that."

"I was trying to."

He yanked his satchel free from the tangle of vegetal detritus, slipping book and waterskin inside with a practiced motion. Then he hesitated and looked back. "Should I destroy the rest?"

"I'll handle it," Tanxi said. Her light spell flared, illuminating every ridge of the engraved maze on the wall. "You go to the chapter house. Maybe . . . maybe wash up first."

He nodded once. "Thanks."

"You be *careful*," she warned. "This one's bad. They'll be watching you now. Harder than ever. We thought plants were safe."

He gave her a disbelieving look. "No, *you* thought plants were safe. And no one ever listens to me."

Four days, he'd been gone. The children were going to skin him alive.

Math hurried up the stairs, past the broken flagstone marking the antechamber entrance. The stone was carved with a single word, as it had been since before Math was born: —WISDOM.

CHANGE

Math didn't go to the chapter house—not yet. First, he had a stop to make. The dorms were supposed to be empty—novitiates in class, teachers distracted. A perfect window to change clothes, scrub off the worst of the grime, and maybe pretend he hadn't just spent days in a forbidden ruin.

The dorms *should* have been empty.

"Math!" a voice screamed as he tried to cross the main room. "You're back!" A few seconds later, a body collided with him. "Where *were* you? We looked everywhere for you!"

If that wasn't true, it was only because none of the children—or Master Wadera, for that matter—would've considered searching the off-limits maze antechamber.

"I was doing secret stuff," Math said. "But why aren't you in class?"

Jaiik was twelve and, like Math, had lived at Isofal Cenobium most of his life. He was small for his age, with dark brown skin and hair he wore braided in thin strips across his scalp. In a year or two, he might stop being adorably cute, but he hadn't reached that stage yet.

Jaiik stepped back and rolled his eyes. "I'm supposed to be, quote, 'meditating on my mistakes.'"

"Ah yes, the old 'meditate on your mistakes.'" Math nodded sagaciously. "I know it well."

"I don't understand why I should be punished. I wasn't the one who was being mean."

The young boy crossed his arms over his chest for emphasis, like an adorable little exclamation point.

Math paused. "Who was being mean?"

Jaiik avoided Math's gaze. "It doesn't matter," he said too quickly.

"Doesn't sound like it doesn't matter," Math responded.

Jaiik balanced on the edge of puberty. Just on the edge, too, of manifesting his weapon, always the hope amongst the novitiates. But Jaiik wasn't the normal sort of novitiate, even at Isofal, notorious for being the last place in the entire Order where one might find a normal novitiate.

"Did someone hurt you?" Math asked. "Just tell me who I have to kill."

"Math! You can't! You're still a novitiate!"

"That just means I can't manifest a weapon." *Yet*, even if it seemed less and less likely with each passing year. "It doesn't mean I can't use one."

Nobody messed with his kids.

Jaiik's expression turned even more stubborn. "Nobody hurt me," he insisted.

Math sighed. "Jaiik. What have we said about lying?"

The young boy paused. "Don't do it."

"Right," Math said. "Don't do it." Since he wasn't a complete hypocrite, he tacked on: "Unless it's important."

"Unless it's important." The boy grimaced. "Knight Huraiik didn't hit me. He said he was teasing, but he wouldn't stop calling me Jaya, even after I told him to stop. Said I was still a girl and that meant I was useless."

Math sighed. This again. "You told us who you are. That's all that matters. No one gets to take that from you." Math paused again. "What part about this is making you unhappy? That he said you're a girl? Or . . . are you having regrets?"

Jaiik narrowed his eyes. "No! Never. I'm a boy because that's what I want to be!"

That was the crux of the matter, of course. Technically speaking, what Jaiik had done verged on heresy—using magic to reshape one's own body wasn't precisely orthodox. But it hadn't hurt anyone, hadn't been done to anyone unwillingly, and most of all, had been done by Jaiik himself *intentionally*.

Intention was everything, in the Idallik Order. Once Jaiik manifested his weapon, there'd probably be a fight over which section would claim him. He had *potential*.

So had Math, once.

He tried not to think about it.

"Yes, we've noticed. I'm more concerned about what's going on up here, though." Math tapped the side of the boy's head.

Jaiik made a half-hearted attempt to dodge the motion. "I don't care what Huraiik calls me." The boy paused as he tried to find the right words. "It's just that he made it sound like being a girl is a bad thing. Like I should be ashamed. And Taris is my best friend and there's nothing wrong with her just because she's a girl. Never mind that she can kick my ass."

"Language," Math scolded from habit.

Jaiik ducked his head. "Sorry. Anyway, you understand what I mean, right? There's nothing wrong with her. So, there's nothing wrong with the idea that I used to be a girl, either. I'm just *not* one anymore."

"No, you're not." Math paused a moment. "Sounds like he deserves a lesson in manners."

"Don't."

Math put a hand to his chest. "Me? Oh, no. All I'll need to do is spread word he told you that girls are useless. Pretty sure there's a half dozen captains and lieutenants who will be more than happy to give him *that* lesson. My hands will be clean."

Jaiik laughed.

Math squinted. "So, Knight Huraiik said mean things to you and you're the one being punished?"

"Maybe . . . he said mean things and—" Jaiik made a face. "I maybe . . . kicked him in the balls."

"Ah, I see." Math tried very hard not to laugh. Given the proud twinkle in Jaiik's brown eyes, he didn't think he succeeded. "And how were you feeling when you did that?"

The boy screwed up his face. "Upset?"

"Did you let that show? Yell or cry?"

He drew himself up. "Nope."

Math mentally exhaled. "Good man. Remember: an Idallik Knight masters their emotions, not the other way around. So when this happens again, what are you going to do?"

Jaiik considered. His brow furrowed in mock seriousness. "Kick him harder?"

Math raised an eyebrow.

"That wasn't the right response, was it?" Jaiik said.

"I think you already know the answer to that," Math replied, although he wondered if maybe Jaiik had been spending too much time around the Sword section knights. "It's a matter of being true to yourself and respectful of others."

Jaiik studied him for a long moment. "You mean like how you insult people to their faces?"

Math decided to pretend he hadn't heard that. "Just remember that if you want to become an Idallik Knight, these are the people you're going to be relying on to watch your back in battle. So maybe getting into fights with them isn't the best idea."

"You and Lieutenant Nuhzar are always fighting, but you're always going on missions with him."

Sometimes Math really wished that the younger novitiates were a little less observant. "And am I a knight? No, I am not. So maybe you don't want to be like me, hm?"

Math's gaze flickered over to the door to the children's cribs. He didn't dare enter; Master Wadera was likely inside, and Math was pushing his luck as it was.

"You're back now, right?" Jaiik tugged on his sleeve, casual as a whisper. "Because the babies miss you a lot, and they're always complaining about it." Meaning Jaiik had missed him but didn't want to admit it.

Math placed a hand on the boy's shoulder. "I'll try to be back as quickly as I can, and I'll talk to Master Wadera about Knight Huraiik. But right now, I'm late, so I need to go. Remember, if Master Wadera asks where I am . . . ?"

Jaiik rolled his eyes. "Is this important?"

"Yes."

"Then I never saw you."

Math grinned at him. "Good man."

CAPTAINS

Math pushed open the chapter house door and squinted against the mage-light glare. Normally, the room was lit by candlelight. But during a captains' meeting, each captain summoned their own light, flooding the hall as bright as day.

Math silently cursed his sister as his eyes adjusted. She'd mentioned the commander. She'd neglected to mention the entire library's section captains were here.

Every single one of them.

"—sure it's not a prank?" someone was saying.

Conversation ceased. Sixteen people—Commander Talu, fourteen captains, and Lieutenant Nuhzar—turned to stare at him.

Math swallowed and bowed. "Commander, Captains, Lieutenant, please accept my apology for being late. Novitiate Mathaiik Kaven, reporting as ordered."

"Ordered by who?" Lieutenant Nuhzar growled. "This is a captains' meeting."

He stood inside the darker stone square in the floor where knights and petitioners received orders or judgment. In the lieutenant's case, the former. In Math's case, usually the latter.

"Commander Talu called for me, sir."

Murmurs shifted through the room as eyes turned toward the commander. Talu raised one imperious eyebrow.

"I did ask for Novitiate Kaven—over an hour ago."

Math bowed lower. "My apologies, Commander. I was meditating on my mistakes, as required for penance."

An elderly woman with a scrunched-up face and white hair pinned tight to her skull spoke loudly. "Penance? What's he done now? Wasn't that boy in trouble just last week?"

"I believe it was the same trouble, Captain Danvi," the man beside her offered.

Being scrutinized by the entire leadership of Isofal Cenobium was enough to break a sweat down Math's spine.

Captain Lilah of Mending frowned at him, then turned the same expression on the commander. "That was four days ago. He's been meditating four days? Uninterrupted? Do you need the healers?"

Math bowed his head. "Thank you, Captain, but I'm fine. If I'd gone four days without interruption, I doubt I'd be able to stand."

"Yes, but where *were* you?" Captain Jantu of Fields asked. "We looked everywhere."

Math didn't answer. He looked instead to Commander Talu, who met his gaze without blinking.

The leader of Isofal Cenobium was a man of sixty with the vitality of someone half his age. People spoke of him as if he'd been here since the grim lords ruled the world. His white hair and dark brown skin gave him a statuesque air, and his hawk-nosed profile might've been chiseled from granite. His sharp brown eyes missed nothing. His voice could cut through an army like a sword through a training dummy.

Talu had ordered his penance. Talu had known exactly where he was. And had said nothing.

Still said nothing.

The silence stretched. They were all waiting—expecting the familiar story of some minor infraction, some barely tolerated breach.

Fine. Math cleared his throat. "I was in the antechamber of the maze, Captain."

That did it. Fifteen voices rose at once. Noise swelled through the chamber like a struck drum.

Math found himself relieved he wasn't usually required to attend captains' meetings.

When the chaos ebbed, Captain Qin of Riddles stepped forward. "Who gave you permission to be in the antechamber? Novitiates are not allowed down there."

Novitiates weren't allowed down there. Monks weren't allowed down there. Knights weren't allowed down there.

Only two people could authorize access to the maze: Captain Qin, or . . .

"My apologies, Captain. I was under orders from Commander Talu."

Captain Qin turned to Talu. The commander raised an eyebrow and shrugged: *So what if he was?*

The rest of the captains took a careful step back.

"Commander," Captain Qin said after a taut pause. "I must protest."

"Noted, Captain. And overruled. Novitiate Kaven, your penance is officially over. Go stand in your place."

Math bowed and moved to the position just behind and to the right of Lieutenant Nuhzar.

"To return to the subject at hand," Commander Talu said, "no, I do not believe it's a prank. Kegomar Lumber has always maintained a serious mien. We must assume things have gone terribly wrong and treat it accordingly. You have your orders. May the Tri-Mother bless us all. Novitiate Kaven, stay behind. I would speak with you. Afterward, you will join Lieutenant Nuhzar's team."

If Math froze, it was nothing compared to Nuhzar's reaction.

"Commander? He's not a knight."

True enough. Most who failed to manifest by eighteen chose the monk's path, but there was no rule that said a novitiate had to stop trying to become a knight.

No rule—but plenty of pressure, silence, and looks just like the one Nuhzar was giving him now.

Commander Talu narrowed his eyes. "Yes, Lieutenant. I expect that hasn't changed in the last four days."

Lieutenant Nuhzar straightened. "Yes, Commander. But he's not—"

"You know we're under strength."

"He shouldn't be in the field."

Math clenched his fists behind his back. He had no choice but to stand still while they talked about him like he wasn't in the room.

"An opinion you've shared before, Lieutenant," Commander Talu said coldly. "Thank you."

"Quit while you're ahead, Alik," Captain Rabu cautioned.

Lieutenant Nuhzar's jaw clenched, but Rabu was his commanding officer. The lieutenant bowed. "Apologies, Commander. I'm only concerned for the mission's success."

"As am I." Talu's expression didn't thaw. "Which is why I want him to accompany you. He's the only person in this cenobium who's encountered anything like what you may face today."

"Yes, Commander."

Commander Talu made a small, sweeping gesture. "Then be off. Kaven will meet you in the stables and brief you en route."

"Yes, Commander." Lieutenant Nuhzar bowed again, spared a scathing look of contempt for Math, and stalked from the room.

Once the door closed and only the commander's mage-light remained to light the room, Talu said, "Come closer, lad."

QUEST

The commander forbade sitting during meetings—said it encouraged sloth and endless debate. Which was probably why he made straight for a chair the moment everyone else left.

A row of velvet-padded, high-backed chairs stood by the hearth—old enough to date back to the Age of Blood. Mathaiik ignored them. Commander Talu hadn't given *him* permission to sit.

Talu studied Math as he approached. "Sending you along with the others was not my original plan. Alik Nuhzar isn't wrong: you've no business being in the field on a job like this."

Math's throat tightened. "Yes, Commander. It's just . . ."

"It's just what?"

"I don't know what the mission is."

Talu chuckled lowly. "Of course. You missed the briefing. Your sister didn't tell you?"

He didn't want to throw her under the cart, but Commander Talu could sniff out a lie better than anyone. "Only that plants were involved, Commander."

"Aye," the old man agreed. "Plants are involved. This morning we received an alert by messenger bird that a local lumber camp had been attacked by 'plant grimmocks.' By the time we received the message and Captain Danvi scried the location, everyone at the scene was dead. It's not clear who or what was responsible. I'm dispatching Captains Rabu and Yihura with their people to find out what happened." He shook a finger at Math. "Your job is not to fight, but to provide information. If you cause Lieutenant Nuhzar any problems, he'll send you back home the long way."

Math shifted uncomfortably. He'd been at rigid attention ever since the commander had confirmed the plant grimmocks. "Commander. You know how important this is to me."

"I also know you still haven't manifested your resonant weapon. Elemental manifestation is one of *the* foundation stones of our order, and I'm supposed to let a novitiate who still hasn't mastered that fight beside knights?"

"You let me—"

"I sent you out on minor investigative cases because our backlog is overflowing and we don't have enough knights. Last week was not supposed to have put you up against grimmocks."

They weren't grimmocks, Math stopped himself from saying. He silently counted his breaths.

He'd learned long ago how often senior members of the Order said things just to test someone's self-control.

"When you came here, we all thought you'd be the next Vesgariik. That your knighthood was simply a question of time. And now . . ." The look in Talu's eyes was worse than anger. It was pity.

"Alik Nuhzar's report on your last mission is one of the most scathing pieces of writing it's ever been my displeasure to read. You must do better. Do I have to spell out just how thin the ice underneath you is?"

Math swallowed. "No, Commander."

"Now, as for earlier . . . you don't expect me to believe you were late because of your punishment, do you? You weren't meeting with a paramour, were you?"

All the blood rushed to Math's face. "I, uh . . . I don't . . ." He swallowed. "No, Commander. I am chaste as the Order demands."

Commander Talu rolled his eyes. "How quickly people forget that I, too, grew up in the Order and remember being young."

Math shifted. He preferred to think of Izhiik Talu as someone who'd never been sexually active in any capacity. "Yes, Commander."

"If not a paramour, then what? And in case you were curious," Commander Talu drawled, "this is the part where you volunteer an explanation."

Math cleared his throat. "Thank you, sir. I was late because I couldn't wake. I was caught in an enchanted trap." He bit his lip, debated how much to say. "We were wrong about the wall map of the antechamber, sir. It's not the safe route through the maze at all. Just the opposite."

Commander Talu leaned forward in his chair, firelight haloing his white hair. "Explain."

Math opened his journal to the right page and handed it over. "I sketched the map on the wall first. Then I tried a third-circle translation spell, which did nothing—"

"And has been tried many times before." The commander handed the journal back.

"Sure, because it's not language. So it came to me: What if I tried a seeing spell?"

Talu gave him a single, slow blink.

"I know what you're thinking, but it worked!"

"Compose yourself, Novitiate."

Math straightened. "Yes, sir."

"You used clairvoyance on an object right in front of you?" Talu frowned. "That's a fifth-circle Sky spell. You don't have the experience or skill to handle a spell of that rank."

"Is it? I didn't know. It didn't feel that hard . . . I just sort of figured it out."

Talu pursed his lips. "Do not do so again. It is too dangerous." He tilted his head, then gestured. "Continue."

"I triggered the map's enchantment. Which gave me a series of visions, each containing a choice between two options: life and death, violence and peace, things like that. Each time I chose, a new vision began. It went on like that until I . . ." Math's voice trailed off. "Well. Until I woke."

"And you endured this for four days?" Commander Talu's expression was inscrutable.

"No," Math lied quickly. "I just, um, no. I didn't figure out the seeing spell trick until yesterday."

Talu didn't react. Didn't call him out. Which meant either he believed it—or he knew, and chose not to press. That was almost worse.

"Ah."

"The important part, though, is that when I woke up, the map on the wall had *changed*." Math fought not to grin. "We've always assumed the bas relief showed the safe passage through the maze, but what if we have it backward? What if the map doesn't reflect the correct path through the maze—*it controls it*. You can only solve the maze if you first solve the map."

The commander looked poleaxed. "I never would have imagined . . . wait. Did you?"

"Did I what? Oh. Did I solve it? Tri-Mother, no. I wasn't even close."

There was a pause—long enough that Math wasn't sure if he should brace for rebuke or thanks.

The commander nodded thoughtfully. "I see." Then: "Still, it's excellent work. I would not, perhaps, tell anyone just yet, nor mention the unauthorized magic. No one has to know you were involved. I'll take it from here once the Captain of Riddles has calmed down."

"Captain Qin was pretty angry," Math agreed.

"Idallik Knights are never angry, only righteous," Commander Talu rebuked.

"Then I'd say he was feeling incredibly righteous, Commander."

The corner of Talu's mouth quirked. "Yes, I suppose he was. Now go. I trust you to behave appropriately. And hurry: I doubt Lieutenant Nuhzar would appreciate being forced to lag behind waiting for you."

VINES

Lieutenant Nuhzar was indeed waiting for him. His expression was placid, but Math knew better; that was just Alik's way of sneering.

"You shouldn't be coming with us," the knight said in lieu of greeting. He then threw a bundle straight at Math's head.

Math caught it with the ease of long practice.

"So you said ten minutes ago." Math glanced down at the bundle: his jazerant mail shirt, which was basically a chain shirt disguised as a padded jacket. Just the thing for going on missions where propriety demanded only full knights wore armor.

Math would've thanked the man, but Nuhzar had only done it to keep Math from delaying their departure.

"It's still true. You're not a knight. You're twenty-two years old and still a novitiate."

Math ignored him, at first. He headed to the stables, where the knights were readying to depart.

"You belong with the children, not out in the field. It's a disgrace."

Math swung back around. "Do you really want to start something right now? Think carefully before you get your ass handed to you by a *novitiate*."

"You are *not* a better fighter than me."

"Funny. You didn't say that two weeks ago when I dropped you in front of half the yard."

"How you do in a practice yard differs greatly from how you do in the field. Which we both know."

"We both know what happened last week had nothing to do with *fighting*."

"Calm yourself."

"Am I shouting?" Math narrowed his eyes. "I know you don't like me. That's fine: I feel exactly the same about you. But it doesn't matter. The commander gave us orders."

"Oh, so now you'll follow orders?"

Math tossed his jacket over on top of the rosebushes and then pushed hard at the center of Nuhzar's breastplate. The lieutenant took a step back to keep from sliding on the polished stone floor of the colonnade.

"Those were *children*!"

All around them, everyone stopped. Math stepped back, dropped his hands, stilled his expression into something less furious. Math could feel the judgment of a dozen knights pressing down on him—not for what he'd said, but for how he'd said it.

Idallik Knights master their emotions. They do not let their emotions master them. Jaiik had done a better job of hiding his anger.

The look on Nuhzar's face screamed how pleased he was by Math's faux pas. He straightened up, smoothed his tabard. "They weren't children," Nuhzar said in a far quieter volume. "They were grimmocks. And we have a duty when it comes to monsters: we eradicate them. Now, this time, follow orders, or I'll make damn sure you're punished by something a lot worse than *meditation*."

Nuhzar swanned off.

Math slipped into his chain shirt and had no choice but to follow.

Unsurprisingly, he was the last person. They'd even readied a horse for him, although not to do him any favors. Someone had instructed the grooms to find the sorriest nag in the whole stable, an old, spiteful mare named Calamity, who kept eyeing him like she hadn't decided whether he was edible.

Math's only consolation was that with so many captains watching, no one dared mess with his saddle or kit. Rabu's Sword knights certainly would have otherwise, and then claimed they'd had no choice but to leave Math behind when his horse faltered.

Nuhzar was the one exception. He would never.

That would have required Nuhzar breaking a rule.

As Math waited in queue, a rider and horse pulled up next to him.

"What form do you think the magic's going to take this time?"

Math glanced sideways, then glanced again when he realized who it was: Huraiik. "I don't suppose we'll be lucky enough to see velvet-lined carriages again."

"That never happened."

"Oh, it did." Math kept his attention focused forward. There would be little warning once they started moving, and little tolerance for anyone left behind. He did, however, tilt his head in the knight's direction. "I hear Jaiik won ball tag this week."

Huraiik barked out a laugh. "Little bastard hits like a rhinoceros."

"Which you deserved."

Huraiik's voice lost its cheeriness. "If he's going to be an Idallik Knight, he needs a thick skin. Wadera coddles his children too much. Just look at you."

Math's hands tightened on the reins, but he controlled his temper. Huraiik didn't get under his skin the way Alik Nuhzar did.

"What's *she* doing here?" Huraiik's question interrupted any cutting response Math might have delivered.

Math twisted in his saddle.

"She" was Captain Danvi of Idols, the captain who'd scried the logging campsite. The old woman made a querulous complaint as someone helped her up into a saddle.

". . . coming with us?" Because that did seem to be what was happening.

Huraiik scoffed. "She's as old as the cenobium! She can't go out into the field!"

"*She* can hear you, young man." Captain Danvi's high voice carried as she settled on her horse. "And I suggest that if you mind your own business, I'll do likewise."

Given that Captain Danvi was the most skilled scryer in the cenobium, that was a threat with teeth. Nobody liked the idea of a captain literally watching their every movement.

Huraiik blanched. "Yes, Captain." He lowered his helmet over his face like he was hiding from the nanny.

Math leaned over. "I take it back. *She* just won ball tag."

"Circles up," Captain Rabu called out. "We don't know what we're going to find. Be ready for anything."

All around him, Math heard quiet mutters as knights said sacred words and moved fingers, hands. Math did as well, although he had to start over when Huraiik kicked his leg, startling Calamity.

Huraiik laughed. "Oh, I'm sorry. I hope I didn't mess up your preparations for a family reunion."

Math gave the knight a thin smile. "Your insight into how families work is yet another example of our founders' wisdom in insisting on chastity."

"Wait—"

"Sir Huraiik, fall back. I'll be riding next to Novitiate Kaven."

"Yes, Lieutenant Nuhzar." Huraiik gave Math a mocking salute and pulled his horse out of line, while the Lieutenant of Swords took his place.

Nuhzar wasn't riding a nag. In fact, Nuhzar rode a gorgeous coal-black stallion who Math adored, although he'd sooner eat hot rocks than admit it. Or rather, Math adored everything about the horse but his name: Inquisitor. That had always struck him as a bit much.

"You can't miss me already," Math said.

"Everyone ready!" the Captain of Fields called out.

Nuhzar's reply was left hanging.

"Ride out!"

The entire group—horses, riders, and equipment—turned ghostly and translucent. When they began riding, the countryside blurred. Math suspected they would ride right through any travelers they overtook. The horses didn't spook at the radical change, part training but mostly magic.

Math discovered a problem, however: it was impossible to talk. Wind and the speed of the riders ripped away any noise before it could be deciphered. He tried briefing Nuhzar, but he might as well have been shouting into a storm. Nuhzar's attempts to shout back were as unsuccessful.

Fortunately, it didn't take long to reach the logging camp.

Math identified it initially by smell. The horses tossed their heads and flattened their ears.

Burned bombard powder, first of all, a sharp slash through the nostrils but not enough to cover the scent of blood or voided bowels. Underneath, almost undetectable, lingered green cut wood and spilled sap.

Save for the rustling wind in the trees, the only sounds were the ones they'd brought themselves: hooves against grass or mud, the tin-bell sound of metal against metal from shifting armor and tack.

Someone had set off the bombard field. Many someones, as there seemed to be no bombards remaining. Great rents gouged the earth where the explosions had done their best to rearrange the landscape. Rainwater from some recent, brief shower had filled the tiny craters, reflecting blue sky in shining flashes.

No one had to point out how unusual this was. When grimmocks annihilated themselves on a bombard field, they left behind a field capable of continuing to fend off attacks. These explosions had been total, so destructive that they'd toppled or shattered the heavy log palisade around the camp.

"Someone had a party." Captain Rabu laughed, and his knights laughed with him.

Captain Danvi of Idols did not laugh. She gazed at the scene with narrowed, sharp eyes. "This is not what I scried earlier," she declared from atop her horse. "The tree line has moved one hundred feet closer to the camp since this morning."

Everyone stopped laughing.

Captain Rabu motioned to his people. "Take positions. Stay alert. Captain Yihura, this is all yours."

Lieutenant Nuhzar turned to Math. "You've been through this before. What should we expect?"

Math's throat felt sticky. With great difficulty, he swallowed down the temptation to remind Alik Nuhzar that he'd been *five*. How much did they expect him to remember?

"They won't—" Math pressed his lips together. "They're not like normal grimmocks. They're ambushers. They'll attack from underground, from the branches. They'll lure you into traps, trip you, take advantage, then lure you into the next trap."

"You make them sound intelligent," Nuhzar said.

Math stared. Hadn't that been obvious?

"Novitiate Kaven, over here," Captain Yihura called.

Captain Yihura of the Forest was a tall, thin woman of the sort that encouraged people to make comparisons to willow trees. Math didn't see it, but he understood the appeal of the pun. Like Math, she had a Wood resonance, although in her case that magical facility was bent toward putting arrows through targets the size of flower petals at distances too far for most people to see. She could also put that same arrow through most trees.

Math dismounted, handing the reins of his grouchy horse to a knight, who would have refused if there weren't four captains and a lieutenant watching.

Captain Yihura motioned for Math to join her, and together they approached the tree line. Math forced himself to do so calmly, in spite of how uncomfortable he felt.

"Any thoughts, Novitiate?" Captain Yihura's gaze was clear and steady.

It was a test. Captain Yihura was one of the people who had hoped to add Math to her section, a hope that remained unfulfilled as long as he failed to manifest a weapon.

Math placed his palm flat against the tree trunk. "I don't see any sign of violence. No blood, no bodies." He studied the tree. "The trunk feels warmer than I would expect. Almost like . . ."

"Yes?"

"Like the tree has a pulse." The idea sent an icy shiver across his skin. The tree looked normal, but his every instinct screamed that was a lie. It would look normal right up until it didn't.

Captain Yihura startled at his comment. She set her hand next to his, just for a second, and then drew it back quickly as if she'd been burned.

"Stay away from the trees," she told the other knights. "Let's search the camp."

While she'd looked at the forest, the other knights set up a temporary picket for the horses. The cordon was just a few wooden stakes with rope strung between, but all the horses—even Calamity—had been trained from birth. They'd never wander off under normal circumstances.

The knights didn't remove the horses' bridles or saddles—just in case they needed to leave in a hurry. The horses would be brushed down later, when it was safe.

Everyone entered the logging camp.

Math swallowed bile. Few surfaces weren't painted with blood, now thick, black, and tacky. Sometimes, he didn't even realize he was looking at a body. Mostly, it was just parts of bodies. Globs of flesh left to cook in the sun. Clouds of flies drifted like black mists between piles of butchered flesh.

"This is . . ." Lieutenant Nuhzar's expression mirrored Math's for once—horrified, disgusted.

Somehow, none of the knights threw up. Possibly because this massacre was so far removed from anything identifiably human, it was easy to pretend it was something else.

Captain Rabu of Swords picked up a man's foot, still clad in a thick leather workman's boot, and tossed it to the side. "Hey, Novitiate."

Math raised his head. "Yes, Captain?"

"This how your family died?"

Math felt his whole body tighten. "No, Captain. They were strangled . . . and impaled."

The Captain of Swords grunted. "Kid-glove treatment. Weapons didn't cause this. Not even beast claws. They were pulled apart, but I've never seen wounds like this before."

Captain Yihura of Forests raised an eyebrow. "You've seen that many people dismembered, have you?"

"There was that giant grimmock out in East Castinion, remember? That thing was ripping limbs off with its bare hands." He shook his head, genuinely perplexed. "That's the thing. Dismembered would be normal. Disgusting, but normal. It's like tearing apart a chicken. The wings and the legs—the arms and the legs here—everything comes apart at the joints."

The Captain of Forests lifted her eyes to heaven. "Tri-Mother save me. You're saying these bodies weren't dismembered . . . ?" Her voice trailed off, as the knight captain more closely studied the remains.

"Yeah, that's right. I can't tell how they did it, what made them—" The captain made a breaking motion with his hands.

Math squatted down next to a fleshy mass, examining it with what Captain Rabu had just said in mind. Rabu might not be the smartest knight that had ever roamed the stacks, but he was good at his job, which was slaying grimmocks. If he said these deaths were even more abnormal than "dismembered" . . .

Math waved away flies as he identified someone's shoulder, an upper arm, a chunk of the chest, all of it poorly wrapped in the bloody remnants of wool broadcloth. He could see what Captain Rabu meant. The bones were *intact*. The upper arm bone was coated in congealed blood, unbroken and still attached to the shoulder socket. The soft tissues, the muscles on that upper arm: those had torn apart, too raggedly for saw or sword, too violently for something that had left the bone underneath pristine.

He hunted around until he found a splinter of palisade fence, and then used that to push aside the muscle fiber. No, it wasn't his imagination. Nothing had damaged the bone. What ripped apart muscle while leaving the bones whole? Mostly whole, anyway. Despite Captain Rabu's comment about joints, the bones on this arm had separated at the elbow, although he had no idea what had become of that arm, since it wasn't in the immediate vicinity.

He noticed a flash of green.

Math paused to see if anyone was paying attention, but the knights had split up. Half were combing the camp to see if they could find anything more useful than blood and viscera. The other half watched the tree line. No one paid any attention to him, not even his usual babysitter, Nuhzar.

He pushed aside muscle fibers, saw green again, and this time made a much easier identification. Math's whole body froze, his breath catching, an icy dread gripping him.

It was a plant vine.

Part of him noted the vine with calm precision. Another part—the part that remembered what this might mean—froze in horror.

He reached for it with the splinter, realized that wouldn't work, reached for it with his hand, and remembered he was wearing thick leather gloves. He stripped off a glove so he could pull the fragile-looking plant free from where it had lodged in a vein.

He felt like he wasn't squatting next to a mutilated corpse, but looking over his own shoulder, studying the scene with clinical disinterest. This wasn't the only vine: he counted seven just on that arm. Separated from the horror of it all, the sharp sense of personal danger, of shock, he saw this wasn't the same.

Wasn't the same as him. Wasn't what happened to Math when he lost control. *His* plants didn't clog up arteries and veins. They didn't . . .

They didn't rip their way out.

Then someone shouted: "We found a live one!"

WOODS

They discovered the man buried under a collapsed section of palisade fence. He was sweaty, dirty, babbling, but otherwise unharmed.

Physically.

Mentally was a different matter.

"No, no, no," the man muttered, rocking back and forth. "For the Queen, for the Queen, we must be good for the Queen. Everything is for the Queen."

Captain Yihura raised an eyebrow. "You mean the empress?"

"Gray and gray and gray and then green, green everywhere. You understand, yes? The time of gray is over. It's green from now on." The survivor stared up with wide brown eyes, but he didn't look at the surrounding people so much as through them. He wrapped his arms around his legs and continued rocking.

He wasn't a lumberjack—not large enough, not dressed for it. His shirt was too fine; his skin was too soft. He looked like a banker caught somewhere he didn't belong.

Captain Rabu rolled his eyes. "What's your name? And what in all the seas happened here?"

The man's eyes snapped up. "The Green."

"What?" more than one person asked.

"The Green," he repeated. "The Green happened here." His gaze dropped. "We hurt the Queen. We woke up the Queens. I tried to apologize, but they didn't understand." A tiny frown dropped the corner of his mouth. "Or they don't care. Probably that last one. I never realized trees were so . . ." He shook his head. "Green."

More than one knight inhaled with ill-concealed exasperation.

Captain Yihura bent down next to the man. "What's your name?"

He hesitated. "I used to be called Catimus."

"Used to be?"

He turned away and refused to say more.

Captain Rabu rubbed his chin. "Great. I'm unsettled."

Lieutenant Nuhzar cleared his throat. "We found another body, Captain. Dead, but intact."

The banker's eyes widened; he leaned away from the lieutenant.

Captain Rabu noticed the motion and pointed to the man. "Someone take him away. Put him with the horses." He gave a considered look to Captain Yihura, as if to say: *What next?*

"I walked the perimeter of the bombard field," she replied to the unasked question. "No sign of bodies being moved. No drag marks or blood trails." She gestured around the camp. "There should be over a hundred bodies here. This isn't more than a few dozen."

"How can you tell?" Lieutenant Nuhzar muttered.

"I'm guessing the majority never made it back to camp." Her shoulders slumped with exhaustion. "Let's go look at the intact one, then—" She glanced back at the tree line. "I have a theory I want to test."

Lieutenant Nuhzar directed them to the intact corpse. Now this was a lumberjack, dressed in sturdy—if blood-splattered—clothing, with massive shoulders and arms thick from hard labor. The partial collapse of a storeroom had shielded the body. It lay positioned on its back, perfectly straight, as though someone was readying it for burial.

The man had only died that morning, but the body was already bloated and stretched taut against his shirt until it resembled an ill-fitted sausage casing. The man's skin was livid near his shirt neckline. His fingers were plump worms, shapeless and fat.

The three captains, Mathaiik, and a handful of knights all stared down at the revealed body.

Captain Rabu sucked on his teeth as he examined it. "Okay, I give up. Anybody got a clue what killed him?"

That . . . did seem to be the question.

The body was undeniably dead, but lacking any visible injuries. But in a worst-case scenario—if he was right about how the plants had been killing people—the plants targeted unprotected skin. This man hadn't left much available. He'd been bundled up from foot to neck.

Math tilted his head, carefully stepped backward and around the others, so he could look at the body from a different angle.

He saw it: the man had punctures in his boots, one on each side, right between the hard leather soles and the softer upper lift. The holes would be easy to overlook, easy to discount as normal signs of wear, or a poor cobbler's work.

But it wasn't any of that. Math's mouth felt dry.

Why wasn't the body ripped to pieces?

Then he noticed a detail that rabbited his pulse and raised all the hairs on his skin.

No flies. None at all. Not even buzzing near the corpse. It was wrong, like even decay had been warned away.

The world seemed to slow down, stretch thin and taut and so fragile, as Math watched Captain Rabu reach down to turn the body over. "Injury must be on his back . . ."

"No, Captain! Don't—"

It was too late. Captain Rabu grabbed a shoulder and tugged. The body moved with a horrifying, wet, meaty sound, too flexible, too soft. It sloshed. Not like flesh—like something *inside* it moved. A wrongness that didn't belong in anything human.

Captain Rabu let the body fall back, making a disgusted sound. He then gave Math a questioning stare.

Math flushed. "There aren't any flies," he tried to explain. "I thought it must be a trap." He felt his face growing redder by the moment.

Lieutenant Nuhzar stared at Math with undisguised incredulity. "Only you," he sneered, "would be fool enough to think that a rotting corpse could somehow be a trap."

Math knew better than to defend himself. That only made them dig deeper.

"Nah," Captain Rabu said. "Leave off him, Nuhzar. He has good instincts. Remember how that last flare-up with the Kaliri had them putting bombard mines under the bodies of our people, rigged to blow if they're moved? Pretty sure grimmocks aren't capable of something like that, though." He gave Math a wink.

Lieutenant Nuhzar's eyes hardened at the captain's correction, although nothing else about his expression changed. "Yes, Captain. With your permission, I'd like to check the perimeter."

Captain Rabu waved his lieutenant away.

Nuhzar spared Math a lethal glare as he passed, as if Math had committed the unforgivable crime of not embarrassing himself enough in front of his commanding officer.

Captain Yihura gazed off toward the woods, her expression pensive. "Funny you should mention the Kaliri . . ."

Rabu raised both eyebrows. "You're kidding."

"Maybe not," the Captain of Forests said. "The distress summons said grimmocks, but these people couldn't tell a grimmock from a giraffe. They were being attacked by things that shouldn't attack them. That's all they knew. Everything here looks normal. The trees are healthy. Nothing's growing here that shouldn't be. It's just a theory. But it makes more sense than grimmocks evolving coordinated ambush tactics. A grim witch using their powers to *control* plants is more likely."

"And the missing men have been taken prisoner?" Rabu set his fists against his hips and cast his gaze around the camp. Clearly, he liked this theory more and more with every passing second. "The Kaliri did it" was an explanation with which the captain had experience.

Math was equally certain that was *not* what was going on, but no one would take him seriously if he said so.

After all, everyone knew how Math felt about plants.

"It doesn't explain why we can't find footprints." Captain Yihura pointed toward the shifted tree line and raised her voice. "Betan, Calxi, cut one of those trees down." To Rabu's perplexed look, she explained, "Tree rings will tell me if these were grown recently."

Math still squatted next to the only intact corpse, tapping his fingers on a knee. Why was *this* one left whole when all the others had been ripped apart?

The small green vines were what was truly bothering him. They were too horrifyingly familiar. If Captain Yihura was right and this was the work of Kaliri witches, that was a problem, too, because it meant the Kaliri had developed an attack that would be difficult to defend against. At the same time—

A loud crack of splitting wood filled the air. Simultaneously, someone screamed.

Math stood and turned toward the noise, toward where everyone's attention was focused.

A tree, the one that Captain Yihura's people had wasted no time cutting down with magic. Both knights seemed hale; it wasn't clear who had screamed.

A gushing stream of crimson poured from both sides of the felled tree's trunk. It wasn't sap. It looked like . . .

Was that blood?

Math's view was blocked by the knights, jockeying with each other to see what had happened.

Captain Rabu raised his voice. "What in the Tri-Mother's garden is going on over there?"

"We found the body of a lumberjack, Captain," a knight answered. "It was still alive inside the tree trunk."

"*Was*," someone else agreed.

Math felt a frisson of horror. He couldn't have been the only one, either, because the field grew quiet. Everyone studied the copse of trees that Captain Danvi said hadn't been there earlier.

Math was willing to bet that there was one tree for every missing man. Also, that the Kaliri had nothing to do with this.

"Call everyone back," Captain Rabu ordered. "We'll stay in the camp where it's safe."

At which point, the corpse they'd been standing next to exploded.

SPORES

A shockingly loud bang erupted as the bloated corpse popped, like an overinflated bladder. Purple dust filled the air in an enormous cloud.

No, not dust. Spores.

He was poisoned. That much, at least, was real.

Math leaped backward, covering his mouth, but he wasn't fast enough. Everyone who'd been standing around the corpse—himself included—breathed the spores.

Confirmation came a split second later, when the world began to shift and deform, separate and recombine. Melting glass seen through a kaleidoscope prism.

Oh. The spores must be hallucinogenic.

"Back away—" Captain Danvi tried to cry out. "Don't breathe—" She verged on collapsing, not because she was falling unconscious but because her sense of balance had been obliterated. The world was thus about to slap her in the face.

Math heard laughing. Or was he the one laughing?

Or . . . was that screaming?

He felt good.

His whole body tingled pleasantly. He had to fight the urge to sit down, or maybe lie down, and just enjoy himself. It seemed better to be closer to the ground. Less likely to trip or fall. It would be easy to do that—fall—because the world was shifting, rocking from side to side like an unsteady boat on tumultuous seas.

Stuff was happening around him. He wasn't sure what, but it was loud stuff, making lots of noise. Sometimes that noise was music and sometimes it was screams and sometimes it was apples.

Across from him, Captain Danvi kneeled, one forearm on the damp, bloody ground. A knight managed to stand, before tripping off out of Math's line of sight. Captain Rabu stared up at the sky, screaming that his hands were on fire, which they most certainly were not.

Captain Danvi tried to right herself. She must've jostled something, though, because without warning, her skin melted from her face in a slow slide, revealing a radiant, prismatic skull beneath. The eyes, still wet and human, rolled in confusion.

Math was probably supposed to be scared. Maybe normally he would've been, but right now everything . . .

Well. Nothing was real, was it?

Captain Yihura held a cloth over her face as she rushed in to pull Captain Danvi to safety.

Past Yihura, Captain Rabu stood, the screams having switched to growls. The Captain of Swords manifested his weapon. His eyes were wild, his face twisted in fury. He looked like a grimmock.

Math laughed at the idea. There wasn't much difference between an out-of-control Idallik Knight and a grimmock, really.

Maybe no difference at all, except the knights looked human while they lost control and slaughtered everyone around them.

Just like Rabu was losing control.

Math had always thought it ironic. The Captain of Swords did not himself use a sword. Rabu's resonance was Land, and in a fitting detail, he manifested a giant war hammer. Then Rabu spotted one of the other knights, shouted, and charged.

"Captain, no!" The hammer caught him in the shield, splintering it, and drove through, tossing the knight into the air and sending him sailing a good ten feet away, although he turned into a crow before landing, and flew away.

So he was probably fine.

Captain Rabu kept attacking, this time bringing down his hammer on the bloated dead body—which puffed out yet more purple spores. The sound the hammer made when it hit the body was the stuff of nightmares. Math had crawled too far away to breathe any in this time, but he was . . .

What was he doing?

Math spotted Alik Nuhzar, who'd manifested his ice halberd. He was freezing and then shattering trees. As if a tree had ever hurt him.

Except, no. Those trees were trying to hurt him, weren't they? At least Nuhzar had been too far away to breathe in the spores.

Captain Yihura was a giant flower pile, which was pretty, but Math didn't think she should stay so close to the rampaging bear with the giant hammer swinging at everything. Math asked the vines to bring her closer, which they did, because plants were good like that.

Math himself tripped over something, although he caught himself before the stumble became a fall. He looked down to see a pile of leaves, strangely wet and making the oddest sounds when he nudged it with his foot.

A small voice whispered: *Don't be a fool. You know those aren't leaves.*

Math could only hope that was an old body part, and not a new one. Not one of the knights.

That was possible, given the strength of Captain Rabu's swings. He'd wipe out his own people long before the trees got to them.

The trees. They were forgetting about the trees.

Math searched the area as best he could through the floating, colored fogs and the strange shapes and the dripping lines.

Not everything was distorted. The trees were normal, except for the part where they moved.

He blinked as a vine rose from the ground near a knight. Several vines. They acted in concert, working together to grab the knight's arms and legs in a moment of distraction. As soon as she was immobilized, still another vine shoved itself through the gaps in the knight's helmet, flowing down . . .

Some instinct told Math the vines were using every opening, every orifice. The green plants flowed and rushed and grew like an inescapable tide, a drowning, lethal flash flood of foliage.

It happened so quickly. By the time Math understood what he was seeing, it was too late. The vines had finished their journey. They exited again, erupting from arms, legs, torso, tearing her entire body apart. Only the straps and fastenings of the knight's armor kept the pieces from flying off, as they had with earlier victims.

Oh. So that's how those lumberjacks died.

Some instinct he couldn't name alerted him. His hand snatched the vine sneaking up on him.

"Stop that," Math snarled, tearing the vine in two. The thing jerked back, as if it was a scolded dog, and then retreated underground again.

He spotted another vine, about to attack another knight. Unacceptable. He demanded it return to its mother soil.

It did.

He stepped on something that looked like, but was almost certainly not, a set of stairs. Math spotted Huraiik.

He was dead, too, one open eye recognizable from a face otherwise torn to pieces.

Rough hands grabbed him by the shoulders. He blinked as Alik Nuhzar's face lurched into view—too close, wild-eyed and spitting. "Fucking grim, Kaven! Get ahold of yourself. I know you're a damn third circle in Wood. Fix yourself! Purge the poison!"

Math blinked.

Fix himself. Right. Wood, third circle. He knew the spell. Knew the sigils. His hands remembered even if his head didn't.

Lieutenant Nuhzar didn't wait for an answer; he had trees to chop down. He ran away, leaving cold frost wafting behind him in the air. He cast spells as he went, magics to turn the trees brittle and frozen.

Nuhzar's resonance was Sea, particularly glaciers, ice.

What was Math doing again? Oh, right. He was watching the trees.

The trees.

They weren't . . . they weren't trees, were they? They looked like trees, if trees could move in the way trees never did.

Almost never did.

Math had, in fact, seen trees move like this once before.

The attacking creatures *were* trees, an enormous collection of oak, ash, and thorn with some rowan and pine sprinkled in. But underneath the bark . . .

Somehow, they were the lumberjacks.

Math didn't know how this had been done, why these men had been turned into these monsters while the ones in the camp had been torn to pieces. Were these men still alive? Were they aware and capable of agency? He didn't think so. Whatever had happened to them was as good as death.

In the far back, though . . . past the vines and the walking trees, there was something else. Someone else.

Three trees less like trees than all the others.

These beings were aware, awake, intelligent. He felt them like a light shining into his eyes, searing and red even with his eyes closed. They each resembled a tree, yet were as unlike actual trees as a painting of a fire was unlike the real thing. They weren't attacking or making any movement toward the camp at all. He felt them watching, knew from the roots of his hair to the tips of his toes that each one was a ruler, a matriarch.

A queen, one might say.

One of the Queens was injured, the bright white slash of a wound where someone had taken an axe or saw to her side. He had the hysterical thought that if only he'd kept a first-circle Wood spell ready, he might've fixed it.

The new trees—the ones made from the lumberjacks—weren't alive in the same way. He could control the newborns. Maybe not all of them, but enough to set them to attacking their siblings instead of Idallik Knights. He forced them to do that in a moment of lucidity. Or what felt like lucidity.

Some things were so clear. So beautifully, crystal clear.

Everything else was mud.

And then something brushed his mind.

Not a voice. Not a thought. A presence.

You're unexpected.

Whatever had just spoken to him hadn't used words or language. Ideas, emotions, had appeared in his mind, tangled with his thoughts.

"The Queen," Math murmured to himself. Someone had said that recently, right? He didn't remember who.

Her touch felt familiar.

He remembered . . .

Math swallowed down bile and memories of running, tears streaming tracks down a face still throbbing from his father's backhand. Memories of screaming and pain. The knowledge that he was broken, that his mother demanded that he be fixed . . .

Branches moving over his head like a hand brushing a child's hair . . .

No.

Math opened his eyes, not realizing he'd closed them in the first place. He cast an ugly gaze at the attacking forces trying to hurt his people, his knights.

"Go home," Math screamed. "Go away!"

Some did. Not all. The trees rallied, but there had been a decided pause. The knights had taken advantage. They pressed forward, attacking with blade or fire or, in the case of Captain Yihura, carving away wood with her bare hands.

Math hefted his axe to help when a wave of exhaustion overtook him, forced him to his knees. He didn't think he'd been doing anything that would tire him out. Had he?

He mumbled something, twitched his fingers, felt a wave of energy spread up from his feet, push at the fuzziness and the dripping wet glass of his perception.

Math stared across the battlefield. The trees were close to being felled, the tree men laid to a more final death than their first.

They'd won. The Idallik Knights had won.

But he didn't see the Three Queens. No sign of them at all. It was as though they'd never existed.

He felt the air shift—just enough to turn. Then something slammed into his back, and everything turned black.

MENDING

When Math opened his eyes, the first thing he saw was undyed canvas. The second was the tabard of a knight of Mending, muttering low words and circling a healing spell over Math's arm.

He froze. His shirt was gone, and so were the vines. That meant the healers had seen them—had cut them from his body. It meant he couldn't hide.

He struggled to sit up, pausing when his back flared with pain. His head throbbed. "What—"

"Hey now." Zahraiik, one of the healers from the Halls of Mending, pushed Math back down on a cot. "Stop behaving like you're in Swords. You need to give yourself at least a few minutes for the spells to finish working. You know how this works."

Given that they'd taken off his shirt in order to treat him for whatever had hit him in the back, it was impossible that the healers hadn't seen those inexplicable bits of plant growth. Math was naked, so he could assume Zahraiik had treated his legs as well.

At least the man had thrown a sheet over his lower half in deference to modesty.

It was darker inside the tent than outside, suggesting it was still daylight. Shadows moved against the tent fabric as knights hurried around outside. He heard the muffled sounds of industry, of people working and talking and carrying things. So many more knights than they'd originally brought.

A captain must've called for help, if not with the fighting itself, then with the cleanup.

In a way, he'd gotten very, very lucky. Normally, there would've been no explaining this away, no justifying it. At least this time, he had a ready-made excuse: the trees had done it. If those vines hadn't dug into his flesh in the same way they had for the other victims, didn't look *exactly* alike, they still wouldn't think Math was responsible.

His thoughts shied away from the attack itself, from the hallucinations.

He hadn't . . . he hadn't *really* controlled those plants, had he?

Math didn't want to know. In any event, neither the plants nor the twisted visions explained how he'd been knocked unconscious. The vines hadn't caused blunt-force injuries, and at no point had the trees been behind him. The only people behind him had been more knights . . .

Oh.

"Captain Rabu hit me?" Math asked.

"Like a damn rhino, sad to say," Zahraiik informed him, chuckling. "Fortunately, he didn't hit you in the head. Also, you had almost two dozen knights right there, so no permanent damage. You're lucky, Novitiate." He pointed a scalpel at Math, pointing out the various places on his body where small bandages marked all the other incisions the medic had already made. "The other four people who had those things crawl under their skin didn't survive the experience."

Math didn't hide his shudder. Four knights dead, just like that. It was . . . it was a stunning blow for the cenobium, already stretched so thin trying to cover the increasing rise in grimmock attacks.

"I'm done here," Zahraiik told him. "You. Stay down for at least fifteen more minutes. When you can sit up on your own, and only if you can breathe easily, you may leave."

"Yes, sir," Math said.

"And stay out of trouble. How are we supposed to grab you for Mending if you get yourself killed?"

"Nobody's grabbing me until I figure out how to manifest."

Zahraiik nodded, gave him a sympathetic clap on the shoulder, and then left the tent to tend to someone else's injuries.

Math waited, if not patiently, because the pain provided excellent motivation to not move. When he managed to sit, he noticed a small table next to the cot, which held several dishes containing various medical supplies. Another dish held a collection of small, slender plant vines, sprinkled with drops of blood. They looked tender, delicate, harmless.

Zahraiik, or one of the other healers, had left him clothes, which was good, because his own clothes, dumped into a sackcloth bag and thrown in a corner, were completely ruined.

More ruined than they should've been. Even his jazerant chain coat was ruined, the chain that normally lay safely tucked between two layers of padded linen now so corroded and worn that the links snapped from the force of their weight. Someone had used third-circle Storm spells on his clothing until they were so rusted and worn they could be ripped off his body with ease.

Math knew exactly who.

"Damn it, Nuhzar," he growled.

At least the bastard had left Math's boots intact. Small favors—it still meant that Math wasn't going back into the field until he could replace the coat, which wouldn't be a high priority for the Isofal smiths. Commander Talu wouldn't send him into the field without armor, and he wouldn't be allowed to wear anything that would have him mistaken for a knight.

Nuhzar's sabotage would prove nastily effective.

Math barely recognized his location when he stepped outside. He wasn't sure how long he'd been unconscious, but it had to have been hours.

The logging camp was gone.

All the bodies and parts of bodies had been removed. The entire area's soil had been turned under, hiding the blood and gore that had soaked the ground. To the south . . .

Math couldn't help but feel offended, even if he understood the necessity. The knights hadn't cut down the entire forest, but they'd made a good stab at it—nearly a quarter mile from the camp was now nothing but felled trees, uprooted whole and lying on their sides. The Idallik Knights had wanted to make certain they'd found all the lumberjacks—or whatever they'd become.

The knights' deaths must have shaken the Order badly.

Math searched until he found a captain—Captain Rabu, in fact.

The captain was casually carrying a whole tree thrown over a shoulder to a stacking pile. Math had the fleeting thought that the cenobium really should bill Kegomar for all the free logging.

Rabu pointed at Math and barked out a noise. "I didn't kill you! That's good!"

"We're in perfect agreement, Captain Rabu." Math bowed. "Might I have a moment? I have a concern."

"What?" The captain squinted at him. "Normally I'd tell you to go talk to one of my lieutenants, but since I almost killed you today—talk fast." Rabu made a face at his hands as he began walking back to collect another tree. "My hands are covered in sap."

Math didn't feel his input was needed on that. "I was wondering if we killed—or maybe the right word is felled?—the three leaders?"

Math already knew they hadn't, but . . . he wanted to be wrong.

Captain Rabu stopped walking. "What leaders? The Kaliri? Did you see any Kaliri, boy?"

Mathaiik raised his chin and squared his shoulders. "I saw three trees, Captain. In the back. Much larger than the others. Directing the fighting."

Rabu kept staring, then he exhaled sharply through his nose, much like a bull. "Kaven. I saw the sky melt, and a dancing elephant turned into a winged horse and flew away. Maybe don't pay too much attention to what you 'saw' while you were under the effects of"—he waved a hand vaguely—"that purple stuff."

Captain Rabu swung another tree onto his shoulder and turned around, so Math had to duck if he didn't want to be clobbered a second time in one day by the Captain of Swords. "You probably saw Kaliri and were just too burned to realize it. Witches, I'd wager."

"I didn't—" A muscle in Math's jaw twitched as he bit back the rest of the sentence. It was futile, a waste of breath, to argue with Captain Rabu. He'd already decided: anything odd they'd seen or experienced was a hallucination.

Captain Rabu either didn't notice or didn't care to notice Math's faux pas. As far as he was concerned, their conversation was over: he returned to tree delivery.

Math couldn't go over the man's head and just barge in to see the commander, either. He'd already jumped a rung he shouldn't have. The rigid structure of mission protocols demanded problems be reported up the chain of command. He was expected to inform a lieutenant—specifically, Lieutenant Nuhzar—who would then decide whether to escalate the matter to Captain Rabu.

Rabu hadn't made a fuss about it, but he would if he was the one being skipped.

Math knew this wasn't the Kaliri, though. Isofal existed to repel the Kaliri, and there wasn't a single knight of the Order who hadn't had at least one run-in with Rokasmaa's "friendly" neighbors.

They liked to use forbidden magics, it was true. They also liked to ambush. A trap like that corpse, overripe with hallucinogenic spores, could represent an escalation in Kaliri tactics, except . . .

Except it hadn't triggered when Captain Rabu had moved it. Shouldn't it have? Wouldn't that have made sense?

No, the corpse hadn't exploded until Captain Yihura's people chopped down the first tree. Not an ambush, but a retaliation.

These weren't Kaliri.

They were something much worse.

CELEBRATION

The return to Isofal Cenobium was a solemn and silent ride. That trend continued when they reached the fortress itself, as word rippled out through the ranks of what had happened.

When Idallik Knights died, the Order marked the occasion with honey on the table, cheese, fruit, and—for one night—permission to speak freely at dinner.

Which guaranteed there would be at least one table full of cheer.

"Tell us what happened," demanded Iduan, bright-eyed leader of a trio of adorable monsters. Her partners in crime, the twins Yasib and Mudiya, solemnly nodded in support of their sister novitiate.

Taris, the oldest girl in the novitiate dorms, leaned over the table at this. Her "whisper" was loud enough to make Master Wadera frown. "We heard there were grimmocks. Were there really? What kind?"

To which little Ayiad added, "Were they the same kind that killed your parents?"

"Ayiad!" Master Wadera scolded. "That is inappropriate."

A wave of heat slammed through Math. For a second, the table blurred, muffled. He blinked it away.

He hadn't told that story to Ayiad, so one of the older novitiates must have.

Children were the worst gossips.

Math pointed his fork at Taris. "First, yes. There were grimmocks. They were a kind we've never seen before and very dangerous." He started to tell the children that the monsters looked like trees, but Tri-Mother help him, if he did that the younger ones would panic every time they went outside.

Math shifted his attention to Ayiad. There was no point in avoiding the question. Even if he distracted her, one of the others would demand an answer. Yasib was tenacious when he sank his teeth into a mystery.

"I doubt these were the grimmocks that killed my parents," Math told the little girl. "Because it's unlikely that the grimmocks who killed my parents stopped with them. That means some knight, either from this cenobium or another, must have found and destroyed them."

Then Satu, one of the quiet ones, whispered: "I heard four people died."

The table fell quiet.

Math and Master Wadera exchanged a look. This was a delicate subject when dealing with children expected to one day face such risks themselves.

Wadera tapped a knife twice against his cup. "Four knights died," he said. "But a great many more than four *people* died. We should not forget that. Their losses are not less meaningful just because they weren't knights."

Satu looked down, embarrassed. Math's lips twitched in irritation. He didn't disagree with Master Wadera, but it was hard enough to get the boy to speak up as it was.

Math caught Satu's eye. "It's okay. You didn't know."

The little boy gave him a small, sad smile.

"You killed the monsters, though, right?" Jaiik asked, in keeping with the boy's need to know justice had been served.

Math hesitated and hated himself for it. "We did," he said. "We killed the monsters. I'll tell you all about it later."

Taris squinted at him, skeptical, before sharing a look with Jaiik. Her arm moved—she'd probably taken Jaiik's hand, under the table. Math said nothing. It was long past the point where it would do any good.

Those two were inseparable.

At least, for now. They would, of course, be separated at some point. It was pretty much inevitable, if for no other reason than because the dormitories were separated by gender.

Why was he thinking about this? It was depressing.

Math covered for his disquiet by eating, and while the children didn't entirely get the hint, they moved to other topics, if only until "later" arrived.

The serious turn in conversation reminded Math that he'd come to dinner with a goal. So he scanned the great dining hall for Captain Yihura, who he found wasn't sitting with her own section, but over next to Captain Rabu.

Speaking of problematic behaviors . . .

They sat too close. Captain Yihura laughed, throwing her head back, glass catching the light. Whatever Rabu said, it probably hadn't been that funny.

They were not being subtle.

Math could understand why. Both captains had lost people today. They wanted to commiserate.

Math sighed. If he knew Nuhzar—and he did—the lieutenant would keep his captain from doing anything too foolish.

On a more personal level, though, it meant two things. First, that Rabu wasn't likely to change his mind about "Kaliri grim witches" if it meant contradicting a theory Yihura had suggested in the first place. Two, that Math would have to avoid his favorite sleeping spot in the garden.

He felt it building again—that creeping pressure behind his ribs. Maybe not tonight. But soon. Something was coming, and no one else seemed to feel it. He hadn't seen Tanxi all evening, so he couldn't go to her for advice.

He needed someone to believe him.

Math finished his meal and picked up his dishes to return to the kitchen. On the way, he paused next to Master Wadera. "Do you need me tonight?"

The older man glanced at the children. Specifically at Hamu, who wasn't the youngest, but was blind and prone to seizures. "I have everything well in hand. You should rest."

Little Nula pulled her thumb out of her mouth for long enough to give Math a sulky look. "No stories?"

He kneeled down next to the toddler. "Not tonight, Nula. Tomorrow night, though? I'll tell you a great story tomorrow."

She pouted at him, because "tomorrow" was an impossibly long period of time to a three-year-old. That pout was seconds from turning into a full-blown tantrum.

"If you're patient," Math told her, "I'll tell you the story about the three hyenas and the dragon, hmm?"

She contemplated this idea with adorably grave seriousness. She didn't want to wait, but it was her favorite story.

"Hey, Newt," Jaiik called out to her. "I can tell you a story tonight."

That settled the matter; she nodded in emphatic agreement.

Math waved goodbye to the children and headed to the most important place in the entire cenobium, the one place he could always count on to find the solution to any problem:

The libraries.

He couldn't go straight to the commander. Not without evidence. Talu would laugh, ruffle his hair, and assign him to the stables until he died. No—he needed proof. And in Isofal, proof meant books.

Fortunately for Math, he happened to live in the middle of one of the largest libraries in the known world.

Protecting the archives was, after all, one of the main reasons the Idallik Order existed. Without those archives, mankind would still be hunting with sticks.

It was just a matter of finding out if the Queens were already recorded in the records somewhere.

The Forests section dealt with the practical: lumber types, pests, sap rot. What Math needed wasn't the practical, but the mythical—folklore, legends, and histories.

Math went to the Lore section.

Normally, there would be members of the Order in the libraries even this late. Visitors came during the daytime and left by sunset. The evenings were for the Order members themselves.

With the celebration, though? The stacks were empty.

Or, at least, they should've been. Instead, he saw the summoned light of a Sun spell betraying someone lingering at a reading table: Captain Danvi of Idols.

The old woman had spread out books across the entire considerable table length. She'd also dragged a stuffed chair closer and propped her feet on the table's edge, one leg crossed over the other. She glanced up when Math approached with his own light, then snickered. "Well, if it isn't Commander Talu's favorite pet."

Math froze, unsure how to reply in a way that wouldn't get him into trouble for using rude gestures.

She waved a hand. "Teasing. It's not my business who the commander mentors—so long as that's all it is." She looked up from her book. "That *is* all it is, yes?"

Math flushed. "That's . . . yes. That's all that happens."

He'd received more than a few inquiries over the years as various members checked to make sure no one was taking advantage of him. They usually took longer to get to the point.

"Good. Glad to hear it." Her eyes returned to her book. She turned a page and, without looking up, said, "I assume you're here for the same reason I am."

"Same reason?"

Captain Danvi snorted. "Yes. You saw them." She peered up over the book's edge. "The tree women."

"I—" He bit his lip. "I told Captain Rabu about them, but he thought it was a hallucination caused by the spores."

She nodded absently as she turned a page. "Going to Rabu was your first mistake, Novitiate. But honestly, I doubt any of the captains would've believed you. The consequences are too terrible."

Math tilted his head. "Consequences worse than this being a Kaliri magical plot?"

She turned another page, then another, before answering. "Did you know the earliest depictions of the Tri-Mother show her with leaves in her hair? Specifically, as a tree goddess."

Math's mouth felt dry. "But that's got nothing to do with—"

"Doesn't it?" She glanced up again. "If you compare the religions of Kalast to the other continent, Navre, I think you'll find tree-related divinities are significantly more common in *our* religious faiths than any others. Even the Kaliri, before they decided worshipping grim lords was a fine idea, worshipped tree goddesses."

"I . . . didn't know that." He frowned at the table, then belatedly realized how judgmental he must look, staring at the woman's feet.

She slapped a hand against her thigh. "Don't worry about me breaking the rules. I have permission. Bad veins in my legs—helps if I keep them elevated. Anyway, what were we talking about?"

"Heresy."

"Right. Yes, so we were." She waved a hand. "What if, my young novitiate, those early pagan religions were an attempt to propitiate genuine threats? Not gods, but forces beyond their comprehension? What if the reason we've never heard of these tree creatures before isn't because they're new but because they are, in fact, exceedingly old?"

"You're saying those weren't grimmocks."

"My dear boy, grimmocks aren't what we think they are, but yes, that's exactly what I'm saying."

He pulled out a chair and sat down. "With all due respect, Captain: What?"

The old woman's eyes lit up with delight before they dropped back down to her book. "A grimmock is supposed to be a creature made by grim magic. Necromancy, if you believe the old texts." She flipped a page. "But tell me, Mathaiik—how many of the monsters we face today look like corpses to you?"

"None," he admitted softly.

"Exactly. And yet we still call them grimmocks. Because we must."

Math frowned. He was pretty sure the Order's charter covered more than . . . "Oh. You mean the Innalova Accords."

"Yes, I mean the Innalova Accords. If we're only allowed to use magic against grimmocks, it stands to reason that the definition of 'grimmock' must occasionally expand to fit our needs." Captain Danvi made a moue at her book before flipping to the back. "Does this damn thing have an index . . . ?"

Math reached for a book. "If they're not grimmocks, what are they? And how can I help?"

"That is the question, isn't it? So grab a book and start circling first-circle Sky spells. We're looking for any mention of tree people."

Math nodded and cast the spell, which didn't improve perception so much as comprehension. In a quiet place with minimal disturbances, its major benefit was the ability to read fast.

Just the thing for an order obsessed with books.

QUEENS

Several hours later, Captain Danvi made a soft noise. "Interesting," she murmured. "Listen:

"'Folktales of the Valmaki region are a fascinating inversion of typical tropes concerning the Green Mothers and the Gray Lady.'"

Math raised his head and paid closer attention. Isofal was in the Valmaki region—along with the Parnassa Forest and his hometown of Sounalla.

She continued: "'The Green Mothers are always a triumvirate of nature spirits, and the Gray Lady is always a personification of winter. Despite what one might assume, the Green Mothers, sometimes called the Forest Queens, feature as the villains in these folktales.'" She shrugged. "Interesting, but not much help."

"I don't know. We both saw them. And that man from the logging camp—what was his name?"

"Catimus Abhigan."

"Right. He kept ranting about 'queens.' What if these Forest Queen stories are based on the tree women?"

"That man is a library stack with all its books dumped out," Danvi said amiably. "But it's possible those folk stories share a root with the creatures we saw."

"I think I heard stories as a child."

"That's right. You're a local boy, aren't you?"

"Yes, Captain." He wasn't sure whether to feel embarrassed. "One moment." He retreated to the stacks.

When he returned, he carried more books and a large, obsolete map—the oldest he could find of the Valmaki region. It listed the library fortress as under Kaliri control, with the unfamiliar name "Deshayrs." Most interesting was the area that centuries later would become a lumber camp.

The captain tapped the map. "Here, I believe, is where today's events transpired. Isn't that interesting?"

"'Old Queens' Hill,'" Math read. "Queens. Plural. But what you said about the Tri-Mother had me thinking . . ." He showed her another book: *Census of the Doctrine of the Faithful*. He pointed back at the map. "If these tree women shaped stories and legends, maybe they influenced local religion too. The church used to care about that."

Math grinned. "Listen to this entry for Gebra: Father Dariik requests help with locals. 'They are persistent in worshipping Cadras, a regional variant of Kilsha, instead of the Tri-Mother. They must be reeducated.'" He searched again. "Here's a letter to the matriarch asking advice on a sect near the Parnassa Forest worshipping the sky goddess—called Cadras, not Kilsha."

Danvi made a face, as if Math had stepped in something unpleasant. "Yes, I see. Fascinating, but inconsequential. That has nothing to do with trees."

"Nothing to do with trees, yes. But everything to do with their enemy: 'The Gray Lady.'" Math read from another book: "'In Valmaki County, near the Parnassa Forest, locals refer to Kilsha as Cadras. In this form, the goddess is "cloaked in a mantle of winter clouds" and "wearing dresses of mist," unlike her form elsewhere in Rokasmaa.'" He tapped the book. "I think Cadras is the Gray Lady, and the locals worshiped her—maybe because they remembered her saving them from the Green Mothers, and—" He paused. "What's that look for?"

Danvi chewed her thumb, glancing at the books. "This is a false trail. Interesting, but Cadras is more heretical than you realize. The church wouldn't care about a name swap. No. Cadras is heretical because she's the local name for the *Kaliri* goddess Kideris." She flicked her fingers. "Or as we know her, the *grim lord* Kaiataris. And *her worship* is forbidden."

Math slumped. "Oh."

"Indeed." She returned to her book. "Maybe there was a battle between these 'Queens' and a grim lord. It would explain why they hate us. But think before you make such suggestions. You joked about heresy earlier. *This* is not a joke."

Math chewed that over.

The grim lords had been worse than slave owners—tyrants so brutal their slaves hadn't even found freedom in death. They'd nearly wiped out humanity.

He opened his mouth, then shut it again.

"Right," he said. "So . . . I'll just go back to stories about the Green Mothers, why don't I?"

She gave him a knowing look, pulled a key from her coat, and tossed it to him. "Get it out of your system." She gestured down a row. "You know where the restricted books are." At his look, she added: "Not much on Kaiataris, but plenty on the Kaliri faith."

Math didn't run, but it was close.

The Kaliri and Rokasmaa had fought over this border for centuries. Control of the archives meant power. The Kaliri had never forgiven Rokasmaa for taking "their archive."

Math read what he could on Kideris. Not quite the Kaliri goddess of the sky, she ruled clouds, rain, winter, ice, masonry, and stone—all gray things. She arrived or left with the cracking of ice, the avalanche, fury, noise, and thunder.

She didn't sound friendly.

He moved on to Kaiataris.

Danvi hadn't lied: only three books mentioned her. Math dismissed the first—it relied on hearsay. The second, though primary, offered only a passing reference to statues in Tralos (now Bashan), depicting Kaiataris as exceptionally beautiful—or vain.

The third book was gold.

As Math read, a shiver of dread crawled through him. He scanned the pages, then returned to Danvi's base camp.

She glanced up. "You found something."

"I think so. It's not . . . good." He opened the book.

"'There is little merit to these peasant tales. Kaiataris Von insists she achieved a great victory against these tree people of the Parnathi, even that she drove them into hiding, but she presents no meaningful evidence of her so-called great deeds. She claims even if her own experience is doubted, the evidence lingers in folktales and myth—'"

"Is that Lord Torum the Foul's journal?" Danvi asked. "Even for a grim lord, his writing has a certain unmistakable bombastic stench."

"Yes, Captain." Math continued: "'This is prattle. Scarcely a village lacks an idol to a mother tree. These stories of walking trees and their existential threat are primitive superstition. Worship of the Three Mothers—'"

Danvi snatched the book.

She stared at it for several moments, then slammed it shut and set it aside. "You didn't read that."

"No, I don't suppose I did." He swallowed.

It was unsettling. If Torum was right, Kaiataris hadn't just encountered the Forest Queens—she'd beaten them. And if Torum hadn't believed her, it was only because these tree beings were ancient and mythical *even then*.

That wasn't the worst part. The worst was the reference to the "Three Mothers." Not far from "Tri-Mother."

Heresy, through and through.

"I'll tell the other captains the Queens' existence dates to antiquity. But don't mention Kaiataris or this book again. Understood?"

Math nodded. "Yes, Captain."

"Good boy."

As he stood to leave, he noticed the book of folktales Danvi had been reading. Half-buried under another, the visible page showed a blond sorceress leaning from a window, likely beckoning some poor knight to his doom. Only part of the banner could be seen: —WISDOM.

He pushed the top book aside. The revealed text read: IN SILENCE, WISDOM.

"They sure got that one wrong, didn't they?" Math murmured.

"Pardon me?"

He flashed an apologetic smile. "The Gray Lady. There's nothing quiet about her if you believe the Kaliri. She's all noise."

"I suggest you stop thinking about an evil necromancer who's been dead for centuries."

"Right. Yes, Captain." Math bowed. "Thank you for letting me help, but I should really—"

He pointed toward the entrance—a gesture that could be interpreted as a plea for either food or sleep.

She waved him off. "Go ahead." She opened her mouth, hesitated, then shook her head and returned to reading.

Math left—but didn't return to the novitiate dorms.

He knew he should leave it alone. He shouldn't dig in dangerous soil. He just . . .

He just had to solve this one last mystery.

Math ventured to a different library that housed foreign language dictionaries. He searched until he found several in the Kaliri tongue.

Kideris had no direct Kaliri meaning, but "Parnathi" was, hilariously, Kaliri for "forest." "Parnathi" had morphed into "Parnassa," which meant Kaiataris's hated enemies had been active in the same forest as the slaughter earlier that day.

"Deshayrs" meant "avalanche," and—

Wait.

The Kaliri name for Isofal meant "avalanche"?

That made no sense. Isofal wasn't near the mountains. But he recalled how the Kaliri goddess always arrived or left with an avalanche. A translation error? Not coming or going "with deshayrs" but coming and going *to* Deshayrs—a base of operations near the Green Mothers she warred against.

Calling it "Avalanche" still made no sense, though. It should've been something like "Ice Fall," the poetic name that preceded "Isofal." The fortress sat atop Gorsin Falls, which used to freeze over when winters were once harsher.

A horrible thought struck.

With racing fingers, he searched for the Kaliri word for "ice fall." They had none. They used the same word for it as for avalanche: "deshayrs."

The Kaliri weren't trying to retake Isofal because of the archives. They fought to recapture it because Isofal was the holy fortress of their grim lord goddess.

Pulse racing, he returned to the maze.

Or rather, he tried to return to the maze—but someone had posted a guard.

The knight seemed bored and irritated. No wonder, when everyone else was enjoying good food and company.

"Captain Qin of Riddles must not like you." Math walked forward to the man.

The knight straightened reflexively, realized it was just Math, and then gave him a murderous glare. "Oh, it's you."

Math smiled.

"Orders are orders. The maze is closed to unsupervised novitiate children," the knight muttered.

Of course it was. Captain Qin of Riddles was the one throwing a tantrum, but Math was being snidely lumped in with the "children." The commander had let Math near the maze without Qin's blessing, and Qin couldn't technically keep Talu out—but Math? Math was fair game.

Unless Math had some sort of writ of authority he could present—which he didn't—the guard at the door to the antechamber could cheerfully say he was just doing his job by not letting Math inside.

"Lucky for both of us, I didn't want inside."

"Huh?"

Math's gaze wandered downward until it reached the flagstone the knight stood upon.

The maze lay at the heart of the cenobium, a giant array running underneath the fortress monastery. Only upon close examination could one discern the division between the ancient Illuminated stonework and more recent construction.

On this tile, though? It was easy. Part of the stone had broken away, obliterating its inscription, leaving behind only a single word: WISDOM.

Math had been taught it originally said "The Path to Wisdom." It was a fitting introduction to an unsolvable maze.

"You know how it is," Math said idly. "Sometimes when I'm feeling out of sorts, I find it helpful to walk around and appreciate the beauty of simple things." He flashed the knight a brilliant smile before focusing on the tile.

"In Silence, Wisdom" would also fit the same space. It would fit perfectly.

Math couldn't breathe.

The quiet of the cenobium pressed in around him, the hush of a place meant to hold sacred things only to instead shelter secrets and monsters.

This wasn't evidence. Just scraps: a children's tale, a broken inscription, a few quirks of language. A sneering grim lord mocking a rival for her obsession with walking trees. A heretical theory: that Cadras was Kideris was Kaiataris Von, grim lord villainess.

And the Kaliri? They believed she'd lived here—in Isofal. Or Deshayrs, as they once called it. A name they'd fought to reclaim with the zeal of true believers.

And let's not forget the part where Kaiataris had been the sworn enemy of the Green Mothers, also known as the Tree Mothers . . . or Three Mothers.

Or . . . or possibly . . . Tri-Mother.

It left him sick. No. He couldn't contemplate it, refused to believe it. Just, no. That part wasn't true. The Tri-Mother was not some twisted reflection of an ancient group of entities that had resurrected themselves with gory, bloody abandon earlier that day. The Three Queens were just . . . monsters.

Grimmocks.

Math had a harder time dismissing the idea that Kaiataris Von might have used Isofal as her headquarters. It made sense. Which led to a question almost as heretical as the one about the Tri-Mother. Namely . . .

What if the Illuminated weren't responsible for building Isofal? What if it had been an evil necromancer instead?

If Kaiataris was the architect, he shuddered to think what might have happened if he'd succeeded in opening the maze. What horrors she might have left behind. He could only be grateful he hadn't figured out how to use the maze map, or he'd have . . .

His gaze strayed back to the carving of "wisdom."

Damn it.

Math cursed to himself. He knew *exactly* how to open the thing. The grim lord had left instructions, hadn't she?

She'd carved them in stone.

"You can't stay," the knight told him.

Math raised his head. He must've looked a fool, staring down at the floor for who knew how long.

"Don't worry," Math told him. "I wasn't planning to. In fact, I'm—" He laughed. "I'm not planning to ever go back. Do you want me to send someone over with food?" He'd have offered to bring the food himself, but he didn't think the knight would trust it wasn't a trick.

The knight shifted his head, surprised. "That's kind, but I already ate."

Math nodded. "Have a good evening, then."

He felt cold, and not from the night air. Shuddering, Math walked back to the living quarters.

WARNING

No guard was posted outside the commander's chambers because if some person were so foolish as to interrupt him without an excellent reason, Commander Talu would make sure they suffered for it. No more security than that was required.

Math knocked, hoping the commander wouldn't be too upset. He was debating whether to knock again when the door opened.

Commander Talu, in his nightclothes, was still as terrifying as a knight in full armor on the battlefield.

Talu asked: "Yes?" in a tone that meant: *This had better be good.*

"It's about the maze," Math said.

The older man stared at him, his expression unreadable, then opened the door wider. "Come in, then."

Math exhaled in relief and did so.

He'd never been inside the commander's quarters before. Commander Talu's room was only slightly larger than most, with a bed, desk, wardrobe, and armor stand. Only a set of puzzle boxes on the desk suggested any personality.

The puzzle boxes made sense though, if one understood that Talu had been the Captain of Riddles before he'd been promoted.

Talu frowned at Math. "Well?"

Math inhaled. "Sir, we can't solve the maze."

The commander raised both eyebrows. "I believe that's common knowledge."

"No, I mean we can't *ever* solve the maze. We need to stop trying." He grimaced, because equivocating would do nothing to help his case. "The maze wasn't built by the Illuminated. It was built by the grim lord Kaiataris."

Commander Talu's stare turned razor sharp. "That's a serious claim. The Illuminated built the repository, including the maze, to preserve knowledge for future generations. The grim lords, in contrast, attempted to destroy everything that represented, and would've been content to turn the land to ash while they commanded their legions." He narrowed his eyes. "If you have evidence to the contrary, present it."

Math stood perfectly straight and concentrated on not fidgeting.

"I was investigating the trees we encountered today, Commander." He amended: "I was assisting Captain Danvi of Idols."

Commander Talu sighed. "I see. Continue."

"We found—" Math swallowed. "Records. Folktales. A journal by a grim lord. Linguistic patterns. It all points to the same thing: Kaiataris operated locally, and she was the sworn enemy of a race of 'tree people.'" He hesitated.

Commander Talu gestured for him to continue.

"What the Kaliri used to call this fortress is the same word they used to associate with their goddess's dwelling place."

"A coincidence, I'm sure."

"I don't think so. I think she took over this fortress and made it her headquarters. She had a motto: 'In silence, wisdom.' Which is interesting because the Kaliri associated her with loud noises, and I think it's what's carved on the flagstone just before the maze antechamber—"

"Breathe, my son."

Math did. "Do you know how many local bedtime stories involve children getting lost in mazes?"

"There's a perfectly reasonable explanation for that."

"Yes, but maybe it reflects more ancient memories, too." Math held up a hand. "I'm not suggesting that she built the entire archive, but if she built the maze, how safe could it possibly be to go inside?"

Talu closed a box on his desk. "I appreciate your enthusiasm, my boy, but it has been a very long, very unpleasant day, and besides—your concerns are unwarranted. We have no way to safely navigate the maze." He leaned on the table with his knuckles. "Go to bed."

"I know how to open it."

Talu stilled. "What was that?"

"I figured it out," Math protested. "I told you the map is magical, and trapped. And I told you that it was showing me images, making me choose between them."

"And you said there was no pattern."

"But I was wrong," Math enthused. "I wasn't thinking about sound!"

"Calm yourself."

Math cleared his throat and straightened. "In silence, wisdom, Commander. As I said, the Kaliri seem to associate Kaiataris with loud noise, and I realized that every scene I'd been shown while I was trapped, no matter what the subject matter, had also been a choice between quiet and loud." He shrugged. "Pretty sure all you have to do to solve the puzzle is pick the quiet choices. Which we'd know if that flagstone hadn't been damaged. The instructions on how to open the maze were left at the entrance to the antechamber."

Commander Talu's face looked pinched as he picked up a different box from his desk, fiddled with the puzzle sliders, then set the thing back down again. "Have you tested your hypothesis?"

"Not yet, sir. I came directly to you."

"Might be nothing," the man mused. "It feels right, though. In silence, wisdom."

A good motto for a library, Math thought.

Or a graveyard.

The commander closed his eyes and rubbed at his temples, as if vainly attempting to stave off an oncoming headache. He sighed heavily before opening his eyes again. "Have you told anyone about this hypothesis of yours? How to open the maze?"

"No, Commander," Math replied.

"Not Captain Danvi?"

"No, Commander. I didn't fit the final pieces together until after I'd left the archive."

The commander studied him for a moment longer, trying to gauge his honesty, before he nodded. "Very well." He threw a thick robe over his nightshirt and picked up the largest box from his desk. "Come with me then."

Math frowned, that feeling of dread clutching at his chest once more. "You're not . . . Commander, you're not thinking of trying to solve the maze, are you? It's too dangerous—"

"Were you suddenly promoted and I missed it? Do you think you're in a position to give me orders?" Nothing about the commander's manner was friendly.

"No!" Math lowered his head. "No, Commander." It took everything in him to bite back on adding: *But this is still a terrible idea.*

"Then come along," he ordered, and began walking swiftly down the hall.

Math had no choice but to follow.

The cenobium was quiet. Celebrations had ended, and most were asleep. Distant lights moved through the yard. Above, the stars glittered like jewels. The air was icy; Math wished he'd brought a cloak.

"We're going the wrong way," Math said.

The commander grunted a noncommittal noise. "Come along."

Commander Talu led Math out of the officers' rooms and across the bailey, past the stables. He took Math to one of the warehouses set into the curtain wall. Talu circled a light spell as he entered, although it wasn't necessary, because the knights already there had their own. Both people straightened from where they'd been sitting, clearly uncomfortable to have been found in a moment of idleness.

Talu pointed at a door. "Is that where we're keeping Mr. Abhigan?"

"No, Commander. He's in the next room. Are we sending him back tomorrow?"

"Yes. Unlock this door, please."

A knight did so, looking at both the commander and Math with curiosity. Commander Talu walked inside and motioned for Math to follow.

Inside was an undecorated storeroom.

Math's stomach twisted, an ugly feeling beginning to itch its way up his throat. "What's going on, sir?"

Talu rubbed a hand over his bearded chin. "After the meeting this morning, your sister came to see me. You were scaring her, you see. And she showed me these." He opened one hand, revealing a few wilted green shoots.

No. No, no, no. Tanxi wouldn't have done that. She knew what it would mean, what would happen. She would never—

Math fought to keep his expression placid. He knew he was failing. His heartbeat raced.

"But I wasn't alarmed until this evening, when a knight of Mending brought me identical samples—the plants that he'd pulled from your body. Which means you knew about the plants *before you went to the logging camp*."

Math's eyes widened. "No, that's not true. I can explain."

"Can you? I would be surprised," Talu said. "Then you come to me with this ridiculous story about the Kaliri religion and grim lords. Suddenly Rabu and Yihura's theory about Kaliri witches is starting to seem plausible." He shook the wilted green plants. "Perhaps you're trying to divert attention away from yourself. So you're going to stay here for the night, without fuss, and in isolation. Tomorrow, we'll send you to Bashan. They will find out the truth."

"Commander, no. I'm not—I'm not a traitor!"

"We'll find out, won't we?" Commander Talu stepped back out into the hall. "No one enters without my presence. No one talks to him. He is to be treated as an enemy combatant, understood?"

"Sir?" The knight didn't sound happy.

"Is that understood?"

"Yes, Commander."

"Good." Talu didn't even look at Math as he slammed the storeroom door shut, plunging the room into darkness.

"Commander!"

If Talu heard Math shout, he didn't respond.

The worst part was . . .

The worst part was, he could understand Commander Talu's logic. It looked *damning*, didn't it? Who would look at everything that had happened and think he was innocent?

Except he *was*.

At least Talu didn't think he was a grimmock. No, not a grimmock—just some kind of Kaliri spy and traitor.

He took some comfort in coming to Talu at midnight, when the commander was alone. Otherwise, Talu would've come for him in the morning, with the children present. That would've been a disaster. This way, the novitiates didn't have to see him placed into custody firsthand.

Math circled a light spell—small lightning bugs flitting about—and found himself a seat on a pile of donated frippery slated to be used for papermaking. It was shockingly comfortable.

Now he just had to figure out how to prove his innocence.

SAP

Math had been awake for hours, with no solution in sight—unless exiling himself to a cave counted. Then came a strange noise from the back of the storeroom.

He directed the light to hover in that area. Several stone blocks in the middle of the wall were crumbling, pushed aside to tumble to the ground. A small figure forced his way through the hole, grunting and grinding his teeth.

Catimus Abhigan.

"What are you doing?" Math demanded. He momentarily forgot his own imprisonment, overwhelmed by indignation. Someone had torn a hole in one of Isofal's walls. Somehow, *this* man had managed it.

Abhigan lifted his head, giggling.

Math felt a chill.

The man's bright green eyes were mad. Black juice stained his mouth and dribbled down his chin. Then he grinned, making it more obvious that the juice wasn't black so much as dark green.

Catimus Abhigan lifted a hand to his mouth. A finger was gone—the stump jagged, chewed. Math reeled. Abhigan hadn't lost it. He'd *eaten* it.

"You came," Catimus said, voice singsong. "That was smart." He pointed, oblivious to the missing finger. "The Queens want to talk to *you*."

"The feeling isn't mutual." Math circled a brighter light spell and studied the man again by summoned gaslight. "What have they done to you?" Math wasn't sure the man in front of him even qualified as human anymore.

He realized, dull and thick, that Catimus was a grimmock. Not the undead definition, perhaps, but certainly a living being corrupted and cursed by magic.

"Me?" The man giggled again. "I'm awake. It's so nice. The Green wakes," he giggled. "The Queens are coming. Their day is roots and rot and rain."

"So you said before." Math carefully edged his way around the man and slammed his fist against the door. "You better get in here! That guy we brought back from the logging camp is being really weird!"

Math already knew he'd be ignored.

Meanwhile, Catimus scuttled over to a wall and began running his hands up and down the surface, muttering to himself.

"What are you doing?"

Catimus ignored him.

"You need to stop." Math contemplated just how much trouble he'd get into if he used magic on the man. It seemed the lesser of two evils.

Kill the full-grown. Bring the saplings back to us.

Math's mouth opened in shock. That hadn't been a sound, not even words, but pure intention—heavy, relentless—delivered straight into his thoughts.

Math swallowed painfully, an ugly, heavy feeling dragging at his stomach. They hadn't won against the trees at all, had they?

The Queens had just been taking their measure.

The worst part, though . . . the worst part was how something inside of him wanted to obey.

Gravefuckers, it was the damn spores, wasn't it? They'd done more than cause hallucinations.

The small man grinned at Math as he wiped black-green blood away from his mouth. "You might want to duck."

Still grinning, Abhigan bit down and tore open the veins in his wrist.

Dark green sprayed onto the wall and ran down in rivulets, flowing into the mortar grooves between the stone blocks.

The blood didn't flow the right way. It didn't drip like blood at all, but moved like something alive, something with purpose.

It split, and split again, growing lighter in color as it did until the emerald streams were clearly identifiable as sprouting plants. The crawling vines dug their roots into the mortar with extraordinary speed, doing the work of centuries in a matter of seconds. The vines didn't burst—they slithered. They twined through the mortar like arteries leading to a heart.

Abhigan was expanding, bloating up in a manner not unlike the corpse at the logging camp.

Math dove behind the fabric bales just as Catimus Abhigan exploded.

The explosion wasn't what took down the curtain wall. Rather, it was the blood that wasn't blood, seeping into the stone foundations, transforming into a writhing mass of violently expanding foliage.

The stone groaned. Then it split—deep, like a snapped tree limb. Dust roared outward. Math staggered as the fortress wall tore apart behind him.

A bellowing noise rang out, all too recognizable as Captain Rabu.

Math circled wind-based Storm spells to push falling masonry away from him. Shouts and screams rang out. He couldn't tell if those screams were from the knights stationed outside the storerooms or from some other group. The noise was deafening; Math slammed into a plant-weakened wall just as the ceiling collapsed behind him, filling the air with choking dust. The wall gave way; all the walls gave way. Math fell among shattered stone and rubble in the inside bailey of the cenobium.

Behind him, a giant section of curtain wall vanished.

The cenobium interior was wide open to anyone who might feel like strolling inside. Math didn't need a light spell to know that a whole lot of somethings did indeed feel like doing so.

He heard the trees moving.

Bring the saplings back . . .

The saplings . . .

Math scrambled to his feet. They hadn't meant plants, seedlings, or sprouts. They'd meant the children.

Whatever else, he wasn't letting *that* happen.

RETREAT

Even in peacetime, Captain Rabu's bellow echoed from anywhere in the cenobium. In battle, he was impossible to miss.

At first, Math was happy to hear him, because it meant Rabu was awake and already fighting back the invaders. That was until Math saw that Rabu was attacking *the other knights*.

Rabu was being controlled by the Queens.

This was a disaster. If those Queens were using the purple spores to control everyone who breathed them, that number included dozens of knights and two of the cenobium's strongest fighters. Who could stop Rabu?

Math spotted Lieutenant Nuhzar.

"Nuhzar! Alik!" Math shouted. The man glanced his way and summoned up his halberd, but in the dim light, Math couldn't tell how much armor he wore. Not his full set, certainly.

"They're being controlled!" Math yelled. "Everyone who breathed in the spores is being controlled!"

Nuhzar, thankfully, hadn't been nearby when the spores had spread.

Maybe Nuhzar would've questioned Math more, since Math, too, had breathed in those damn spores—but a violent scream cut the air as Rabu's hammer sent a knight flying across the courtyard.

Nuhzar ran toward his captain.

Math might not hold any fondness for Alik Nuhzar, but he would be the first to admit the man was murder in a fight. Captain Rabu had more experience, not to mention avalanche-like ferocity, but Nuhzar favored precision and speed. He might not win, but he'd distract Rabu until other captains arrived.

Captain Yihura, the archer, was the more serious problem.

Math had already passed two knights with arrows threaded cleanly through the slits in their helmets, dead before they finished falling. Yihura would pick off anyone foolish enough to cross into the open.

Or . . . almost anyone. She'd already had several clear shots on him—each opportunity ignored.

Apparently, the Queens really did want to talk to him.

Meanwhile, they were going to kill everyone he cared about. Maybe not the kids—but their fate wouldn't be much better. And given that Math had been like an older brother to most of them, he couldn't live with the idea of just accepting that outcome.

Thunderclaps boomed. Blinding white light blazed across the courtyard as a bolt flew down from heaven and slammed into a running knight. The man was tossed aside and didn't stir again.

Rolling, violent storm clouds now cloaked the stars that had been visible just hours earlier. The scent of rain-soaked stone, lightning, and freshly cut lumber filled the air. But for the smoke and blood, it might have been beautiful.

The Queens were using magic. That probably made them witches, but the old definitions didn't feel like they applied.

A burst of movement caught his eye—Tanxi, half-dressed, was sprinting down the aerie stairwell, still tugging on her breastplate.

Her gaze slid past him, then snapped back. Her face was a battleground of worry and relief. "Who's attacking?" she demanded, stepping into the courtyard.

"No!" Math grabbed her arm and yanked her back. A second later, an arrow slammed into a nearby pillar—right where Tanxi's head had been.

Tanxi answered with a second-circle Storm spell. Wind howled around her, flinging arrows off course and pelting Math with grit and stone. It wouldn't stop a certain captain from using her manifested weapon.

"Stay under cover. The trees are attacking." Ridiculous, but it was the only explanation he had. "They're controlling Rabu and Yihura and some of the knights." He tightened his hold on her arm, ignoring the stinging debris. "Did you send off a bird?"

"Are you joking? I sent them all."

"Good. Tanxi, I . . ."

He had questions. *Why* had his sister gone to Talu? Had she any idea what was going to happen to him?

She looked worried, not guilty—certainly not like someone who knew she'd betrayed him.

This wasn't the time.

"I overheard some of the knights being controlled. Their orders are to kill the adults, but capture the children and bring them to those monsters. I don't know why, but if it's anything like what they did to the lumberjacks back at that camp, we have to stop them."

"Does Commander Talu know this?" Was he imagining the hesitation in her voice?

"I don't know where the commander is." That, at least, wasn't a lie. "You go find him. I'm taking the novitiates to the—"

He paused.

If this were an ordinary army, there were protocols: secret exits, fallback positions. But the Queens? One might be waiting in ambush at any exit.

When escape was impossible, a different protocol took priority.

"I'm taking them to the maze antechamber," he finished. He'd apologize to that knight on watch if they both lived. Apparently, he was going back there after all.

"Don't be a fool," Tanxi said. "I'll come with you. You aren't wearing armor. You don't even have a weapon."

True enough. If he could summon one out of thin air, he wouldn't be a novitiate.

He almost argued, but Tanxi might be safer at his side.

"Fine," he said. "Let's go."

SILENCE

They caught up to Master Wadera as he was herding his charges to one of the postern gates. Math and Tanxi intercepted, warning the old man that the path might be compromised. The antechamber, they said, was safer.

Master Wadera didn't argue. Perhaps the idea of navigating steep, rain-slicked stairs in the dark while carrying toddlers was reason enough. He passed Jura and Shavru to Math and Tanxi, while he kept Hamu on his hip, muttering reassurances to the blind boy. Jaiik and Taris were shepherding Ayiad and Khariik, while Iduan held hands with the twins, Yasib and Mudiya, and Satu and Fahura had death grips on Master Wadera's cloak.

The children were barely constrained chaos on a good day. Tonight? A storm screamed outside, punctuated with flashes of lightning. Thunder shook the very stones. In the distance, metal clashed against metal . . . or wood. The children were upset, verging on tears. Math could hardly blame them.

They rushed into the hallway outside the antechamber. The knight posted earlier was gone.

Math, Tanxi, Master Wadera, and even some of the children all circled Sun spells for light. No one spoke, but the awkwardness wasn't silent: the raindrops hitting the stone outside the window echoed with disturbing volume, breaking up the low whimpers of crying children.

Tanxi's voice cut through the sound. "Math." She glanced up at the small window. "Will this room be secure?"

Math followed her gaze. There were only two ways into the room from outside: the doorway they'd just used and that tiny window. It overlooked the river, impossible to access from the outside . . . for a human.

Not impossible for something made from roots, branches, and vines.

"No." Math grabbed her arm and yanked her aside, aware that everyone else was staring.

"Hey!" Tanxi made a half-hearted attempt to free herself.

"Did you tell Commander Talu about my plants?"

She flinched. "Math—"

"Tri-Mother. You did."

"I was trying to help."

"By handing him the vines to hang me with?"

"I thought it would prove you weren't part of—"

"He's accused me of being a traitor, Tanxi." He hadn't meant it to sound so raw, but the words tore out of him, bloody and wounded.

She wrenched free. "This isn't the time—"

"I never thought it would be you," Math whispered. "Not *you*."

He could've taken it from Alik. Might have even expected it. But Tanxi? She'd been the one lecturing *him*, the one who knew exactly what it would cost Math if the Order decided that his lack of control pushed him out of the category of "knight" or even "monk" and into something best described as "grimmock." She *knew* how much he hated waking up after losing control.

After all her scolding, *she'd* been the one to go to Talu.

Tanxi knew what they might call him if he lost control again. And still, she'd gone to Talu. Did she really think he couldn't hold the line?

"Sir Tanxi? Math?" Wadera's voice cut in, calm but wary. "Everything all right?"

Math stepped away from his sister, face hot. "We were just—"

"Talking strategy." Tanxi's voice was clipped, professional. She'd pulled herself into an Idallik Knight's iron-straight posture.

Wadera didn't look convinced, but was too busy corralling the children to press further.

"Are we going to die?" Satu's eyes were the size of coins. Two of the children began crying.

Wadera kneeled and wrapped an arm around the boy. "What was that? No, no, no. This is a safe place. Now everyone gather around. I'm going to tell you a story."

No one cheered, but the children stopped crying.

Math turned back to Tanxi. "This isn't over."

"No, but it has to wait." She tilted her head. "What now?"

As if Math hadn't been improvising the whole time.

Math's eyes caught on the yawning black doorway leading into the physical maze. He turned his head to study the maze map on the wall.

There were only two ways into the antechamber, but there was a third way *out*.

Except, even if Math had figured out how to open the maze, would that be safer? If he was right about the grim lord Kaiataris, who knew what monsters she might have left waiting in the center of her maze?

But he already knew what monsters advanced on their position. He thought about people trapped inside trees, torn apart, turned into living bombs.

If they stayed in the antechamber, they'd die. Slowly. Horribly.

The maze? At least they stood a chance in the maze.

Math pointed to the wrought-iron gate locking the entrance to the maze. "Tanxi, cut that open, please? We're hiding inside the maze."

"We're going into the maze?" Jaiik half asked, half shouted with wide eyes.

A dozen kids stared like Math had just announced dessert for breakfast. He really should have remembered that nothing motivated a child like the opportunity to do something forbidden.

"Yes," Math said. "We are."

Wadera gave him a thundercloud glare. "Mathaiik Kaven, that maze isn't safe—"

"I can find the safe path." Math gestured to the surrounding room. "We can't stay here. It's not secure."

Tanxi didn't hesitate: she summoned her sword and carved through the gate as if it was made of ice. The bars melted and fell.

Master Wadera grabbed Iduan before she could dart inside. "No," he told the girl sternly.

"But he said—"

"I need to solve the maze first," Math told her. "If you go now, you'll get lost and starve to death in hideous agony. Why don't you help Master Wadera keep an eye on everyone? You know how Jaiik gets."

Iduan crossed her arms and glared at him like a tiny little displeased queen. "I see what you're doing."

Math grinned. "I'm counting on you."

"Fine!" She rolled her eyes even as Master Wadera let her go. She stomped back over to the others, flicked Jaiik and Taris on the head, and declared, "I'm Captain of Safety and you're my lieutenants and we're going to make sure no one goes into the maze before Math is ready."

Jaiik gave her an unimpressed stare. "You're eight."

"And still Captain of Safety!" she screamed.

Ayiad pulled on her sleeve. "I'll be your lieutenant," the slightly younger girl suggested.

"Nope," Jaiik said. "That's already taken. I'm Lieutenant of Safety."

More haggling, arguing, and accusations broke out immediately.

"Hurry," Master Wadera mouthed.

"I'm working on it," Math said. "Watch my back."

Tanxi started to say something, but glanced at the children and closed her mouth. She tried again, saying: "I'll wake you if . . . you know."

If they were about to die.

He nodded as he sat, crossed his legs. The children's bickering faded into a background hum.

He would've liked more time, would've liked to be more certain about his theories, but he had no choice. He didn't know how long it would take for the trees to find them, if the captains retained enough of their faculties to remember the maze antechamber under the library sections.

There was no time.

The map loomed in front of him. He focused and circled the scrying spell that Commander Talu seemed to think was beyond his abilities.

First intersection: a chaotic, hectic battle scene contrasted with a flowering meadow. He chose the meadow. Next was a silent graveyard versus a group of children, playing under a tree. He picked the graveyard. A rushing river, loud and vibrant as it flowed over rocks. A lake frozen over in winter. The lake.

Each vision offered a choice that looked like a test of character—grief or joy, life or death, justice or mercy. But none of it mattered. The only truth was volume. Pick the quiet path, and the maze let you move forward. Pick the clamor, and you were kicked back to the maze's beginning.

In silence, wisdom.

At last: a peaceful beach with crashing surf and screaming gulls, or blackness. Not an empty void, but a space filled with stars and spheres, jewel-like and beautiful, dancing around him in absolute silence.

Math chose silence.

The map immediately ejected him.

Math opened his eyes to see light, the antechamber, his sister's anxious brown eyes.

"It kicked me out. I don't . . ."

"No. Look." She pointed to the map carved into the wall. "You solved it."

The map now hardly qualified as depicting a maze. The correct path ran from the start directly to the map's center. To solve the maze would require no turns at all.

Just walk a straight line.

Math rushed to the entrance to the physical maze, that yawning black doorway. He tossed out a light spell. The spell pierced all the way through, the way it never had before, illuminating a straight corridor that ran straight to the center.

"It's open," Math breathed. "Let's go."

"But what about—" Wadera began.

"It's not trapped," Math reassured him. It never had been before. The only trap had been the maze itself. "Anyway, we don't have time. We need to get inside, right now."

"Mathaiik!" Tanxi made his name a whole lecture.

"We can argue about it in the center," Math snapped. "Go!" He shooed everyone forward.

The children needed herding, but the maze held no more illusions. They followed the corridor to another door—one that hadn't existed before.

Everyone hesitated.

Math walked forward, light spell in hand.

He felt something as he did, a strange bubbling energy that pulsed through him, pushed at his mind. He couldn't identify it, except that it felt like a last barrier—one last defense to keep out interlopers.

He pushed back, harder. The barrier broke, melted into something warm, even pleasant.

Math paused, but felt no other strange sensations.

Then he saw the room.

It looked like what the Idallik Order had always thought lay in the center of the maze: a library. Wall-to-wall shelves of metal-bound books, the last unopened archive in the entire world.

A treasure trove of unimaginable proportions left behind by the Illuminated for those who valued knowledge—or power.

In one way, though—in one particular, specific way—it was nothing like the Order's legends, and everything like what Math had feared.

In the room's center, on a marble slab, lay a girl.

AWAKEN

The moment Math passed the threshold, crystal lanterns flared to life, casting shards of soft light into every corner.

"It's a girl!" one of the children exclaimed.

"Yes," Tanxi replied. "We can see that."

No, Math thought. Not a girl.

A grim lord: Kaiataris Von.

Of all the things he'd expected to find in the heart of the maze, the woman herself wasn't one of them.

It had to be her, though.

Kaiataris provided the only color in an otherwise stark room of white marble, silver-clad books, transparent crystal, and gray metal. If her skin had been white, he might've mistaken her for one of the statues they carved atop funeral caskets in the west. Her skin was that smooth, her body that still. She appeared no older than Math, and never in his entire life had he seen someone who looked less like a "necromancer."

Her golden-brown skin and angular eyes were typical of the Souna people from the Rokasmaa grasslands. Her lips and nose were small. He couldn't see her eyes, but suspected they would be a brown so dark as to verge on black. Her hair, kissed with sun-streaked highlights, wrapped her head in intricate braids. She wore a flowing gray dress so thin it scandalously outlined every curve. Golden rings, chains, and bracelets crossed her arms and circled her throat.

Writing carved into the slab's edge completed the quote that began outside:
IN SILENCE, WISDOM IS KNOWING THE DIFFERENCE BETWEEN THE LIBRARY AND THE TOMB.

Math was unnerved at how closely his thoughts had mirrored the infamous grim lord's.

He could already feel how his life would forever be divided into two parts: before first seeing Kaiataris, and after.

Also, she hardly needed armies of the dead to defeat her enemies. A coy look would've worked just as well.

He'd assumed the author who'd commented on the beauty of her statues had been exaggerating. Instead, they'd undersold it. Someone should have mentioned that Kaiataris was the sort of beauty that heroes from legends once went to war over. Lisadre and the Sea Serpent or Cyala of the Halkanis Wars.

Someone tugged on Math's trousers. He glanced down to see little Jura. "Is she sleeping?" the little girl asked, holding out her arms to be picked up.

"No." Math dragged his gaze from the dead woman. He lifted Jura to his side.

"This must be a tomb." Master Wadera's hand hovered over his collar as though he hadn't decided whether he wanted to clutch his robes or his beard. "She must be one of the Illuminated."

Math didn't trust himself to answer. If she was one of the Illuminated, then everything the Order believed was wrong.

"We need to reset the maze," Tanxi said. "So they can't follow us inside."

Math exhaled. "You're right. Let's spread out and look for a map or switch—something simple. Captain of Safety," he shot a theatrical look at Iduan, "your job is to make sure no one touches anything."

The little girl bounced in his arms. "Are you going to kiss the pretty lady and break the spell?"

Math blinked. "What?" He glanced at the body, then away. "No!"

Jaiik piped up, "Can I kiss the pretty lady and break the spell?"

Tanxi burst into tense laughter as Taris smacked Jaiik's head.

"No! You can't— Tanxi, stop laughing." Math glared at his sister, who'd covered her mouth but whose eyes still betrayed her amusement. Worse, Master Wadera was laughing too.

Math groaned. "No one is kissing anyone. We are the Idallik Order. We don't *do* that."

His sister stopped laughing and stared flatly at him.

"Work with me here," Math muttered. "I'm trying to set a good example."

"Whatever you say, little brother."

Ignoring her, Math pointed at the unmoving, still, hopefully dead woman. "No kissing the scary dead lady. Understood?"

"I don't know if I'd call her scary," Tanxi said. "A little underdressed, maybe, but that's more tempting than frightening. Though . . . Never mind. Idallik Order. I stand corrected: terrifying."

Math sighed in frustration, hugging Jura before handing her back to Taris. He pulled Tanxi aside. "She's scary because she's a grim lord, Tan."

Her eyes flicked to the body. "What? I'm sorry, you just said . . . *what?*"

"That's Kaiataris. *The* Kaiataris. No one goes near that body. Ever."

A loud thud echoed from the distance—something slamming into the antechamber door. Math and Tanxi turned toward it. Something was trying to break in. Maybe it was Captain Rabu. Maybe it was a giant animated tree.

Neither option was ideal.

Before Math could shout orders, a movement caught his eye. Iduan was making a mad dash for the grim lord's body, apparently having decided forgiveness trounced permission. Or maybe she'd convinced herself touching the woman's jewelry wasn't the same as touching the woman herself.

"Iduan, no!" Tanxi shouted.

Math ran faster than he'd ever run before. He grabbed the girl's waist and swung her out of the way, narrowly avoiding the marble slab. His hip slammed into the edge, a bruise forming even as he held Iduan away from the body.

"What did I just say?" Math hissed, fighting not to shout. Iduan's eyes widened, ready to unleash the most effective weapon in her arsenal and start crying. "No waking the scary death lady, okay?"

Iduan's only response was to flinch as a thunderous boom echoed from the far side of the antechamber beyond the maze.

Then the wall exploded.

The children whimpered; the older novitiates summoned their courage.

"Jaiik, Taris," Master Wadera called. "Get the children behind the stacks!"

"But we can help!" Taris protested.

"You can help by staying out of the way," Math ordered. "Make sure no one else touches anything."

Master Wadera gave him an approving look as the older man summoned his staff. "Well said."

Math grabbed a sword from the wall. Another crash drew his attention back to the maze.

The trees were coming. All too quickly for something that creaked and groaned and shouldn't move at all.

Math could feel them, even before he saw them. Roots writhed on the stone floor, sending out waves of murderous intent. The trees were angry. One of them was recognizably one of the giant trees Math had seen at the logging camp—a Queen. Math felt the same sense of wrongness he had the first time he'd seen them: the feeling that he gazed upon something of vast, terrible intelligence, more horrible for taking a shape so familiar.

Underneath the dark shadows of her looming branches, Captain Rabu advanced.

"Captain Rabu, you can resist this!" Math shouted. But the captain wasn't listening. He was too far gone.

Math didn't know what had happened to Lieutenant Nuhzar, but he feared the worst.

Tanxi pushed herself in front of Math, her sword a white-hot bar of light. "Come any closer and it'll be your last move."

Captain Rabu laughed. "Surrender, monster, and I'll make it quick."

Math wondered what the captain thought he was seeing.

Master Wadera tapped his staff against the ground, causing a rumble. "Think, Captain. This isn't you."

Math's gut clenched as Rabu advanced. Both Wadera and Rabu had Land resonance, but Rabu was younger and stronger. Taking him alive would be near impossible.

Rabu's first swing missed but demolished a bookshelf. Math felt a spike of panic, but no cries followed; the children were hiding elsewhere.

Math worked around the edges of the fight, dashing in to breach Rabu's defenses and make small cuts that he could only hope would have a cumulative weakening effect. Tanxi was making quick work of many of the smaller trees, but she was tiring.

Rabu's second swing landed with a gut-wrenching crunch against Master Wadera. Despite the obvious injury, the elderly knight stayed on his feet, slamming his staff against Rabu's shoulder. The captain staggered, but fury replaced the pain as the captain rallied.

But Math had lost track of the Queen in the chaos—a costly mistake.

The ground under Master Wadera vanished. Wadera fell five feet before the stone returned. The old master screamed.

Math screamed too. He rushed forward, hoping to distract Captain Rabu from killing the man who'd raised him. Math was as surprised as anyone when he slipped his sword under Rabu's arm and found a weak spot in the man's armor. A second later, Rabu shoved Math away with casual disregard, tossing him backward, straight against Kaiataris's marble slab.

The captain turned back to the still-struggling Master Wadera and raised his hammer.

The sound of Master Wadera's death would haunt Math forever: a slick, wet splatter and a crunch of splintering bone. What remained no longer looked human. It was nothing more than meat.

Math found no comfort in the way Captain Rabu staggered after, as if he'd finally noticed his own fatal injury.

Math grabbed the edge of the marble slab and pushed himself to his feet. He glanced at it, distracted. Then a cold spike of fear pierced him, washed away any anger. The marble slab lay empty.

The necromancer's body was gone.

Math shoved down his panic, an emotion that helped no one. He would deal with the implications later. He would—

A woman's hand, clad in gold jewelry, touched his shoulder.

Time stopped.

Math glanced up and stared straight into the necromancer's eyes.

He'd been right about their color—blacker than the deepest woods at night.

He could scarcely describe the feeling of looking into her eyes, a strange combination of horror and fascination. The sort of allure one might feel at the top of a cliff when some darker, destructive part of the soul whispered how easy it would be to step off into the abyss and lose oneself forever.

"Worry not, fair knight," she said to him, oh so gently. "I did not expect to be woken by the sounds of battle, but you have done your job this day."

He should attack her. He knew he should attack her, but—

A child screamed.

Math's head whipped back to where the trees had pushed aside a stone bookcase to advance on the children. Jaiik stood in front of the group, trembling but defiant, holding a javelin that crackled with lightning.

Jaiik's resonance was Storm. He'd manifested his weapon.

It wouldn't be enough.

"Get away from them!" Math shouted.

Then a soft voice cut across all others, as if every other sound belonged to events happening miles away.

"Has it truly been so long that you have forgotten what it means to attack a graven wizard in her own domain?" Kaiataris floated above the slab, her hair rimmed with ghostly light.

Her eyes rolled back into her head, revealing whites glowing the same hue. Crackling pops of energy, something that might have been mistaken for lightning without Jaiik providing a reference of the real thing, danced over her metal jewelry before radiating out to touch the walls, the floor, the ceiling.

Those surfaces, too, glowed with fine lines, forming traceries that merged into symbols and glyphs, raced from her fingertips to encompass the totality of the room. The walls—the maze itself—pulsed with her power.

The trees *burned*.

Something else was happening, too. A feeling of abandoned graveyards and the hair-raising certainty that something ugly and unnatural had just opened its eyes.

A dead knight rose back to his feet. He began attacking the tree people he'd been helping before Tanxi had slain him.

He was only the first. Others soon followed.

Captain Rabu staggered and fell to one knee. He bled freely, a steady stream of red coloring his silver armor. The captain choked, although not from any obvious cause. Then Math noticed that sweet, sad little Satu had poked his head from behind Taris's leg, his face twisted with hate in a way that Math had never seen before. Tears streamed down the little boy's cheeks.

Satu wasn't summoning a weapon. He was summoning water—inside Rabu's lungs. The Captain of Swords was drowning on dry land.

The exact moment of the captain's death was easily pinpointed, too, because Rabu barely collapsed to the ground before he was rising again as one of the dead. His hammer vanished, but he didn't seem to notice or care, instead using his bare hands to tear apart bark and flesh.

Then the Queen screamed.

The sound was a piercing stab inside his head. Every tree or controlled person on the battlefield recoiled. The Queen thrashed as she tried to run, but the maze had her trapped. She turned into a pyre, collapsing to the ground with the scent of burning wood.

Math turned to Kaiataris.

The grim lord no longer floated, but stood atop the marble slab, staring at the scene with distaste.

"Was Ice Falls destroyed?" she asked Math. Her accent was archaic, but her manner was congenial, as if she was catching up on gossip with an old friend. "All of it, destroyed save for these small spaces: my sanctum and the maze?"

"You keep away from him!" his sister yelled as she ran over, brandishing her sword.

"Tanxi, stay back," Math warned. He hadn't forgotten how much damage the necromancer had done and how easily she'd done it. How she'd animated the dead—for all he knew, was still animating the dead.

Said necromancer gazed at his sister with bemused ambivalence. Math could feel the frustration and annoyance boiling off of Kaiataris for all that none of it showed in her expression.

"It is done," Kaiataris said.

A further disturbance from the antechamber drew everyone's attention. None of them wanted some magical surprise that might turn their hard and painfully won victory into an equally bitter defeat.

Luck was with them, however. Instead of more trees, more knights arrived, knights Math knew weren't infected, including Lieutenant Nuhzar and Commander Talu. Much as Math was pleased for the reinforcements, he couldn't help but feel dread: Math wasn't supposed to be there.

As he tried in desperation to come up with some excuse, any excuse, that might be acceptable, he heard a sharp exhale from his sister. "What the . . ."

Math turned around and stared.

The grim lord Kaiataris Von had disappeared.

TRANSPORTATION

In the morning, Math watched as they dragged bodies into the open. It was painfully clear how many of the dead had fallen to other Idallik Knights—men and women he'd known, trained beside, laughed with.

It was just as clear how many of the living thought Math was responsible for the dead.

"He was under arrest last night, too, and look how much damage he did." The knight wasn't shouting, but only just. A knot of them had gathered in the courtyard, righteous and vengeful. Math had no doubt what kind of justice they thought he deserved. "He killed Captain Rabu."

"And a good thing, too," Captain Danvi called out from across the courtyard.

Math was relieved she'd survived—though she'd only done so because she'd fallen asleep at her desk in the Library of Legacies and missed the fighting entirely.

"Captain Rabu killed half the people lying over there," Commander Talu said, voice clipped. "You'll need a better argument." He turned away from the protestor, back to Captain Qin of Riddles, who had already shackled Math into the back of a wagon. "Stick to the main roads. I doubt the creatures will attack again so soon, but that's hope, not certainty."

Math didn't ask why they weren't quickening their journey: the body of the Captain of Fields lay with the other corpses. The only other person who could cast that spell (at least as far as Math knew) was Commander Talu. He'd left at first light and was already back with reinforcements, but Talu was stretched thin. He was hardly going to waste time personally escorting a suspected traitor who'd thrown in with the Kaliri . . . or whoever was controlling those plants.

A sharp voice rang out behind them. "Wait—please."

Tanxi.

Math closed his eyes. He hadn't seen her since last night. He'd hoped, selfishly, that she was asleep or occupied elsewhere, sparing them both this moment.

But there she was, limping slightly, one arm bound in a sling, dirt and dried blood staining her cloak. Her face crumpled when she saw him in chains.

"Commander—please, don't take him like this. He hasn't even been—"

"You should be resting, Tanxi," Commander Talu said without turning around. "You're letting your emotions get the better of you."

"But he's not—" Her voice cracked. Tanxi swallowed, struggling to get herself under control. "He's not what you think. It wasn't—"

Math thought she was smarter than this. She couldn't save him. All she could do was put herself in the same cage.

Well, at least he could stop that from happening.

"Just stop," he growled. "Don't pretend you care. You just don't want to feel guilty."

That landed like a slap. She flinched.

"I was trying to protect you," she whispered.

"Funny how you've never once managed that," Math said viciously.

Tanxi's breath hitched, but she didn't argue. She just stood there, shattered, as the knights finished securing the wagon. Then, slowly, her expression froze, hardened, turned to stone.

She spun on her heel and stalked away.

Math slumped in relief. At least no one was going to think she'd been colluding with him now. Maybe that she was naive and too trusting, but not a traitor.

"I didn't do this, Commander," Math said, not for the first time. The words tasted like ash. He shifted in the cage to keep a gear bag from jabbing into his back.

Talu shot him an annoyed look. "We'll find out, won't we?"

Captain Qin swung into the saddle. The knights fell into formation.

Math gave the courtyard one last look. Mud and blood. The scent of smoke. Bodies were still being carried out of the maze. Most people ignored the wagon as it rattled into motion.

He had spent nearly his entire life at Isofal Cenobium.

He never thought he'd leave like this: not hailed as a hero, but hauled away like a villain.

He shut his eyes and looked away before he lost control.

The snap of reins, the nickering of horses, and the soft jerk of the wagon as it started rolling were the only goodbyes he received.

No one spoke for hours.

They stopped a few times, just long enough for someone to unlock the shackle on Math's leg and loosen his hands so he could relieve himself—always under close guard, weapons drawn, a spear tip grazing his throat.

Math didn't blame them. He would've done the same. Who wouldn't suspect a magically trained member of the Order over a gibbering civilian when half a fortress wall came crashing down?

But there was no way that the Queens were a Kaliri plot. These creatures were older than Kaliri or Rokasmaa.

The memory of Catimus Abhigan's face rose again—bright with mischief, fully aware. Not enthralled or dull, vacant and under magical thrall. Not afraid, but proud and exultant.

Insane? Absolutely. Mad as a sack of shrieking hyenas, but not scared. Not the slightest bit scared.

Math hunched deeper into the corner of the wagon. The ache in his wrists had faded, but the rawness in his chest hadn't. He couldn't stop thinking about Tanxi's face—shocked, stricken, guilty. He hadn't even looked at her at the end.

The horrible thing is that Tanxi thought she was protecting him. She probably really had thought she was helping. It hurt to think about her lecturing him on controlling himself only for her to turn around and go straight to the commander.

Talu hadn't hesitated.

And that hurt more than he could admit. Talu had taught him to cast his first spell. Had trained him, scolded him, praised him. He'd never called the man "Father," but in the deepest corners of himself, Talu had worn that label right alongside Master Wadera.

Now one of those men was dead and the other had branded him a traitor.

"There was a time I thought you'd join my section," said Captain Qin from the driver's seat, his voice so soft Math nearly missed it.

They'd been riding all day. The sun hung low in the sky, its amber light slicing through the tree canopy.

"There was a time I wanted that too, Captain."

"What changed? Or was it ever in question? Some of the knights were whispering that you must have Kaliri blood in you."

Math scowled. "I'm from Valmaki County. Everyone here has *some* Kaliri blood. They make sure of it every time they invade." His throat closed up again. "But I'd never—*never*—betray the Order."

"I'm not the one you'll have to convince," Qin said, not turning around.

Math sat straighter. A spike of emotion surged in his gut—panic, fury, dread. It made no sense. He wasn't feeling that way—

They weren't *his* emotions.

"Someone's nearby," Math warned the captain.

The Queens? Was he feeling the Queens? No, he didn't think so. This didn't feel alien the way they had. This felt all too human.

Qin didn't answer. "I hear the regent's people are very good at pulling the truth—"

A chain of sharp, thunderous cracks split the air.

The back of Qin's head exploded in a burst of blood and bone. Something slammed into the wagon's rear wall, splintering it apart. Horses screamed. More cracks echoed—deafening, unnatural. The panicked team of horses bolted, tangled and bleeding, then collapsed mid-run. The wagon lurched and crashed into their bodies, hurling Math backward into a heap of armor bags.

Knights shouted. Strange voices answered in a foreign tongue, fast and clipped. The air filled with the smell of blood and sulfurous black powder.

The ambushers were deliberate. They picked off the horses first, then calmly and efficiently reloaded before executing the knights pinned beneath the fallen beasts.

Math twisted toward the wagon's side, scrabbling for cover, working frantically at his bindings.

The shackle on his ankle was still locked. Useless.

He'd just freed his hands when a man rounded the wagon and aimed a long wood-and-metal tube directly at Math's face.

The man was Kaliri.

Math had never seen a Kaliri in person, but the Kaliri had been too ever-present a threat for him not to recognize the descriptions.

Talu had been right?

Math had no idea how the weapon the Kaliri was holding worked, but considering how Captain Qin had just died, he could guess. Judging by the smell, it used black powder—and Kaliri was the only country that had refused to sign the Innalova Accords forbidding the use of black-powder weapons.

Math circled a Sun spell and set the man's coat on fire.

The Kaliri startled, probably more worried about the powder charges he carried than the flames. But instead of screaming or patting himself down, he *circled his own spell.*

And the fire vanished.

He's a mage, Math thought with horror. *He's a Kaliri mage.*

The man smirked, lifting the weapon again, eye aligning with the barrel.

Then a horse reared and smashed its hooves into the man's skull.

Math would've promised the stallion all the carrots in the world, except he didn't think the horse would care. The horse was already dead.

Its side had been torn open. It shouldn't have been able to stand, let alone charge. Yet it did—glass-eyed, bleeding—and trampled the Kaliri assassin before turning on the others.

Math peered over the side of the wagon.

Fog had drifted in from the trees, pale fingers snaking through the ditches. The setting sun painted twisted shadows across the forest floor. Everything looked stretched, surreal.

The horse wasn't alone.

Knights were rising, one by one—some missing limbs, others with crushed torsos. Captain Qin's face was a mask of gore, one eye rolling blindly. Still he moved, just like the others.

They attacked the Kaliri in grim silence, unflinching and methodical. Math watched one knight get shot point-blank in the chest, stagger back—then snatch the weapon and beat its wielder to death with it.

None spoke as they went about killing their murderers with great industry.

The ambush had turned into a rout.

Math's wrists were free, but his ankle wasn't. He could use magic to erode the links, given time—but he didn't *have* time.

He glanced around for the key. In theory, the captain had it, but Captain Qin's corpse had wandered off.

Then the sound of the fighting stopped. He didn't hear a groan or a breath: the silence was complete.

Math sat up, heart hammering.

Bodies lay scattered everywhere: Idallik Knights, horses, Kaliri assassins. All were still and lifeless.

Something moved behind him.

He turned—and found himself face-to-face with the thing he feared most.

She hadn't changed much since the night before. Her hair was windblown and tousled now, but her dress was still scandalously thin. Midnight eyes watched him without apology or shame. Her presence . . . pulled at him, like a rope knotted behind his sternum he couldn't untie.

The grim lord Kaiataris dangled a familiar iron key from her fingertip. "Need this, fair knight?"

"Give that to me."

She tilted her head, smiling faintly, then descended from the berm like a noblewoman trying not to dirty her hem. She handed him the key. Her brow arched at how violently he snatched it away from her.

Then she turned her back and began picking through corpses.

Math frowned. He was pretty sure he'd just been dismissed as inconsequential.

Math unlocked the shackle and scrambled out of the wagon. He snatched up the long, thin not-a-bombard from the Kaliri agent who'd unsuccessfully tried to shoot him. The weapon was essentially a metal tube attached to a wooden stock of the crossbow type, designed to make it more comfortable to seat against one's shoulder. A covered chamber filled with black powder sat at the beginning of the metal section, itself capped by a small, mirrored half dome. Underneath the metal tube was something similar to a crossbow's release mechanism. Delicate whorls and patterns had been engraved into the metal to resemble smoke.

How to use it seemed obvious enough: he braced the weapon against his shoulder and aimed it at Kaiataris.

"These aren't bandits, are they?" she asked, not bothering to look up.

"No."

Math tightened his grip on the wooden underguard. He didn't put his hand on the trigger just yet—he was unsure how much force was required to set it off. Honestly, he wasn't sure that would work—he'd always been taught that bombards required lit fuses to ignite the black powder, and he saw nothing like that here. Then again, bombard cannons were giant monstrosities as large as a full-grown adult lying on their side, while this was a previously unknown handheld variety.

A previously unknown but undeniably lethal variety.

Kaiataris kneeled beside Captain Qin's body.

"Get away from him."

She paused, turned, papers in hand. Her eyes flicked to the strange weapon. "Are you angry at *me*? For what possible reason?"

"That was a captain of the Idallik Order. I won't let you desecrate his body with—whatever obscenity you're planning."

She tucked the pages under her arm and stood. "Shall I remind you that the obscenity I just committed was saving your life? Twice in the last day, if memory serves."

"It's not—" The weapon wavered. "Why would you even *do* that? Why would a grim lord save anyone? Let alone *me*?" He gazed at all the corpses littering the battlefield. "My order is *never* going to believe I'm not a traitor now. This is going to look like the Kaliri attacked to recover their agent. Were they under your orders?"

"My orders?" she scoffed. "Did I not just slay them all?"

"They *worship* you. You could order them to their deaths and they'd go gladly."

"They what?" Her voice leaped to a pitch of incredulous outrage. "They *worship* me? Why would they worship *me*?"

"Because you're a grim lord? You lot *love* that kind of thing!"

He didn't understand what he was feeling, but he didn't like it. The emotions pouring into him were raw, overwhelming: confusion, panic, disgust, wounded pride.

She studied him long and hard, then said quietly, "Then I suppose I should start with the obvious."

"Oh? What's that?"

"What in the world is a grim lord?"

ASSASSINS

Math didn't lower the weapon.

"You're seriously asking me what a grim lord is?" he said, scowling.

She smiled, but it was thin and cold. "Be honest: Did they give me a knight who's exquisitely beautiful but not very bright? You can tell me. I won't even be offended." She stomped a foot, splattering mud. "If I already knew the answer, I wouldn't have asked!"

His jaw dropped. *Give her a knight?* Did she honestly think he was a *gift*?

He might've brushed it off as a figure of speech—but with *her*, that didn't feel like a safe bet.

"You should know the answer," he said. "*You're* a grim lord. One of the necromancers who enslaved humanity." He gestured to the corpses. "And don't pretend you're not. After this and what you did last night? Textbook evil necromancer."

"Evil necromancer," Kaiataris mouthed. "You *mean* it. Dear stars, how long have we been asleep?"

"Asleep?"

"Yes," she snapped, her irritation unmistakable. "From our enchanted slumber—the spell we graved to save humanity from the solstice. How long—"

"Since when is a *solstice* a threat to humanity? We have them twice a year!"

She blinked, outrage flaring. "Not the seasonal kind. The *magical* solstice." Her expression turned to horror. "Except you have no idea of what I speak, do you?"

"No, and I probably wouldn't believe you if I did, because *you're Kaiataris*." His nostrils flared as he shoved down panic and rapidly spiraling dread. "You *are* Kaiataris, aren't you?"

"Yes!" Kaiataris took a deep breath and said in a more normal tone of voice, "Although it's pronounced KAI-at-aris. The first *a* is part of a diphthong, and the second two *a*'s are monophthongs. So 'Kai' rhymes with 'lie' and 'at' rhymes with 'bet.'" She shrugged. "At least the way I pronounce those sounds. *You* have an accent."

Math stared.

"Don't look at me like that." She crossed her arms over her chest. "I've overslept for a few centuries and wake to find that people have dubbed my order 'grim lords' and I'm being described as an 'evil necromancer.' The least you can do is pronounce my name correctly."

"You *did* raise the dead. Twice. *I watched.*"

"It's hardly my fault that corpses are so convenient to animate. They come pre-articulated." She glared. "And again, both times, it saved your life. A little gratitude wouldn't be amiss. Didn't your parents ever—" She stopped. He felt her sudden embarrassment. "Apologies. I wasn't aware that was a sensitive subject."

He stepped back, appalled. It wasn't his imagination, was it? He'd *felt* her embarrassment—felt it as though it were his own.

What had she done to him? She must have done something.

Kaiataris's expression turned worried, troubled. He watched her take a deep breath to steady herself.

Now he felt her chagrin, her concern. This was starting to scare him, and he wasn't sure what was worse: the fact that he could feel her emotions or that apparently *she could feel his, too.*

She wasn't gloating, though. He would've expected more gloating from an evil, beautiful necromancer who'd just enthralled a new slave. Come to think of it, he would've expected more blind obedience from said enthralled slave, and that didn't seem to be happening, either.

Case in point:

"Just go." Math shifted his grip on the black-powder long arm. "Thank you for saving my life. I'll return the favor by pretending I never saw you."

She looked visibly taken aback. "But what will you do?"

Math didn't answer right away. He squatted beside Captain Qin's body, setting the black-powder weapon against his shoulder. From a pouch at the man's belt, he pulled a small carved disk.

"I'm waiting here. Isofal will check in on our progress using this. The next time they do, they'll see the bodies and send reinforcements. Someone needs to explain what happened. The Order needs to know the Kaliri are using these new weapons."

She tilted her head. "This is new?"

"The Innalova Accords ban category-one weapons, except Kaliri never signed the accords. And this"—he nodded at the weapon—"I've never even *heard* of anything like this." Math scoffed. "As if we didn't have enough problems."

"So you wish to warn your peers. Commendable. But you can't stay."

"I *have* to. If I run, I look guilty."

Kaiataris sighed and offered Math the bundle of folded paper she'd taken from a Kaliri corpse. "That will not change if you stay."

Math grudgingly took the papers and unfolded them. The first few pages were completely unintelligible, since Math couldn't read Kaliri.

The last page was a sketch of Math's face.

The illustration was alarming for all the obvious reasons, but it wasn't what made Math's breath catch. No, his distress was caused by something much simpler: the paper.

Like most cenobiums, Isofal manufactured its own paper. Over time, each cenobium developed its own personal style. Most people couldn't tell the difference, but for someone raised in the Idallik Order, each cenobium's paper was as distinctive as a family member's face.

This was written in Kaliri *on Isofal paper*.

"This doesn't look great," Math admitted. "But I can't read Kaliri. It could say anything."

"Not *anything*, I should think. I rather doubt it's a wedding invitation."

He glared. "Can *you* read it?"

"Of course. It's an assassination order," she explained helpfully. "They were supposed to kill everyone—but most especially you, Mathaiik Kaven."

"It's pronounced Math-EYE-ik KAV-in."

"My apologies." She then continued, "But as I was saying, they were then supposed to take your body when they left, so it would appear that you'd escaped. And as these orders include a very thorough list of your escorts, their names, descriptions, and their abilities, well. I can only assume they had an accomplice."

"They might be trying to frame someone." He winced. "Yes, fine. That sounded ridiculous the moment I said it out loud."

He pointed to the captain. "You said it lists his abilities? Then who's he and what can he do?"

She gave the bloody ruins of the man's face a distasteful look. "You said that was your captain . . ." She scanned the second page. "Kin? Cheen? According to this, he can summon a chain made of darkness." She paused. "I will assume that is some kind of euphemism, as darkness is not a quality but an absence of such. It also says that he's smart, capable, and an excellent spellcaster, but habitually removes his helmet when not under threat, so an ambush would be the most efficacious way of dealing with him. Shall I tell you what it says about the others?"

"No, that's not . . . that's unnecessary." He swallowed thickly. "None of us said his name. He never summoned a weapon." The only way she could've possibly gotten those details right is if those papers really said those things.

He couldn't go back to Isofal. Not like this. Not knowing someone had handed over names and mission details. The "accomplice" could be anyone.

What were his choices? Flee and become a hunted exile, or go to Bashan and report to the heads of the Order. They needed to know.

Reaching Bashan would be the hard part.

His gaze fell to Captain Qin's body. The man hadn't been wearing plate, only a hauberk for comfort. His full armor was still in the wagon, where it had been poking Math's ribs for most of the ride.

They were about the same size.

Kaiataris cleared her throat.

Math narrowed his eyes. "Yes, *my lady*?"

"You may stop *that* at any time. I have never worn the title of 'lady' before in my life, and I don't intend to start." She gestured with the papers. "Now that we've established that you can't stay, we should follow that to its logical conclusion and be on our way."

Math kept rifling through the captain's pouches. He found spiral-locked letters from Commander Talu, and a writ of passage.

"You're welcome to do what you like." He walked to the wagon, opening gear bags until he found the captain's. "But we're not traveling together."

She crossed her arms. "You cannot simply leave me."

"Watch me." He hoisted the equipment bag off the wagon, stopping to throw the tracking stone as far into the woods as possible. He threw the bag over one shoulder and picked up the Kaliri weapon. The higher-ups in Bashan would want to see it.

"Although really, I would rather you didn't," he added.

"You're making a dangerous assumption, fair knight."

"You can stop calling me that any time you like, too. I'm not a knight." He turned back around with a sigh. "Fine. What assumption?"

"That I followed *you*."

Math frowned. "I . . . okay. Why would you be here if you weren't following me?"

He could still feel her worry, only why would she be? The Kaliri were dead. The knights were dead. Reinforcements wouldn't arrive for at least an hour.

Who was left?

Wind rustled the treetops. And Math knew.

"You weren't following *me*," he said. "You were following the trees."

"I call them the Parnathi." She pointed to the nearby hill. "But they *are* following *you*. They sit just over that rise. Why they haven't attacked yet is a mystery. Perhaps the noise from the black powder made them hesitate."

"Or," a third voice said, "they were waiting for me to catch up. Sorry. I grew as fast as I could."

Math knew that voice. Except it couldn't be . . .

"Huraiik?"

The man who crouched up high on the branch of a sturdy oak did indeed look like the late Idallik Knight Huraiik.

It's just that he was also a plant.

THORNS

The trees back at the logging camp (the trees who'd attacked Isofal Cenobium) had been horrible, but they'd still been trees. Animated in ways trees shouldn't be, but undeniably trees. Even the Queens, despite brief illusions suggesting femininity, had appeared primarily as trees.

This was not a *tree*.

This creature seemed more like someone had used Huraiik as a blueprint, reconstructing him from vegetation instead of flesh. The imitation wasn't perfect: leaves replaced hair, branches grew from skin, and thorns substituted for nails. Math couldn't tell if Huraiik wore clothing made from plants, or if his body had grown foliage to mimic garments. He didn't look like a tree—but he certainly didn't look human.

Yet, much like Catimus Abhigan, there was mischief and intelligence in the creature's dark eyes. The smile was the worst, though. Math knew that smile—he'd known it most of his life.

"Huraiik" jumped from the tree branch, landed lightly on his feet, and pirouetted in place before bowing. "Don't be so dour, Math. I thought you'd be happier to see me, if only for old times' sake." His eyes didn't blink; he no longer had eyelids.

Math dropped the equipment bag and aimed the black-powder weapon at the creature. "I saw you die, Huraiik."

"That's not your friend," Kaiataris warned.

"Yeah, I figured that out on my own, thanks."

Huraiik chuckled wickedly. "Oh, but you're wrong. I *am* your friend. Or as much as we ever were. I mostly tried to make your life miserable." He shrugged. "It was something to do. Honestly, I wasn't very happy as a knight."

Math had told himself Abhigan had been corrupted or controlled—still fundamentally human beneath the grimmock magic. But what did that make this creature? It looked and acted like Huraiik . . . yet couldn't possibly *be* him.

"I don't know why you're here, but crawl back into whatever hole you grew out of."

"No, don't feel like it. And what's that tube thing you're pointing at me?" Huraiik studied the weapon curiously.

"It's what killed every Idallik Knight here, so maybe run before I use it on you." Math was bluffing. The Kaliri agents had reloaded their weapons after each use, which meant that even if he could make this work, he only had one shot. After that, it would become nothing more than an oddly shaped club. Math had no other weapons; none of the fallen knights had carried anything larger than a dagger. Why would they when they could manifest their preferred weapons out of thin air?

Uncomfortably, Math found himself hoping Kaiataris would raise the dead again, but she seemed reluctant to act. He glanced briefly toward her, but she had stepped back, out of view—though not out of awareness. He could still sense her.

She was angry, frustrated—but mostly, *afraid*.

Damn it all. Why did he know she was scared? *How*?

"No need for threats," Huraiik continued cheerfully. "The Queens thought you'd be more receptive to a familiar face. They just want to talk."

"Like they 'talked' to you? To the loggers? To Catimus Abhigan?"

Huraiik laughed—a strange, rustling sound. "No. You're apparently *special*." He raised both hands in mock surrender. "I tried telling them you're basically useless and can't even manifest a weapon, but they don't think that's important."

"Kind of you. Thanks."

"Anytime. Just looking out for you." Huraiik waved him forward. "Come on. I'll introduce you."

Math tightened his grip on the weapon. "No, thanks."

Huraiik rolled his eyes. "It's not actually a request, Math. Why do you always have to be so difficult—" He tilted his head sideways, peering behind Math.

Realizing what had caught the monster's attention, Math shifted to block Kaiataris from view.

"Huh," Huraiik murmured. "Who's she?"

Unfortunately, he wasn't asking Math.

Our enemy, said a voice that echoed strangely in Math's mind. *The only real threat to our plans.*

"That little thing?" Huraiik scoffed. "I'd never have guessed *that*." His expression hardened as the voice spoke again.

Destroy her.

"Introductions will have to wait," Huraiik told Math. "I have a little thing to take care of, first."

Math felt Kaiataris's spike of panic as clearly as if it were his own.

The legendary, terrifying grim lord ran for her life.

"Oh, no you don't." Huraiik manifested his weapon—a fiery sword—and began to chase.

Math froze. Each knight's manifested weapon was unique to them and them alone. And that was *Huraiik's sword*. A fake copy of the man shouldn't have been able to summon it.

Math raised the stolen weapon, aimed at Huraiik's back, and squeezed the trigger.

Nothing happened.

There was no resistance when he pressed the latch, no sign that the damn trigger did anything but jiggle. There was no fuse, no flame—nothing obvious to ignite the powder.

"Gravefucker!" he snarled.

Huraiik laughed without breaking stride. He'd nearly caught up to the necromancer when she spun around, clutching a necklace with one hand while thrusting the other hand toward him. A burst of white energy enveloped Huraiik's head and then condensed into a metallic silver coating.

The vine man screamed and doubled over, clawing at his face. His sword vanished.

Kaiataris resumed running, but Math knew the distraction wouldn't last long.

Math studied the weapon desperately. He'd seen the Kaliri assassins fire them repeatedly. Had he missed a step? How did one light the black powder with no fuse? It was impossible, short of using magic...

Short of using magic.

Math snorted. Sure, why not? If you were already going to break half of the Innalova Accords, why not break the other half, too? Black powder was classified as a class-one weapon.

So was magic.

He set the stock firmly against his shoulder as Huraiik straightened, preparing to chase again.

Math circled Sun, channeling heat through the weapon. A sharp crack echoed and smoke billowed.

Huraiik collapsed.

Math didn't wait to see how long it might stop the creature. He suspected the answer was "not very."

Then a fierce, stabbing pain erupted in his ankle—as though he'd twisted it badly. But he hadn't moved, hadn't tripped.

Glancing down, he saw nothing wrong. Yet the agony was vivid.

Off in the distance, he watched Kaiataris pick herself up off the ground where she'd fallen, and move away, slower now. Limping.

He wasn't feeling his own pain. He was feeling hers.

What else had she done to him?

Still holding the now-useless club, Math chased after her, furious and afraid in equal measure.

She hadn't gotten far.

She'd been smart enough to avoid the forest, but she was also limping. If Huraiik chased after her, she'd be easy prey.

The wind picked up behind him, except it wasn't wind. It was the sound of countless tree branches moving on their own as they marched.

"Math!" he heard Huraiik scream from behind him.

Math grabbed Kaiataris's hand as he caught up to her. "You know, if you were going to raise the dead, back there was the right time."

She growled at him, her composure finally broken. "I would have, were it only an option."

"You did it before—"

"In my sanctum, my place of power, graved and prepared centuries before! Out here, I'm not strong enough to do more than—"

She looked past him—and blanched.

He didn't need to ask why.

"Understood. In that case, don't kill me. You'll just be hurting yourself."

"What are you—?"

Math threw her over his shoulder and ran.

She screamed to shake the sky, but didn't hex him, which he took as a win. He circled spells one-handed as he went, searching for any advantage. Master Wadera would have been proud.

"Do not run into the forest!" Kaiataris yelled at him.

He ran into the forest.

Math might have been more confident just a short time earlier. The trees hadn't moved swiftly. But Huraiik—who had all the gifts he'd possessed as a knight, and now whatever abominations the plants had granted—was a different matter.

He was more than capable of catching up to Math. When he did, Math would be without any weapons other than a club and a necromancer who couldn't necromance.

Not ideal.

So he did what he'd sworn never to do: He went home.

"Put me down! I can heal my foot. Put me down at once!"

He didn't argue. Carrying her over Valmaki terrain wasn't sustainable, even if she *was* petite.

He set her down. "Ten seconds. Then I'm picking you up again."

She bit back a retort and instead moved her fingers over one of her bracelets, tracing the pattern. A faint, pale glow circled the gold metal, then wrapped around her ankle before disappearing.

She straightened. "There. A considerable improvement."

He felt it—the lessening of her pain.

"Good." He grabbed her hand and ran.

Math slowed his pace to match the woman's shorter steps, the rhythmic slap of her sandals a constant reminder of her unprepared state of dress. He helped Kaiataris over roots and warned her away from troublesome briars, navigating by instinct.

At least he no longer had to carry her. He needed that advantage: the full darkness of night was fast approaching. When that happened, Math would be forced to risk a conjured light guaranteed to betray their position.

He hadn't seen this place in years, yet it felt unchanged. The scent of poplars and damp earth, the twilight calls of cuckoos and crows, every turn of trail and abandoned path tugged at bright and bitter memories.

Then he saw it: a low, ruined silhouette of an abandoned cottage, ivy-draped and half-swallowed by undergrowth. Birch and elms surrounded it, along with countless rowans, a few ancient yews, and miles of blackberry and briar bushes. The wind through the branches felt like hello.

Part of him was glad for the dark, for how it concealed the glade's beauty.

It made hating this place easier.

"Math!" Huraiik again, much too close.

Math pushed Kaiataris toward the ruins. "Hide in the house. Just ahead."

"You cannot fight him." Her voice was taut with fear, fury—*concern*.

Concern for *him*.

He didn't know what to do with that. He couldn't reconcile the stories of the grim lord necromancer, the horror stories told to children, the definition of power and darkness, with this fragile, furious woman in a torn silk dress and broken shoes.

The woman who, according to the Queens, was the only one who could stop them.

"You're right," Math said, "but I won't have to. It's a trap."

He ignored the voice of doubt that questioned why he thought any of this was a good idea. He buried those feelings deep, exactly the way he'd trained to do for years.

She could probably feel his emotions, anyway.

Kaiataris gave him a flat look.

Huraiik called out: "Math, come on. Don't drag matters out like this. You're embarrassing yourself. She's a necromancer! What would Tanxi say?"

The look Kaiataris gave Huraiik was pure hatred. If she'd had power enough, she would have turned Huraiik to ash.

"Go!" He pushed her toward the cottage ruin.

She didn't resist. The leaves rustled as she climbed over a low section of broken stone wall.

Math turned around.

He circled a light spell, but it was largely unnecessary; Huraiik's sword blazed brighter than any torch. That light revealed that green pus oozed from a gaping hole in Huraiik's chest—an injury that should've been fatal.

Evidently, he either didn't have a heart, it wasn't in the right place or, like many trees, "heart" had a completely different definition. His eyes wept something silvery and metallic.

Neither of the two remaining Queens or their servants had followed. As Math had hoped, the former Idallik Knight had been the only one fast enough to keep up.

"Huraiik, I'm giving you one last chance. This time I'm aiming at your face. Turn around and go back." He raised the black-powder weapon again.

Huraiik didn't know Math had no way to reload it.

Huraiik raised a hand, forming a shield of vines. "Not falling for that again. Unless you've finally manifested your weapon, you're out of tricks."

Math lifted his chin. "Did you really try to convince the Queens that I was useless?"

The plant man smirked. "What was I supposed to tell them? You're fantastic with the kids?"

"What did they say?"

Huraiik's expression turned vacant again. He looked up and past Math. Math didn't hear his words—but the Queens answered.

As it was, so it shall be. The time of the Green grows, as do her children.

Huraiik blew out a long, frustrated breath. "You know, honestly, it's kind of hard to understand them sometimes? Not their fault, it's just that they were never human. It doesn't help that everyone's talking all the time."

"Everyone?"

"You know: the plants. Chatter, chatter, chatter, constantly. They do not *ever* shut up. Berry bushes are the worst." He dismissed the sword for just long enough to mime a flapping mouth. Then Huraiik frowned as he glanced around the small clearing. ". . . that's it. That's what's so weird about this place. It's quiet. None of the plants are saying anything."

"They haven't decided whether they like you," Math explained.

Huraiik threw him a confused look. "What?"

"You can't just barge into someone's house and expect a warm welcome." Math made a face. "How does that work, anyway? If you're all plants, shouldn't you go dormant when the sun's down?"

Huraiik chuckled. "We're more than just plants, you realize. Just like your race are more than just animals."

"Yesterday, you weren't a plant at all."

"Strange, isn't it? A day makes such a difference." Huraiik seemed amused by the thought, rather than horrified. "So I guess this is the place you wouldn't shut up about when you were a kid. Where your parents died."

Math flushed. This *thing* knew everything Huraiik had ever known—and Huraiik had known a lot.

"Yeah," Math finally said. "Maybe you should've paid more attention."

An elm branch slammed into Huraiik, knocking him sideways. Huraiik retaliated immediately, but for every branch cut, three more appeared.

Another branch strike hit harder, forcing Huraiik to lose concentration on his manifested sword. Roots erupted from the ground and buried themselves again, wrapping around him, pinning him in place.

"Math!" Huraiik roared, again unleashing magic. It wasn't a flaming sword this time, however. He channeled lightning through his fingers, the air crackling as he launched the stroke at Math.

It was too powerful for Math to deflect.

Kaiataris grabbed Math's hand, and a white wall of energy shimmered into existence around them both. The lightning slammed into the barrier and dissipated into weak sparks. Immediately after, the wall of white light faded into nothingness. A necklace around Kaiataris's neck turned black and flaked away.

Math made the mistake of half turning in the necromancer's direction.

It was all the opening that Huraiik needed.

One of Huraiik's whips lashed out, but not aimed at Math. Instead, Huraiik attacked the one target the local plants wouldn't protect: Kaiataris herself.

A vine lash flew past Math and buried itself straight into Kaiataris's chest. Their eyes met, and a stunning wave of pain radiated from her to him.

Kaiataris collapsed.

Math knew just how much pain she was in. He felt it all. He felt everything.

Math whirled back to Huraiik, furious and helpless, weaponless and desperate—

The forest moved first.

The plants of the glade wrapped around Huraiik's arms, his legs, his neck. Then they pulled in different directions.

There was a moment of tension, then sudden, violent release. The plant man tore apart, dismembered as surely as if he'd been tied to racing horses. Huraiik didn't scream, but made a sound like the cracking of tree limbs brought down by too much snow in winter.

Math dropped to his knees beside Kaiataris.

She was pale and blood pooled beneath her. His own chest burned with pain, even though he wasn't injured.

"Why did you do that? Do you want to die?" Math pulled off his shirt and pressed the fabric to the wound. "Don't move, damn it! I need to stop the bleeding."

She was losing too much blood.

Kaiataris gave him a weak smile. "Do you still think me undead?"

"No," he snapped. "I think you're a *fool*. I told you to hide!"

"You would have died."

"You don't know that— Okay, yes. Fine. I probably would have, and then Huraiik would've really gotten it from the damn Queens because he wasn't supposed to kill me." Math cursed at her injury. "I can heal skin. That's easy. But if I do that and you're bleeding internally—which you *are*—you'll still die."

"But I shall leave such a fair corpse," she whispered.

"That is *not* funny."

"'Tis so." She coughed, winced. "Heal me, my beautiful knight."

"I *can't*."

"You can," she said softly. "You are a wild mage. And we are bound."

"Apparently so. I don't know exactly what that means, but I hate it!"

"It means that you should . . . you should gather plants. Bring them back. Lay them on my wound, and then . . . you shall . . . imagine, truly believe, that this is healing me. See it in your mind as reality and you will . . . make it so."

She lay back, brow slick with sweat, as though that speech had taken everything from her, most especially her ability to stay conscious.

"That's not how magic works!"

She scoffed and then winced. Math felt the sharp stab of pain as she'd stifled the instinct to laugh. "No. 'Tis not how *my* magic works."

Math pushed himself back to his feet and stumbled away. He searched near the cottage, plucking leaves, petals, vines, and weeds, at random.

He returned to the woman and kneeled beside her, layering those same plants over her wound.

She had closed her eyes. Her pulse was rapid, her breathing shallow. Math tried to let his own confusion distract him.

She was so fragile, so delicate, so *mortal*.

Now he understood her fear of Huraiik. She'd known she wouldn't be able to protect herself.

Math set his hands on the wound and thought about Kaiataris being healthy and whole. He concentrated on the lack of pain, on the connection between them. He told himself pretty lies: that if this magical bond between them meant that they could feel each other's pain, it also meant that neither of them could die while the other still lived. And if that was true—and it *was* true, he *knew* it was true, it *had* to be true—then she couldn't die here. Math had a few scratches, but nothing life-threatening.

He was fine; thus, so was she.

Math believed. He had to believe.

It was only when that was done—when Kaiataris's chest rose and fell with peace instead of pain—that Math understood what he'd done in spite of the fact it went against everything he'd ever been raised to believe.

What he'd done without hesitation. Without thinking.

He'd just saved the life of a grim lord.

SOLSTICE

While Kaiataris lay unconscious, Math worked with the grim resolve of a man tidying a massacre. He shoved Huraiik's severed limbs into the underbrush. He circled spells to clean the blood from his shirt and from her silk dress—though part of him hated that kindness. He even mended the broken strap on her sandal.

The air was still. The glade smelled like blood and green sap.

She looked like something out of a child's tale—but not a happy one. A cursed princess, laid out in a bower thick with shadows, the hush of it too deep, the breeze too absent. The quiet made his skin prickle. It was a nightmare dressed up in innocence.

Not inappropriate, considering their location.

When the necromancer stirred, it was with a child's startled gasp, a full-body twitch. Then she stiffened, her breath trapped in her lungs.

Her eyes flicked to him, wild, as she realized her limbs were caught in living vines—still faintly pulsing, as though they too remembered her pain.

"Don't," Math said, before she could do more than open her mouth to scream or curse—or both. "I can't trust you. Not after you neglected to mention the spell you cast on me."

Kaiataris's lips pressed together. Her dark eyes flicked across the clearing, lit with Math's magic.

"I had every intention of mentioning it," she said, her voice tight. "You may recall, however, that our conversations have been rather rudely interrupted."

"I can feel your pain," Math accused. "Literally."

She bit her lip but said nothing.

Math dug a fingernail into the flesh of his palm, hard enough to sting. She flinched.

"And that," he said coldly, "is why I can't trust you."

He braced for an excuse. A lie. A sidestep. Instead, her fury hit him like a slap.

"You cannot trust *me*?" she snapped. "You, who command the forest? And I am to presume you bear no allegiance to the Parnathi? Am I to be grateful that the person bound to my protection consorts with my enemies?"

"Consorts with them?" Math laughed. "The torn-up little pieces of Huraiik disagree with you. You get the same speech he did. I don't command the plants. They happen to like me, which isn't the same thing."

Kaiataris twisted against her bonds as she glared at him with narrowed eyes. "Tell me you're not gullible enough to believe that."

"It's the truth."

She scanned the glade—the gouged earth, the scarring roots. "Is it?"

"Yes!" The word burst out louder than he meant. Her skepticism was a pressure in his chest, scratching under his ribs. "They want to protect me, but they don't obey me. There's a difference."

"Have you tried giving them a direct order?"

He bared his teeth. "If I were working with the Parnathi, I wouldn't have healed you."

She quieted. The fire in her dimmed, replaced by something harder to identify.

"That is . . . a fair point," she finally said. "Thank you."

"What bothers me," he continued, "is that I shouldn't have rushed to your aid, yet I didn't hesitate. I didn't even consider doing anything else."

Her gaze sharpened, struck. "Would it have been better had you let me die?"

Math flushed. A proper Idallik Knight would've seen her for what she was and acted accordingly. Beautiful or not, she was a grim lord.

Even if she had saved his life three times now.

She touched her chest, just above the now-healed wound. "I did not stay silent concerning the spell to deceive you. I stayed silent because it is not working as designed."

Math tilted his head and waited for her to continue.

"The bond was meant to be one-way," Kaiataris explained. "You would feel *my* emotions. *My* pain. If I grew distressed, you might fetch a cup of tea. Perhaps a nice biscuit. If I found myself in danger, you'd come to my rescue. It was not meant to be . . . reciprocal."

"Sure. Because why would you care what your *thrall* is feeling?"

"You are *not* my thrall," she replied, with imperious frost. "As I should think is proven by my current predicament." She tugged her arms against the vines, not so much to escape as to make her point.

"So what went wrong?"

Her glare deepened. "*You!* You went wrong. You turned the spell back upon me. Which should be impossible, but since 'should be impossible' defines your style of magic, I have no choice but to accept the result."

"And if one of us dies?" Math pressed. "Was that part of the design? Bind me to your survival so I can't walk away?"

She looked appalled. "No! That is a vile suggestion. I would never—"

"But you *don't know*, do you?" His voice dropped. "The spell isn't working right. So what *happens* if you die? If *I* do?"

Kaiataris turned her face away, shame rippling through their connection like heat from a forge. "You were supposed to *know* if I was hurt. Not *feel* it."

"Answer the question."

"I can't! I cannot say what happens at the edge of death."

"Fantastic," Math muttered. "Love that. And undoing the spell? How easy is that? Don't take this the wrong way, but my life is basically over if I find myself permanently bound to a grim lord!"

"I am not a grim lord!"

"Trust me when I say you are the *only* person who believes that."

She gave one of her bound hands a vicious yank. "Let me out of this."

"Answer the question. Can you undo the spell?"

"Of course," Kaiataris snarled. "It was never meant to be used on an unwilling subject, only a volunteer."

Math barked out a bitter laugh. "Since when does *walking through a door* count as volunteering?"

"Were you shoved, then? Sent through blindfolded?" She sniffed with indignant disdain he could both see and feel.

"I'll repeat it again." Math stepped closer. "If I untie you, will you remove this enchantment?"

She studied him with a gaze that seemed to see more than it should. "Yes," she said finally. "I shall."

He unwound the vines. He pretended not to notice the way they slithered away into the underbrush like shamed servants.

Kaiataris rose slowly. She brushed off her dress, straightened her back, and ran her hands down her arms, brushing away every leaf like a queen regaining her poise.

"Your turn," Math said. "Undo the spell."

But she didn't. Instead, Kaiataris regarded him cooly. "First, I must pose a question. It is relevant, I promise. How long has it been since the destruction of these 'grim lords'?"

"All the grim lords but you, you mean."

She visibly clenched her teeth while shoving down her anger. "If you insist. Yes, all but me."

Math frowned. "A thousand years. Maybe more."

He felt the ripple of her panic, though it never showed on her face. "And how . . ." She exhaled a shaky breath. "How long did they rule?"

"Centuries. I don't remember the exact number."

"How *many* centuries?"

"At least four."

Kaiataris closed her eyes. "Fourteen hundred years," she whispered. "By the stars . . ."

She looked as though the ground beneath her had cracked open, as if the axis of the world had shifted beneath her feet.

She looked so small in that moment, so lost—and the emotion that welled up in his chest made him furious. Math didn't want to pity her. Pity made her real. Pity made her human.

He forced the emotion down, strangled it.

"This explains everything," she said at last, drawing herself back together like gathering tattered silk. "Why I am so diminished and weak. You see, the world's magic flows in cycles between two great forces—"

"Necromancy and—"

"No," she snapped. "Absolutely not. Order and Chaos. Everything is Order and Chaos. The rest is nothing but dressed-up superstition. Order and Chaos diametrically oppose each other, a cycle of waxing and waning power that lasts exactly two thousand years between crests."

"And when one's at its peak, the other's at its lowest . . ." he murmured. "That's what you meant by 'solstice.'"

She glanced at him, surprised. Her pleasure and approval was a warm, tingling sensation across his skin. "Yes, exactly so. The solstices are terrible, dangerous times when the magic of the universe is horrifically out of balance. The last solstice belonged to Order—"

"That doesn't sound so bad."

She gave him a long look. "What is more orderly than death?"

That shut him up.

"Nothing that breathes or dreams or changes should have survived the last solstice. The only reason that you and I are here to argue the matter is because we—myself and my peers whom I presume you would also classify as 'grim lords'—wove a spell powerful enough to carry life through death's nadir in a magical slumber. We would wake when the tide of Chaos had risen high enough to support life again. After which we would have over a millennium to prepare for the next solstice, the one that Chaos brings."

She gestured to the dark rents and burned patches of woodland floor where

Math and Huraiik had fought, already half-reclaimed by roots. "But I have woken too late."

"The Green grows," Math murmured. "They meant the rise of Chaos."

"Naturally. Chaos is life. But imagine, if you would, that life *without death*. Mutation. Madness. Growth with no end, no limit. War without peace. Violence without end. A world that devours and regurgitates its children in infinite, brutal variation."

He swallowed hard.

"That's what the Queens want," she whispered. "They've been waiting for it, anticipating it."

Math couldn't stop himself from shuddering. Then he blinked, and gave the beautiful dark-eyed woman a hard stare. "And that's bad," he agreed, "but I can't help but notice you haven't explained what any of this has to do with removing the damn enchantment on us."

Kaiataris stepped backward. She turned her head, startled, as a vine shifted against the wall behind her.

She calmly looked Math in the eyes. "Haven't I?"

"Stop playing games," Math hissed. "You haven't explained a—"

He paused.

No.

He shook his head in horror, denying a truth even as he spoke the words. "You . . . you use objects for your magic, don't you? The walls of the maze, your jewelry, the map. You tie your magic to things that are permanent. Stable."

"Orderly," she agreed. "The less likely to change, the better."

"Which means you—" He pointed a finger at her. "The spell triggered last night, when I entered the maze, but that's not when you cast it. That's not when you've cast any of these spells. You did that when 'Order magic' was at its most powerful—"

Kaiataris's mouth flattened with concern. "Perhaps you should attempt to remain calm."

"Fuck remaining calm!" Math swore. Trees creaked behind him in response, bark groaning like it might split. Somewhere deeper, a low thrumming began, like roots dragging across stone. The forest had heard him. Worse, she had too—and he could feel her dread rising. "You can't remove it, can you? It's not that you won't. It's that you literally *can't*."

She swallowed visibly and looked out into the darkness. "I can. Eventually. But it will likely take years—"

"Years? Years! Ha!" Math picked up his Kaliri-weapon-turned-club and slung it over his shoulder. "My country is being invaded by evil, magic-throwing intelligent trees and grim lord–worshipping cultists using some kind of horrible new black-powder weapon. I don't have years. I doubt I have weeks."

Math could still feel her anger, except it wasn't hers at all. He was feeling his own anger, reflected back at him like a mirror. "I would undo it if I could," she whispered. "I have no desire to keep someone by my side against their will."

Math closed his eyes. The horrible thing—the really awful, twisted, ugly thing—was that he knew she was telling the truth.

Honestly, he wished she'd been some vile witch out of a fairy tale. That would've been so much easier. Why did she have to be like this? She was beautiful and smart and so, so *brave*. She couldn't have known for sure that Math would heal her, that Huraiik wouldn't give her an immediately lethal injury. She'd done it anyway.

"I believe you." Math turned away, hands on his hips. The flower-strewn glade stretched before him like a forgotten memory. The ruins of his childhood home crouched under vines and moonlight.

He couldn't stay here.

Math didn't turn to look at Kaiataris, but he felt the weight of her stare.

"So this is where we part," Math said.

She straightened, shocked. "You cannot be serious."

"I couldn't take you with me even if I wanted to. I have no coin. No gear. No horse. All I've got is a writ of passage tied to a dead captain, and even if I looked like him—which I don't—there's no one on the continent who's going to mistake *me* for a decorated Idallik officer. The Queens are hunting *you*. The Order is hunting *me*. If we travel together, we double our chances of being caught."

She folded her arms over her chest. "Do I have to remind you that the Queens were not, in fact, following *me*?"

Math sighed. "Fine. Everyone's hunting me. You still stand a better chance without me."

"Or," she said slowly, "I could aid you."

"I don't see how."

"What if I could help you impersonate your captain?" Her voice was beginning to take on the tense edge of desperation.

Of course, Math realized. She didn't have anyone else. She didn't know anyone else. And she'd just woken up in a completely unfamiliar world only to discover that everyone *hated* her.

He yanked his thoughts away from that road. The last thing he could afford to be was sympathetic to a grim lord. Even if that person might not have ever *been* a real grim lord. What had she called herself? A graven wizard?

"Mathaiik?"

Math ran a hand through his hair. "How would you help me? I had to leave his plate armor behind, and it's not like I can go back for it. I don't know if I'd find Idallik Knights, Kaliri assassins, or very angry trees, but I guarantee you that site's guarded by now."

"Yes," she said with exaggerated patience. "And I told you I am not completely powerless. Just because I lack the strength to raise the dead again so soon does not mean I am devoid of *all* magical ability. You want to reach your superiors, do you not? I want to prevent a second extinction. Our goals are aligned."

Math shook his head. "I can't. I'm sorry. Thank you for helping me. I wish you luck."

He turned to leave.

Her voice chased him. "I can help you disguise yourself as a captain. Then you will be able to use your writ to reach your superiors quickly and easily."

Math stopped.

She continued: "The Parnathi travel faster than you do. Another Huraiik will be here soon enough."

He turned around. "You have some kind of magic?"

She stepped forward, raised an arm. Bracelets gleamed in the light. She slipped one free—a wide, flat band of gold etched with flowing script that shimmered with Math's reflected spell light.

"It is the primary difference between your magic and mine. Wild magic is raw, impermanent, difficult to control. The effect vanishes the moment you stop concentrating. Ordered magic anchors itself to objects—and those objects may be shared."

She extended the bracelet toward him. "This will suffice. If you trust me."

Math stared at it.

He knew what he *should* say. He should say no. Should turn his back, walk away, find some rational path through this madness.

But then he thought of the Queens. Of the way the vines had peeled Huraiik's original human body apart like wet bark. Of the sound of that metal slug blasting through Captain Qin's head.

The Order needed to know. They needed warning. Right now, Math wasn't sure that anyone at Isofal even understood the threat. Maybe Captain Danvi, but Math didn't think she'd be able to convince enough people.

Someone had to warn the Order's leaders.

And yet, this wasn't a compromise. Accepting help from Kaiataris was heresy with a pretty face and an outstretched hand. Everything he'd been taught said to end her. Instead, he was bargaining. Worse, he was starting to believe she didn't want to hurt anyone at all.

Slowly, he nodded. "Fine. We have a deal. For now. If this thing can make me *look* like Captain Qin, I can get us both tickets on the train to Bashan. We can part ways before I head to the Bashan chapter house, and no one has to know you were ever there."

Kaiataris brightened. "Brilliant," she said.

Then paused.

"... only ... what is a train?"

STATION

"Are you sure these constructions aren't magical?"

Math couldn't see Kaiataris's expression. No one could just then, because apparently if one gave her around fifteen minutes to store up enough magical energy, she could turn herself invisible.

Just herself, unfortunately.

But he didn't need sight to sense her mood—she was nearly giddy, delight radiating from her encounter with something wonderfully new. Her excitement prickled at the back of his neck, alien and intrusive.

"Completely sure," Math whispered. "They're powered by steam."

He'd never visited Sounalla's train station before; it hadn't existed when he was a child. Now the empire was littered with stations, part of the empress's new initiative for "linking the continent."

Kaiataris seemed more intrigued by trains than anything they'd encountered yet. Her curiosity rippled through their bond, mingling uneasily with his anxiety. Even invisible, he knew she'd gravitated toward the tracks for a closer look, heedless of danger.

In most countries, iron trains—if they had them at all—were reserved for goods or soldiers. Only Rokasmaa was opening trains to public use.

"Now stop talking," Math whispered. "You're invisible, not inaudible."

He was garnering stares as it was—not because he was doing anything strange, but because he *was* something strange: an Idallik Knight. Most had never seen one, but all recognized the distinctive armor and tabard. Thus, Math—or rather, Captain Qin—was the most exciting thing to happen in Sounalla since the arrival of the train itself.

He forced himself not to fidget, unease crawling between his shoulder blades.

The station was busier than he'd expected, but trains traveled at all hours. Many of the travelers wouldn't be residents of Sounalla, but rather people passing through, on their way to bigger, more important places.

Or so Math assumed.

He was assuming too much lately, none of it comforting. Whenever he'd left the cenobium before, it had been to hunt monsters, not marvel at imperial technology. He could admit (at least privately) that he'd always wanted to see a train up close, just as he'd dreamed of exploring Bashan illuminated by gaslight. Yet now, with his wish fulfilled, a creeping dread shadowed every step since meeting Kaiataris.

The station loomed far larger than he'd expected: tall, vaulted, cathedral-like. Metal arches soared overhead, intricate iron lace supporting huge glass panes. By day, sunlight would flood the space; at night, glass bulbs cast clinical pools of light.

He heard Kaiataris's soft voice: "Could it be that I am misinterpreting the unfriendly stares you're receiving?"

Math sighed. "No."

"Perhaps I should rather ask: *Why* are you receiving such looks?"

"It's not me," Math whispered. He grimaced. "Five years ago, the emperor was assassinated. Rumor says an Idallik Knight opposed to his reforms did it." He turned toward a wall, pretending to inspect a pouch, feigning nonchalance even as tension tightened his shoulders. Captain Qin had carried enough money for a night's stay in Sounalla—enough, hopefully, for food if he could find someplace still open.

"And was he?"

"Was he what? Oh." Math swallowed, glancing around nervously. What worried him most wasn't the suspicious civilians, but the group of Rokasmaa soldiers who'd clearly been drinking. They looked exactly like the sort to cause trouble.

"My sister always thought so," Math admitted softly. "But I never wanted to believe it. It's true the reforms weren't popular among certain knights, though." He failed at keeping disapproval from his voice—not that it mattered. She could feel it anyway. Her curiosity only sharpened in response.

He was upset for reasons beyond reminders of why Rokasmaa citizens might distrust Idallik Knights, however.

Specifically, the small brick ticket booth just inside the station entrance sat dark, a CLOSED sign in front of a lowered shade.

Why had he assumed tickets would be sold all night?

Because trains ran all night, obviously. But while Bashan might offer round-the-clock ticket sales, Sounalla, famed only for hot springs and pottery, did not.

"Oh dear," Kaiataris whispered, noticing the same problem.

He briefly considered boarding the next train using the stolen writ, claiming an emergency—which was true—but he didn't know protocols. Idallik Knights rarely took trains, preferring magic for rapid travel. He might face a conductor's scrutiny, and Kaiataris's illusion might fade at precisely the wrong moment.

Even with funds for overnight lodging, he dared not remain. The Queens could be tracking him. Even if not, someone in the Order would realize this was his logical next stop. His neck prickled; he imagined enemies closing from every direction.

He couldn't be in Sounalla when either group arrived—and desperately hoped quick departure would deter pursuit entirely.

"Maybe it should be the Idiotic Order, huh?" a too-loud voice called from behind him.

Math sighed. He knew exactly what he'd see when he turned around. He felt a flare of apprehension from Kaiataris, mirrored by his own dread.

The group of Rokasmaa soldiers he'd spotted earlier had stopped to watch him, laughing and elbowing each other. Four of them—three men and one woman. Math didn't recognize ranks, but all wore Rokasmaa uniforms. No armor, but they were armed.

All of them were drunk.

"No, no," the woman giggled. "Idyllic Order."

This confused the first soldier. "Wait. Isn't that their name?"

She laughed and slapped his chest. "No! Idallik . . . it means . . ." She frowned. "I don't actually know what it means."

"Death knight," Kaiataris whispered, too quietly for anyone but Math to hear. Her words sliced through his nerves.

He forced himself not to react.

The soldier wasn't finished mocking him. "But that's not important! What matters is *idyllic* means peaceful. You know . . ." The woman paused, giving Math a thoroughly hateful look. "Because you all sit on your asses and don't *do* anything."

"Of course they do something," another man sneered. "They take people's money, don't they?"

"We don't do . . . anything," Math said slowly, watching carefully. Normal soldiers, likely stationed near the Kaliri border or embroiled in the conflict with Vilsenor. No armor, just uniformed, tipsy, and clearly aggressive. They'd had their fun—tavern drinks and a dip in the hot springs. Now, back at the station, they waited for the train to take them back to their posts. Their luggage was piled in an untidy heap in a corner.

He glanced up at the destination sign above their heads.

They were waiting for the train to Bashan.

"That's not your fancy knight's weapon, is it?" A quieter man pointed to Math's Kaliri weapon. "I thought it'd glow at least."

"Yeah, where's your sword?" Loudest demanded.

"It's not always a sword," the woman reminded him.

"Still want to see it. That's just a stick. Summon your weapon," Loudest sneered. "At least you'd be good for a laugh."

"I don't want a fight," Math warned, tension winding through every muscle.

"So don't make one," the woman said, smirking. "We just want to see your . . . sword." She giggled, deliberately twisting her words.

"If I manifest my sword, I'll use it," Math said quietly, coldly. "And that means I'll kill with it."

The four soldiers exchanged glances, drunk bravado briefly wavering. Loudest recovered first. "You threatening us?"

What were they thinking? As far as they knew, Math wore plate armor, could summon a weapon at will, and used magic. He was no one to pick a fight with.

Math eyed their uniforms—baggy cotton trousers tucked into high boots, linen shirt under a thigh-length vest, covered by a wide, tasseled sash of imperial-blue silk. If they'd been in the field, they likely would have covered all that with a jazerant coat, much like Math's own. As it was, they wore full, high-collared coats of dark gray wool. It wasn't quite one-size-fits-all, but it came close.

All four soldiers wore swords.

Math raised an eyebrow and smirked, challenging recklessness masking real dread. "Yes, I am. Any of you cowards going to do something about it?"

Loudest lunged, staggering forward. Math dodged easily, heart pounding. He couldn't let them touch him and risk revealing the illusion.

"You want a fight, grave scum?" another soldier shouted, advancing. He hadn't drawn his sword yet, but surely would soon. "You're asking for it!"

"What are you *doing*?" Kaiataris hissed, panic flaring sharply.

"Getting you a coat," Math whispered.

He backed toward the doors, waiting until the soldiers chased—then ran.

Normally, Math would've been arrogantly certain of his ability to handle an enlisted soldier, but being unarmed and outnumbered evened the odds. Math's confidence had always been ironclad, but tonight—weaponless, exhausted—he felt that certainty cracking.

Fighting openly in the brightly lit train station, in full view of witnesses, was out of the question. Fortunately, even a town the size of Sounalla had plenty of alleys—none lit after dark. In the shadows, those alleys pressed closer, narrowing into uncertain traps.

Math wasn't surprised when Loudest rounded the corner first. Judging by his footsteps, he'd outpaced his companions. Loudest took the wooden end of the Kaliri weapon directly to the face, staggering back with a broken nose. Math grabbed him by the coat and slammed him into the alley wall. The soldier crumpled.

Math pulled the man's sword from its sheath and retreated deeper into the shadows.

One soldier paused at the sight of his fallen companion, but instead of instilling any sense of caution, Loudest's injury just made it personal for the others. Now they had something to prove.

"Come out here!" another soldier shouted. "Fight us like . . . like an Avansi!"

Math nearly scoffed aloud. Fighting like an Avansi didn't mean fighting foolishly.

He waited until the soldiers stepped forward, then kicked over a stack of wooden crates destined for firewood. The boxes crashed down, striking one man on the shoulder, sending him sprawling into the muck. Before he could recover, Math slammed a knee into his back, grabbed his head, and bashed it into the ground.

When Math stood again, the woman faced him, sword drawn.

But Math had a sword now, too.

She hesitated, and that was all Math needed. While she'd had some training, Math had wielded swords his entire life. Math lunged, pressing his borrowed blade against hers until she lost her grip. With no intention of killing a Rokasmaa soldier, he stepped close and knocked her unconscious with the sword pommel.

He heard the last man fleeing. Gravespit. If the soldier called for help, Math's problems would multiply swiftly.

But as he ran after the soldier, a soft cry preceded the thud of a body hitting the ground. Math rounded the corner to find the soldier sprawled in the dirt, and Kaiataris, visible once more, dropping the loose board she'd wielded.

"Nice job," Math said, kneeling to check the man.

"Thank you," she replied primly. "Only why did we pick a fight with these people?" Her unease threaded through their bond, a stark contrast to her earlier joy at the train station. Her curiosity had sharpened into wary uncertainty.

Math held up a finger. "One moment. Help me drag them together."

She didn't argue, focusing instead on pulling the unconscious woman toward her companions. Once the group was clustered in the dark alley, Math checked to ensure none were fatally injured. Every passing second felt eternal. Anyone might stumble upon them—guards, witnesses, or worse, someone from the Order—and no disguise would save them if that happened.

Head wounds were tricky. A blow strong enough to render someone unconscious was strong enough to kill.

Once Math confirmed the soldiers would wake with nothing worse than headaches, he began removing clothes. Not everything—just two coats, the critical blue sashes, and boots for Kaiataris to replace her useless sandals. Not the woman's boots, interestingly, but one of the men's, who had surprisingly delicate feet.

He glanced up at Kaiataris, though he saw only the faintest silhouette blocking starlight. Her disapproval radiated, which Math found darkly amusing.

What was his life when he had a necromancer judging him? He hesitated, hand hovering over a coin purse. Master Wadera's lessons on honor echoed loudly, condemning this once-inviolable boundary now crossed.

Yet survival left him little choice.

"What are you doing?" Kaiataris broke the silence.

"Breaking the law for the first time in my life," Math muttered, patting the soldiers down, relieving them of extra money and train tickets. "We need money, tickets, clothes." He gestured toward the unconscious soldiers. "The Tri-Mother provides."

"I hadn't imagined we'd so quickly resort to brigandage."

He hadn't missed her use of "we," and he wasn't sure how he felt about it. Part of him liked it, and he was deeply uncomfortable about the fact that part of him liked it. Her presence was both comforting and disturbing.

"They picked a fight with someone they thought was a fully armored Idallik Knight," Math said. "Someone they knew could summon magic and weapons. How will they learn without consequences?"

She scoffed, but he felt the fondness lurking underneath her pretend outrage.

He circled a few basic spells to clean the grime. It wouldn't do to arrive at the station looking like they'd rolled in an alley.

"Your order seems popular," Kaiataris remarked dryly.

"I'd never thought about it much, but it's never a good omen seeing us at your doorstep. Especially after that business with the emperor . . ." He tossed her a coat. "Put this on. They left suitcases on the platform. We'll take their bags and use the station restrooms to change."

Which was what they did.

TRAIN

They had no trouble at all boarding the train. They'd claimed their stolen luggage and retreated into restrooms to change—Math into a slightly fancier version of the standard uniform, and to his shock, Kaiataris into completely civilian garb. She met back up with him wearing a deep red chemise over pillowy gathered ochre trousers, all of it under a tight-fitting blue wool vest.

It flattered her. He hated that he noticed.

She'd hidden her hair under a red-and-blue print scarf, a "disguise" that seemed to amuse her for all that a flicker of uncertainty ran underneath. She pulled a red felted kuweian cap over his head like a joke, but was unable to hide the careful distance in the gesture.

"I'm told married couples cover their hair." She gave him an odd look when he choked. "A woman in the restroom was kind enough to explain things."

"We can't—" His face turned red.

"Can't pretend to be married?" Her confusion and embarrassment were sharp, made worse by the fact that she could feel his embarrassment, too. Math knew it must be like staring at a cracked mirror—everything reflected, warped, too close.

Math forced himself to calm down. Being able to feel what she felt was making it difficult for him to wrestle his own emotions under control. "No," he said. "You're right. People will ask fewer questions if they think we're newlyweds. I was caught off guard. The Order demands a vow of chastity."

A vow that virtually no one obeyed, but even so.

Her eyes widened. "Chastity? *Why?*"

"Tradition?"

She scoffed as she dragged him over to the man checking tickets.

A red-coated conductor gave them a single glance and stamped their tickets. "Anywhere in the first three carriages, but seats are first come, first served." His gaze slid to Kaiataris and lingered. "No sleeping berths."

Math's smile turned icy. "Thank you."

Kaiataris leaned into him after they walked onto the train. "Why was that man staring at me like that?"

"The usual reasons, I suppose. First, because you're Souna. They're not often seen this far east."

She frowned at that, accompanied by a less obvious spike of concern. "That wasn't worth mentioning earlier?"

"I don't care if you're Souna and I don't care what he thinks."

Her lips twitched. "That was the first reason. What might the second be?"

"You're beautiful."

She flushed at that, but also frowned. "Are you *sure* you're chaste?" She wasn't flirting: this was suspicion, a cautious testing of boundaries neither of them understood.

"I said the Order demands chastity. I never said I was any good at it."

Inside the first passenger carriage, they found two rows of padded benches, separated by an aisle down the center. Each bench sat next to a small window, which could be opened to relieve the stuffy air. It didn't strike Math as comfortable, but he supposed this method's chief advantage was speed.

The most troublesome part was that passengers who'd already boarded—here or earlier—had claimed most of the seats. Technically, there was room for everyone, but single passengers had spread out, each claiming a full bench rather than share with a stranger. So either they'd have to split up or move to the next car and hope for better seats.

As Math understood it, any carriages beyond the third had no benches—from that point, passengers stood.

Math felt a flash of annoyance at their impending separation—then caught himself. Why would he be upset about sitting apart from the necromancer?

As those thoughts ran through his head, Kai leaned over an elderly lady seated alone. The old woman wore a wide-brimmed hat adorned with flowers—once fresh, now wilting—and was quietly embroidering more blooms onto white linen stretched in a wooden hoop. Her supplies were neatly arranged beside her on the bench.

"I am so sorry," Kaiataris said to the woman. "But my husband and I were hoping that we might be able to sit together. I've never been by train before, and he promised he'd hold my hand."

The old woman lowered her embroidery hoop and gave Kaiataris a shrewd once-over, then turned the same keen scrutiny on Math. Whatever she saw seemed to satisfy her. "Of course! I wouldn't dream of breaking the two of you up. What an adorable couple you make."

She promptly stood, grabbed her embroidered bag, and headed for a new seat—a bench occupied by a middle-aged man sprawled so wide his knees claimed the entire bench. The old woman fixed her gaze on his crotch until, flustered, he pulled his legs in and made room.

Kai slipped into the old woman's seat and gestured for Math to join her once he'd stowed their stolen luggage and the Kaliri long arm. (Miniature bombard? Small cannon? He really needed a better name for it.) As soon as he sat, she took his hand. Across the aisle, the old woman gave them a conspiratorial wink.

He didn't pull his hand away. Too many people had heard their excuse—that was the reason, he told himself. Not the warmth of her fingers. Not the way it made something inside him feel breakable. Instead, he leaned in as if to murmur something tender. "Why did you say Idallik means 'death knight'?"

Silence, heavy with Kaiataris's refusal to discuss it.

He repeated the question.

"I heard you the first time," she whispered. "And I said it because that's what the word *means* in Irrahan: death knight."

Math suppressed the uneasy twist in his stomach. "It means..." He searched his memory for his Irrahan lessons—every member of the Order knew at least some, since it was the archives' original language. "Death dealer. It means death dealer."

"No." She shifted, tucking one leg beneath her to lean in closer and whisper. "The word is a contraction of *idal* and *alla*, with a suffix indicating someone who performs a role—so the correct translation is 'death knight.'" She shrugged. "Yes, that makes 'Idallik Knight' technically mean 'death knight knight,' but that manner of linguistic redundancy is surprisingly common."

He stared straight ahead. The train felt claustrophobic, entirely too cramped. "Maybe it wasn't originally an Irrahan word."

She didn't respond for several long heartbeats, although he sensed her frustrated sadness. The entire carriage jerked and began moving forward.

Around them, passengers busied themselves with books, newspapers, embroidery, and knitting. Some had brought food, its smell a pungent reminder that Math hadn't found dinner for them.

He hoped some enterprising soul had brought enough extra to sell.

Kaiataris's quiet words cut through his musing. "I told you that we placed ourselves in an enchanted slumber, but you must understand that someone else had to wake us, yes? A group outside of the spell. The solstice would stop all life, so the only beings that might endure would be artificial constructs—which are unreliable—or people already dead but magically sustaining themselves. So what do you think we called those people?"

In a flash, he understood exactly what she implied—and it was so unacceptable he tried to stand, as if he could physically distance himself from the idea. Every instinct urged him to flee, to be anywhere else.

She had a steel grip on his coat; he wouldn't be able to escape the truth without a fight.

So Math turned, grabbed her coat collar in return, and pulled her close enough to feel her breath on his face. "If that were true, the Order would—"

"Tell you? It has been a thousand years. I rather doubt they know the truth themselves by this point. Or that anyone who mentions such a thing would not be immediately labeled an apostate."

"There's no way! The whole reason the Order exists—"

"Whisper, my fair knight." She wrapped her arms around his neck. "We aren't alone."

Math froze and swallowed hard. To any onlooker, it must have looked like a lovers' embrace—and he had no doubt people were watching, whether they pretended not to or not.

The problem was, it *felt* like a lovers' embrace. And it couldn't be. She was a grim lord—the kind of person he'd been taught since childhood to see as inhuman. Dangerous. Her warmth burned through layers of cloth. Her face was far too close.

Someone behind them cleared their throat with pointed intent. Kaiataris lifted her head just enough to level a withering glare at the source and snapped, "We've only just wed. Look away if our love offends you."

After delivering that scolding, Kaiataris slipped from his arms and faced forward. Math shifted, adjusted his coat, and pretended her embrace hadn't affected him.

Neither of them said anything for a long time, after that.

Not forever, though.

"The Order exists to destroy grim lords," Math said at last, his voice low. "And you're suggesting we were the monsters all along."

"Absolutely not. The Idallik Order were *heroes*—soldiers and graven wizards who were sacrificing their very lives to protect humanity. And clearly, some members of the Order tried to do that. The rest, though . . . ?" Out of the corner of his eye, he saw her lift her chin with quiet defiance. "Evidently, the rest decided they would rather be *tyrants*. So yes, I do imagine those knights who stayed true to their vows would have focused the Order entirely on eradicating the 'grim lords' who betrayed us."

"Us? You mean graven wizards?"

"No, I mean *humanity*." Kaiataris turned to face him, although she remained a safe and proper distance apart. "That's your question answered. Now it's my turn. Why aren't you a knight?"

"Pardon?" Math shot her a quick, surprised glance, then turned his attention back to the front of the train.

"I've seen you fight. I've seen you cast spells. If you're not good enough, I shudder to think who is."

"Didn't you hear Huraiik? I can't manifest a weapon."

"I heard the words," she admitted. "'Tis the meaning that eludes me."

Math made a face. "Every knight can summon—manifest—a weapon, something unique to themselves, a reflection of their souls. And I... I've never been able to. Simple as that."

"I see." She leaned lightly against him, and Math tried not to react. Her presence was too vivid, too familiar—like a song he'd memorized by accident. She couldn't control what he felt, and he couldn't stop her from knowing. And she did know—he could feel her amusement. "Let me assure you of one thing, my fair knight: that is utter and complete rubbish."

"Excuse you. I haven't called your magic rubbish."

"No. Just evil."

Math had no response to that.

"You're wild mages," Kaiataris whispered. "The flavors of your magic have nothing to do with the qualities of your soul—it's about your *belief*. You've all convinced yourselves that you know the rules, when for you, there are no rules. It's just willpower." She gave a quiet scoff. "That's likely the entire point: imposing order on something inherently chaotic. It works because you believe it must. And I imagine a great deal of effort goes into ensuring you never think otherwise—because letting you *question* it would be dangerous."

Math thought of all the restrictions—never allowed to drink, lose his temper, grow too excited. Above all, never allowed to lose control. He thought of children raised like dangerous weapons.

Math thought of what he'd done—what all the knights had done—under the influence of those spores, and he shuddered.

"Your turn," Kaiataris said.

"My turn," he repeated before he realized she'd meant it was his turn to ask a question. "What about your magic?"

"What of it? Unlike yours, mine has rules."

"No," he replied, fighting to keep from losing his temper. "Mine has rules you don't understand. Does yours always have to be written?"

She'd called herself a "graven wizard" when she first woke, and though his mind had been elsewhere, he knew enough to recognize that "grave" was an archaic form of "engrave"—an unfortunate homonym for a group historically linked to necromancy.

"Yes," she said. "Always—though not always permanently. I once graved a spell into snow. But yes, the writing shapes the magic stored in the object." She paused. "That's how we accomplish extraordinary things—we can spend days, weeks, even years storing magic, then release it precisely when we choose."

"But nothing spontaneous?"

"No, nothing spontaneous. And it works best with items that change little—stone and metal being ideal."

His gaze drifted to her jewelry, to the intricate patterns he'd first mistaken for decorative design. Then he looked at the bracelet on his own wrist—the one she'd given him for his disguise, which he still hadn't returned.

He stood, reached up onto the overhead luggage rack, and pulled down the Kaliri long arm.

The engravings weren't identical, but they were similar. To his untrained eye, similar enough to have similar origins. He held out the weapon by the haft. "What about this?"

She took the weapon, rested it across her lap, and examined it carefully. By the time she handed it back, both her expression and emotions had shifted to clear irritation. "It's sloppy work," she muttered.

Math put the weapon back up on the rack and sat back down again. "But is it graved?"

"Oh yes. Someone's keeping the craft alive, at least." She leaned toward him. "If you're wondering about the purpose of those gravings, they appear—at a glance—to enhance accuracy and range. The device would be far more precise over longer distances than its construction suggests. But nothing in this graving would propel a bullet forward."

He slumped back against the bench. "No, that's the black powder's job."

He wasn't sure why the idea surprised him—that the Kaliri, long accused by the Idalliks of grim lord worship, had kept practicing the same magic as their necromancer overlords. In hindsight, it would've been stranger if they hadn't.

"Wait. You said your magic is weakening."

"It is," she said through clenched teeth. "That"—she waved toward the rack where the weapon rested—"is a simple modification. The ball's already being fired, the weapon already aimed. The spell just tells it 'travel farther' and 'strike true.' Even so, once its magic is spent, I would expect it to take some time to grave a new enchantment." She arched a brow. "And do not think I have missed you slipping in at least three questions on your turn."

Math huffed. "Fine. Ask."

"What were inside the packages?"

He frowned. "Packages? What packages?"

"The ones you took from Captain Qin. The little paper packages."

"Oh! The letters—I nearly forgot about those." He reached into his coat and pulled out two small, neatly folded pieces of paper. From the outside, they looked almost identical, both written on Isofal Cenobium's linen stationery and folded into precise rectangles.

Math pursed his lips as he examined the letters. This was a complication.

"*Those* are letters?"

"Sure. It's ... look." He turned to face her on the bench and held out one of the notes. "You write the letter, fold it, then thread a thin strip of paper—still attached to the page—through the folds like a needle. The ends are sealed with wax. The result ..." He turned the small paper packet between his fingers. "You can't open it without tearing the paper and revealing it's been read."

"It's impossible to open without magic, you mean," Kaiataris corrected.

"You could've said you'd heard this joke before." He grinned. "Even with magic, it's tricky. You can't just fix the paper—you also have to restore the marbling, the doodles, or any writing that spilled past the margins. I'm good at that. With time and a sharp knife, I could open both, read them, and reseal everything without anyone noticing. But we have neither, which means ..." He sighed, dug his thumbnail into the wax seal of the first letter, and pulled until it tore free—ripping the paper with it.

He unfolded the letter and read the whole thing. He read it a second time, but the message didn't change.

"This ... this is all wrong."

Kaiataris raised an eyebrow. "Do you wish to explain that, or shall I guess?"

Math scoffed and handed it over. "Commander Talu doesn't grasp the real threat. He thinks—" Math paused. "It's an account of what happened, but everything's skewed to make it look like the Kaliri are plotting something. He claims they've got a new grim witch who can control plants and trees. He doesn't even mention the Queens—not even the possibility they *exist*."

"In his defense, it does seem the Kaliri are 'up to something.'"

"Yeah, but not *this*. They aren't responsible for attacking Isofal." Math chewed on his lip. "He doesn't mention you, either."

"Respectfully, I cannot find it within myself to be much upset at such a revelation."

"Yeah, I don't blame you, but you'd think the resurrection of a ..." He shrugged apologetically. "You know."

She was unimpressed. "Yes, I know."

"Given that stopping grim lords is the entire reason our order exists—"

"The Order doesn't still protect the archives, then?"

Math froze. He closed his eyes and sat still for a moment, listening to the murmur of conversation around him, the clatter of iron wheels on iron tracks, the creak of shifting wood.

He felt Kai's chagrin and then concern.

"Math, I did not mean—"

"No, it's fine. Of course the graven wizards built the archives. You were trying to preserve life. Why not make sure knowledge survived, too?" He scoffed. "The Illuminated. That's what we call the people who built the archives. You're one of the Illuminated."

"That is a far more flattering name than 'grim lord.'"

Math shook his head. "I finally know who the Illuminated were, and no one will ever believe me." Still turning that over, he broke the seal on the second letter and read it, too.

"Gravespit." Math lowered the paper in disbelief.

"Worse?"

"Worse." Math handed her the page.

It was an order for his execution.

STOP

Math spent the next hour explaining the Rokasmaa legal system to Kai, who had no shortage of scathing opinions—especially about the part where a cenobium commander could order an execution without trial or evidence.

He reluctantly pointed out that there *was* evidence, which promptly killed what little urge to keep talking he had left. Though, if he were honest, exhaustion played its part—he hadn't truly slept in two days. Unconsciousness didn't count.

Which was probably why he *did* fall asleep, despite the hard bench and looming danger. Math only woke when someone tugged on his collar and pressed a soft kiss to his temple.

He snapped awake.

Kaiataris stood over him, watching—and casually eating half a flatbread stuffed with cheese and grilled lamb. His stomach grumbled in jealous complaint.

Still . . . "Did you just kiss—?"

"Such a sweet couple," the old woman with the flowers said.

Math forced himself to relax, to smile. They were being watched.

"We overslept, my heart," Kaiataris explained.

Math blinked and sat up straighter. Morning sunlight poured through the windows of the motionless train. In the distance, voices carried, birds sang, and someone was chopping wood.

It was a sound Math had grown all too familiar with lately.

Math didn't know exactly what Bashan looked like, but he was fairly certain this wasn't it.

Kaiataris offered him her remaining bread and meat. "Madam Leadur was kind enough to share her meal with us."

Math reached for the offered food, giving a grateful nod to the old woman, evidently Madam Leadur.

"Madam?" the old woman scoffed. "Mrs. Leadur, dear. Don't be giving me airs." She pushed the bread back toward Kaiataris before presenting Math with the other half of the flatbread. "You eat yours, sweetheart. Your husband can have his own."

The man the old woman had shared a bench with was gone, and in his place Mrs. Leadur had set a woven picnic basket, the source of the stuffed bread.

"That's very kind," he told her.

The old woman waved off the gratitude. "Figured this was going to happen again, and wanted to make sure I had enough for the trip." She made a moue. "But I overpacked. Food's just going to go bad if it's not eaten."

Math ate slowly, forcing himself not to devour the food like a starving wolf. But after a few bites, her words caught up with him. "Happen again? It's happened before?"

"You haven't been reading the papers?" The woman tsked, then carried on as if he'd answered. "I love these new trains—so much more comfortable than carriages—but every other day something's blocking the tracks. Last week, when I visited my granddaughter, it was an entire herd of giant birds. Birds! Some new species. And today? A wild bramble patch bigger than the train. Sometimes I think the Tri-Mother's had quite enough of us."

Math stomped on his panic. A wild bramble patch . . . "We were supposed to be in Bashan by now," Math murmured.

"I hate to disappoint you, young man, but 'supposed to' doesn't often visit the present," Mrs. Leadur said, shaking her head. "They claimed it would be a six-hour delay—that was five hours ago—and they've barely made a dent. Personally, I think we'll be here all day."

Math hurried to the door and leaped off the motionless train. The chopping he'd heard earlier came from a group of men with axes, hacking at a massive briar of twisted branches—easily as tall as the train—that had overtaken the tracks. The brambles looked ancient, though Math knew they had to have grown in just a few hours.

"As the solstice nears," Kaiataris said, standing beside him, "this will become more common. The giant birds she spoke of would almost certainly be because of such increases in chaos."

"Last week, the Queens hadn't woken yet."

"Indeed. It's equally possible the Queens had nothing to do with these brambles, either."

"Possible, but not guaranteed."

"No, not guaranteed. Now that the Parnathi have absorbed people from your world into theirs—all the people they've killed and taken—the Queens will understand exactly how disruptive blocking these routes could be, and that it buys them enough time to catch up to us."

Unfortunately, Math couldn't find a single flaw in that reasoning. He clicked his tongue, then waved down a train conductor pacing nearby with a worried look on her face.

"Excuse me," Math said to the woman. "You wouldn't know where we are right now, do you? How far away from Bashan we might be?"

The woman sighed. "As soon as the obstacle is cleared, we'll be on our—"

"But where *are* we? What would have been the next train stop if the tracks weren't blocked?"

The conductor blinked. "Oh—Cherkiss. But it's still twenty miles from here. You're better off waiting. We should have this cleared in a few hours."

Math looked past her to where workers were still hacking at the thicket. A few passengers had joined in, driven by the sensible belief that speeding things up served everyone—and helped ease their boredom. Math studied the tangled mass of branches and gauged their progress.

He shook his head as he turned back to the train conductor. "You're not going to get out of here for at least another ten hours."

Probably half that, if he helped. The problem with that idea, however, was that it meant he'd still be trapped here for another five hours. Which was absolutely not an acceptable idea should either the Queens or Idallik Knights show up.

"It's better than walking," the woman said.

"I'm going to miss my daughter's wedding!" a man nearby shouted. A woman muttered about demanding a refund. Soon the entire group had erupted into argument.

Math returned to Kaiataris, who'd been standing close enough to hear the brief exchange. "If I start now, I can reach Cherkiss by nightfall and catch another train."

Several of the other passengers heard his declaration. Their expressions turned thoughtful.

Kaiataris narrowed her eyes. "If *you* start walking?"

Math gestured for her to follow him away from the tracks, putting distance between them and any curious ears. "The Idallik Order isn't after you, and while the Queens might recognize you, I doubt they can track you. The safest thing would be for you to stay here. Wait for the tracks to clear—we can meet in Cherkiss, or Bashan if it comes to that. There's no reason we both have to be uncomfortable."

"Have we not already discussed why I have no wish to be parted from your side?" Kaiataris scoffed. "You shall not be rid of me that easily."

He threw an arm up over his head. "I'm not trying to get rid of you—"

"Excellent. Then I'll fetch our bags so we can be on our way." She was heading back to the train before he could finish the sentence.

He muttered: "Of course. How could I refuse?"

Then Math followed after her—it would look strange for a newlywed husband to let his wife carry their luggage alone.

Since Math knew the way to Cherkiss no better than Kaiataris, they agreed the most sensible choice was to follow the train tracks. The tangled brambles that had stopped the train were far less effective at halting those on foot—they simply skirted the edge and kept moving.

They weren't alone. Around two dozen others had made the same choice, scattering along the tracks like glass beads from a broken string. Loose pairs and trios walked at their own pace, never too far apart, never quite together.

Taking this route meant giving up the chance to catch a passing wagon, but with so many people on foot, it would've only led to arguments over who got a seat. As it was, following the tracks kept them off the main roads when the Idallik Knights came searching. Math was happy to do so.

Despite the grim purpose and pressing urgency, the day was stunning. The sky stretched in a clear, brilliant blue; the landscape burst with the vibrant greens of spring, accented by elegant, unexpected touches of color—a solitary cloud, scattered yellow wildflowers, the dark line of train tracks cutting through it all.

Under other circumstances, he might've mistaken their group for tourists out on a leisurely hike.

"So, when did you first decide to become a knight?" Kaiataris gripped her borrowed suitcase with one hand, careful to keep it from bumping her legs as she walked.

Math glanced around them, but no one was close enough to hear. "It doesn't work like that. It's not a 'decision.' If a child starts demonstrating magical ability, they're given to the Order to train. Of course I want—" He halted, flushed.

He'd *wanted* to be a knight. Past tense.

Because it sure as the oceans wasn't going to happen now, was it?

"You're forced into this as *children*?" He felt her outrage, even as she must have felt his grief.

"Can we talk about something else?" he snapped. "*Anything* else?"

Kaiataris came to a full stop, casting him a shrewd, assessing stare. "Very well." As she resumed walking, she added, "There's something I've been wondering since we boarded the train—a question about the behavior of men in this era."

"Yes?" He already didn't like where this was going.

"Is it truly so common in this era for men to sit as if you are royalty on a throne?" She glanced down—not at his legs, but his hips. "With your legs spread wide open as though some invisible lover is nestled between them, about to give you a—"

"Kai!" If he laughed, it was purely shock. He immediately lowered his voice. "Kaiataris, I mean. You can't . . . you can't just ask a question like that."

"I cannot?" The look of utter innocence she gave him was as false as a painted smile on a doll. "But you asked me to talk about anything else. Don't you remember?"

He inhaled, starting to feel irritated. Or was she the one who was feeling irritated?

No, it was definitely him.

"We have got to break this bond," he muttered. "Or we're going to kill each other."

"You haven't answered my question."

"Are you serious?"

She lifted her chin. "Absolutely. It was a very serious question."

It wasn't. He could feel her amusement, even now, but also a stubborn obstinacy and refusal to give ground. The question itself wasn't serious and didn't matter; the fact that he refused to answer it? *That* part mattered.

"It's probably cultural," Math finally said. "I've never given it any thought. Personally, I just find it more comfortable."

She made a noncommittal noise. Neither of them said anything else for a period as they walked.

His only warning was the sudden spike of Kai's amusement just before she said, "No, I apologize, but I can't think of anything else. It's the size of your testicles, isn't it?"

Math choked on air so hard he stopped walking until he wrangled his coughing fit back under control.

"I take it back." Math glanced around, but none of the passengers had wandered close enough. "There are *two* things I don't want to talk about."

"Don't you mean three?" She was almost smiling.

He raised his face to heaven. "Tri-Mother help me. Stop."

"Very well." She glanced at him sideways. Her annoyance was slipping, but her amusement still felt sharp and dangerous. "In the spirit of friendship and generosity, I shall refrain from a discussion of seating customs in the future."

"That's not what I meant and *you know it*—"

"You said earlier that the Idallik Order demands chastity of its members, but why is this left to chance? Why would they not use certain potions or drugs or . . ." She made a snipping motion with two fingers. "Hmm?"

"You're doing this on purpose."

"Yes, as it happens, I am indeed responsible for which words leave my mouth. Now I would appreciate an answer. I promise I am not asking purely to make you blush, no matter how fetchingly you do so."

Math took a deep breath. She wasn't lying. Or at least, wasn't completely lying. He could sense her curiosity; she wanted to know.

As it happened, he had a ready answer—this question usually landed somewhere between number eight and fifteen on the list most commonly asked by novitiates, once they discovered that, for an order demanding celibacy, the cenobium libraries held an astonishingly robust collection of books on sex and sexuality. (When it came to a conflict between the Order's rules and preserving knowledge, knowledge always won.)

"We—" Math sighed. "*They* used to do that. At various points in the Order's history, they've used anything from drugs to mutilation. It just doesn't work."

She swung around, walking backward for several steps. "Doesn't work? Whatever do you mean, it doesn't work? Generally speaking, if one removes a body part, it stays removed."

"You'd think that—" Math eyed her uneasily until she flipped back around to walking the right way. "You'd be right to think that, but don't forget: the Idallik Knights are a military order. Healing spells are a priority—and those spells can be indiscriminate. So, no, if one removes a body part, it doesn't always stay removed."

"Oh. Oh, I see." She chuckled. He didn't need to look sideways to see her smile. He could feel it, warm and glittering in the back of his mind, prettier than the day.

"Right. So current doctrine is that it's better to train members to understand temptation and its consequences than think ourselves immune." He shifted his grip on the Kaliri long arm. "Some have an easier time of it than others."

"I would imagine." She pursed her lips thoughtfully. "Just as I imagine the Order practices a great deal of nonprocreative sex that everyone can pretend doesn't happen as long as no one ever speaks of it."

Math cleared his throat but didn't answer. He didn't think he needed to.

Kaiataris tilted her head. "This does, however, bring me back to what I was saying about testicles."

"Tri-Mother," Math muttered. "I thought we weren't going to talk about that?"

"I never promised any such thing." She blithely continued on. "It's a question of fertility, you see. As we approach the Chaos solstice, I would expect a commensurate increase in fertility levels. Which, for human males, would logically manifest in the form of larger male . . ."

"Just stop." He really needed her to stop, because he was going to start laughing pretty soon, and that would absolutely wreck all his efforts to pretend he didn't like her.

Wait.

Not *pretend*. He wasn't pretending. If she was likable, it was only a sign of how dangerous she was, never mind the whole "under an enchantment" aspect to their relationship. She had him under a spell. It was as simple as that.

"If you truly want me to stop, I will," she said. "But I don't get the sense that you actually do." Kaiataris paused and Math felt a spike of chagrin and self-rebuke. "Let the record show: that is not a sentence I ever imagined saying aloud, and I hate myself a little for having done so." She stopped walking, her gaze fixed on his back until he turned. "I would never force you into anything against your will. You know that, don't you? This bond can't make you do anything you don't choose."

"I don't . . . I don't think that. I was just surprised, that's all." Math set down his luggage and the wooden Kaliri weapon. "I've enjoyed the flirting. I have. It's been flattering, and if you were a member of the Order—" He huffed out something between a laugh and a scoff. "If you were a member of the Order, I'd be in a lot of trouble. But you're not. You're a grim—"

"Please do not call me a grim lord. I'd rather you just called me Kai. I like that."

"You do? Oh. Well, I . . . okay. I'll remember that. Call me Math."

"Thank you. I shall."

Math wrestled his feelings back under control. That entire exchange had basically been the opposite of what he'd meant to accomplish. "Just . . . you're not someone I can be involved with. You understand that, right? I'm going to go back to the Idallik Order to warn them about the Kaliri and the Parnathi, and if you're smart—which you clearly *are*—you'll do what you need to do and then stay as far away from the Order as possible."

She looked up into his eyes, and her own would've been unreadable if he hadn't been able to feel her resentment, her irritation, her regret. "In truth, I am not overly fond of sexual encounters divorced from any emotion or romance, and that seems to be the only kind your order tolerates. So you're right: nothing between us can ever happen."

"Exactly. I'm glad we agree." Math picked up the luggage, the weapon, and began walking again. A quicker pace this time, to catch up to the others.

Kaiataris didn't follow right away. He could feel her standing still behind him, emotions knotting together in a quiet storm: pride, regret, frustration . . . and something she was trying very hard not to let him name.

By the time her footsteps started up again, she'd smoothed herself into something composed and distant.

They walked in silence after that.

The sun was still shining. The sky was still impossibly blue. And somewhere between the spring wildflowers and the sound of their boots on the gravel, Math tried very hard not to imagine what it would've been like to walk beside her without a thousand years of mangled history between them.

As predicted, it took most of the day to reach Cherkiss. Everyone was short-tempered about it, but they all had to admit that there'd been no sign anyone had successfully cleared the tracks.

At no point did any trains pass them.

At last, the station came into view—easily recognizable, as it looked much like the one they'd left behind. Their fellow travelers, who had spent most of the day strung out in a loose, uneven line, regrouped as they neared Cherkiss. They'd agreed they'd have a better chance negotiating the next steps—like getting the train company to honor their original tickets—if they stuck together.

Ahead, trains waited, including one that looked like it only needed the all-clear before it would race as fast as it could back toward Sounalla to make up for lost time.

The rest unfolded as expected. They bargained for tickets, and everyone boarded the new train bound for Bashan. It was much easier to find seats this time. A quiet camaraderie had settled over the group—still strangers, but strangers who'd shared a small ordeal. They laughed, joked, and teased one another, and for a moment, it all felt oddly normal. Math almost forgot who he was, or what he was running from. He was just a young soldier headed back to the capital with his beautiful new wife.

That idea was far more appealing than it had any right to be. He wondered what the children would think of Kai, now that she was awake. Jaiik would want to know if he'd kissed her.

Kai gave him a funny look. Math internally winced, reminded himself not to think about such things, and went back to watching the crowd on the train platform.

That's likely the only reason he saw the flash of white surcoat, the red hexagon symbol of the Idallik Order, on the station platform.

Math grabbed Kai's coat and pulled her away from the window. "There's an Idallik Knight out there."

She didn't look. "Could it be a coincidence?"

"I don't think so, no." Math slowly reached under the bench and pulled out his stolen coat, the Kaliri long arm. "Start walking toward the back."

People were still settling in, still stowing their luggage, still dealing with the exhaustion of walking such a distance just to put themselves on another cramped, uncomfortable train.

That was the only reason Alik Nuhzar wasn't able to immediately close with Math the moment the knight stepped into the first carriage, scanned the aisle, and spotted them.

"Mathaiik Kaven! You are commanded to turn yourself over to the Idallik Order. Hold up your hands and surrender now!" shouted the newly appointed Captain of Swords for Iscfal Cenobium.

"Definitely not a coincidence," Kai murmured.

BALLS

Cherkiss was labeled a town rather than a city only because it lived in Bashan's shadow. In truth, it was a county seat—which meant the train station bustled with people who had little interest in or connection to a delayed train from Sounalla.

They had one chance to disappear before the knights closed in—and the station crowd was their best cover.

Captain Nuhzar shouted again, and once more Math feigned ignorance, calmly collecting his things as if the man couldn't possibly be addressing *him*. The absence of panic left the crowd confused—people glanced around uncertainly, but no one edged away from him and Kai.

That would change within moments, as people did the only sensible thing when faced with an armored knight wielding an obviously magical weapon—they'd get out of the way.

Kai's focus hit him like a blade drawn bright and honed. She turned, pulled a ring off her finger—Math barely had time to blink—then murmured a few words and hurled it.

Some people ducked, although it was unlikely they understood exactly what they were ducking. Nuhzar's expression was contemptuous as the ring flew right past him and pinged against the front wall of the carriage.

Then: chaos.

People shouted in dismay and confusion. Some grabbed on to benches but most were flung down the length of the carriage to slam into the knights. Nuhzar and his people fell back into the far wall as though hit by an invisible tidal surge. A hurricane had blown through the carriage, but without any wind, just motion.

"What did you do?" Math demanded.

"I changed the definition of 'down,'" Kai said. "Don't stop. It will not last. Gravity does not like being told what to do."

Math ushered them through the back door of the carriage and over the narrow bridge to the next.

"Can you do that trick again?"

"I only possess two more, so we best ensure they count. Might we be able to slip out the back?"

"Maybe," Math hedged. "If we exit through the standing-room-only carriage, maybe we can lose ourselves in the crowd trying to board."

They didn't slow, dodging passengers entering or exiting in a chaotic dance.

Outside the windows, Math glimpsed flashes of Idallik tabards as knights circled the train. Reinforcements, no doubt. At any moment, those knights might burst into their current carriage, and matters would grow more complicated.

They passed several water closets, but Math dismissed them. Hiding in a bathroom was a perfect way to be cornered and captured in the most unpleasant possible surroundings.

By the time they reached the first of the standing carriages, most of the crowd had already disembarked. Their only stroke of luck was that a lot of soldiers and knights were too busy running toward the front of the train to pay any attention to who was leaving.

"The spell hasn't faded yet," Kai said, a little surprised. The flicker of satisfaction she felt echoed down the thread of their bond. "How unexpectedly delightful."

Math grabbed her hand. "Then let's go. We won't get a better chance."

They stepped onto the station platform.

The hardest part was *not* running. Math forced himself to walk slowly, to smile at Kai, to look tired and eager to be home. Her effort to project calm brushed against his skin, paper-thin and straining.

They passed a knight on the way out. Nuhzar had seen Kaiataris back at the maze, but he had no reason to suspect they were traveling together—or that they were disguised. For now, the knights were looking for one man, not a couple.

They hadn't taken more than five steps beyond the station before Math heard Nuhzar shout.

Math pulled Kai into an alley, where they crouched down behind a stack of delivery crates. Armor jangled as the knights ran past down the street.

Kai started to rise, but Math pulled her back down. He held up a finger, signaling silence. Another set of footsteps followed—slower, more deliberate, followed by the scrape of metal and a long pause.

Math didn't need to look. He knew it was Nuhzar, scanning the area one last time.

"I really hate that man," Math chuntered.

He would be back. As soon as Nuhzar realized he'd lost them, he'd circle back and search every gutter.

"Follow me," Math whispered.

They crept deeper into the alley. It twisted and bent, narrowing their line of sight—but also hiding them from pursuit.

"How did they find us?" Kai asked softly. "How did they get ahead of us?"

Math paused. These were not rhetorical questions. Her unease buzzed against his ribs like a trapped insect. If they didn't find the answers, they'd risk repeating this disaster.

"How they got ahead is the easy part," he said. "Idallik Knights can move incredibly fast when needed—sort of like your gravity trick. If they know their destination, a journey that should take days can be done in minutes." He ran his tongue across his teeth. "As for tracking . . ."

He rifled through his coat and pouches. He hadn't been foolish enough to keep Captain Qin's scrying token—that was the standard focus for such spells. The clothes he wore had been stolen after fleeing the cenobium. His boots were his own, but far too generic to serve as a scrying anchor. The cenobium paper was distinctive, yes, but with thousands of identical samples in circulation, it made for a poor target. He had some money, a water canteen—but nothing quite *distinctive enough*.

"What are you looking for?" Kai asked.

"We use objects as scry—tokens. Something unique. If someone slipped one into my things . . ." He shook his head. "But I don't see anything that would work."

Kai didn't respond right away. Then she tilted her head, studying him. A surge of realization snapped straight through the bond like a cord pulled taut.

"What is the range for this scrying?" she asked. "And how many of those Kaliri weapons do you think might exist?"

He looked down at the weapon in his hand. His stomach sank. The bond echoed with her mirrored dread.

He had no idea how many of these things had been built by the Kaliri, but given that it took a mage to use them, he didn't think so many of them could exist inside Rokasmaa borders.

They'd left a mess at the ambush site. It was entirely possible someone had counted the dead, counted the weapons, and realized one was missing.

And that missing weapon was with him.

That would be more than unique enough.

Math pressed his thumb to his temple, exhaled slowly, then tossed the Kaliri long arm into a nearby garbage bin. It rattled loudly before settling. Kai's quiet relief fluttered across the bond.

"You're right," he said. "That's how they tracked me."

A sound echoed from the mouth of the alley. They both startled, then hurried to keep moving. Math kept his eye open for an exit, any door they might use to leave the alley and lose their pursuers.

They were lucky in that the alley was not a straight line, but twisted and turned, making it difficult to see who else might walk ahead or behind. Still, they heard noises.

More specifically, the sound of their pursuers.

"I don't suppose we could take them," Kai murmured.

"Who? The knights?" Math let out a grim chuckle. "Absolutely not. Not like this. And definitely not Nuhzar."

"He seems utterly delightful," she said dryly. "An old friend?"

"If childhood bully counts, then sure."

They rounded another corner and saw a cluster of produce carts. Workers hauled boxes into a tall building through a side door. The people in question looked like cooks, or at least some kind of helpers at a restaurant.

Kai gestured for him to strip off his soldier's coat, sash, and scarf, and stuffed them into a trash bin. Her urgency scraped raw along their connection. Once he looked less immediately recognizable as a soldier, Kai grabbed his arm and walked straight through the door.

When someone called after her, she waved them off and said, "I *know*! But you can't expect me to walk all the way around to the front, can you?" as if that was a sufficient excuse.

Except, apparently, it *was*.

No one tried to stop them. Everyone was too busy with their own jobs to pay attention to a group acting like they were supposed to be there.

The rear of the building contained some sort of kitchen, attached to a full restaurant. The hallways bustled with cooks, assistants, clattering pans, the aroma of food.

Kai seemed temporarily distracted by that, taking a moment to stop in the middle of a hallway and inhale.

"We have to keep going," Math reminded her.

She raised her hand. "Just one moment."

She seemed to be counting something, listening for a pattern in the chaos. Maybe she heard something he didn't.

Kai pointed down a hallway. "This way."

He followed. She clearly had a plan. He didn't. That feeling was only emphasized when she opened a small, narrow door into a large room filled with metal basins, washboards, and clothes pinned to lines.

It was a laundry.

She quickly plucked several sets of clothes from a line and tossed them in Math's direction. "Quickly. Before anyone notices."

They both ducked into a closet to change. It said something about the seriousness of the situation that Math was too busy worrying about their pursuers to be distracted by the beautiful woman undressing behind his back.

He swapped out everything he could, moved essentials into the new clothes, and hoped no one noticed his mismatched boots.

They emerged in black uniforms that looked like those worn by domestic staff. Kai's fit perfectly while his was decidedly a bit snug. Still, it would do.

Kai pointed. "Back this way, if I'm not mistaken."

Before Math could reply, a sharp voice cut through the hallway. "What have I *told* you people about lazing around? Those appetizers won't serve themselves!"

A tall, stern woman appeared, gray hair bound in a gold-and-black scarf. She wore the same severe black uniform that they did, but she wore hers with a difference.

She was pointing at them.

Math ducked his head. "Yes, ma'am."

They'd wandered into a side hall off a larger corridor—and the woman had caught sight of them.

Behind the woman, other servants bustled past carrying trays. Marble tiled the larger hallway, which was further covered with an elaborate silk carpet runner of green and blue. Orchestral music drifted in from farther down the hallway.

The woman clapped. "Well? Go!"

They went.

The woman directed them to a staging area just off the main corridor. Within seconds someone shoved trays into their hands and pushed them through a set of double doors.

Math no longer had any idea where they were.

He'd thought it was a restaurant. Then a hotel. But now?

Stepping through those doors, he revised his guess again. If this was a hotel, it was the fanciest he'd ever seen.

The room was massive, lit by crystal chandeliers and gas-lamp wall sconces. Mirrors lined the walls, interrupted only by doorways and enormous masterpiece paintings. The ceiling soared overhead, at least forty feet above. A double set of stairs swept from the main floor to a balcony mezzanine and another set of double doors.

A small orchestra played music, servers circulated through the crowd with food and drink, and several hundred sumptuously dressed men and women laughed and danced beneath lights that glittered almost as brightly as Kai's amusement.

"Don't say it," Math warned.

Kai bit her lip, eyes sparkling, and the swell of barely contained laughter buzzed through the bond like champagne fizz.

"But—" She gave him a pleading look.

"Fine," Math grumbled. "Go ahead."

She cleared her throat, straightened her borrowed uniform, and asked sweetly, "Are *all* your balls this large?"

GOSSIP

"Perhaps we're overthinking this," Kai said, her voice light. "Let's just walk out the front door, shall we?" She drifted in that direction, pausing now and then to smile demurely as guests plucked orders from her tray.

Math's stomach clenched. "No. That's—no."

Captain Nuhzar had just entered the ballroom.

Kai made a faint sound of dismay. Through their bond, he felt her irritation flicker hot, tempered by a measured wariness. "He's becoming tiresome. Damnably persistent, that one."

"He thinks that's a virtue," Math muttered, scanning the room without looking like he was scanning the room.

The party itself was a blur of silk, laughter, and chandeliers. Wealth and power thickened the air, but Math lacked the context to gauge how much—only that it was enough to make his own presence absurd.

Retreat was blocked. The servant overseer guarded the kitchen doors with razor focus. Without empty trays, they'd be turned back. And Nuhzar still loomed near the front entrance. Gods knew how many knights waited outside.

That left only one path: the grand staircase curling up to the second floor and the gilded double doors at the top. As Math watched, a server carried a tray of pastries up, knocked on the door, and was allowed inside.

He tugged on Kai's sleeve. "We'll have a better chance if we split up. I'll meet you at the top."

She shifted beside him, elbow to elbow, their trays aligned like shields. "Remember that you're a wild mage," she murmured. "Your limitations are self-imposed."

"My inability to manifest a weapon begs to differ."

"My magic doesn't care about my belief, but yours *does*, and you countered a spell I cast at the height of my powers without even trying. Don't undersell yourself." Her amusement sparked bright for a moment—then she vanished into the crowd before he could argue.

Math worked his way along the dance floor's edge, head lowered, tray balanced. He let the ambient murmur wash over him. Guests discussed the usual: Vilsenor's provocations, Cinoparan skirmishes, Valdea's diplomatic silence. Pirates. Lomar. King Sanistral's ambition to annex everything that moved.

Nothing about Kaliri. Nothing about trees.

He began quietly circling defensive spells. If things went wrong, there wouldn't be time to cast later. Kai's words echoed. If she was right, his limits were lies the Order had trained into him.

He'd been told knowledge was power. But if Kai was right, ignorance was the real secret.

Kai traded trays with another servant and moved toward the stairs. Math watched her pass directly behind Nuhzar, and nearly had a heart attack. She didn't even break stride. Nuhzar, thankfully, didn't notice.

She reached the top, knocked on the door, and was admitted.

Math inhaled once, steadying himself, and followed.

The door cracked open when he knocked. A woman in a white-and-sky-blue uniform regarded him, the lion of Rokasmaa gleaming on her chest.

She didn't ask his name. Just gave him a squint, lifted her chin, and said, "What do you have?"

Math glanced down at his tray. "Fruit tarts?" he offered, a touch too hopefully.

From the foot of the stairs came a sharp bark: "Kaven!"

He didn't flinch. Didn't turn. Didn't even breathe.

The guard barely reacted—too much noise, no reason to think the shout was meant for the man with the pastry tray.

She smiled. "Perfect. Those are her favorite."

The guard opened the door and ushered him inside.

The moment Math crossed the threshold, he wondered if he'd made a mistake. Not about escaping Captain Nuhzar—that part was brilliant. But this? This had all the hallmarks of jumping off a tree branch only to realize it had been growing from the edge of a cliff.

The room wasn't a room, as much as an opulent upper foyer: gaslit, marble-floored, lined with polished woodwork and velvet drapery. Hallways stretched left and right, unmarked doors lined the walls, and a sweeping balcony opened onto the city of Cherkiss. Whether palace, hotel, or private manor, it catered to the elite of Rokasmaa.

And it was crawling with soldiers.

All of them wore the formal white-and-blue colors of the empire. A jeweled sword hung from every belt. Math counted a dozen before he stopped trying.

The woman who'd opened the door gestured him toward a linen-draped table. A severe man in scholastic robes was transferring food from Kai's tray with the reverence of a priest arranging an altar. Nearby—

Math mentally stumbled.

That was an Idallik Knight.

She wore no armor or tabard, but instead a luxurious gown that wouldn't have looked out of place among the dancers downstairs. The gold-embroidered crest on her dress declared her allegiance, as well as the fact that she was busy circling spells on the food—poison warding and toxin detection. The sort of thing one might do when protecting someone important.

Next to her, another servant waited to ferry dishes to some unseen location.

This wasn't a staging area. It was a buffer zone for someone important enough to warrant this level of paranoia.

Someone important, yet also someone not mingling with the guests below.

Then he saw it: a tiny hand snaking up from behind the table to steal a pastry.

Math made a decision.

He stepped sideways, closer to the Idallik Knight. "Excuse me, ma'am—are you one of the knights? Because there's a man downstairs claiming he's one, too, and he wanted to do something to my tray. Is he one of yours? Should I have let him? He got so mad when I said no."

She looked up sharply, one hand drifting beneath the table as if to reassure herself of the location of a weapon.

"No," she said flatly. "He's not one of mine."

Someone began pounding on the doors.

"Open up! This is an Idallik matter!" Nuhzar's voice roared.

Soldiers snapped into motion. Half of them rushed to the door, pulling Math and Kai behind them. The rest formed a defensive wall in front of the food table.

The knight swept out from behind the table with a great swishing of skirts.

In her absence, a small face peeked over the edge of the table. Large, dark eyes took in the scene. Math pretended not to notice.

Had it been just the soldiers, Nuhzar might have bullied his way through. But with another knight present—one of high rank—that wouldn't happen. She'd force Nuhzar to explain himself.

Across the room, Kai caught Math's gaze. She pulled a ring from her finger—identical to the one she'd used at the Cherkiss train station—and glanced at the balcony. The message was obvious.

He nodded.

At the door to the ballroom, a narrow crack opened.

"Do you have any idea who you're disturbing?" the knight asked, her voice low and lethal. Math wouldn't have heard it without the sensory-enhancement spell he'd cast earlier.

"Go," he murmured.

Math and Kai ran.

Shouts erupted behind them, but the soldiers were normal humans—fast, but not fast enough. As they reached the balcony, Kai made the same gesture she had on the train, whispered the same phrase, and hurled the ring.

It struck the outer wall—and gravity flipped.

Math's stomach lurched as the world turned sideways. Suddenly, "down" meant the sheer stone façade of the building. He and Kai leaped over the railing and landed running, boots skimming the vertical surface as though it were flat ground.

They were higher than he'd realized—four stories, maybe more. Below them, another rooftop waited two floors down. Beyond that, steam rose from the station's idling train engines.

They hit the lower roof at a sprint. Math heard startled shouting from behind them, but it was already fading.

They ran.

ICE

Math let himself believe they might actually escape.

It didn't last long.

The rooftop was too exposed. The magic Kai had used to shift gravity still clung to the walls and stone behind them—an open trail of breadcrumbs easily followed by their pursuers. And while Kai couldn't run as fast as Math, Math couldn't run as fast as Alik Nuhzar.

He heard the knight's footsteps before he saw him.

Down below, the train they'd glimpsed earlier let out a shrill burst of steam. It had cleared the tracks and begun to roll—in the wrong direction, away from Bashan, back west. Math didn't care. Any train would do.

"Can you make it to that train roof?" Math called.

"I'll manage. Can you?"

He offered a crooked smile. "Someone has to stall Nuhzar. I'll catch up."

They both knew that was a lie.

"I'll be quite cross with you if you don't." Kai pushed the sleeve up around her wrist to reveal the largest gold bracelet she wore. She glanced over at the train slowly pulling away from the station and slid a finger across the bracelet's surface, skimming over the etched symbols.

She vanished.

A heartbeat later, she reappeared, unsteady but upright, on top of the slowly moving train.

Math exhaled, impressed despite himself. So *that's* how she'd escaped the maze. He wondered how often she could do that, but then immediately answered himself: not often, or she'd have used it when running from Huraiik.

"Kaven!" Captain Nuhzar landed on the station roof, armor ringing. "Surrender!"

Math turned, plastering a false smile on his face. "Alik! What a surprise. What are you doing *here*? Did you already strangle every kitten in Parasir County?"

The man ignored the jab, his breath heavy but his posture unshaken. "Stop running. You're just putting me in a bad mood."

"I can't take credit for that, Alik. You're always in a bad mood." It was a good thing that Kai had been able to get away on her own, because at the moment, Math's greatest magical power was angering the man chasing them.

Nuhzar advanced. "Surrender."

Math's smile vanished. "How are the kids?"

The question caught Nuhzar off guard. His shoulders stiffened. "They're fine."

"They're not," Math snapped. "They just lost Master Wadera. *We* just lost Master Wadera. There's no world where any of us are fine."

Gods, he might hate the man, but they'd grown up as novitiates together; Alik was only a few years older and Ziik Wadera had raised them both. The old man's loss was a foul emptiness that threatened to trip Math anytime he lowered his guard.

The knight's jaw clenched. For a breath, Math felt it—that cracking surface. Grief, quickly smothered. It was the smallest slip of the mask. After, Nuhzar's face was once more carved from the ice he resonated with.

"People die," Nuhzar said flatly. "Focus on your own situation." Ice bloomed in Nuhzar's hands as he summoned a halberd made of ice, luminous and deadly, glowing silver in the moonlight. "Again, *surrender.*"

Math shifted his footing. Ice had already begun to form beneath his boots.

"What's my incentive to surrender, exactly? Commander Talu's already signed my death warrant."

Nuhzar hesitated. "He did *what*?"

"I may not have killed Captain Qin—and please note that I *didn't*—but I read the letters he carried. One of them ordered my execution—courtesy of Commander Talu."

He could only assume that Talu had sent Math away for it in the interest of not upsetting the Isofal Cenobium members Math had grown up with. Math wasn't sure how many of those people were even still alive . . . but Talu hadn't even told Nuhzar.

"That's . . . He shouldn't have done that."

"Huh. I guess you and I *can* agree on something. I'll have to run an announcement in the paper."

"I am your only chance of surviving. I'm not your enemy."

Math stopped long enough to raise an eyebrow and give the knight an incredulous look. "Try again, Alik. You've been my self-appointed enemy since I was five."

Captain Nuhzar took another step. "What happened at the ambush? You're the only witness."

"You're not just assuming that I'm a Kaliri traitor? Are you feeling well?"

Tri-Mother, he wished he could trust Nuhzar. Unfortunately, it was entirely possible that Nuhzar wasn't accusing him of being a traitor because Nuhzar himself held that role.

Math repositioned himself when his foot began to slide again.

Nuhzar scowled in irritation. "We found black-powder weapons and signs of necromancy. Was it the grim witch?"

"No, we were attacked by the Kaliri. Using grim magic, yes, but it wasn't her. They had orders to kill me, and a description of all the escorting knights, written in Kaliri—on *Isofal paper*."

The man's eyes widened. "Do you still have the letters?"

"Of course I do. And as soon as I get to Bashan, I'll be turning them over directly to the head of the Order." Math scowled. "Maybe the regent, if I can figure out a way to see her."

"If you'd wanted to do that, you've already missed your chance."

Math blinked at Alik once, then glanced back toward the hotel they'd run from. He remembered the woman he'd seen: an Idallik Knight dressed like a noblewoman, with imperial soldiers obeying her every word.

"Gravespit. *That* was Regent Shovan?"

"That was the regent. Just turn yourself in, Kaven. We'll figure this out."

"I'm going to turn myself in—just not to you." Math glanced around, hoping to spot some advantage.

"You don't have a choice," Alik reminded him. "You have nowhere to run. You don't even have a weapon."

"I'll always have my razor wit." Math glanced around, all the while keeping his opponent in his field of vision. There were cranes at the far end of the station, used for loading cargo onto train carriage beds. If he could reach them, he might be able to use the ropes to swing across to Kai's train.

"Damn it, Alik. You may not like me, but you can't really believe I would betray the Order, can you? I'm innocent."

"I believe what I saw," Nuhzar said, taking another step forward. The ice wasn't impeding *his* footing any. "Every person exposed to those spores betrayed us—except you. No, instead, you woke a grim lord so she could destroy our attackers."

"Do I need to explain what 'betray' means to you? Because saving Isofal is the opposite of that." He paused. "You're admitting she saved us? Really, who *are* you?"

"She's still a grim witch who has you under a spell." Alik twirled the halberd in his hand so it trailed ice crystals in the air.

Ah. Technically true. "I don't suppose you'd believe me if I said she doesn't?"

Nuhzar's expression didn't change. "No."

That was the problem, wasn't it? An Idallik Knight lived or died by their convictions, their beliefs.

Math's pulse raced, his arms held out for balance as he tried to keep from slipping on the icy roof. His breath plumed in white puffs in front of him from the sudden drop in temperature. He heard shouting in the distance: more knights, reinforcements on the way.

He would've been tempted to just let himself fall, except that's what Nuhzar wanted, the reason he'd iced over the roof. The moment he fell, Nuhzar would pounce.

The cobblestones below him looked hard. None of the local landscaping was of the soft and welcoming variety. Then a flash of green from a side street caught his eye, so startling that he nearly gave it a disastrous second look.

Huraiik?

No. It couldn't have been.

Nuhzar lunged.

Math dodged, while the halberd scraped past, leaving a trail of ice. "Careful there. You can't interrogate a corpse."

Nuhzar sneered. "True, I'd need Kaiataris, wouldn't I?"

Math backpedaled. "First of all, it's pronounced KAI-et-eris. Second: Did you just try to make a joke?"

The knight attacked again. This time, the blow connected, a stinging strike to Math's legs. He buckled and fell, sliding down the icy rooftop.

Panicked, Math circled the first-circle Land spell, Balance, and rolled back to his feet.

It was only after he'd stood again that Math realized he'd cast it entirely without words or hand gestures. Just will and purpose.

"I'll take that as a no," Math said, mostly because he *knew* Nuhzar hated it when he kept talking during a fight. He used to complain about it after every sparring match.

Math grinned. Knowledge was still power.

Maybe he no longer had the blind faith of the average Idallik Knight, but he knew he didn't need the hand motions, the sacred words, even the time to focus. He *knew* all his limitations were in his mind.

Even if that didn't equal instantly unlocking all the secrets of magic, Kai's advice still burned inside him with a fiery joy.

Math ran, circling spells with every stride. He didn't limit himself to three—an act that should have been impossible if the Order's teachings held true. Magic surged through him in a dizzying, intoxicating rush, sharp as lightning in his veins. He moved faster, his footing sure despite the ice, casting gusts of wind behind him to slow Nuhzar's pursuit.

Also, he set the roof on fire.

Math wasn't exactly proud of that, but there was a water tower nearby, and this close to Bashan, the city was sure to have a competent fire brigade. Besides, it would keep the other knights busy.

Then he saw that he'd misjudged the distance between the edge of the roof and the crane. He'd never make that jump, not even using magic, but if he stopped running—

It didn't matter anyway. The train had pulled too far from the station. He couldn't make the jump.

Someone was shouting. A woman's voice.

He speed-circled a spell to heighten his senses and heard:

"The hole! Jump into the hole!" Kai was screaming from the top of the nearby train, waving her arms wildly.

What hole?

He looked down at the boardwalk below. A rough square was missing from the wooden planks. The interior resembled a pool of water reflecting the stars.

"Jump!" Kai screamed.

Nuhzar was right on his heels, too close.

Math jumped, aiming for that dark square, praying he didn't break his legs when he hit the ground.

But he didn't hit the ground at all: he fell *through* the square.

Down became up, then down again. The world twisted. For one awful second, he was nowhere, then he slammed onto the top of the train. It was more embarrassing than painful. In front of him was the open portal he'd fallen through, partly reflecting the soffit of the train station roof.

Kai hauled him to the side while she used her skirt to smudge part of the chalk square drawn on the roof.

The portal vanished.

The roof returned to being a normal roof again, if a normal roof on a vehicle moving at considerable speed. The wind streaming past made his eyes water.

"Math, what has happened? You look feverish—"

He stared at his shaking hands. His skin felt reddened, as though he'd been in the sun too long. Sparks hovered just beneath his skin, waiting to catch fire. He felt manic, hyper, a clock wound too fast. Something more intense than feverish. Burning up.

"I don't feel great," Math admitted, voice unsteady.

"Drop your spells," Kai ordered. "Now."

He tried.

The world exploded into a thousand points of burning, pure light.

SEEDLING

When Math woke, daylight streamed through a small box window, slanting directly across his face. The world rocked and swayed beneath him—disorienting, until he remembered he was on a train.

It looked like a cargo carriage—boxes, crates, and sacks lined the walls, stacked high and lashed down with thick ropes.

In that context, the window seemed oddly placed—but he was too disoriented to dwell on it. He forced himself to focus.

Strangely, nothing hurt. He glanced down, expecting to find blood and tears in his trousers, but there was no sign of injury at all.

"You're healed," Kai said. Her voice was off, her emotions a tangled mix of concern, anger, and dismay.

"What happened?"

"You nearly died. Because of me."

Math ran a hand through his hair. "Don't be ridiculous. You had nothing to do with Nuhzar—"

"I do not refer to Nuhzar," she murmured. "'Twas not blood loss that so nearly spelled your doom last night. Your injury was not so serious, and yet, you skirted catastrophe by the narrowest of margins."

Math frowned. "What are you talking about?"

"Magic," she said bitterly. "I speak of magic. I told you how power radiates into our world from waxing and waning sources—but our ability to hold and channel that energy is another matter. Gravers like myself draw it slowly, storing it in objects until we've gathered enough to act. It's a method that demands patience, but carries little danger. You, however—"

"Wild magic doesn't work that way?"

"Wild magic does not work that way," she agreed. "Your kind stores power in your own flesh, and you draw on that power all at once." Kai's jaw clenched. She looked away, her body rigid with emotion. "In my arrogance, I thought your order's spellcasting rules were anachronisms. I see now—they are safeguards. Last night, you channeled so much power, so quickly, that you—"

She shuddered. "There are no limits to what you *can* draw. But your body has limits. And you nearly exceeded them."

"It felt like I had a fever," Math murmured.

"Oh, indeed. You might've boiled your own blood. Burst into flame. Transformed into something monstrous."

Math shuddered.

"Do you grasp how close it was? One more spell, and—"

Math raised a hand. "Please. I get it. Just—stop blaming yourself. You didn't know."

The revelation smothered what little excitement he'd felt about casting without limits. Fine. He could go back to doing magic the old way. That was still an option. Probably.

"I *did* know," Kai snapped. "What I failed to do was think. There's a wide gulf between knowing and understanding."

Math gave a faint smile. "Honestly? I feel fine. Like nothing even happened."

"I'm not surprised," she said coolly. "But that's a different concern."

She leaned forward, lifting her hand into the sunlight.

A slender green vine unfurled in her fingers.

Math's stomach dropped. He didn't need to ask where she'd found it. It had come from him. Grown *through* him.

"This is yours," she said softly. Her emotions were a churn of horror, shame, and something very close to hatred.

"When the sun rose, this—and others like it—sprouted from your body and slipped through the gaps in the floorboards, gathering up the sun like any proper plant."

She let out a bitter laugh. "I remember what that knight said—that you'd been exposed to Parnathi spores. I dismissed it."

Then he recognized what he felt through her: the tangled fury of someone betrayed, the quiet shame of being made a fool. The inverted anger of someone appalled at their own gullibility.

Math was furious with himself. He *could* have told her—should have. But hiding his condition had become second nature, so ingrained that the thought of telling Kai hadn't even crossed his mind.

"I didn't breathe in enough spores to matter," he protested.

She slid off the sack in one smooth, dangerous motion. "That's a lie."

Math winced at the rage burning through her. "It's not."

"No?" she snapped. "Then you're deluding yourself. There is *no* safe level of exposure. The spores aren't poison or toxin—they're a connection. A *bond*."

Her voice cracked. She shut her eyes.

The grief bleeding from her was cold and hollow, ice packed around an open wound.

She tried again. "It matters not how little exposure exists, nor if you cure the spores. Once that bond forms, the Queens gain access—and then they change you. Reshape you into something else, which has clearly already begun in your case."

"Then why didn't you—" He stopped short. If she believed he was infected, why hadn't she killed him?

But he already knew. She hadn't because they still didn't know—not with any iron certainty—that his death wouldn't become hers as well.

"No." He pushed himself to his knees, lifting a finger. "This thing with the plants—it started when I was a child. You saw the woods near my house. That isn't the Queens. It doesn't happen all the time. Just when I'm asleep and in danger. Or wounded. Sick." Or had nightmares.

There was a reason he went out into the garden to sleep so often.

He exhaled. "It's gross, sure, and the Order—the Order would jump to all the wrong conclusions if they knew, precisely because it only happens when I'm *not* in control. But the wounds heal. Everything returns to normal. The Queens haven't touched me."

Saying it hurt—maybe because it felt too true. He hated that.

He turned away, hoping to hide the twist of dread in his expression, then remembered: it didn't matter. She could feel every shred of his emotions, anyway.

Damn it, he hadn't betrayed the Order. He hadn't turned on his own people. He was still himself.

He had to be.

"You're a wild mage," she said sharply. "If there's something you can't do—if your power falters—it's not because of law or limitation. Only your body's threshold. Only what your mind believes is possible."

"I *can't* control plants—"

"No—*you believe you can't*. But when you fall unconscious or take ill or are injured, the part of you that knows the truth takes over."

"Damn it, I'm *telling* you—I'm not one of them!" he shouted. "Those things killed my parents! There's no way—"

His voice broke. The words collapsed in his throat, leaving him gasping.

"I don't believe you."

"Then it's a good thing your belief doesn't matter, isn't it?" His voice was raw. "It doesn't change what's true."

"No. No, it never does." She laughed—soft, quiet, and sharp as shattered glass. "Still, a lack of faith for a lack of faith . . . a fair trade, is it not?"

He frowned. "Excuse me?"

She didn't look at him—just stared out the window.

"Did you think I couldn't feel it? The doubt. The constant reminders you give yourself that I'm not to be trusted. That you must never let down your guard with me. Never fully believe me."

The words cut like a razor. Math flinched before he could stop himself. Whatever reply he might've given caught in his throat and stayed there.

She wasn't wrong. That only made it worse.

"Now, at last, we're equals." She said it like a sentence passed down from a judge. "You don't believe I'm not a grim lord. And I don't believe you're not Parnathi. How beautifully balanced."

Math shut his eyes. If he looked at her now, he'd break—shatter into a thousand pieces that could never be healed.

He heard her rise, quiet and deliberate.

"Perhaps I'll see if this grand machine holds other occupants. A change of surroundings might do us both some good."

She walked away without waiting for an answer.

"Thank you for healing me," Math said, more out of a sense of politeness than genuine gratitude—Master Wadera's training, showing itself.

Kai paused at the doorway, turned just enough to look back.

"I didn't."

FIRE

Math sat in silence, more wretched than he'd imagined possible without a wound to show for it. He stared out the window Kai had left open, watching the grasslands roll past in golden waves. His thoughts drifted to the children at Isofal—likely relocated to another cenobium by now. He hated the idea, not because he feared they'd be treated unfairly, but because he knew they wouldn't.

The instructors would put the Isofal novitiates through the same grueling regimen as their own. And when the children faltered—or worse, failed—they wouldn't understand why. Math wouldn't be there to shield them. And the only other person who might have—Master Wadera—was gone.

Just that—the loss of Wadera—was enough to make his chest tighten. But thinking about what would come next made him want to scream. There was nothing he could do. Even if the Idallik Order were willing to listen to a failed novitiate's opinion—and he knew they wouldn't—he was still a fugitive, riding a train in the wrong direction.

And if that wasn't a metaphor for his entire life—helpless, off course, and heading somewhere he didn't choose—he wasn't sure what was.

And then there was Kaiataris. Too late, he'd begun to understand what he meant to her: a lifeline. She'd woken into a world worse than the one she'd left—no longer merely dismissed or doubted, but reviled. A villain. A monster. Something to be destroyed. She had no family. No allies. No one but him.

And now she believed even that had never been true.

Math had no idea how to convince her otherwise. He *did* have this horrible connection. He *could* hear the Queens talk.

Maybe he could have convinced her if she'd seen Huraiik's broken body, but he'd buried the pieces, hadn't he? Like a proper gentleman.

He regretted that now. Bitterly.

As he brooded, Math gradually became aware of the landscape rolling past the window.

Grasslands.

The train had left Cherkiss heading west, but Math had assumed that it would turn south, down the spur that led to Sounalla. That, however, wouldn't have taken them through grasslands.

Only one line did: the southern route—so named not because it ran south, but because it skirted the southern border of the empire. One of the longest rail lines in Rokasmaa, it wound west through Pastan, then into what used to be the Vormadaak Desert—now lush grasslands.

After Pastan, only one stop remained: Ashahr. Miss that, and the next station wouldn't come for over two thousand miles, not until the line reached Okiakosaa on the Bay of Ayya.

If they didn't disembark at Ashahr, Nuhzar wouldn't need magic to track them. Their destination would be obvious.

The only question was whether they'd already passed it.

He had no way to know.

As he absently scratched at his skin, Math realized the problem hadn't gone away. Kai had only removed a single vine. The rest of the growths remained, quietly anchored beneath his skin.

Why would she have done more? To her, they weren't a sickness or a curse. They were proof. Confirmation of what she feared he truly was. Maybe she thought tearing them free would cause lasting harm. She definitely knew it hurt.

Whatever her reasoning, it didn't change the fact: the vines had to go.

He rifled through the carriage, uncovering crates stamped with military seals—supplies bound for the isthmus. One box of swords raised his hopes, only for them to crash when he drew one and found it to be ceremonial: dull-edged, gold-gilt, made for parades or decoration, not for fighting. He found blankets, tents, canteens, leather satchels, and piles of belts and boots—useful, but none of it the kind of help he needed right now.

Math rearranged the crates, carving out a small alcove beneath the open window Kai had made while he slept. He liked to think he was decent at this sort of thing—years of helping novitiates build blanket forts had to count for something. From the outside, it would look like nothing more than a dense stack of freight. Only by climbing the boxes and dropping down would someone discover the space, which was just large enough for two people to lie side by side.

He suspected he was being optimistic. Kai wouldn't want to share close quarters, not after this.

Math told himself that was fine. He'd have more room to sleep.

He lined the alcove with coarse wool blankets, muttering a few quiet spells to anchor them against the crates and block any telltale slivers of light. Then he peeled off the ill-fitting servant's uniform and set to the far more unpleasant task of extracting the vines embedded in his skin. Without his tools, he could only manage a rough job of it, and he had no illusions that he was getting everything. Still, the light from the window helped.

He'd just finished tugging a long, wiry vine free from between his shoulder blades—biting his teeth at the pain—when a quiet, startled gasp broke the silence from above.

He whirled, half-crouched and reaching for a sword he didn't have.

Kai stood above, at the mouth of the alcove, clearing her throat in apology. She tossed down a bundle of clothing and a tightly rolled scroll, her cheeks stained crimson. He could feel her reaction almost as vividly as his own—mortification, yes, but also a deep flush of heat and shame. She kept her eyes pinned to the window, as if the scenery had become suddenly, terribly important.

But she'd been looking before. He could feel that too.

Normally, he might've made a joke—should've, even—to defuse the tension coiling between them. Maybe that was what embarrassed her most: not the sight itself, but the betrayal it implied. She'd decided he was the enemy. Wanting him—*desiring* him—didn't fit that narrative at all.

"How long have you been lurking there?" He yanked the torn remains of his shirt over his lap, a poor substitute for modesty—though truthfully, his smallclothes would've done even less to preserve it.

"Oh. I . . ." Kai waved vaguely at the bundle of clothes, her gaze still fixed anywhere but him. "I found a crate of garments that I thought might suit you. I should have—well—I mean, it would've been courteous to announce myself, but I was . . . distracted." She wrinkled her nose in frustration, an expression that might've been charming under less humiliating circumstances.

"Is that what they called it in your time?" Math asked, doing his best to ignore the warmth still radiating from her side of the bond, like a handprint pressed to skin.

Kai looked away and didn't answer.

Math wasn't a virgin. Hadn't been for years—not with how the Order handled "tension." Commander Talu hadn't been wrong: those encounters were always in the dark, wordless, forgettable, with a mutual decision to pretend they'd never happened. Like most in the Order, Math had kept mostly to his own sex—less risk of complications, fewer chances for whispered scandal, and if two young men stumbled back from the woods flushed and disheveled, everyone accepted "sparring" as a convenient fiction.

It had all been pragmatic and transactional, stripped clean of emotions so they could all pretend it was just another kind of training exercise. Nothing personal. Nothing lasting.

Which meant Math had never been wanted—just convenient. Every partner he'd ever had had been chosen for ease, not longing. He understood sex well enough. But not once had he looked someone in the eye and seen their desire for *him*, specifically.

It should have been intoxicating. Maybe it still was. But the person who'd looked at him like that was also the one who'd just called him a monster. Her anger hadn't vanished—it had simply been overwhelmed by a hotter and more humiliating fire.

None of it made him feel good. Not like this.

He dressed in silence, choosing to ignore the sharp tug of the vines still buried beneath his skin. That pain could wait.

Neither of them spoke as he began to fasten the buttons. The silence was heavy, thick with everything they weren't saying. He nodded toward the roll of paper. "What's that?"

"A map," Kai said tersely. "Something that may improve our situation." She cleared what little space there was and unrolled the scroll—revealing, to Math's surprise, not a regional layout or even a map of Rokasmaa, but a full world map, complete with both continents and the borders of every nation.

"First," Kai said, eyes on the paper, "is this accurate, to your knowledge?"

Math crouched beside her, pretending not to notice how she angled away from him. "Close enough. It'll be less precise outside Rokasmaa, but . . ." He pointed. "There's Cherkiss, where we started. The line heading south goes to Sounalla. We're somewhere along the line west, probably not far from Pastan." He traced the rail to the next city. "If Nuhzar guessed we boarded this train—and we should assume he did—he'll be waiting either there or at Ashahr. Or he'll have warned another cenobium to catch us further down the line."

"Is there a closer cenobium?"

Math grimaced. "Kudawan. Smaller, but still big enough to hold us if we're caught. And Bashan's not going to take us seriously now. Not after I refused to let Nuhzar take me in. Even if we reach them, I don't know how to make them listen."

"Then perhaps we don't go back to Bashan," Kai said, and pointed—not to a city on their map, but to a large country that ran down the center of the other continent to the west. "What if we went here instead?"

Math blinked. "Lomar? *Invade-everyone* Lomar? The only reason we don't hate them more than Kaliri is because we don't share a border. Yet."

Kai's expression didn't waver. "I used to have a mentor named Sanis."

". . . all right," Math said slowly, already suspicious.

"Sanis was short for *Sanistral* Lomar. At that party, I overheard much discussion about King Sanistral of Lomar." She looked at him significantly. "That cannot be a coincidence."

"It may not be, but he's also Sanistral the Twenty-Seventh, and I bet he doesn't have the faintest idea who you are."

"But a descendant of a graven wizard is far more likely to take us seriously than the Idallik Order," she pointed out. "And unless I've missed an announcement, Lomar has yet to issue an order for your execution."

"That you *know of,*" Math muttered. "Lomar's not exactly a bastion of virtue, Kai. Maybe not as bad as Kaliri, but that's not saying much. And it's a sovereign nation—what do you expect? Even if King Sanistral believes you, Rokasmaa's not going to welcome foreign troops crossing its borders just to help with 'a little tree problem.'"

"But if he really is descended from the Sanistral I knew, he may give us access to resources we sorely need." Her exasperation flared, sharp and bright. "It cannot possibly be a worse plan than throwing yourself on the mercy of people who've already decided you deserve to die."

"I already said I wasn't turning you over—"

"I meant *you*, Math."

His mouth closed with a click.

Math didn't trust his voice. He stared at the map without seeing it, his throat tight. He hadn't realized until that moment how deeply he'd assumed she was the one in danger. That he was the shield. The protector. Not the one standing before the edge of a blade himself.

"It doesn't matter," he said at last, though his voice came out rougher than intended. "Lomar is still thousands of miles away. Even if we reached the border, and even if they let us in, there is still no guarantee their king will believe us—let alone offer aid."

Kai's lips curled faintly—not into a smile, but something smug. He felt it just as much as he saw it.

"What?" Math asked warily.

She tapped a spot on the map—an unmarked patch near the empire's center. He squinted. "There's nothing there."

"But there *is* something there," she said. "The absence of a label gives me hope it remains undiscovered—and therefore, usable."

"It's been a thousand years. What could possibly still be—" He cut himself off mid-question as the answer struck him. "An archive. You think there's an *Illuminated archive* still intact?"

She made a moue. "No. A more accurate description would be an undiscovered Illuminated waystation. I told you that my people have nothing like this . . . train . . ." She gestured around them. "But that does not mean we lacked methods of transportation. The world was once bound by a network of waystations, each a magical portal linked to every other. If this station still functions—and if a descendant of Sanis has kept their node intact—then Lomar is not thousands of miles away. It is seconds away."

"That's a lot of ifs, Kai." He folded his arms. "You don't even know if it *still works*."

"I do not," she admitted. "But I know the option is superior to any you have suggested. Or do you plan to knock on the gates of Bashan and hope your execution order has expired?"

Math scowled. He didn't want to admit it, but her "lot of ifs" sounded better than his.

Neither of them said anything for a few minutes. Math glanced back at the map. He was pretty sure that they'd reach the city later that evening. With luck, the darkness would make it easier to flee if it came to that.

He hesitated, then said: "We could split up."

He was unsurprised when Kai gave him a hurt look.

"It's . . . it's logical," he argued. "Alik wanted to arrest me, but weirdly, he also listened to what I had to say. And he didn't just blindly agree with Commander Talu's execution order, either. That was a surprise. I just wish I could be sure he wasn't a Kaliri agent."

"It can be most difficult to prove someone is not a thing."

"Don't I know it."

"Even if he is not, though, I thought you said that man loathes you."

"He loathes grimmocks more," Math said while simultaneously stamping down hard on the tiny little voice inside him that was pointing out that by most of the definitions Nuhzar cared about, Math himself qualified as a grimmock, too. "He might not want to help me, but he won't turn his back on a greater threat just to spite me. Again, that's assuming he's not a foreign agent."

"What of this Commander Talu? How certain are you *he* is not a foreign agent?"

Math blinked. "Talu? Impossible."

She stared at him, unimpressed.

Math exhaled. "Okay, fine, not impossible. Just . . ." Math scoffed. "He's the cenobium commander, Kai. If he was a Kaliri agent, why didn't he throw open the gates of the fortress to them years ago? And why jeopardize his position and the secret of those weapons the Kaliri have developed just to kill *me*?"

She didn't reply for nearly a minute, lost in thought. Finally, though, she said: "I do not know, but just because I cannot imagine a motivation does not mean it cannot exist. Of all the people you have described, he is the one whose behavior seems most inexplicable."

Math made a face. "Except it's not. He found out the same thing you did, Kai." He gestured to himself. "The thing with the plants. And because there were members of the knights who fell prey to those spores, it would've been easy to assume I was one of them. Not really me at all anymore, but something that just looked like me. Much as I may not like it, I can't blame him for jumping to the conclusion I couldn't be trusted."

"'Couldn't be trusted' dwells a long way down the road from 'should be executed.'" She raised a hand to forestall his rebuttal. "I understand your point and I shall keep myself from leaping to judgments," Kai said, "but I ask that you do so as well."

"I've known him all my life, Kai. He's been like a father to me."

Her eyes took on a sharp, flinty look, even as he felt her conviction. "Let us hope that means he cannot also be a villain."

SINKING

At Ashahr, they hit an unforeseen snag.

Kai had carefully rebuilt the train carriage, restoring the wooden walls to their original windowless condition. They'd prepared themselves, dressing in stolen military uniforms and availing themselves of stolen rations. If one or both of them decided to get off at Ashahr, they'd pass themselves off as soldiers, just as Math had at Sounalla.

There was just one problem: the train didn't stop.

With no window, Math only realized something was wrong when the rhythm of the wheels shifted—twice—without the train slowing. By the time he found a knothole in the planks, Ashahr was already behind them.

"This significantly simplifies matters," Kaiataris stated crisply.

Math glared at her. He felt the faintest pulse of satisfaction beneath her calm—a dry, bitter spike that wasn't his. It made his own frustration flare hotter than it should have.

"We also needed the train to stop if we were going to investigate your waystation, you know."

"Were we going to do that?" She raised an eyebrow. "I rather thought you were determined to go running back to your order."

Her tone was sharp, but the burn of resentment came through the bond like a slap. Not just irritation—betrayal. Oh yes. She was still angry.

Then again, so was he.

"It's not just about me, Kai," he snapped. "And despite what you think, I'm not trying to abandon you. There's a dozen kids back in Isofal that I will probably never see again if the Order thinks I'm some foreign agent, and running off to the one nation that Rokasmaa considers an even bigger threat than the Kaliri isn't exactly going to convince them otherwise!"

She stilled. Before she spoke, he felt the change: the heat in her presence dulled, gave way to something cooler—uncertainty, maybe. Regret. It slid into his chest like cold water.

"I . . . I did not realize you were their caretaker."

"Technically, Master Wadera was their guardian. Unfortunately, he's also the one who got his head smashed in when you were woken." He waved a hand. "I worry about them, okay? Everyone knows the misfits are sent to Isofal, except now that it's been torn open, they'll be sent somewhere I can't protect them."

"Are there any more like you?"

Math's eyes narrowed. A flicker of tension spiked from her, like a breath held too long.

"Would you like to clarify that?"

"Are there any more children who might be specifically targeted by the Parnathi?" She raised her chin, and to his surprise, her concern felt genuine and raw-edged. "People with an unusual connection to plants."

"No. I don't know." He swallowed down his distaste at the unspoken foundation of that question—that the Parnathi were absolutely targeting him. That even if he wasn't *one of them*, they wanted him to be. "I'm Wood resonant. So are a lot of people, but I've never heard of anyone else with my . . . plant issues."

Mostly because anyone who couldn't control their powers in a similar way would be classified as a grimmock and "removed."

"That is good." She crossed her arms and looked away. Her feelings were a tumult—guilt, worry, something sharp and self-directed. "We will likely have to jump from the train when the time comes, but I can create a pair of charms to protect us. They will only last a few seconds, but I suspect that is all we'll need."

He didn't answer. The anger had drained from her—but now there was discomfort threading between them, an echo of shame that wasn't his and too strong to ignore.

"Math."

He exhaled and nodded. "Yes, of course. I trust your skills. You do that, and I'll—" He pointed a thumb at his back. "I'll see about getting rid of these plants."

He both felt and saw her surprise.

"Should they not heal of their own accord?"

"I can't say. I've never had the stomach to find out what happens if I leave them alone to keep growing."

She swallowed, tried not to look as sickened as he knew she felt. He could feel it clawing at the edges of her composure like nausea.

"Ah."

"Exactly."

Kai cleared her throat and, apparently deciding there was nothing else she could say that wouldn't be exceedingly awkward, changed the subject.

"How long do you think it will take to cross the continent? Our 'stop' should be somewhere in the middle, as close as possible to the volcano." She amended, "It was called Mount Dabaluin in my time. It may be called something else, and perhaps others have grown since, but . . ."

"Mount Topalawon," Math said. "It still exists."

"Brilliant. Then that shall be our target." Her manner turned more guarded, more uncomfortable. Her emotions dimmed—sheathed, like a knife returned to its scabbard. She eyed him up and down, then looked away.

"I shall leave you to your privacy."

"Kai."

She turned back. "Yes?"

"If you come across any more food—" He gestured to the small amount she'd found. He was fine going without food for a few days; the plants made sure of it. He didn't think Kai could say the same.

Her smile turned to genuine amusement. He felt it, light and fleeting.

"Not all the cargo on this train is of the inanimate variety. There are soldiers in the second carriage, horses in the third, and thus the provender for both in the fourth. I believe I should be able to find us something."

"Be careful."

Kai's eyes met his. The bond hummed, quiet and even. No anger or shame, but a thread of wary understanding, drawn taut between them.

Slowly, she nodded.

She left him alone to pull his weeds in private.

The next two days were uncomfortable in the extreme. Not physically; Kai's opinion on the ease of gathering food proved true, and they'd made a little nest for themselves in their crate fort.

No, the discomfort was entirely emotional, as both Math and Kai tried to navigate their feelings, and worse, did so in the company of someone who felt every swirl of passion, fear, or anxiety as though it were their own.

On the morning of the third day, they readied themselves for their leap from the train.

Except here, they ran into a different problem.

The train stopped. It didn't do so in the traditional way, with a squeal of metal on metal as the brakes slowed the vehicle over a long period.

Rather, when the train stopped, it did so suddenly, and all at once.

Math found himself flung violently forward toward the front of the train, smashing face-first into the wall of wooden boxes. Something hit him from behind. Something hard—probably the crate-turned-stepstool they hadn't secured. It didn't matter though: even the secured crates slammed against each other, against him, the fastenings twisting and snapping. His ears rang, his vision swam in spots. The light spell he'd been using to illuminate their tiny refuge winked out the moment he smashed into the wall.

He couldn't see anything, and was terrified to realize that he didn't know if it was because of an injury or because he was buried under too much wreckage. He only knew it was dark, and nothing was moving now.

"What . . . what happened?" he gasped, although he couldn't hear himself. He tried to conjure a light, but his hands shook too much.

He heard the sound of wreckage being moved. Light dazzled his eyes, blinding in a different way. Something tugged at his sleeve. He shook it off, but it returned a moment later. Confused, disoriented, he swung his fist and was rewarded with the feel of an impact on flesh and a flash of pain that cut through the general panic he was feeling, he realized now, from multiple sources.

"Stop that!" Kai screamed above the roaring in his ears. Only, if the roaring was in his ears, how could she talk louder than it?

The sound, he realized, was only partly in his head. The rest was coming from outside.

He took a deep breath, almost vomited. He held the breath for a moment, trying to force his hands to stop shaking. Eventually, he circled a weak light.

Kai gasped. The little nest was devastated; crates had fallen, torn free of their moorings. Some had emptied, some simply shattered. Broken wood, twisted nails, the contents of several boxes formerly filled with small metal folding mess kits. The ground was inches deep in what he could only refer to as "stuff," too chaotic for identification.

He turned to Kai when he felt her shock and horror.

She was looking at him. Specifically, at his face.

He touched a hand to himself, felt something wet. As he pulled his hand back to look at it, he found himself suddenly terrified that the blood wouldn't be red. That it would be black, or more specifically, a dark, forest green.

It was red.

"Thank the Tri-Mother," he whispered, and then swayed. Sitting seemed like a fine idea, only to be outdone by lying down. Lying down was a stroke of genius.

Kaiataris slapped him, hard, across his untorn cheek. "No! You must not fall asleep. Do you not hear the noises outside? Something is happening, and we cannot stay."

"Right," he agreed numbly. Math desperately wanted to sit down and close his eyes, but she was right.

"Come, then." She grabbed his arm and pulled him after her.

Leaving their crate fort wasn't difficult, since it no longer existed. It was more a matter of shoving boxes across the angled floor—the *sharply* angled floor, which meant the carriage must have derailed.

Sadly, he suspected his vertigo was less to do with the angle of the floor than his concussion.

A sliding door on the side of the carriage had been ripped open, jagged metal twisted and sharp from where the slide on the ground had torn it asunder. They crawled through the gap and slithered through the dry dirt and gravel until they could stand again.

Outside, it was daylight, for which Math was partly grateful, but mostly resented. Grateful because he always liked sunlight, but resentful because of both the stabbing pain in his head and what the sunlight allowed him to clearly see.

Death, first of all.

Neither people nor animals had done well in the crash. Math suspected he could count himself as one of the lucky ones, since he could walk and see and breathe. From the smell, the faint moans, the bloody evidence spread out in random abandon, that wasn't true for many others.

He stared in blank, numb horror as a crying soldier staggered over to a shuddering, mortally injured horse and cut its throat. The man immediately collapsed, after, his head in his hands.

Then Math heard roaring, shouts, and a familiar voice.

"Math, we must fly." Kaiataris pulled on his sleeve. He saw she carried something in her other hand: it was one of the dress swords he'd found days earlier. He had no idea where she'd been hiding it.

"That's Huraiik," Math explained. He turned back to her, although he wasn't sure exactly what he would have said, what he needed her to understand. How could that possibly be Huraiik? Then he stopped.

Looming behind Kaiataris was a . . .

Plant. Creature. Thing.

It looked for all the world like a topiary lion come to life, a topiary lion made of a thornbush. It saw them, and lifted a paw. The foreleg elongated as the vines lashed out. Thorns raked the arm he hastily threw up to defend himself, and Math cried out.

"Catch!" Kai yelled.

He didn't. The sword struck his shoulder and bounced away—mercifully still sheathed. He scooped it up, barely registering its garish hilt before he yanked it free and swung the wide, curved blade at the lion.

He sheared through several vines—not because the sword had edge or weight, but because his momentum did. Like snapping a dry root with a boot heel. The lion closed the distance, lashing again. This time, when Math struck, vines coiled around the blade and pulled. The weapon fought him briefly, then slipped free from his hands and vanished into the creature's body, swallowed whole.

"Gravespit!" It hadn't been a good sword. He'd held it for less than two seconds, and already he missed it with an absurd and wholehearted passion.

"Catch!" Kai yelled again.

This time, he caught it. Another costume blade, of course. He had just enough time to glance over and see that she was standing beside an entire opened crate of the damned things.

Blood from his scalp wound kept trickling toward his eye. He wiped at it with his left hand, but that one was already slick with blood from the claw wound down his arm. His vision remained speckled with bright spots. The dizziness had not relented, even though the ground beneath him was now perfectly flat.

He felt rather than saw the next attack: a full pounce, launched from ten feet away. Math let the vertigo take him. He dropped and rolled, the impact of his shoulder against the ground knocking loose another breath. It probably saved his life. It did nothing for the ache in his skull.

He pushed upward. Tried to rise. His knees obeyed; his balance did not. He stayed crouched, sword tip braced against the dirt.

The lion turned, coiling for another strike—but the blow never came.

A wave of heat surged past his left side, close enough to lift the edge of his collar. The grimmock ignited all at once, fire threading through its body in lines like glowing veins. The vines blackened and cracked as flame consumed them.

It didn't scream. Or perhaps it did, and he simply couldn't hear it.

Huraiik had said plants were chatty.

"Thanks," Math croaked, voice rasping.

Kai's hand was still raised. Her arm trembled slightly, whether from effort or shock, he couldn't tell. "You are most welcome," she said. "But I fear I have little more magic to offer. This was all I could restore during our time on the train . . ."

A second passed with nothing trying to murder him and Math decided he was done reacting.

He stood. Or tried to. He swayed, stumbled, and fell back to his knees.

"Gravespit," he muttered. "Hang on. I just need . . . I just need a minute."

"You mustn't fall asleep!" Her voice cracked. Her fear surged through the bond, sharp and cold and insistent.

He needed to heal. Properly. But he didn't know how, and she didn't have enough power. The irony stung: if he did the very thing she feared—if he gave in and let sleep take him—his plants would come.

Whether they'd come quickly enough to save his life was a different matter.

He remembered what she'd said. That he could control them. That he always could. He knew that was true, didn't he? He'd done it before—at the lumber camp, drugged and barely conscious.

It was a beautiful day. A sky of cloudless blue. A sun that soaked the skin with golden warmth. And the only thing keeping him from healing was his own logical mind.

If he couldn't cross that threshold—if he faltered now—he would die. Or worse.

And if he became what Huraiik had become, then his first act would be to kill Kaiataris.

SPEAR

Math pushed himself to hands and knees and tried to concentrate—tried to shut out the crash sites, the dying men and animals, the groan of roots shifting, trees snapping in slow collapse. He reached inward, toward that buried core that had always thrummed with a deeper resonance to plants than most Idallik Knights could fathom.

His skin prickled. He didn't need to look to know: small green shoots were already creeping from his sleeves, climbing toward his collar. The sunlight, which had felt warm before, now seemed charged—sparkling, extraordinary, alive with potential.

The dizziness ebbed. The spots cleared. The bleeding slowed, then stopped.

But he didn't have time to finish.

A man's voice—one of the soldiers—called out, "Hey! Are you all right? You there, on the ground!"

Damn. He'd really hoped to do this without anyone noticing.

If that soldier came any closer and realized what was happening . . .

All the energy he'd been pouring into healing rerouted at once, became the delicate work of pulling away—of trying to disconnect himself.

"Please, if I might implore you to—"

Math nearly shouted at Kai to shut up. Just shut up. Nobody spoke like her anymore. Certainly no *soldier* spoke like her anymore. And if that soldier came closer, his questions would turn to realizations, and that would turn swiftly to violence.

Even as Math lifted his head, even as Kai kept talking, the soldier's expression changed. His mouth opened, eyes gone wide with something worse than surprise.

"Look out!" the soldier yelled.

Math rolled sideways, biting back on a scream as he surged forward into a crouched rise. He more felt than heard the popping sound of vines ripping from his flesh, painful and bloody. His gaze flicked to the gaudy show sword still lying where he'd dropped it. Before he could move to reclaim it, a vine whip lashed from the tree line and snapped the blade in half.

Huraiik stepped into view like an actor stepping from behind a curtain.

He looked unchanged from the last time Math had seen him—except that all signs of injury were gone. He seemed even less human now, if such a thing were possible. His movements were too fluid, each limb swinging with whip-like grace, twisting and bending in ways no skeleton could permit. Vines rustled with each step, dragging behind him like something forgotten.

"Nice day, isn't it?" Huraiik said cheerfully. His voice hadn't changed: wry, half-bored, as if this were still a sparring match in the training yard, and he was simply showing off.

"I saw you die. Twice."

"People say that to me a lot. You're not special, Math." He tilted his head. "Though I will admit, I missed your charming scowl."

The bond jolted—sharp and cold, panic slicing through his ribs like a sliver of ice. Kai. He moved before he thought, stepping between Kai and Huraiik like a shield.

"You don't seem surprised to see me."

"Should I be? Did you think we derailed the train for sport?" Huraiik's grin was maddening. "Come now, Math. You're smarter than that." He winked. "So—are you ready to talk to the Queens? Come with us. No one else has to die."

"You know," Math said, "I might've considered it—if I thought your definition of 'death' matched mine."

"Ah well." Huraiik shrugged. "It was worth a shot."

Then he lunged.

Math dodged backward, unarmed and rapidly running out of options.

Kai no longer stood beside the crate of swords. He couldn't blame her—she knew Huraiik would try to kill her if he could—but her absence meant he was well and truly alone. No more replacement swords. No backup.

"Hey!" a voice called. The soldier from earlier. "Catch!"

Something heavy spun through the air toward Math.

Math caught the weapon by the haft on reflex. A battle-axe. Not a toy weapon for show, this time.

As Math caught the weapon, an arrow lanced from the tree line and slammed the soldier so hard it sent him hurtling backward and stapled him to a nearby tree. The man was dead before he had a chance to scream.

Math knew exactly one person who could shoot a bow like that.

That thought flickered through the chaos like a spark in dry tinder—bright, unwelcome, and best buried quickly. He had to focus on Huraiik, or it wouldn't matter if Captain Yihura was lurking nearby.

Math let the momentum of catching the axe swing him around. The axe edge sank into Huraiik's shoulder, biting deep into the layered stalks that passed for muscle.

"Ow," Huraiik remarked, tone flat, gaze drifting to the embedded axe. "Jerk."

Movement ghosted into Math's peripheral—a flicker of fabric, a presence realigned in the bond. Kai had circled around behind him. He hadn't seen her approach, but he felt her now, solid and sharp at his back.

Her arm rose and one of her rings flared with the misty white color of her magic. Then Kai's eyes widened and she dove to the side, the glow of her ring guttering and dying as she abandoned the spell.

A second arrow tore past her, slicing the air close enough to flutter her hair. She jerked aside, again not having enough time to launch her own counter.

She evaded—barely—and the bond ignited with her panic. Fear, sharp-edged and focused, pressed against him like a second heartbeat.

"I can't keep this up," Kai gasped. "She's too fast."

Math didn't have the time or breath to respond. He tore the axe free just in time to block the next strike—but his footing was wrong, thrown off by the sudden spike of Kai's fear in his head. The impact jolted up through the blade, rattling his arms and shoulders. He stumbled, barely keeping his balance.

Another vine lash followed. Huraiik's other arm snapped around, the whip catching him across the side. Cloth and skin tore. Blood welled instantly, hot and fast.

"You're bleeding," Huraiik observed, head tilted.

"I was bleeding when you got here," Math growled, pivoting to keep the axe between them. "You're not special."

Another vine came for his face. He ducked—late this time. The edge of it grazed him, just shy of slicing his cheek open again.

The bond flared. Not just fear now—Kai's fear braided with determination, hard-edged and fierce. It coursed through him with a force that wasn't his, threading through his bones like a second pulse.

It wasn't the panic that unsteadied him. It was how he couldn't stop himself from responding.

"She's making you sloppy," Huraiik said. "You'd be better off without her."

Math swept the axe toward Huraiik's knees. The strike missed, but forced the creature to shift its stance. Bark strained audibly. A fine fracture opened near the ankle, sap beading along it—thick and green, with a sheen like oil gone bad.

"Not going down as easy as last time, am I?" Math said, breath short and rough.

"Easy?" Huraiik caught the axe's edge with a looping vine. His voice was calm, but his eyes had narrowed. "You're still predictable."

Math wrenched the weapon free and spun low. This time, the blade struck true. It sank deep into Huraiik's flank, carving through bark with a sound like aged wood cracking in frost. Slivers scattered. Sap bled slow and heavy, darkening as it flowed. The smell hit next—compost and alkali, sharp enough to curl his stomach.

"Still going for the legs," Huraiik mused. "I think I remember that."

Math froze for half a breath. Not at the words, but at the way Huraiik said them—like someone reciting historical events from one of the libraries' books who wasn't sure they were remembering the right dates. I *think* I remember that.

There wasn't time to dwell on it. The fight hadn't paused just because Huraiik was starting to slip.

Math turned just in time to block another downward strike. The force rattled down his spine. Another vine followed, low and sharp, raking across his thigh. He stumbled, teeth gritted, but didn't fall.

He sucked in a breath. Centered himself. Then he pivoted—not toward Huraiik, but toward the tree line. Math reached out toward one of the trees with all his will and gave it a new target.

Yihura.

It wasn't much more than a distraction—these weren't anywhere near the same caliber of tree as the ones back in Sounalla—but the moving branches cut through her sight line. Yihura flinched. The bow dipped for half a heartbeat.

"Kai—now!"

"I see her," Kai said, voice tight.

The next arrow came without warning. Kai raised her hand. The gold ring ignited, bright and sudden.

The arrow froze mid-flight. It hovered for an impossible moment—then twisted and reversed, a flash of motion in the wrong direction.

It struck Yihura in the ribs and knocked her into the underbrush. The violet shimmer surrounding her cracked and failed.

But in focusing on Yihura, Math had left himself vulnerable.

Huraiik pressed his assault, advancing with fluid violence, limbs twisting into unnatural arcs, thorny ropes cutting the air. One of those vines wrapped around the shaft of the battle-axe and yanked.

Huraiik tossed the axe aside, where it buried itself deep in the trunk of a tree. Ten paces away. A lifetime at this range.

Math found himself without a weapon.

Then pale, ghostly fingers of white flame wrapped around the haft of the weapon. The axe shivered. Kai gestured with the same hand she'd used to send Captain Yihura's arrow screaming back to its source to send the axe back as well.

Math's eyes widened as he ducked out of the way of the flying axe, grabbed the haft as it passed, and let momentum swing the weapon into Huraiik's path in a brutal arc.

The blade sheared cleanly through Huraiik's outstretched vine-limb, severing it at the elbow. Pale sap spattered across the stones, viscous and slow.

Yihura rose again.

Her body moved without intent. Her limbs jerked through patterns of remembered violence. Her bow hung slack in one hand—until her fingers flexed, found the string, and began to draw. She wasn't aiming at Math.

"Kai!" Math screamed.

A cloud of shimmering purple spores pulsed around Yihura, thick and luminous, and then drifted forward—not dispersed, but moving with purpose. They curled toward Kai like smoke caught in a draft.

She froze—only for a breath.

The bond twisted, a thread drawn taut with revulsion. Math felt the disgust radiate from her, just as panic must have flowed through him. He remembered Abhigan, Rabu, Yihura herself—all Kai needed to do was inhale so much as a single spore and the Queens would have her.

Kai stepped back, her breath catching. Then her hand rose. White fire surged across her skin. The magic wasn't gentle this time. It burst outward in a sharp, controlled arc, slicing through the advancing cloud.

Wherever it passed, the spores unraveled. Filaments of violet light twisted, frayed, and vanished. The pull toward her snapped like a severed cord.

Yihura staggered. Her mouth opened, soundless. Her bow slipped from her fingers. Then her legs folded beneath her, and she collapsed beside it.

This time, she didn't rise.

Math nearly dropped his guard. The flare of Kai's fear had been sudden, seizing; the echo of it still clung to his ribs. For a heartbeat, his vision tunneled—not from blood loss, but from the sick, shivering awareness of how close he'd come to losing her.

Huraiik didn't wait. He lunged at Math.

Math dodged out of the way, taking advantage of the opportunity to land a second strike. Math cut him with a vicious swing to the head that sliced almost all the way through from left temple to right cheek. While he had no illusions that such an injury would kill Huraiik, at least the fact that his jaw was half-severed kept him from talking.

The sound that followed was not pain. It was fury, a roar torn from something that had forgotten how to be human.

The shout faded—but the noise did not.

New cries broke through the haze, high-pitched and panicked—human. Yelling echoed through the wreckage, distant but rising fast. Then came the thunder of hooves, not behind them on the shattered tracks, but ahead, pounding from the tree line. A new force was entering the battle, mounted on horseback and riding fast.

"Math!" Kai shouted. "Arrows!"

Those arrows were already cutting the air above the carriages, hissing down into the wreckage. It was impossible to tell if those arrows were meant to kill the train wreck survivors or the Parnathi tree people attacking them.

Possibly, it was both.

Math reached instinctively for a Sky spell, moving to shape it into a shield against the volley.

That was a mistake.

Huraiik sensed the hesitation. One vine whip feinted high, drawing Math's focus—while another curled low, fast and unseen, wrapping around his leg and yanking.

His foot caught on the shattered debris. Gravel slid. He dropped hard to one knee, ribs jarred from the landing.

Huraiik loomed above him, one arm raised high, bark limbs twisting together into a crude weapon. The blow would split his skull.

Math didn't wait.

He circled Sea—not to draw water from the air, but from Huraiik himself. From the sap, from the wounds, from the deep fibrous threads already frayed by the axe. Then, fast as thought, he layered Storm over it, unraveling the inner structure.

Moisture fled the monster's body in sudden force, siphoned through cracks like breath through reeds.

"Wad?" Huraiik slurred. His limbs seized—not with surprise, but rigidity. Old vines, dry and brittle, could not bend. "Dad wond zhdab me," he rasped.

"I know," Math said. He circled Sun.

Fire bloomed in the hollow center of what had once been Huraiik.

This time, the scream came.

It tore through the wreckage—loud, raw, unmistakably human. Flame surged higher, consuming bark and root, igniting the last veins of sap. Huraiik writhed as the vines that made up his body curled inward, twisting against the fire hollowing him from within.

Math dropped to his knees. He'd won. Huraiik was gone. If they could survive the Souna riders attacking them, they might even escape this.

Kai screamed.

Pain lanced through Math's center, sharp and seizing. For a moment, he was sure one of the plant monsters had reached her. The spike of fear, the jolt of alarm—it had to be hers. Then he understood: it wasn't her pain.

It was his.

A burning vine whip connected him to the center of Huraiik's pyre. With his last act, Huraiik had echoed his previous attack on Kaiataris, this time driving a vine straight through Math's body.

Math looked down. The shaft was still smoking, embedded deep in his abdomen. He coughed in surprise as blood flooded into his mouth.

"But—" he tried.

Darkness claimed him before he could finish protesting that this wasn't how it was supposed to happen.

He'd already won.

DEALS

He smelled the smoke first—a strange, almost pleasant tang of overheated iron and burning wood, layered over the stink of roasting meat and spilled offal. He opened his eyes to what should have been blue sky. Instead, the firmament churned with greasy clouds—billowing gray and black smoke from the burning train and, somewhere nearby, an enormous bonfire.

He watched the scene unfold, feeling hollow. Their rescuers—if they could be called that—weren't Avansi. They wore bright, embossed leathers, and their small, powerful horses bore even more colorful saddles, glittering with tiny mirrors and crystal. Most carried wickedly curved bows.

The Souna, his brain finally supplied. They'd been taken by the Souna, who famously hated their Avansi conquerors—and were just as famous for not taking prisoners.

The Souna were burning the bodies from the train.

He hurt. Tri-Mother help him, he hurt. The ache had grown so deep it blurred into numbness, as though his body had given up trying to warn him. Either he'd gotten the message, or he never would.

He heard a faint, pained sound nearby. Kai stood close, one hand pressed to her stomach, her expression strained. She was speaking to one of the Souna—a woman.

"Did I not tell you they would live?" Kai said.

"Pity. I was hoping to make a necklace from their teeth."

Math's eyes widened. He tried to sit—only to abandon the effort as dizzying pain swept over him. He bit back a sob, echoed a moment later by Kai.

"Please stop moving." Kai's voice was weak and thready.

Math obeyed.

She turned back to the woman. "Math is not one of them."

"We remember the stories of the tree people. We saw the plants. They're cursed."

"If that were true, would they have fought? The tree people stabbed them. They are not the tree people's ally."

"They're Avansi," the woman said, though without conviction.

"But not soldiers. We stole the uniforms." Kai's voice had slipped into pleading.

He shouldn't be able to understand them. He didn't speak whatever language the Souna used, and he doubted they would bother ever learning Ginren or Irrahan.

"That is also a pity," the woman said. "If they were a soldier and lived, we could ransom them. But you say they aren't. And I say they'll not live—not with an injury like that."

"We just have to wait," Kai insisted. "When the smoke clears, when the sun returns, they will heal. I know they can. They healed me once, from a wound just like this. They will live."

"They'd better," the woman growled, "or Souna or not, I'll leave you burning on their pyre."

She turned and stalked away, heading back toward the cluster of horses.

"She seems nice," Math whispered. "It's good that you are making friends."

Kai rushed over, kneeled on the gravel beside him. She was very pale, a little gray, and sweat beaded on her brow. Tear tracks had cleared two paler lines down her face. She was in a great deal of pain—all of it his.

Kaiataris gave the smoke-filled sky a sullen, resentful glare, then picked up his hand and held it in both of hers. "I need you to hold on."

He almost asked if she still thought he was one of the enemy, but thought better of it. She had come to a better decision about him at some point that morning, probably after the crash and during the fight. He would rather she not have any reason to second-guess that choice.

"I am not going anywhere." For many reasons, not least of which being he doubted he could walk. Not just due to his injuries, but because he suspected his plants had rooted themselves, drawing energy from the ground instead of the sun. He could think of no other reason he was awake at all.

"Can you heal yourself?"

Such a good question.

Math felt unreal and disconnected, simultaneously aware of all the tiny aches and pains of his body and yet numb to all of them. Time stretched out, soft and slack as pulled dough, each moment an excruciating draw of air through searing lungs. It hurt to breathe; he wondered if Huraiik had nicked a lung, then remembered the ash and smoke in the air.

He had healed himself just earlier that day. He knew he could do it. Of course, that had been when the sun was full and bright, with sunlight pouring down . . .

Except why did he even need sunlight?

He wasn't a plant. He wasn't a tree. He didn't need light to survive. The blood spilled down his chest—now a sticky, awful mess along his back and legs—had started out as red as any other man's.

The plants were symbols, the same way ice was a symbol for Nuhzar. A way to wrap his mind around the power at his command. Wild magic might be limitless, but the human mind was not. Chaos could not be embraced without structure.

The paradox of chaos was that it needed rules, just as the paradox of order was that using it to enact change was, by definition, an act of chaos.

So be it. He was lying on the ground, surrounded by wildness, with nothing but plants growing nearby for hundreds of miles.

He could do this.

Sometime later, Math opened his eyes, which he had not realized he'd closed. Time had passed—how much, he could not say. All he knew was that he saw nothing but leaves and flowers overhead, blocking out the sky. The plants had surrounded him like a cocoon. A womb.

He pulled air into his lungs.

It didn't hurt.

"All right," the woman said from somewhere beyond the plants. "You might be onto something. Let's get your friend out of this mess—then we'll talk about what comes next."

CAMP

What came next was being taken prisoner.

He wouldn't claim to be an expert, but it was easily the nicest experience he'd had being taken prisoner.

The Souna gave him enough time to extract himself from the tangle of plants—though, embarrassingly, the plants detached themselves the moment Math commanded it, as if they'd been waiting patiently for him to just ask.

No one accused him of being a traitor. The Souna even gave him a new coat—a Rokasmaa soldier's, of course—and a waterskin.

Still, the plains riders also made it very clear that if he tried to ride off, they'd shoot him so full of arrows they wouldn't need extra wood for his pyre.

Kai's connection to these people was even more obvious now that Math had a whole troupe for comparison. She was a more petite version, but the resemblance was undeniable.

Their leader was a grim-faced woman named Oltaxath, who clearly would've preferred they'd left the crash site hours ago.

"What did you promise her?" Math asked quietly.

"Them," Kai corrected.

"What?"

"Their language doesn't use gendered pronouns." She rubbed her arms through the wool sleeves of her coat.

"Fine. Them. You're changing the subject," Math said. "What did you promise *them*?"

"One of Oltaxath's parents is ill. They promised to protect us—and even escort us to our destination—if we can heal them."

"I can't promise I can do that." Math wasn't a fool—he kept his voice to a whisper.

Kai seemed genuinely surprised for a moment, then shook her head. "It matters not. These are not . . ." She paused, scanning the crowd. Most were on horseback; the rest were looting the parts of the train not yet on fire.

Math wondered how many aboard the train had survived. It was entirely possible those not killed by the Parnathi had been finished off by the Souna—a bitter kind of joke.

"These are not my people," Kai said at last. "They might resemble them, but too much time has passed for that to be true. I speak the language—though apparently with a terrible accent—but I do not understand their ways. They are a hard people, used to violence. If we are to get out of this, we must make ourselves too valuable to kill."

"Is our bond the reason I can understand them?"

"Yes." Her lips quirked. "Did you think I speak *your* language?"

A Souna rode over, leading two horses—one black, one dun—both already saddled. "For you to ride," the man explained.

No one asked Math if he was okay with the bargain. He wanted to protest, but there were at least forty people in this band, all of them armed—mostly with halberds and spears, though some carried the wicked-looking bows they had used to such deadly effect earlier. None of them looked like they would take kindly to being told "no."

The leader rode back to them. "You can ride, can't you?" The question was for Math; Kai's skills were assumed.

"I can," Math said. He almost pointed out that he was an Idallik—of course he could ride—but he was not sure how the Souna leader would react. Kai hadn't mentioned his affiliation when describing their abilities.

The horse sniffed at Math as he approached, decided he had no treats for her, and lost interest. She was calm and made no trouble when he climbed up.

Nothing about the horse kit was strange, except for the saddle, which had a much higher pommel and cantle than he was used to. Kai examined her horse with a pensive, resigned expression before pulling herself into the saddle as well. Apparently, the assumption about her riding skills had not been entirely wrong—though she didn't seem as confident as usual.

"When was the last time you rode a horse?" he asked.

She tossed him a tight smile. "I am told it has been at least fourteen hundred years. Shall we ride?"

They headed south and west, toward Mount Topalawon, near the Jokokala border.

It was exactly where Kaiataris had wanted to go. From the occasional flashes of smug amusement he felt from her, she had figured that out as well.

The camp was a hectic, chaotic place, with people preparing food, mending clothing, sharpening weapons, and practicing fighting. Children laughed and played. Dogs trailed their owners, often butting heads—sometimes playfully, sometimes not—with the large hunting cats that lounged throughout the camp. Some of the Souna even kept hunting eagles.

All eyes were on him as their party entered the camp. They might have stared at Kai as well, but if they did, it was with far less hostility than the glares reserved for him.

They'd hardly walked twenty feet when Oltaxath grabbed a woman's arm, whispered something, and pointed at Kai. The woman's eyes widened, and she rushed off.

In the meantime, they were taken to a small, single-room dwelling—a cross between a tent and a hut—constructed by stretching leather over a wooden frame. It stood apart from the other dwellings, far enough to make the isolation unmistakable.

They were very sick, Oltaxath had said.

As Math dismounted, he hoped he hadn't just volunteered to expose himself to something deadly. He'd never tested his self-healing against an infectious disease.

Inside the hut, it was too dark to see. Math spelled up a light, though it was little brighter than a candle.

A pile of stuffed fur pillows rested on a thickly woven rug in the center of the room. A man lay there, barely aware of his surroundings. His hair was white, his complexion pale with illness. He was far too thin—except for his grotesquely distended stomach.

The odor was unbearable—a mix of bodily waste that suggested the hut had not been cleaned in a long time, and even then, poorly.

Math immediately turned on Oltaxath. "Haven't you been feeding them?"

Oltaxath bared her teeth. "They're my parent, Dulbach," she spat. "Anything they eat comes back up. They can only stomach gentle broths. So yes, I'm feeding them. And yes, they're still starving to death."

Kai kneeled beside the dying man. "How long have they been like this?"

"Not long." Oltaxath stared anywhere but at her father. "They were fine a month ago. It happened fast."

"And they didn't eat anything poisonous? Didn't encounter anyone else who was sick first?" Math asked.

"No! Nothing like that."

"Then why keep them like this?" Math gestured to the tiny, cramped hut.

The leader gave him a contemptuous, narrow-eyed stare. Then, speaking as if to a small child, she explained, "Demons cause sickness. Everyone knows this. As the victim grows more ill, the demons search for new hosts. If there is no one nearby—no new victims. I would be a poor leader if I risked my people."

Demons. Math clenched down on the urge to scoff. Depending on what was wrong with the man, isolating him might well have been the right call. That the chieftain had done it out of superstition did not negate the benefit.

"Math, come here, please," Kai called to him.

Math turned away from the Souna leader and kneeled beside Kai, trying with all his power to ignore the urine-stained rug.

"We need to discuss this," she whispered, switching to Ginren. "This man's sickness is a concern."

"Any ideas?" he asked. "I'm not exactly a member of the Mending section, but there are several diseases that could cause this—"

She shook her head. "It is cancer."

"Are you sure—" He didn't know much about her background, her training.

"Yes."

Math drummed his fingertips against his thighs as he thought it over. The old man—Dulbach—was conscious, his gaze drifting repeatedly to Math and Kai. Math had to fight not to shudder. Not because the man was thin or frail, but because of his eyes. He was not looking at them, but through them, staring at something only he could see. Math had only ever seen that look in the eyes of the dying.

Math fought the urge to gag. The air tasted like rot and piss.

"Kai, I can try, but I don't know if anything I do will help."

"Just the opposite," she whispered. "I promised your aid without understanding our challenge. You have told me your healing does not discriminate. It regenerates all—which would only cause the tumor to grow. I fear your aid would worsen matters considerably."

Math closed his eyes for a moment and tucked his chin. "Great. Just fantastic. I'm looking forward to telling that leader we can't do a thing to help their father. I suppose we can at least take the pain away."

"If I had enough time, I could cure it." She lowered her head, her expression twisted.

"How much time would you need?" That was not a consideration in the kind of spellcasting he was used to. Either one could do a thing, or one could not. Waiting accomplished nothing.

The room was silent, save for the too-loud sound of the old man's breathing—an ugly contrast to the children playing outside. Kai stayed quiet, her gaze fixed on the floor, as if weighing what to say.

"I am not like you," she whispered. She raised her head again, as if realizing what she had just said. "Obviously, I mean. But ordered magic is not . . ."

He waited.

"We do not draw upon our source with the ease you do yours," Kai said at last. "Even at its height, it is a stream to your river. But as the Chaos solstice nears, even that stream begins to dry. This is not an unclimbable obstacle, however. The source may be weak, but since I am shunting the result into a kind of holding tank, even a small trickle will fill a pond—given time."

"How long?"

She considered. "A week?"

Math grimaced. A week was forever with the Queens and the Kaliri doing only the Tri-Mother knew what back home. "And there isn't anything you can do to go faster? Or would you risk a magical overflow like I almost did last night?"

Kai's expression turned appalled for a moment, then she laughed. "No, I fear that is not at all what befalls a graven wizard who grows too greedy. We do not burn, we—" She paused, searching for the word.

"Freeze?"

"In a sense. We suffer enervation. If we are fortunate, it manifests only as malaise or paralysis. If not"—her tone remained composed—"it may begin as calcification, petrification, or the necrosis of flesh. I am told the first free-willed undead came into being when an enervated wizard attempted to survive the feedback rotting the flesh from his bones."

Math stared at her, but she wasn't joking.

"A week," she repeated. "And even then, there is no guarantee. His body may fail regardless, even should the cancer be removed. And that assumes this is sickness alone, not some magical side effect of the encroaching Chaos."

"That's possible?" he asked, utterly appalled.

She shrugged. "I know not. Cancer exists even when Chaos is not gaining power. That said—remember what I said of wild, unsustainable growth. This would certainly fit a theme, but it is not so unnatural that I can say with certainty it must have an equally unnatural cause."

He nodded. That was probably as good as he was going to get.

A week. Damn it. Did they have any choice? Despite Oltaxath saying they'd be released even if they failed, Math suspected their chances would worsen considerably if she found out they were unwilling to try simply because it was inconvenient.

"What do you need?"

She winced. "Therein lies the second difficulty. I require a surface large enough to surround his entire body, with a margin of several feet. It must be flat and capable of holding a precise mark—the more permanent, the better. But out here in the grasslands . . ."

"What about leather?" he asked. "Would that be permanent enough?"

She hedged. "It would require a large and perfect piece, and I doubt these people have recently skinned an elephant."

He smiled, stood back up again, and offered her a hand to do likewise. "You let me worry about that. This, I can handle."

Oltaxath had already left the tent, so Math went looking for her.

"The good news is that it's not demons," Math told her.

"The bad news?" Oltaxath evidently wasn't an optimist.

"Even if we can cure them, there's a chance they'll still die. Their body has suffered a great deal of damage. It's like a battle wound. Stopping the bleeding doesn't guarantee survival."

Oltaxath turned her head, a moment of allowed grief before she toughened herself. "I thank you for your honesty."

"We're going to need supplies for this. And you need to clean up their hut. Take everything out but your parent and the shelter itself. Then I need enough light-colored leather to cover the entire floor and a marking tool for it." He raised a finger. "The leather doesn't have to be one piece, but the larger the pieces, the faster we'll work."

Oltaxath shook her head, and Math frowned, thinking the woman was about to refuse. Instead, she said, "Easy. It will be done. Will we wait until morning?"

"No, we don't dare. We're doing this tonight." He corrected himself. "Or at least, that's when we'll start."

GRAVE

Oltaxath kept her word. Leather poured in from all corners of the camp—more than enough to cover the hut's floor. The donors seemed genuinely pleased to help. Less so the villagers conscripted to clean the place, though none voiced complaint. Math suspected their silence came from shame: an outsider had seen how they'd treated the old man—and found it wanting.

Once the hut was clean—or cleaner—Math began his work.

He used the same spell he'd used on Huraiik—an Order technique for breaking cloth into fibers for papermaking—to seamlessly join the leather. Several Souna helped him tie the sheet onto the hut's skeletal frame, pulling it taut along the ground.

Moving the old man seemed unwise. They worked carefully around him, where he lay suspended between sleep, waking, and death.

"That should do the trick—" Math said.

Someone plucked the hammer from his grasp.

Kai stood behind him, handing him a steaming bowl of soup in place of the tool. "I shall continue from here," she said firmly. "You should eat." Once he had the bowl, she spun an embossing stylus through her fingers, winked, and sank gracefully to her knees to begin drawing.

She must have changed while he'd been distracted—gone was the drab servant's dress. She now wore vivid trousers and a tunic in red and gold, unmistakably herself.

Math hesitated. They had other conversations waiting—but now was not the time.

He backed away carefully, breathing in the pungent scent of leather mingling with the savory aroma of his soup. Cross-legged, he sat nearby, quietly watching her precise movements. He was not the only observer. Villagers just "happened" to pass the once-avoided hut. Their distant chatter and footsteps formed a quiet backdrop, mingling with the playful giggles of children peeking through gaps in the leather walls.

Both Kai and Math pretended not to notice.

After a while, Kai gestured at the elaborate designs she had drawn. "This is nearly complete—the drawing portion, at least. Channeling energy into it shall follow."

"Is there anything I can do to help?"

"Unless you can help me forgo food and sleep for a hundred hours, no." She bent back over the leather, tracing lines. "With such a miracle, we might reduce the completion by two days."

"Too bad I can't just use my magic to power yours," Math said absently—and froze.

Kai noticed instantly. "What is it?"

Math's eyes brightened. "Who says I can't?"

"You know it does not work that way."

"No, I don't know that," Math insisted. "Think about it—the Kaliri weapon, that graved cannon. You said it had to be recharged eventually. But why would wild mages carry a weapon into battle they couldn't recharge?"

Kai frowned. "You misunderstood. The Kaliri long arm was not rechargeable. Once depleted, it reverted to a mundane weapon and the graving would have to be re-created. If those assassins were wild mages like yourself, then that would be far outside their abilities."

Embarrassment heated Math's cheeks, but the idea refused to fade. "Fine. Forget the Kaliri. Just because they couldn't doesn't mean it can't be done. Has anyone tried to recharge Order graving with wild magic?"

Kai blinked, stylus suspended. For once, genuine surprise flickered across her face. "I . . . no, I cannot recall it ever being attempted." Her composure returned slowly, replaced by cautious intrigue. "It is theoretically possible—but wildly dangerous. Order gravings remain stable because they are self-contained. Wild magic would—"

"Require constant supervision," Math interrupted. "Obviously. But it could work, right?"

She paused, clearly weighing the risks. "Perhaps. But this is not like charging metal or stone. Leather will not survive a sudden surge. The magic requires slow, meticulous feeding. Hours at a stretch." Her voice dropped. "A single lapse, and it might unravel—violently."

"If we both did it, you could monitor the process. Ensure I don't move too fast."

"From my experience," Kai replied calmly, "moving too quickly is hardly your flaw."

Math blinked—then caught the tilt of her lips. His heart stuttered. "Wait . . . are you teasing me?"

She looked away, but not before a faint flush rose to her cheeks. "Should I not? If you would prefer I desist . . ."

"No," he said too quickly, then quieter: "No, I like it. I'm just surprised. I thought I was the enemy."

Her smile faded. "Clearly not." She touched the leather gently, her eyes flicking toward the old man. "The Parnathi came too close to killing you for me to think it was staged."

"I shouldn't like it," he added softly. "You teasing me."

Kai glanced over, suddenly cautious.

"Because if I like it," he continued, "it means this isn't meaningless. And I don't get to have things that mean something. Not with someone the whole world thinks I'm supposed to kill."

Her breath caught. "You still believe I am a grim lord?"

"How could you be?" Math scoffed. "You were already asleep before the first grim lord started their reign. Also: you're not dead."

"True enough. A condition I hope continues for some time."

"So no, I don't think you're a grim lord, but I also know what the bond is doing to me. And if a spell is responsible for what I'm feeling . . . well, it's working."

"I see." Her voice was measured. "And if a spell is not responsible?"

"Then it's worse," Math said. "Because then I have no excuse."

For a moment, neither spoke. The hut was filled with the smell of soup cooling and the sound of children laughing outside—distant and painfully ordinary.

Then Kai exhaled softly, a sound too full of feeling for comfort. "Perhaps we ought to continue this conversation later."

"Agreed."

She cleared her throat. "Regardless, your idea is sound. But caution is crucial. We must communicate instantly. If only we shared some form of magical bond . . ."

Math barked a dry laugh. "A bond? Who would dare such a thing?"

"I truly cannot imagine who would be that reckless." Her voice was gentler now, the smile softer—less a weapon, more an offering. "Now, go be handsome elsewhere. I have a grave to finish."

Math winced. "Given the circumstances, maybe don't call it a grave?"

Kai paused. "Ah. Yes. Perhaps a working, then. Please do rest—I shall soon need you at your best."

Math couldn't pinpoint the exact moment Kai finished, but he knew it was late. Most of the camp had gone quiet. The main fire had dwindled to embers, leaving only the moonlight. The scent of ash and dinner lingered—a mixture of pleasant and less-than-pleasant reminders.

He had to admit her work was beautiful, even if its meaning escaped him. The drawing, etched into the leather, resembled a maze threaded with formulas and sigils. It reminded him of the passages beneath Isofal, of the map carved into the wall.

Kai stood, stretched, and then sat down opposite him. Their knees touched. Even through the leather, he could feel her warmth. She was too close, and he didn't move. Beside them, the old man snored and twitched, asleep—if not exactly at peace.

"Normally—" She paused. "Rather, in my time, if gravers attempted a working of this scale, we used a team. A large group channeling at their maximum safe capacity may accomplish almost anything. So I have done something of this kind before—"

"We don't have to do it this way," Math said quietly. "It was just an idea."

"But a good one." She picked up one of his hands and cradled it in both of hers.

Math's breath caught. Her skin was warmer than he'd expected. He ran his thumb along the edge of her fingers, then forced himself to stop. Any more and he would forget why he shouldn't want this.

They sat like that for a moment too long. She didn't let go.

"We shall work for as long as it remains safe," she said, voice quieter now. "If needs must, we shall stop and rest before continuing." She finally withdrew one hand, the absence of it sharp against his skin, and traced the leather's surface as if to ground herself. "Once it is sufficiently charged, I shall activate the spell."

"What's it meant to do?" He could admit he was curious, but the question came out softer than intended.

She looked into his eyes. By the light of his summoned wax candles, hers appeared entirely black.

"Cancer is like your Kaliri spy. A danger to your order, possibly to the empire, but impossible to confront until identified—and it hides well. All I intend is to show the body how to recognize what does not belong, and remove it."

"If only you could do that with the Kaliri spy."

"Indeed."

Math considered her words. They made sense. But...

"We're waiting until morning," he said.

She blinked. "I have already told you—"

"Kai, if this goes wrong, wouldn't you rather it did so in daylight?"

He half expected resistance, but after a short pause, she nodded. "Then we shall begin in the morning. Do we have a place to sleep?"

"We do." He helped her to her feet, their hands lingering for a heartbeat longer than necessary. They stepped out into the cooler night, leaving the old man behind—hopefully still slumbering.

He pointed toward a hut outlined by the glow of a fading fire. "That one's been set aside for us."

"Us? Both of us?" Her eyebrows rose, surprise flickering across her face.

"They seem to think we're . . . together."

"Oh." Though he couldn't see her expression clearly, he felt tensions between them change—her embarrassment flaring, but also a swirl of more heated emotions, quickly banked.

"If that's a problem—"

"No. No, it is not."

"I'm sure I could find somewhere else—"

"It is fine," she said, not looking at him. "We are only going to sleep, after all."

They *needed* to sleep. No matter what he might wish they were doing instead.

"Right," he agreed, his voice rougher than it should have been. Then, needing air—or distance—he asked, "Have your people always been like this? I admit, they aren't what I expected."

"I have not the faintest idea. I was very young when the Parnathi . . ." She trailed off, then shook her head. "I learned the language much later, because I wished to understand something of my people. Their customs were unknown to me. It was never a gendered language, however, so that much hasn't changed."

He couldn't tell how she felt about that—not because she was hiding anything, but because there was too much for easy interpretation. Her silence felt thick with things unsaid.

"Let us try to catch some of that elusive 'sleep,'" Math said.

They were going to need it.

FLOOD

Unfortunately, they didn't get any sleep.

They'd stayed up too late and the camp rose early—the gradually increasing noise acted as an all-too-effective alarm. A second reason, however, was because of each other.

Perhaps if the situation had been more romantic—if they'd removed their clothes, if the bedding had been more than woven rugs and animal skins thrown over a mound of dried grass—then the lack of sleep might have been blamed on more pleasant distractions.

Instead, silence pressed between them, awkward and unfinished. There was a dissonant clash between what they both wanted and what they both knew was inadvisable. Each too aware of the other. Each unwilling to be the one to speak first.

Even if none of that had been true, Math doubted he could've slept. Not after the day they'd had. Lying in the dark, staring up at what was likely a lattice of reeds and leather, he had too much time to think. And mostly, he thought about the plants back at the train crash.

About how he'd controlled them. How they'd done exactly what he wanted.

On the one hand, he could *control* them. That was great. That meant the Idallik Order wouldn't use that as an excuse to announce he was a grimmock. But there was an underlying pain, a threat that this did nothing to lessen.

What did that say about what had happened to his parents?

When predawn light turned the black of the hut's interior to soft gray, Math heard the camp begin to stir. He and Kai dressed, ate the breakfast brought to them, and returned to Dulbach's hut. A few curious Souna lingered outside, but when nothing dramatic happened, most drifted away.

Kai sat beside the leather, one hand resting lightly against it. Math took her other hand. From the outside, they must have looked like a young couple holding hands at the bedside of a sick parent.

Inside their connection, the magic stirred.

That feeling of wrongness he'd first experienced when Kai woke at Isofal returned: rigid and claustrophobic, oppressing and trapping. As Kai pulled in more power, the feeling grew. Her body began to shudder—not visibly, but Math felt it through her grip, through the way her fingers tightened on his.

He squeezed her hand, trying to feed her more energy so she could draw less through herself.

Despite what Kai had originally claimed, the two sources of magic were not antithetical. In fact, once she led him through the process with careful precision, he discovered he could feed power directly into the graving.

Keeping focus was harder. The magic felt like heat in his spine and behind his eyes, like a migraine waiting to crest. But when he wavered, Kai squeezed his hand and steadied him.

They learned quickly: it was more effective for Math to channel energy *into Kai* rather than the graving itself. She could regulate the flow with far greater precision than he could.

She had the knowledge. He had the power.

For a while, that was enough.

For a while.

The stumble caught Math off guard. Though Kai had been drawing from him, she still maintained a trickle of power from her own source—a slow stream barely escaping an ever-strengthening dam. It wasn't much.

Then the dam broke.

Magic exploded through her—not gently but all at once, a great wave of floodwaters bursting through stone.

Kai screamed.

The sound stopped so sharply it felt carved from reality.

"No—!" Math's eyes snapped open.

Kai's eyes had rolled back. She wasn't convulsing. She wasn't moving at all. Her body glowed with a pale white light—not warm or divine, but cold and final. It felt like the onset of winter, like the coming of death. She'd stopped breathing. He suspected her heart had stopped beating, too. Every biological function, frozen.

Math lunged forward and caught her before she could fall. He tried to heal her, but this wasn't a wound. She hadn't meant to take so much; he knew that.

The bond was the worst part, because he felt pain like it was his own, sharp and splitting, knew it meant that she was alive and aware. Her fear thundered through him. His dread surged back in response.

She had walked too close to a metaphysical cliff, and the ground had vanished beneath her.

He cradled her in his lap and poured energy into her blindly. Anything, everything, too much, too fast. His own body reacted and he could feel the feverish burn of a wild magic overdose trying to climb out of his veins.

Some small part of him laughed, dark and detached, at the idea of overdosing while trying to save her from the same.

If someone's drowning, he thought numbly, *you don't give them more water.*

Math released the wild magic he'd been channeling and pressed his forehead to hers. This time, instead of pushing power into her, he pulled.

Gently. Carefully. He reached for the energy flooding her body and drew it back into himself, hand over hand. The current resisted, then yielded. Still—there was loss. A trickle siphoned elsewhere, through the cracks the bond had opened. He felt it like water slipping through a broken seal.

He didn't care. He prayed to the Tri-Mother and all her children that he could pull Kai back before it broke him, too.

Kai gasped.

Her breath returned in a painful rush. She coughed, hard and choking, and winced. "Ouch," she rasped. "That was—" Her voice caught again in another fit of coughing.

Math held her, barely breathing himself.

The bond between them roared. Her pain was his. His relief was hers. Magic still sparked between them, too raw to settle. Her pulse thudded against his chest.

She opened her eyes.

In that instant, they kissed.

That kiss was desperate and hungry. Her hand fisted in his shirt, and he leaned into her like she was the panacea to every poison he could imagine. For one silvered, pure moment, the world didn't exist beyond each other and the certainty of two people who had pulled each other from the gates of death.

His hand was in her hair. Hers dragged down his shoulder.

The bond flared—too bright, too fast, magic and sensation and breath colliding. It was overwhelming.

They broke apart at the same time, stunned and shaken, eyes wide, mouths still parted like they couldn't believe what they'd just done.

Math swallowed, hard.

Kai's eyes darted away, her hand still resting against his chest. Her pulse matched his. He could feel it. The bond hummed with heat and confusion and want—and under that, the terrible knowledge that it meant something. They could claim it was the heat of the moment and always know they were lying.

Neither of them said a word.

Then Kai coughed again, this time half laughing, half in pain. Her gaze tracked upward. "It is always a garden with you."

He frowned, a little embarrassed because it took him a moment to understand what she was talking about. Then he noticed they were no longer in a hut but resting under a living canopy—an enormous awning of vines and wild growth. The plants had consumed the hut, using it like a trellis.

His clothes were in tatters. Vines had curled up his legs, beneath his shirt, around his arms.

"At least now, I don't have to hack my way out," Math muttered, throat raw. He didn't look at her. Couldn't. "How are you feeling?"

"Like someone tried to pour glue through my veins," she said, voice strained but composed. "Otherwise, I am *marvelous*."

"Good," he said hoarsely. "Because if circumstances were even slightly different..."

She turned to him, eyes narrowed. "What circumstances?"

He tilted his head toward the vines. "Can't move."

Kai blinked, as if only now remembering their surroundings. She scanned him, noting the snarl of green climbing his limbs. "Ah. Yes. That would complicate matters."

"I can fix it," he muttered.

She said nothing, only raised an eyebrow and folded her arms.

Math focused. At first, the vines resisted, or perhaps *he* did, but then he forced the plants to release him, one by one. They let go with surprising gentleness. He expected pain. He found none.

The silence after was too complete.

Footsteps approached.

Oltaxath's voice filtered in through the wall. "Is anyone alive in there?"

Math sighed. "We're alive. Just..." He looked back at Dulbach—still asleep—and then leaned closer to Kai. "Maybe we can say there was a problem. That we'll have to start over."

"We *could* do that," Kai said, too carefully. Then her gaze moved to the old man. "But why should we lie?"

Math looked again.

Dulbach's stomach was no longer bloated. His face, once tight with pain, was now peaceful.

"It worked?" Math stared at her. "How could it have worked? How long were we doing this?"

"Not more than a few hours," she said, blinking in wonder. "The graving fully charged. It seemed wasteful not to trigger it."

Not weeks. Not even days. *Hours.*

And yet Math's chest ached.

He could still feel the press of her mouth against his. The pulse of her magic through his bones. And under that, the knowledge that whatever had just happened between them had been a dam breaking in more than one way.

CURE

Dulbach didn't spring out of bed and dance or miraculously seem half his age, but a few hours later—after Math had finished clearing away all the spontaneous growth—the old man opened his eyes.

He immediately snapped, "Where's my lazy, good-for-nothing fool of a child? I'm hungry."

Oltaxath was so happy she nearly wept.

Everyone's attitude toward Math and Kai changed after that. They still received their fair share of strange looks, but people were much friendlier. That evening, the camp prepared a dinner more feast than meal. Oltaxath carried her father out to sit by the fire and eat with them, and the old man actually consumed solid food.

Then, gradually, everyone shuffled off to bed.

In Math and Kai's case, it came with a warning from Oltaxath not to sleep in—they would leave at dawn.

Their second night in the camp felt different. Elevated. Math was given a clean set of clothes, far nicer than his ruined soldier's garb. Between that and Kai's insistence on checking him for lingering vines—some of which had been in *very* inconvenient places—he wasn't wearing nearly as much when they finally retired.

Which made it awkward when Math woke in the middle of the night to find Kai tossed over him like a shapely blanket.

He felt her breathing, the slow curl of her contentment. Her body pressed against him like she belonged there. Through their link, arousal flickered, raw and unmistakable.

He felt like cursing. Like praying. Like pleading.

He should have shifted away. Should have said nothing. Should have buried the thought with all the others he wasn't allowed to feel.

Instead, he lay still, heart pounding against hers.

He wanted her desperately, and it was such a cursed and foolish idea.

Desire wasn't the problem. Everyone in the Order had their quiet arrangements, but so long as no one spoke of it, it didn't exist. No emotions, no confessions—just mechanics.

That was the problem, though, wasn't it? This wasn't mechanical; this was Kaiataris.

What he felt for her couldn't be dismissed with silence or buried under doctrine.

The Idallik Order would never accept him back with her at his side. Even if he was absolved—*if*—she would still be anathema. Heretic. Monster. The living embodiment of everything they'd sworn to destroy.

Even though it wasn't fair. Even though she'd created the Order. Even if she was their only chance of defeating the Three Queens.

She was still a heretic. Still heterodox. Still anathema.

Math lay still, trying not to think about how good she felt against him. The warmth of her body. The temptation to wake her with a kiss.

He failed.

Her breathing shifted. Then she stilled—as if weighing whether to pretend nothing had happened.

"Good morning," he said, voice rough.

She sighed, resting her head against his shoulder. Her hair still smelled like smoke from the train fire. "It seems we were too close when we finally slept."

"You won't hear me complain."

She gave him an intense look, then pushed herself up, her hair a curtain between them and the waking world.

"No. I don't suppose I will. Do you still want to kiss me?"

Despite everything, he didn't hesitate. Math reached for her.

She met him halfway, her hands cupping his face, slowing him—not to stop him, but to savor the experience. He wasn't used to slowing down. Wasn't used to being seen in the light. But now, with her breath mingling with his, a faint warmth from her magic still humming in his chest, it felt undeniably necessary.

Kai kissed like she cast spells: Carefully, deliberately, with intention and purpose.

It made him realize two things. First, her breath was mint-fresh. And second—

"I need to shave, don't I?" He touched her hand, where she was subtly avoiding his stubble. "I also need to brush my teeth." And a few other things better left unsaid.

"And yet *I* would have been punished had I complained—denied those lips while you wandered off to tend to such matters."

Outside, the camp stirred. They exchanged a look.

Kai rolled off him and rose to her feet, brushing herself off. She looked like every person wanted to look after waking, but never did—dewy, red-lipped, hair tousled just right.

Math narrowed his eyes. "Okay. I'll bite."

"Is that a promise?" she asked.

"Stop that." He sat up. "How are you *clean*? We've been traveling for days. You've been stabbed. I've been stabbed. I desperately need a bath. I desperately need a shave. *You* are perfect." He stared. "You're using magic, aren't you? I think I hate you a little."

She laughed. "You do not hate me."

"Not even a little," he admitted. "But I *am* jealous. Can you do that again? Or is this one of those 'you must wait a thousand years' spells?"

"No, I can do it again. The spell is simple. It doesn't require much power. I just need something I can grave—large enough for the pattern, or tools small enough to carve it. I have neither." She grinned. "If I did it for you now, I'm afraid you'd need to carry something the size of a horse."

As she spoke, her hand went to her bracelet. Math followed her gaze. The gravings were so delicate and fine that they weren't easily perceived as writing at all.

"All right," he said. "Back to being jealous."

"It would not solve your issue with shaving," she pointed out.

"No, it wouldn't. I'd ask if anyone here has something I could use, but all the men here have beards."

"No razors for shaving, true—but plenty for scraping leather. Not so different. If not, we'll find something in Lomar."

"Assuming we *can* reach Lomar," he said.

Once dressed, Math turned to her. "Are we going to talk about the wild, rampaging hippopotamus in the room?"

"Which one? I was under the impression we were starting a farm."

He scoffed. "The 'what happened with the magic?' hippopotamus. You said it would take a week. Days, if I helped. It took *hours*. That's impossible, right?"

Kai rubbed her chin. "Perhaps it is a side effect of the bond. Or perhaps the poles do not always oppose one another—they might align. Amplify." She laughed. "Would that not be something? That we are more powerful together?"

"It would indeed."

It would change everything, too. *Everything.*

Math didn't recognize the twist in his chest at first, not until it settled deep and began to grow. Then he did.

It was hope.

They headed north from the camp, away from the volcano. In time, they crossed the train tracks they'd left behind days earlier, though they were now too far west to see the crash site.

They traveled swiftly—not at train speed, but fast enough. The horses weren't confined to rails, and this breed was hardier than ones back home. The Souna were prepared: each rider had four horses, rotating between them to avoid long rest stops.

It took nearly a week to find Kai's waystation, and when they did, it didn't resemble any repository Math had ever seen. There was no fortress or compound. Just a single ruined tower, its top long collapsed and overtaken by generations of roosting birds.

That it still stood was a miracle. So was the expression on Kai's face—a rare, unguarded smile, something that shimmered through the bond like warm sunlight against his face.

"Wonderful," she said. "Let us ascertain whether the entrance remains undamaged."

"Why isn't anyone using this? You'd think somebody would be here."

"I should point out that we have not yet investigated," Kai replied. "Someone might well be within."

"Cursed," Oltaxath said.

They turned.

"The place is cursed," she repeated, matter-of-fact. "Anyone who dares walk inside dies instantly." She studied them both. "You didn't have me bring you all this way to kill yourselves, did you? That would be a waste." She pointed at Math. "I'm willing to forget you're Avansi. You married a Souna. Stay with us. You'd be welcome."

Math didn't smile. Her words hit harder than she likely intended. *You married a Souna.* The bond gave a slight, startled pulse—Kai had felt it too.

He wanted to say it wasn't true—that the bond wasn't that kind of union—but the protest never made it to his lips. The words felt heavier than denial. Oltaxath was offering safety. A life without hiding.

And he couldn't take it.

"If we don't do this," he said quietly, "a lot of trouble will result. This place—and your people—won't be immune."

"What kind of trouble?" another rider asked.

Kai leaned forward in her saddle. "More of the tree women. And their children."

Oltaxath gave a sharp nod. "That is a danger we understand. Thank you."

She pointed at Math. "For healing my father." Then at Kai. "For not cursing everyone."

Kai tilted her head in mock magnanimity. The other riders laughed.

Math dismounted and handed the reins to a Souna. "If it's not too much trouble, maybe don't leave just yet? In case this doesn't work."

Oltaxath stared flatly. "I repeat: Everyone who dares walk inside dies instantly."

Math turned to Kai and offered his assistance. "Are we going to walk inside and die instantly?"

"Absolutely not." She accepted his hand with a faint smile. "I am well versed in disabling traps and unpleasant surprises."

He nodded toward the Souna. "See? We'll be fine. Just wait a few hours. If we don't find what we need, you'll still be here."

Oltaxath grumbled but agreed.

The Souna refused to come closer to the tower. They'd stopped at a respectful distance and stayed there, no matter what Kai offered. She, meanwhile, walked to within ten feet of the arched doorway and stood still, hands lifted, eyes closed.

Math didn't interrupt. He didn't want to walk inside and die instantly, after all.

Kai hadn't said Oltaxath was wrong—only that she could handle it.

The air around the tower felt colder. Still. Like the world was holding its breath. Even the birds had gone quiet.

Kai raised one hand, murmured something, then made a precise gesture. The doorway shimmered. Math stared as thin, silvery lines melted from the stone, bleeding away like water across dust.

Gravings, he realized. Protective magic, dissolving under her touch. She made another gesture. Something clicked.

She stepped inside.

A moment later, her head popped out, and she waved cheerfully to the camp.

"Worry not," she called. "'Tis perfectly safe now." Then, more thoughtfully: "Though I would avoid touching anything, as a basic precaution."

"Very reassuring," Math muttered.

"What we need here requires no theft."

"Lead on."

She did.

The interior smelled of damp stone and ash. The Souna, meanwhile, seemed to be settling in for the night. If something went wrong, at least they'd still be nearby.

Kai made a slow circuit of the room, stopped beside an obvious trapdoor, inspected it, then walked back to the entrance.

"We're fine!" she shouted. "You can go. Thank you again—I am most appreciative. May your ancestors smile upon you."

The riders waved and called back farewells. They completely ignored her invitation to leave and continued making camp.

Math laughed as they returned to the trapdoor. Kai kneeled and pulled it open.

She looked up at him with a grin. "This next part," she said, "will be simplicity itself."

SIGIL

The ladder from the trapdoor descended into a yawning dark. Math summoned a first-circle Sun spell, and a warm flicker of light answered in the form of a small swarm of fireflies, glowing gently, shifting with his steps.

By their glow, the passage revealed itself: tall enough to walk upright, wide enough for two, crafted of time-smoothed stone. It was plain, functional, the sort of architecture common to Illuminated repositories. There was nothing that declared danger or promised death, and no obvious gravings. Math was careful not to touch the walls, anyway.

The hallway ended in an unadorned archway. Kai stepped through first, and he followed into a circular chamber where dim lights sparked to life as they entered. A large sigil was etched into the floor, intricate and geometric, patterns unfurling in spirals that hinted at both art and mathematics. It was the first time he'd seen gravings so large up close, and he immediately understood why Kai hated improvising this kind of magic.

The margin for error must have been thinner than paper.

"For the spell to function correctly," Kai said, her voice low and calm, "one must know their exact location, as well as the precise coordinates of their destination. Even the smallest miscalculation could result in being launched into the air or overlapping with an already occupied space. And I assure you, that never ends well."

Math frowned. "What about continental migration?"

She blinked. "Pardon?"

"Continental migration. It's a new theory. The continents used to be joined, but they're moving, pushed apart by geologic forces. That's what created the twin bays. It must've moved the land's position by at least a few dozen feet in the last thousand years."

Kai smiled. "Ah. A fair question. But yes—it is accounted for." She walked to the far wall and pressed her hand against a smooth panel.

A soft glow bloomed, revealing a map without borders or names, just the bare shapes of continents rendered in faint yellow lines. A point lit in the southwest of the eastern continent, near the edge of the Rokasmaa Empire. Another pulsed in the western landmass—likely Lomar. Three more flickered faintly to the north, west, and east.

"So few," Kai said quietly.

"Does the King of Lomar know about this portal?"

"I cannot be certain, but I see no reason why he wouldn't. It shouldn't be a problem, though—" she began.

Math stepped forward, pointing to the easternmost light. "That's *Kaliri*."

Kai paused. "Ah. I see. That is unfortunate."

"The light means the gate is still active?" He didn't wait for confirmation. "Does that mean the Kaliri have had a hidden path into Rokasmaa *this whole time*?"

She said nothing for just long enough to make his stomach knot. Through the bond, he felt her hesitation ripple—a pause, thoughtful and cold.

"Perhaps," she said finally. "But it has existed for over a thousand years. If they knew, they would have used it."

He exhaled. "Good, but the idea of *Lomar* having one isn't much better. Sanistral could walk an army through here, and no one would know until they were at the capital gates."

Kai looked thoughtful. "True. But if it is Sanistral, I do not believe that would be his intention."

"You don't know that. Sanistral the Twenty-Seventh might not be that nice."

She reached up and pressed the Lomar point. The sigil on the floor flared to life, casting yellow lines across the stone.

"There," she said. "It is keyed."

"You're sure this will work?"

"There is no risk. It will either send us whole and healthy, or it will not activate at all."

She stepped into the center of the circle and extended her hand. Math took it. He wasn't sure it was necessary, but it felt right. A week ago, he wouldn't have trusted her with his life. Now, it felt strange not to.

She laced her fingers through his and spoke the activation words. The world stuttered, folded, blinked.

They stood in a nearly identical chamber.

But this one had been updated. The old map had been painted over with a more modern one—names, borders, nations restored.

And guards.

Six of them ringed the edge of the sigil, weapons already drawn.

"On the ground," one barked. "Now."

LOMAR

"Do not fight," Kai whispered as they lay face down on the stone floor.

Math snorted but kept his mouth shut. For now.

Two guards moved in with practiced efficiency, giving them both a thorough pat-down. They found the Souna daggers easily enough, as well as the bundle of letters Math had kept tucked away. No words were exchanged, just hands and pressure and silent appraisal.

Then they were yanked to their feet, the motion rough and impersonal. Kai straightened with as much dignity as she could muster under the circumstances and said, clear but not loud, "Please inform Sanistral Lomar that Kaiataris Von is calling on him."

The guard who'd lifted her struck her across the face.

Math's breath caught in fury, but then twisted into a low, bitter chuckle. "I wouldn't have done that if I were you."

The same guard turned and raised a hand toward him.

Math only smiled. "Think for a second. We just came through the portal. You wouldn't be guarding it if it were unimportant. So tell me—how many times have you seen someone come through from the other side?"

That gave the guard pause. Hard to read their face, hidden as it was behind a polished black helmet and a hood that dulled their outline in shadow. They were tall, but nothing else about them suggested gender or status. Just a uniform designed to erase individuality.

Not how he'd have done it. Idallik Knights removed their helmets when back at the cenobium—visibility and trust mattered when you were supposed to be seen as protectors. Not even the heat, which pressed in thick and wet, seemed to deter them. The armor must have been unbearable in this climate.

Another guard stepped forward, her voice sharp and distinctly female. "He has a point."

The first guard scoffed. "You are joking. Look at them. They are dressed like . . . like savages."

Math felt Kai stiffen beside him. That word rang sharply through the bond—a spike of old fury, quickly buried beneath cool control. The restraint she showed was impressive.

"I do not care how they appear," the second guard said. "They came through the pattern. That means His Majesty will wish to speak with them. It's not for us to decide what happens."

Math tilted his head toward her and grinned. "Now that's a smart one. She'll go far."

The first guard made a disgusted sound and shoved them both forward.

They were marched through a twisting sequence of hallways, corridors turning sharply, always descending. The architecture was labyrinthine by design, and it didn't take long before Math had no idea where they were relative to the surface. Eventually, a final corridor opened into sunlight.

They emerged onto the side of a massive stepped pyramid. Around it stretched a vast city, laid out like one of Kai's spells—every building perfectly aligned, every color part of a greater design.

Rokasmaa's capital, Bashan, had its own beauty, but it was born of contradictions—soot and gold, noise and grace. Whereas this capital, Monchlen, was quiet. The sky was clear, the air thick with heat but not smoke. The streets smelled of dust and citrus oil, not coal or manure. It was undeniably more elegant. Cleaner. Richer.

And creepier.

People moved briskly through the avenues below, finely dressed in airy clothes that shimmered with embroidery and jewel work. But they didn't smile. They didn't laugh. Their eyes flicked past soldiers with a speed and precision that spoke of habitual fear, like a child who's learned not to make eye contact because drawing a parent's attention is dangerous.

Math shivered, despite the heat.

"What is it?" Kai murmured to him.

"No talking," a guard barked, shoving them both.

They descended the pyramid, crossed a wide stone plaza lined with tall columns, and entered a second structure—less monumental than the pyramid but still grand. The palace. It echoed some of the same architecture but softened the lines: the kind of place people might actually live, rather than only visit to worship.

Inside, the guards escorted them past an elaborately dressed woman whose rings glittered like a warning. She raised a hand to stop them, indignant.

"They just came out of the portal," the second guard explained. "His Majesty will wish to speak with them directly."

The woman hesitated, narrowed her eyes at Kai, and then waved them on. "Third garden."

And so that was where they went.

The third garden was a long courtyard, open to the sky, with fountains and shallow pools flanked by pebble lawns and carefully placed boulders that framed the space like punctuation marks in a well-designed sentence. Canopies offered shade, but there was no greenery. Not a single plant lay anywhere in sight.

A group had gathered beneath one awning, dressed in the local style—soft robes, metallic trim, embroidered belts. One of them stood apart, wearing more: more metal, more color, more presence. A circlet of gold rested on his brow. His face was deeply lined, but strong-featured. His beard curled in stylized loops, oiled and set with gold beads. He was not handsome, but he *was* commanding.

Kai stopped walking. Her voice cracked. "Sanis?"

The man turned.

His expression shifted from mild disinterest to stunned disbelief.

He raised a hand, waved away the people surrounding him.

Math blinked. *No. Surely not.* He'd assumed the King of Lomar must be a descendant. That only made sense: over a thousand years had passed.

But the man was already crossing to them, fast and sure. "Kaiataris," he said reverently. "I never thought I would see you again."

He took her shoulders in both hands and gazed at her like he was witnessing a miracle. Then he pulled her into an embrace.

Math stood frozen, every question in the world crowding into his thoughts. He watched the two of them—ancient sorcerers, old friends, something akin to family—and realized, with a strange, distant clarity, that Kai had been right: Another graven wizard had survived.

And apparently, he'd made himself king.

Math had never seen Kai so happy.

This was a family reunion—far more so than meeting the Souna had been. Sanistral had been her mentor, her leader, her father in all but name.

Eventually, King Sanistral took a step back, noticed Math, and frowned. "Perhaps an introduction would be in order."

Kai smiled, dark eyes bright with laughter. "Indeed, it would. This is Mathaiik Kaven, a knight—"

"A novitiate," Math corrected, although he winced at himself. Technically speaking, he wasn't even that.

"Very well. A novitiate of the Idallik Order." Her smile widened. "Also, my knight. He is the one who woke me."

At this, King Sanistral studied Math more intensely. "Are you? How interesting. And how did you solve dear Kaiataris's riddle? It thwarted all my efforts for years."

"You tried to wake me?" Kaiataris sounded so pleased.

"Of course, my dear." That adoring look again. "Not recently, mind you. It has become more difficult to enter Rokasmaa over the last few centuries." His sharp eyes returned to Math. He hadn't forgotten the question.

Math's instincts warned him against making light of it.

He scratched his neck. "Honestly, it was desperation. If I hadn't guessed the right answer, I probably would've died."

One of the king's thick eyebrows rose. "A lucky guess?"

"And fifteen years or so of research. I've been obsessed with the maze since I was a child."

The man stared at Math with intense focus. Then, with no warning, the expression softened into a smile. Sanistral clapped Math on the shoulder with a grip like a hawk's talons. "Luck is always helped with preparation. I cannot thank you enough for delivering Kaiataris safely. She is precious beyond gold or jewels."

"Sanis, you must not say such things!" Kai was blushing now, and the bond carried a flutter of flustered joy that made Math's chest tighten.

"It has been well over a thousand years, dear one." The king's eyes crinkled. "Watch me." His gaze remained fixed on Math. "You understand what I mean, do you not?"

Math's eyes drifted to where Kai stood, flustered and red-cheeked. There was a sudden, aching contrast between the intimacy of this reunion and his own cautious orbit. "Yes," he said finally. Sanistral was waiting, and still hadn't taken his hand off Math's shoulder. "I understand."

Sanistral nodded. "I thought you might." He squeezed once, then let go. "Why don't we find you both rooms? I'm certain you must be tired after your journey."

"Sanis," Kai said, "there is a great deal we must discuss. The Queens have awoken, no longer content to confine themselves to the forests. They are expanding. Conquering."

The king contemplated this with pursed lips. "I see."

"We tried to reach Bashan to warn the head of my order," Math said. "But we ran into problems. Kai thought you might help—if you were her Sanistral. Which, apparently, you are."

"Lucky me," Sanistral said, amused.

"Seriously, Sanis? You made yourself a king?" Kai sounded incredulous. "How could you—" She waved a hand. "Never mind. That is so far down the list of concerns as to be left off the page entirely. The matter with the Queens is far more pressing."

"I quite agree," Sanistral said. "But I suspect that will be best discussed at dinner, in private. Just us." His eyes flicked to Math. "Just the three of us, I should say."

Math appreciated the clarification because, for a moment, he'd assumed that Sanistral had meant to shut him out. "Thank you, Your Majesty. That's appreciated."

Sanistral's mouth quirked. "Oh, there is no need to address me as such. Certainly, I do not expect Kai to do so without considerable coercion. Call me Sanis." He began walking toward the entrance to the courtyard.

Math had no difficulty believing Sanistral was a king. He had a king's absolute faith that people would always follow him.

A faith that proved well-placed in this instance, too.

The wizard carried himself with enormous dignity. Although by no means a tall man, he possessed a commanding presence. Servants stepped aside without hesitation, bowing their heads. Sanistral didn't notice. He was long accustomed to being the most important person in any room.

Which was the definition of "king," some might argue.

At some point, Sanistral called a woman over. "Diris, these are my most treasured guests. Treat them with every courtesy. They will require refreshment, proper clothing, and quarters."

Math wondered what counted as "proper" clothing in a place like this.

King Sanistral turned back to them. "This is Diris. She will attend to you. Someone shall come for you in a few hours for supper. Should you require anything else, simply ask."

"You are leaving me so soon?" Kai asked.

Sanistral squeezed her hand and released it. "Only for a good cause, I promise. When I return, I shall hear everything, and we shall decide upon a solution together." He nodded once more at Math.

"Thank you, Your Majesty."

The king gave him an amused look but chose not to correct him again. "Until later, then." With that, Sanistral swept back down the corridor.

The serving woman, Diris, bowed deeply. "If it pleases you to follow."

Math didn't think he had any other options. So he did.

MAJESTY

No matter his doubts about King Sanistral, Math couldn't deny the man was a gracious host. He received a table piled with fresh fruit and chilled water, a steaming bath, and tools to shave. The new clothes gave him pause: they were elegant and heavily embroidered, but still made him feel like he was about to dine in his nightclothes.

If the clothes felt strange, Math appreciated how Kai's gaze stopped dead on him when they met again.

As for Kai, he wasn't surprised to see she'd received the full royal treatment. Her dress resembled the one she'd worn when she first woke in Isofal—gold instead of gray, more lavishly decorated. Evidently, a woman more precious than gold and jewels should wear as many of them as possible. Kai resembled a queen out of storybooks, drawn by an artist with a passion for the way gossamer fabrics clung to a woman's curves.

She noticed his look and blushed. "I am not used to wearing so much—" She plucked at a ruby on her bodice.

"You could have left it off?"

"I did not wish to be rude." She brightened. "You are looking very nice, I must say."

He rubbed his cheek. "I had a lot of motivation."

Diris, who'd waited through the exchange, bowed. "Please, my lady, my lord. His Majesty is waiting."

Math took the hint. He offered Kai his arm and motioned for Diris to lead the way.

The palace struck him as odd. He was used to living in a massive building filled with people, but Isofal, like all Idallik Order cenobiums, existed to defend its libraries and support the Order. This place had been built for one man. The halls held only servants.

"Diris, does His Majesty have a spouse?" Math asked.

She looked back, startled. "No, my lord."

"Any children?"

"No, my lord." She looked like her greatest wish was for Math to stop asking questions.

Kai raised an eyebrow. "Are you going somewhere with this?"

"No, no. Just curious. Don't mind me."

When they arrived in the dining room—or rather, the informal banquet hall, since there were several—they found a table set for three, though it could seat eight. Likely the smallest available for an "intimate" dinner.

When King Sanistral said he had to take care of business, what he'd evidently done was instruct his cooks to prepare a feast. The table groaned under the weight of enough food to feed half the Idallik Knights in Bashan.

King Sanistral was already present, which Math was fairly certain was the kind of breach of etiquette that had started wars. The king stood and hurried over.

"I must say," he said, grinning at Math, "after a shave, you bear far less resemblance to a ruffian." He touched his own perfectly coiffed beard. "Though I'm sure you'd wear a beard well. It's the decisiveness that matters. A man should never look as though he couldn't make up his mind."

Sanistral was teasing him.

Math smiled politely. "Thank you. Truthfully, I don't think Kai would have forgiven me if I hadn't."

The king's gaze flicked to Kai, mischief sparkling in his eyes. "I'm sure she'd find it in her heart. Our Kaiataris doesn't bear grudges. You look every bit as beautiful as I remember, dear one."

"You really shouldn't have, Sanis." Unlike when most people said that phrase, Kai meant it. She smoothed the fabric of her dress against her thigh.

"I know," King Sanistral said, gesturing for them to sit as he did. "But one advantage of being king is that when I'm self-indulgent, no one protests."

Math felt Kai's indignation. She started to speak, then shut her mouth with an audible click of teeth.

Sanistral noticed her reaction and laughed. "You haven't changed at all, Kai. Speak your piece."

Kai touched the edge of a crystal wineglass. The plates and dinnerware were gold, each piece precisely arranged. "No one protests—or no one dares?" she said, her gaze fixed on the abundance laid out before them.

"It's not that bad, Kai. I'm a good ruler." He nodded absently as a servant refilled his wine, though his focus stayed on her. "I've kept Lomar from falling into chaos. That's no small feat."

"That's not why we're here," Math said, gently redirecting.

King Sanistral sipped his wine and chuckled. "I can see why you like this one, Kai. For now, enjoy the meal. Then you can tell me all about the Parnathi Queens."

The food was far more elaborate than anything Math was used to—and far spicier. He didn't recognize half of it; several dishes had been cooked to the consistency of jam, their ingredients disguised beneath glaze and garnish. Even the utensils felt unfamiliar in his hands. He kept second-guessing which one to use and couldn't shake the feeling that some of it was meant to be eaten with flatbread or bare fingers, not gold-handled forks.

"How are you enjoying the meal?" King Sanistral asked.

Math looked up, swallowing a bite that might have been eggplant—or something pretending to be. "It's delicious," he said, and it wasn't a lie. "Even hotter than I'm used to."

"I imagine so," the king said. "Your people cook primarily with garlic, do they not? I'm quite fond of those stuffed chard leaves you make."

"You know what they say. You can never have too much garlic," Math said.

"Avansi food used to be far spicier," Sanistral mused. "Back when you were still nomadic. Hot peppers preserved food then—soon they'll be necessary because mold grows so easily. A pity the reasons change, but the need doesn't. And to think—we still have four hundred years to go."

Math felt a flash of dismay from Kai. He couldn't blame her. The thought of four more centuries of magic growing ever more chaotic and uncontrollable was the stuff of nightmares.

"I'd hoped we'd have more time," Kai murmured.

"Yes, just so," the king agreed. "We were meant to wake centuries ago—the gravers, I mean. We might have prepared humanity. But we trusted poorly, and we were all betrayed." His voice was deep and solemn, but also emotionless.

"What happened?" Kai pleaded. "We had contingency plans. Precautions. How did it come to this?"

"Dear one, you ask for nothing less than the history of modern civilization—inasmuch as that term applies. And I was not awake for most of it. What was it you used to say? In silence, wisdom is knowing the difference between the library and the tomb. Methinks much of humanity's history has been both."

Kai stared at him, a flicker of shock breaking through before she buried it beneath carefully controlled silence. But through the bond, Math felt the crack beneath: fury first, then grief. She reached for her wineglass and drank—slowly, deliberately.

"We'll have that conversation another time, perhaps." Kai set her glass down with precision.

"Maybe it would be best if I told you what's happened," Math said. He didn't understand why the king's evasiveness had shaken Kai so deeply, but it had. She was holding it in, but under the surface, her emotions ran riot.

Sanistral's gaze lingered on her, unreadable, before he turned to Math. "Please do."

So, Math did.

He left out a few things: the telepathic link with the Queens, his often-uncontrolled powers, the Kaliri. He mentioned being expelled from the Order. Sanistral didn't react—his expression stayed exactly the same, as if Math were reciting a lesson, not confessing a crisis.

Only when Math finished did the king finally move, sinking back in his chair.

"What a tragedy." Sanistral sounded melancholy. He pushed his food around—he'd barely touched it—then looked to Kai. "The Queens are at war. And they'll win, because Mathaiik's people won't see the danger in time."

"The Parnathi can look human," Math said. "No one knows the Parnathi can take control of someone without leaving any physical clues."

"We know so little about the Parnathi," Kai said bitterly. "There was a time our species coexisted, but even then, we understood almost nothing. We don't even know how they reproduce."

"Through others, apparently," Sanistral said. "More like wasps than trees."

Math rubbed his forehead. Tri-Mother help him, the headache was already blooming. "What can we do? We need to warn the regent. The empress is a child, but someone has to be told."

"I agree," King Sanistral said. "Fortunately, Rokasmaa keeps an embassy here. We could easily summon your ambassador and explain. But I must warn you—it won't be easy. Your people aren't exactly inclined to think well of Lomar."

"If they suspect this is some kind of trick . . ."

"Then we're lucky it isn't."

Math hadn't expected naivete from the King of Lomar.

"I have a question," Math said. "Unrelated to the Queens, as far as I know. We came through the waystation in the Vormadaak Grasslands, and Kaiataris showed me the map of active ones. I noticed one inside Kaliri's borders."

The king tilted his head. "In the interest of specificity: What is the question?"

"Are the Kaliri using their waystation? Could they travel from their country to the heart of mine at will?"

"Ah." King Sanistral dabbed his mouth with a cloth.

Math waited.

"In short: no." Sanistral's smile aimed for kind and fell short. "The longer answer is that I blocked their access years ago. The Kaliri wouldn't have contented themselves with Rokasmaa."

Math leaned back, relieved.

"That you thought to ask speaks to your patriotism. So tell me—what are you willing to do for your country? Would you let yourself be painted a traitor?"

"Sanis . . . ?" Kai's brows drew together.

"Hush, dear one. Let the young man answer."

Math swallowed. "What exactly are you asking me to do?"

"I'm not asking you to do anything. But I am curious what you *would* do to save your people—even at the cost of your reputation." A look of sympathy crossed Sanistral's face, almost apologetic. As if it had just occurred to him that Math might not have much of a reputation to lose.

"I don't . . ." Math reached for his water glass, mouth suddenly dry. "Of course I'd do whatever is necessary," he said—firmer than he felt.

Sanistral leaned back, the picture of regal ease. "Very noble of you." He sipped his wine and gestured lazily with the glass. "But I wonder—what does 'necessary' mean to a man who has never escaped the nursery? You're no knight. What you have is improvisation. Wit. A knack for surviving under pressure. Useful traits, yes—but not ones a kingdom rewards."

Math forced himself to stay still, though every instinct screamed to leave. "I manage."

"I am sure you do." The king's tone was perfectly warm, perfectly bland. "Still, it's a tragedy, what your order has become. Rokasmaa might have stood among the world's great magical centers—if the Idallik Order hadn't treated magic like a secret recipe. Centuries of knowledge, locked behind walls, vows, and dogma. And now, the biggest obstacle to saving your country is the very order sworn to protect it. Poetic, really."

Math kept his mouth shut. He could already hear his mentors' voices—warning, judging. But none of them were here. Only the man who might decide his homeland's fate over a wine course.

"My order isn't—" The words caught, brittle and weak.

"Your order is," the king said gently, "long past its time. And your reluctance to admit it isn't belief—it's loyalty. They're all you've ever known. And if you admit they've become corrupt, hidebound, bureaucratic . . . what does that say about the years—the loyalty, the dedication—you've given them?"

The air turned heavy. Math looked down at his plate. The steam had vanished. He hadn't touched the food in minutes, and now the sauces had thickened, edges crusting. It didn't look like a meal anymore.

"Enough, Sanis." Kai's voice cut through like a blade. "You cannot possibly think to blame Mathaiik for not seeing the sins of those who raised him."

Math didn't look up, but something inside him shifted. He wasn't used to being defended with such quiet certainty.

He hadn't realized how much that mattered.

Sanistral raised a placating hand. "Dear one, of course I don't blame him. If anything, I admire his willingness to remove his order's sad blinders. If only the rest of his countrymen possessed a similarly open mind." He lifted his glass in a slow toast.

Kai didn't return the gesture. She stared Sanis down across the rim of her wineglass, her grip on the stem tight.

"Sanis, what is your point?"

"We must see clearly—and be willing to make difficult decisions. You know I think the world of you, but you've always had a soft heart."

"Compassion is not a defect." The words were sharp, but what bled through the bond was sharper: fury, insulted pride, and something bruised beneath it all.

"In times of peace? No."

Kai's knife scraped hard against the gold plate. "One should not show kindness or sympathy only when it is convenient."

Math spoke before the argument could deepen. "It's about being willing to make sacrifices."

Kaiataris turned to him, startled. For a moment, he thought he'd misstepped—but then she nodded, slowly, almost grudgingly.

Sanistral beamed. "What a remarkable young man you've found, my dear." He stood. "Perhaps it's time I showed you why sacrifices may be necessary—and what we stand to gain. Kai, I believe you'll find this especially interesting."

Kai raised an eyebrow. "However do you mean?"

King Sanistral smiled. "You and I both know the Queens are only a symptom. The real problem is the solstices."

She studied him for a moment, then inclined her head in agreement.

"We fix the solstices," Sanistral continued, "and the rest will follow. I intend to do exactly that. This, my dear, will be the last celestial cycle this world ever sees."

LIBRARY

King Sanistral took them to a library.

Not a cramped, labyrinthine repository built to hoard books in every available inch—but the library of a king. A vast, multistoried chamber supported by ornate pillars and ringed with catwalks that allowed elegant access to the upper shelves.

In the center of the room stood a wide table strewn with parchment, each sheet inscribed with intricate runes and glyphs. Math recognized some symbols from Kai's work, but these were far more complex—interwoven patterns that pulsed with latent energy. Kai leaned in, studying the sigils.

"Sanis, what is this?" Kai's voice was hushed, her mouth slightly agape.

The King of Lomar lowered himself into a chair. "A great working. The greatest I've ever conceived. So great, I haven't dared to attempt it."

Kai blinked. Her surprise bit into Math, sharp and uncertain. Not just at the scale of the magic, but at Sanistral's admission. "Should I be flattered?" she asked, the anxiety under her words unmistakable.

"Yes, I rather think you should." Sanistral leaned toward Math, lowering his voice like he was sharing a secret. "She is truly brilliant, you know."

"I do know," Math agreed.

"Stop, I beg of you!" Kai's cheeks colored as she waved them off. She took a breath and steadied herself. "Please. You were explaining your working."

"Was I?" Though centuries older than Kai, Sanistral looked boyish for a moment, his grin full of wry mischief. "Very well, since we're here. Unless you'd prefer to browse my collection of historic treaties?"

"Sanis."

He chuckled. "Yes, yes, I know. I can't help myself. So—to business. The foundation of what I propose lies in a discovery: that the magical energies that power the solstices can, in fact, be anchored to physical entities."

Kai's surprise curdled into horror.

Math let out a short laugh—then stopped when the king shot him an irritated look. "Sorry," he said. "But are you telling us you've figured out how to make a *god*?"

Sanistral frowned, clearly aggrieved. "They wouldn't be gods."

"How do you figure?"

"Gods arise from belief—rituals, worship, myth. This would be different. A conduit to the solstice energies, yes—but not divine. Just a wizard, taping directly into the source of their magic."

The king straightened. "Don't you see? Right now, we live at the mercy of celestial tides we cannot control—a cycle of birth, chaos, order, and death. But with gatekeepers—people able to open and close the flow—we could regulate that power. We could keep the world in balance."

Kai folded one hand behind her back, studying Sanistral. "Even if such a thing were possible—and I'm far from convinced—it would require an impossible amount of energy—"

"Monumental," Sanistral agreed. "The undertaking of a lifetime. Many lifetimes."

Kai was worried—Math could feel it, sharp and rising, twisting into fear. And if she was afraid, he had every reason to be. For all her affection for Sanistral, she clearly didn't like what he'd just said.

Math didn't fully grasp the energies involved, but he could imagine their scale. Sanistral would've needed a cadre of gravers—or else decades to channel that power alone.

Maybe not decades.

Maybe centuries.

Just how old *was* King Sanistral? Lomar was older than Rokasmaa, and as far as Math knew, it had never been ruled by anyone who wasn't named "Sanistral."

So . . . there was no Sanistral the Twenty-Seventh, was there? Or Sanistral the Fifteenth or Sanistral the Third. It had always been the same man.

"What do you need us for, again?" Math asked.

"I need Kaiataris to check my equations, of course. I'd hate to have made a mistake." Sanistral gave Math a thoughtful look. "I hope you won't be terribly offended when I say I doubt I'll need you at all."

"Not terribly offended, no."

"But I shall need one of the Parnathi Queens."

Both Kai and Math exchanged a glance.

"Why?" Kai asked, turning back to her mentor.

"Because you can't tie both sources to one person, obviously. I suspect this only works if you use individuals with deep—what's the term your order uses for elemental affinities?"

"Resonance," Math murmured.

"Yes. Resonance. You need people who strongly 'resonate' with each pole, respectively. The return of the Parnathi Queens isn't just timely—it's the key that makes this possible." He waved a hand, too casually. "Convincing them is another matter, but I'm confident we'll manage."

Math shuddered—violently—then realized the disgust and horror weren't his.

Kaiataris's face was a mask, offering no hint of what she felt underneath.

"You would offer such power to the Parnathi Queens." Her voice was soft.

Sanistral looked briefly confused, then deeply chagrined. "Dearest . . . I should have remembered how you feel about them."

"Oh yes. I rather think you should have."

He sighed. "Forgive an old fool. I know this is unpleasant. But consider the alternative."

Math wanted to take her hand—but didn't dare.

"Very well," Kai said carefully. "You would anoint one of the Parnathi Queens—a race that sees humanity as little more than seeds for their reproduction. I don't approve, but perhaps a truce is possible. Perhaps one of the Queens says yes. Who, then, do you propose as the candidate for Order?" Her tone carried just enough edge to suggest she already knew his answer.

King Sanistral smiled. "There's only one person I'd trust with such power. You, my dear."

Kai froze, then swallowed. "Me."

"I don't think—" Math started before he even knew what he meant to say.

"She wouldn't be harmed," Sanistral assured him. "Kaiataris is precious to me—I won't see her hurt. But surely it's obvious: Order should be tied to a graven wizard. And between the two of us, I'm not the better choice."

Math couldn't argue. In fact, this trip was going better than he'd dared imagine. Sanistral had been pleasant, helpful, and unusually willing to take them seriously. He even had a plan—not just for the Queens, but for the deeper problems with magic itself. It was all . . .

It was *too* good to be true.

"You've given me a great deal to consider, my old friend." Kai's expression suggested she'd just tasted something sour—or rotten.

"I'm sure I have," Sanistral said kindly. "But it's not a decision you must make tonight. Rest. In the morning, we'll meet with the Rokasmaa ambassador and see whether this must be done the hard way or the easy."

Kai shot Math a worried glance but nodded. "Yes. A proper bed sounds wonderful."

"Excellent." Sanistral stood. "I'll have someone show you to your rooms."

DOMAIN

They said little on the walk back to their rooms. Each time Math tried to speak, Kai shook her head and flicked a glance at the servant.

He took the hint.

At their doors, awkwardness hung heavy. For the first time in days, Math was clean and shaved—everything he'd thought he'd been waiting for, apart from the tangle of emotions now knotted between them.

Kai shook her head before he'd even reached for her. What he felt from her wasn't rejection, but wariness, suspicion, and a thread of deep anxiety—none of it directed at him.

"Sleep well," Kai said. Her expression was calm, but beneath it, her emotions churned—worry and unease roiling just under the surface. "We'll talk in the morning."

"Don't do anything I wouldn't do."

She gave him an odd look, then disappeared into her room.

As Math stepped into the room, every candle and the fireplace flared to life at once. He nearly jumped.

King Sanistral sat in an open-backed chair at the center of the room, waiting.

"How did you—?" Math pointed toward the door. How had Sanistral beaten him here? Some secret passage?

"This is my domain," Sanistral said, clearly amused. "I go where I please."

"Your domain." Math remembered when Kaiataris had woken—how she'd called the Queens fools for attacking her in hers. A graver's domain was the one place they were guaranteed to have enchanted down to the foundations.

"Right," Math said slowly. "That makes sense. So—what didn't you want to say in front of Kai?"

Sanistral smiled. "She did well in finding you, didn't she? But never fear—I mean Kaiataris no harm. Quite the opposite. I should have expected this. Kaiataris has always preferred unorthodox political systems."

Math eyed him uneasily. "I don't think she's thrilled you made yourself king."

"She's always favored meritocracies," Sanistral mused. "I could argue I'm still upholding that—but I doubt she'd listen." He waved a hand. "None of that matters. What matters is restoring balance to the world's magic—and convincing her to help."

For a moment, his frustration showed, though he masked it quickly. "I had hoped she'd be reassured, knowing I intended her to be the recipient."

"She hasn't said no," Math pointed out—though he had a sinking feeling she would.

"I know her too well. She will refuse."

"I don't . . ." Math perched on the edge of the desk, then quickly moved to a chair under the king's parental glare. "I don't know what I can do. I'm not even sure what the right decision is."

"The right decision will require sacrifice."

"Remind me how nearly unlimited power is a sacrifice?"

"Most of us will not be receiving unlimited power, and the Queens are not easy to predict," Sanistral said, his tone patronizing. "They're not human—and they don't think like us. In order to have them agree to our plans, we shall need to explain those plans. To do that—someone will have to enter their collective mind as an ambassador. Unfortunately, it will be a one-way trip."

Math felt the blood drain from his face.

"You want me to do it."

Sanistral looked mildly surprised. "It needn't be you—but it cannot be Kai-ataris or myself. And whoever takes this on must volunteer, which I suspect will be . . . rare."

"I know someone," Math said. "One of the knights they took. I've fought him several times . . . but we've also spoken. Maybe he could be a go-between."

Sanistral's gaze drifted, then locked back onto Math. "How long ago?"

"How long ago what?"

"Since he was killed and returned as one of theirs?"

"Almost a week."

"Then I'm afraid not." King Sanistral said it with the absolute certainty of a man who made a point of never being wrong.

"Why not?"

"Because what the Queens do isn't resurrection," he said simply. "It's easy to believe their victims return unchanged—but they don't. First, they lose their humanity. Then their memories. Finally, even thought. In the end, they're no more independent than your hand is from your body. By the time you see your friend again, he may not remember you at all. Wait longer, and he won't even know how to say so."

Math thought of their last fight at the train crash—how Huraiik hadn't used his manifested weapon.

As if he'd forgotten how.

Math swallowed. "I see."

"If you're worried about your relationship with Kaiataris, I wouldn't be."

Math looked up, incredulous. "How do you figure?"

Sanistral shrugged. "Because there is no relationship. There never was, and never can be. You're both young, attractive, and have endured together—it's natural to think there might be more between you. But it isn't possible. Even if you don't sacrifice yourself, you'll still be mortal. She will not."

His expression was all compassion and pity—which only gave each word a keener edge. Math hated it.

"I thought you said the recipients wouldn't become gods."

"Again, not in a religious sense."

Math stared at the wall. He hadn't predicted "opportunity to become a goddess" would be one of the obstacles they'd have to overcome.

Though he supposed it would solve the "how to stop people chasing Kai for being a grim lord" problem.

The corner of Sanistral's mouth twitched, as if he knew exactly what Math was thinking—and found it amusing. But the amusement vanished in an instant. "I apologize if this seems patronizing," he said, "but it's merely a clearer view of a problem that was always there. The power imbalance between you was never going to be anything but insurmountable."

Math's breath caught—hurt, then anger. "You're right. That *is* patronizing."

"I've known her much longer than you," Sanistral said. "She's more powerful than you and always will be—because a graver's strength isn't magic, it's knowledge. Intelligence. She's smarter, better, and she'll never settle for second best. Eventually, your pride won't survive that. What do you think she's going to do—set aside all her ambitions in favor of defining herself as your wife and the mother of your children?" He scoffed.

"I think you're getting ahead of yourself," Math said. "We haven't known each other that long."

What stung most was how close the man had come to the truth. Math hadn't dared voice his desires—not even to himself—but after only a few days, he already knew how badly he wanted to keep Kai in his life.

Math shook himself. What a hypocrite he was being. He'd hesitated to start a relationship with Kai because he'd hoped to return to the Order. The least he could do was offer her the same courtesy—the same freedom to follow her own ambitions.

"You share a magical bond, so no—I'm not getting ahead of myself. I'm sure she intended it for someone quite different than a strapping, handsome, earnest young man. Still, the emotional connection must have fallen into place easily enough, helped along by physical appeal."

"That might be the most long-winded way anyone's ever said 'she thinks you're cute,'" Math snapped—then caught himself. "I'm not saying you're wrong about the relationship, Your Majesty. We haven't known each other long. Certainly not long enough to talk about true love—" *Liar,* his heart whispered with every beat. "But the reverse is true, too. It hasn't been long enough to say it can never work. What you are wrong about is thinking I need to be in some superior position. I don't."

He figured Sanistral was simply centuries behind the times when it came to women's roles. Before the Order solstice, Kai had probably defied every expectation of what a woman could be. But now? Women led without fanfare. By the Tri-Mother, a woman was in charge of the Rokasmaa Empire.

"Very well. You don't." Sanistral's tone shifted—something unreadable beneath it. "Nor do I expect you to leap to your doom. As I said, it needn't be you—it just can't be *us.* All I ask is that you not stand in the way of Kaiataris accepting her destiny."

He paused. "And maybe persuade her toward the right decision."

Restless, Math stood and crossed the room to the window. He drew back the gauze curtains and stared out at the city, the Monchlen heat pressing close even at night.

The city's lighting struck Math as strange. At first, he couldn't place why—then he realized: only the streets of Monchlen were lit. In most towns and cities, the glow came from homes—hearth fires, candlelight. But here, the houses were dark. Rokasmaa required every home to hang a lantern outside after nightfall. Some cities were moving to gas, but . . . these lights were the wrong color.

Math shook his head, aware he was letting a tangent distract him—mostly because arguing with a king was a terrible idea. But that was exactly what he was about to do.

"You just told me my pride wouldn't let me be with Kai unless I was in charge—and then asked me to help convince her to do what *we* want. I don't . . ."

He trailed off, frowning as he glanced at the lantern on the wall. It had a shutter to dim the light, but the glow wasn't candle flame. This was something else: pure, steady, white. It didn't flicker at all.

"Am I boring you?" Sanistral's tone had cooled—understandably, given the conversation.

Math's gaze snapped back to the window. "No," he said.

The streetlights—same as the lantern. Some kind of graven magic, probably.

Impressive, really. A safe, steady source of light after dark—who wouldn't want that?

If only . . .

If only there were *any other kind of light* out there. That was what unsettled him. There should've been variation—the glow of hearths and candles, bonfires and forges. This was Lomar's capital. Where were the other lights?

Then there was the noise—or the lack of it. He stood at an open window in the heart of the capital, and heard nothing. No barking dogs. No drunken revelers. No carriages. Just . . . nothing.

In silence, wisdom is knowing the difference between the library and the tomb.

King Sanistral sighed.

"I did try." The chair creaked as he stood. "I was nothing but complimentary over dinner, nothing but helpful. I wanted you both on my side. We could have done this the simple way—but you had to be too smart for your own good."

Math wondered how high the drop from the window was.

"It's irrelevant. The window only looks accessible. In truth, nothing more solid than air can pass through. A basic precaution."

Math's gut clenched. He turned to face Sanistral, eyes wide.

Sanistral's lip curled. "I am in *my* domain," he said. "Here, I am god. Of course I'm reading your mind. Another basic precaution."

The door opened. Half a dozen armored guards filed in, weapons drawn.

"She won't be happy if you kill me," Math said. In hindsight, not the sturdiest rope to hang his life upon.

"No, I imagine not," Sanistral said. "Which is why I suggest you don't resist. You might fight back for a time, but you won't win. Come quietly, and at least you'll keep the hope she'll ransom you with her cooperation."

Math ran the odds. Grim, just like the man had said—pun absolutely intended.

Then Sanistral's words sank in, and Math sneered. The bastard had been lying the whole time, hadn't he? If he meant to use Math to force Kai's cooperation, then one thing was clear: he had no intention of handing her power.

The king smiled. Math knew he was right—and that he'd picked the worst possible moment to realize it.

Worse still, his mind served up something even more damning.

"Let me guess," Math spat, even knowing he was being monumentally foolish. "You lied about the Kaliri and the waystation. They can use it whenever they want—and they've been smuggling people into the country. Just like you're the one handing them those shiny new graved black-powder weapons."

Math expected him to lose his temper. Instead, Sanistral looked delighted. "Now, Math," he chided, tone almost playful. "You were raised an Idallik Knight. Surely you remember who authored the Innalova Accords?"

And then the bastard waited—like he was teaching a class.

"The first King Sanistral did," Math said at last. "Which I guess means you, since there's only ever been one King Sanistral."

"Full marks. Indeed. I'm the one who outlawed such barbarity as black powder and battlefield magic. No *civilized* people should ever fight that way."

The mockery wasn't subtle.

Math clenched his jaw, reminding himself he wasn't standing in front of a defenseless man. "Nicely done," he told the grim lord. "You convinced everyone to outlaw the only weapons that could stop you."

Sanistral chuckled and reached out to tap Math's cheek—managing it, even when Math flinched. "Not all the weapons, my boy. But don't worry: the Queens won't be a problem much longer . . . and neither will your Idallik brothers and sisters."

The grim lord gestured to his guards. "Show our guest to his new room in the dungeon."

PRISONER

Math didn't fight.

He'd seen what Kai could do in her own domain, and Sanistral had had centuries longer to shape his. Sanistral might be godlike here—but even without that, Math was outnumbered, outmatched, and weaponless.

He didn't resist as a guard hauled him off. Along the way, he dug his fingernails into his palms hard enough to hurt—really hurt—and tried to project a warning to Kai.

He had no way of knowing if it worked—or if Sanistral had blocked it.

Math watched his surroundings closely—and the more he saw, the more his unease hardened into dread.

The palace lay in darkness. Only the wing where he and Kai had been quartered glowed with magical lamps. Beyond that, the guards led him deeper—into silence and shadow.

The guards didn't seem to notice.

They weren't the only ones, either. In the darkness, Math heard the faint scuff of feet on marble, the rustle of moving fabric. Servants moved through their routines—cleaning, carrying, working—all in utter silence and pitch blackness, not whispering a word.

Maybe that was enchantment, too—but to what end?

"Be honest," he said to the guards. "Does he make you wear those helmets all the time?"

"Shut up," one snapped.

"Yes," the other muttered.

He nearly tripped on the steps, prompting one guard to curse.

"He can't see," the man complained.

"Of course he can't," the woman snapped. "He's still al—" She stopped herself. "Go pull off a damn lamp cover."

He's still . . . what? Still alienated? Still allowed? Still allergic?

Still alive. *He's still alive.*

The stories made grim lord servants sound mechanical—no longer people, just animated husks obeying commands. But these guards had personalities. Not ones he liked, but still . . . personalities.

The room brightened painfully as a guard uncovered one of Sanistral's magic lamps, forcing Math to turn his face away. The light revealed they'd descended deep into the palace—far enough that no windows could reach. He'd stumbled onto stairs made of unpolished stone, far older than the marble above. They led into a dark corridor carved from the same aged rock. The air smelled stale, laced with the faint, sweet odor of long-decomposed corpses.

Math studied the guards. What once seemed like a bad security flaw—fully concealing uniforms—now felt more sinister. Maybe the helmets didn't hide the guards' identities. Maybe they hid that the guards were little better than animated corpses.

"I could make a light, if that would help," Math offered. Maybe if they let him cast something, he could slip in more.

"Shut up," the man muttered—without conviction.

The prison wasn't too bad—just dark and dusty. It didn't smell like any living thing had been here in a long time.

The guards shoved him into a windowless cell, cooler than the swelter outside. That was its only mercy. He doubted they'd remember he had needs like food or water.

He thought of the city lights and shivered. He knew the answer now. Why weren't there lights in the houses?

Because the dead didn't need them. How many people in Monchlen were still alive?

He suspected he wouldn't like the answer.

As soon as the door slammed shut, he summoned a light—proof he could still cast. The room was small and dingy, but dry, and thankfully corpse-free. The walls were bare, but if he were a graver, he wouldn't make his work visible. It'd be hidden—on the far side of the wall, or embedded within it.

To test the theory, Math cast a first-circle Storm spell to dry and weaken the mortar.

But the mortar resisted. Sanistral hadn't barred him from casting—he'd just shielded his property. Math suspected even chipping a single stone would be impossible.

He thought about what Kai might do—

And realized he couldn't feel her at all.

Logically, he knew she was fine. Logically, Sanistral wouldn't hurt her. Logically, the reason he couldn't feel her was because the damn grim lord had spelled the cell to block it. He knew that.

And still, all he could hear was his own pulse. All he could feel was rage. The only thing that kept him from punching the wall was his memory of watching a knight do exactly that after someone smuggled in a little wine. The fool had been circling Land magic at the time. He broke every bone in his hand.

So Math didn't punch the wall.

Instead, he sat down to study the limits of Sanistral's carefully built prison.

Hours later, Math found a mistake.

The mistake was this: he could still see.

He could still see because his light spell was still functioning. His light spell was still functioning because it didn't affect any of the objects that Sanistral had graved.

The grim lord had made his possessions both indestructible and immune to magic, but *only* his possessions. Math could make himself incredibly strong but still couldn't punch his way out. He could light a fire or manifest a weapon (if only), but he couldn't destroy, alter, or damage the floors, walls, or ceiling.

But he could still use magic.

It was a huge flaw. Maybe it wouldn't have been if he were a graven wizard—he'd have nothing to grave but his own skin, after all—but Math was a wild mage. He didn't need a surface to write on, just belief and imagination.

Tri-Mother. Math shook his head. No wonder the Idallik Knights hammered home the idea that only certain spells should be cast, and only with proper understanding. He couldn't even say they were wrong. He thought of little Hamu, calling lightning from the sky as a screaming baby. How destructive that child could be when upset.

The Idallik Knights weren't teaching how to cast spells—they were teaching how *not* to. Training the wild talent out of novitiates so they could safely interact with society.

So why the emphasis on manifesting weapons? Why was that the hallmark of graduation?

Because you only manifested one. And doing it—*only* it, every time—meant more than control. It meant your mind had been honed into something reliable, predictable—safe.

Math shook his head. He was getting ahead of himself—and distracted. A yawn reminded him why: it was an ungodly hour. He considered stopping to sleep, then dismissed the idea. A first-circle Wood spell would keep him awake for days, if needed.

He couldn't waste time. Come morning, Sanistral would summon Kaiataris and demand her answer. Math needed to be free before that happened.

He knew—because he'd seen Kai do it—that one could magically cross a span without traveling the space between. Dangerous, she'd said. If you couldn't see your destination, you had to rely on complex math to define your exact position in the world.

And yes, that sounded dangerous—probably fatal if you got it wrong.

But what if you *could* see your destination? Kai hadn't hesitated to use her graved jewelry mid-fight. If you could see the endpoint, everything was simpler.

So Math tried to copy her spell.

He'd never created one before—but he wasn't inventing anything. The spell already existed. That was the point.

This wasn't a spell any Idallik Knight knew. The idea that he'd grown skilled enough for higher-circle spells was easier to accept than being able to instantly jump between two locations.

Thinking of it that way didn't help. It still sounded impossible. But maybe it made more sense to treat the land as a single, connected whole. On the scale of a continent, what were ten feet? This spot might as well be *that* spot. Maybe they weren't different at all.

Maybe they were the exact same spot.

Math slumped to the dusty floor and thumped his head against the stone wall.

It was *not* the same spot.

Math slammed his fists into his thighs and tried again.

And again.

And again.

And again.

When he finally got it right, it was so ordinary he almost missed it. The only reason he noticed was the ball of light—he hadn't hung it in the center of the cell.

So when the angle changed, he assumed the light had shifted.

Except it hadn't moved. He had.

He'd driven himself into mental exhaustion—shadows had blurred together, and up looked like down.

That time, when he told himself he was on the other side of the room, his body had said, *Sure. Why not?*

It took half an hour to manage it again.

Then ten minutes . . .

Then he did it twice in a row.

In deference to Kai's warnings about burnout, he was careful not to push too hard. As long as he let his body recover and didn't pull too much power at once, he would be fine.

Strangely, it didn't take nearly as much energy as he'd expected.

By the time he could reliably shift across the room with a thought, it was nearly dawn. A lifetime of early mornings tending chores and children told Math the hour better than any clock.

He was running out of time.

Math peeked through the small window set in the door and laughed. It was dark out there, of course—but he could see, and that was enough. He threw a light spell into the hall. When no one reacted, he flung himself after it.

It felt no different than it had in the cell. One moment he was here—then he was there.

The iron-studded door might as well have not existed.

He was free.

Math grinned, cupping the light spell in his hands to dim its glow. Out of his cell didn't mean out of danger—but it was a start.

Shouting rang out behind him.

At the end of the hall, two armored guards leveled swords his way.

Math ran.

Even if Math outran the guards, he wouldn't lose them—he was the only one running around lit up like a festival cart. He needed to find Kai. In another time or place, a narrow corridor might've been ideal for an ambush—but only if he were better armed and armored.

Math tried to retrace his steps from the night before. A few turns later, he found himself in an unfamiliar corridor lined in white marble. Intricate, gold-filled designs covered every surface.

The back of his neck prickled. Magic pulsed from the carved runes around him. Sanistral wasn't hiding his spellwork here. No—he was showing off.

He had to keep running.

At the corridor's end, Math stumbled to a stop. The chamber beyond was immense—jaw-dropping. If not for the guards, he might've stood there gaping like an idiot.

The chamber stretched vast and vaulted, smelling of spice and decayed parchment. Unlike the rest of the palace, this chamber glowed with its own illumination: globes of light spun overhead in slow, lazy orbits. The walls sloped inward—wide at the base, narrowing toward the ceiling—like the inside of a hollow stepped pyramid.

Which it might have been.

The floor concerned him more than the walls, mostly because the floor didn't seem to be in any particular hurry to meet the walls. Instead, a twenty-foot-wide chasm ringed the room, broken only by a narrow bridge from the doorway to the central platform. The drop vanished into darkness—too far to see the bottom. There was no sign of any water, but a fall like that would kill most people.

Assuming they were alive enough to be killed, he added, thinking of his pursuers.

The central platform was pure white marble. He had no idea what the room was for.

Then he looked up—and saw the bodies.

The sloped interior of the hollow pyramid bristled with iron hooks. From each hook hung a corpse—desiccated, twisted, and unmistakably dead. They dangled like a grotesque tapestry collection.

Math had only a few seconds to absorb the sight before noticing something even more disturbing: there were no other exits.

He was trapped.

CRYPT

"You can't run," the female guard called.

Math had already figured that out. He was cornered in a dead end—a pun he might've appreciated under better circumstances—and now faced two people authorized to kill him for trying to escape. A second dead end, if one wanted to be morbid about it.

Also, the hanging bodies were extremely creepy.

This wasn't a proper ossuary—no scattered bones, no piles of ash. The corpses were whole, well-preserved, suspended like meat in a butcher's freezer. Not a drop of blood sullied the marble. There were too many bodies to count.

Math turned around. "Quick question, if you've got a moment?"

His matter-of-fact tone made both guards hesitate.

"Are you serious?" the man asked.

"As death," Math replied. "Which—speaking of—I have to ask. Are you two still alive?"

The woman laughed, sharp and unfriendly.

They advanced. Math retreated, inching back toward the gaping drop behind him.

"Alive by what definition?" the man asked. "We can think, talk, plan. Isn't that alive enough?"

"It's something," Math said, squinting. "But if I had a sword—which I don't—and I stuck one of you with it, you wouldn't bleed, would you? No heartbeat. No breath. You're kept aware and awake by magic."

The man straightened. "I'm being kept aware and awake by universal forces, the same way you are. You're here as the result of deliberate acts and the consequences of those deliberate acts, exactly as I am. So how am I not alive?"

The woman made a noise of disgust. "Isken, stop it. We don't have time for your philosophy lectures."

"But he said—" The man pointed.

"How hard are you to hurt?" Math asked.

"Wouldn't you like to know?" the woman snapped. "Can we just kill him now?"

But the man—Isken—wasn't ready for that. Math had his attention.

"Practically impossible," he bragged. "Even if you were an expert with that hypothetical sword, it wouldn't matter. We can't die. Stab our organs, we keep functioning. Break our bones, we keep moving. We're *immortal*."

"*You* can die, though," the woman added nastily—and quite unnecessarily.

"That sounds terrifying." Math wasn't lying. If this was what the grim lords had been like—all that and deadly spellcraft besides—it was no wonder they were still feared a thousand years later. "But there's something you should know."

The man scoffed. "And what would that be?"

Math shifted—vanished from one spot and appeared on the other side of the guard.

The man startled, his body reacting before his brain caught up—

And Math kicked him, hard, toward the empty moat circling the chamber. After a few seconds, the man's scream cut off with a distant thud.

Math eyed the woman. He'd known from the start she'd be the problem.

"I really hope he wasn't bragging about being impossible to kill."

"You little gravefucker." Her gauntleted hand tightened on her sword's pommel. "I'm going to enjoy gutting you."

Math kept his eyes on her as he leaned toward the chasm. "You okay down there?"

Cursing floated up from the darkness. A positive sign, he thought. The woman took it as a sign he wasn't paying attention. She rushed him.

He waited until the last second and then shifted his position again.

She stopped herself before falling into the pit, but he doubted she liked how close it had been. "Stop doing that!" she screamed.

"If you insist." He circled a Sky spell for wind.

That caught her off guard. She windmilled her arms comically but, unfortunately, still didn't cooperate by falling into the pit. Her sword did, though—slipping from her grip and vanishing into the dark with a faint clatter. She let out a spectacular curse.

Math felt much better about his situation after that. She was still dangerous, but now she was dangerous and unarmed.

Then two things happened at once, and Math wasn't sure which was worse. First, he heard footsteps pounding down the hallway: more guards.

Second, the corpses hanging from the slanted walls opened their eyes.

DAMSEL

Every hanging corpse opened its eyes and whispered—dry, rasping threads of sound that coiled through the chamber.

They made no move to escape their bindings. They only watched and whispered, as if he was an actor messing up his lines during their favorite performance.

The guard took advantage of his shock.

She'd lost her sword, but that didn't make her harmless. A punch or a kick, he might have dodged—but she grabbed his arm and dug her fingers in with such force he half expected to hear bone snap.

Then she crumpled to the ground.

He nudged the body with his foot, but she didn't react. The armor began shrinking, collapsing inward, as if magic alone had ever held it in the shape of a human.

"Math?" Kai stood in the doorway, lowering her hand.

"What did you do?" He knew they should flee, but he had to know. That had been . . . effortless.

"I erased the graving keeping her animated."

"I didn't see any writing."

She shrugged. "I am well-acquainted with where Sanistral conceals his gravings."

"Nice. But you can't stay. You have to get out of here," Math said, glancing warily at the swinging corpses. It wasn't safe. Sanistral might not track his every step, but Kai was another matter.

"*We* must leave this place," she corrected. "Naturally, we shall—"

Her voice trailed off as she noticed the corpses on the walls, still awake, still whispering. If anything, they were louder now.

"I know these people," Kai whispered, her voice hushed with horror.

Math glanced from the guard's corpse to the mummified ones. "How can you tell?"

"Because I last saw them a few weeks ago—or rather, a few weeks ago, from my perspective." Her expression twisted with grief. Rage followed, slower, hotter. "They are my fellow graven wizards. Those who, like myself, entered magical stasis to preserve what remains of humanity. They should not be . . ." Her eyes widened. "They should not be *here*. How can they be—?"

Rage and horror surged through the bond, raw and unfiltered. For a heartbeat, Math couldn't tell which of them was shaking.

Math reached over and took her hand. The contact dulled the edge—just enough for him to speak. "We need to go. If this is the same pyramid that houses the waystation, maybe we can return the same way."

He was asking a lot, but the guard at the bottom of the pit was still alive—or aware, at least—and Sanistral would come looking soon enough.

They couldn't stay.

Math had questions, of course. How had Kai left the palace without Sanistral detecting it? If not for the fact that he could feel her, he would've thought it too good to be true. He sensed her worry for him wrapped around a core of despair and pain that he hated precisely because he understood its exact cause.

If she hadn't figured out that Sanistral was an evil gravefucker before, seeing all her friends and colleagues pinned up like butterflies surely drove the point home.

She didn't protest.

Math focused on getting them out.

They ran. Stealth was pointless—if Sanistral's people hadn't noticed their escape by now, they deserved Sanistral's ire later. As for Sanistral himself . . .

His absence was a looming avalanche that refused to fall.

More immediate concerns pressed in, so Math focused on retracing their path to the gate. Fortunately, that part was simple: exit the ziggurat, climb to the top.

Suspicion and dread prickled his skin when he saw no guards posted. A flicker of unease ghosted through the bond—Kai's, not his—and it told him more than words ever could.

Math stepped in front of Kai, barring her path. "This is a trap."

"No," Kai corrected. "Or rather, not a trap in the manner you are expecting." At his raised eyebrow, she added, "He is allowing us to escape."

"Why?"

Kai raised her hands over the graved floor pattern. "That is the question, is it not? But our options are these: accept this path, or spend months returning to Rokasmaa on foot. Now then—if you will permit me?"

Math glanced back at the pattern. Kai wasn't wrong. But he was struggling to shake the paranoid—yet rational—fear that this would make Sanistral's work easier. That they were walking into their own destruction or playing into some terrible mistake that would doom everyone else.

What choice did they have?

Math took a deep breath and stepped aside.

Math felt the difference between Lomar and Rokasmaa immediately. In theory, the two places should have been identical, aside from the map on the wall. And yet . . .

Something was in the air, scratching at his senses. The air was easier to breathe than it had been mere seconds and thousands of miles ago.

Kai kneeled beside the pattern and began working another spell.

"What are you doing?" Math stepped outside the pattern's boundary. He had no desire to find out what happened to someone still inside when another portal opened.

"Something that breaks my heart," Kai murmured as she worked, "but I cannot have that man so easily following us."

"You just said he let us go."

"He did."

"Then why would he—?"

"One moment, if you would be so kind." Without waiting to see if he would cooperate, Kaiataris raised her hand. The engraved sigils and motifs on the ground softened, like a wooden stamp used so often its edges wore down. Gradually, the worn spots spread until much of the graving was sanded away.

When she finished, Kai turned back to him. "We are safe enough for the moment. You may now proceed with your interrogation."

A flicker of bitterness passed through the bond—cool, controlled, unmistakable.

For a moment, he wondered if the word had changed over the centuries—grown sharper, crueler. Then he remembered the bond. He had heard "interrogation" because she had meant "interrogation."

"It's not an interrogation." Math crossed his arms—then realized he was doing his best impersonation of Iduan not getting her way and uncrossed them again.

"You wonder if you can trust me," Kai said, bitter and resigned. "If he let us go because I had already agreed to help him."

"More like I want to know if you believed his lies."

"Not a single one." Kai closed her dark eyes. For a heartbeat, Math felt the clash of emotions through the bond—despair, rage, sorrow, all churning in silence. "He was my father in all but name. His betrayal would not pierce me so otherwise."

He wanted to comfort her—to pull her into his arms and shield her from all of it.

Math did not.

"How did you know he was lying?" Math asked. "I only figured it out because he told me—after I refused to cooperate." He hesitated. "They were pretty good lies. I believed him, for a while."

She pressed her lips together, gaze lifting to the ceiling—avoiding him, or lost in memory, he couldn't tell.

"I might have, as well," she admitted at last. "But he made a mistake during dinner. Do you remember when he quoted the phrase carved into the stone of my bower? 'In silence, wisdom is knowing the difference between the library and the tomb.'"

"I remember."

"To me, that phrase has only existed in written form for a week, whereas I suspect he has studied it for so long he forgot the context."

The context being that no one who visited the maze antechamber ever saw the full sentence—only fragments: first, "In silence, wisdom," and later, "—wisdom."

In fact, knowing the full sentence would have made the maze harder. It would mislead a researcher, steer them toward libraries, knowledge, books—all guaranteed dead ends.

"You weren't quoting anyone. Not yourself, not some old proverb. Even if someone knew the beginning, they'd have no idea how it ended."

"I did not mean it as a test. But still—I carved the rest of that sentence myself, just before completing the graving for my slumber." She gazed up at him with those dark, dark eyes. "Math, the only way he could have been so familiar with that saying while forgetting that it had never passed my lips would be if he lingered inside my vault *while I slumbered.*"

Math exhaled slowly. That was . . . deeply creepy. Revulsion surged through the bond, hot and bitter. Not hers—his.

"Wait," Math said. "He can't have been there. That's impossible."

"I assure you, there is no other explanation—"

"You said the bond was supposed to trigger with the first person who entered. That was me."

"Consider: I would require no bond if awakened by one of my death knights. And I would *desire* no bond if awakened by enemies."

"Fine, but how does that—" Math stopped himself.

Oh.

There was a simple way to guarantee that outcome, wasn't there? All her enemies were inhuman or dead.

She raised an eyebrow and waited, nothing of her inner turmoil showing on the surface.

"The first *living* human to enter," he said, the word catching on his tongue. "And he's a grim lord, which means he isn't alive."

She swallowed. "I'm such a fool. I was so desperate for one of my own kind to have survived that I refused to consider how improbable such a survival would be. Clearly, he must have founded his kingdom centuries ago, and graven wizards are not immortal, so the simplest explanation is—" She choked.

"That he died a long, long time ago."

"Yes." Kai's voice trembled with anguish. "And to see the undead—writhing, mutilated bodies of my fellow wizards nailed to the walls—it can only be that Sanistral himself betrayed us. That he broke into each vault, one by one, and murdered our fellows in their sleep." Grief surged through the bond, brittle, bright, unbearably raw.

"But not you." The words tasted wrong even as Math said them.

Several long, piercing seconds passed in silence. Through the bond, Math felt a hollow, echoing quiet.

"No. Not me." Her voice was a whisper. "I am like a daughter to him."

"No," Math corrected before he could stop himself. "You're not."

Kai's head snapped up. "Excuse me?" Irritation flared through the bond.

Math swore under his breath. She had enough to deal with, but he refused to lie. "He doesn't think of you as his daughter. I saw how he stared at you. That was not the gaze of a loving parent."

He gestured at her outfit, sparkling and bandage-tight. "He didn't dress you like a princess. He dressed you like a . . ." Math trailed off. Not a queen. More like a consort.

She grimaced, revulsion twisting her features, disgust roiling through their bond. "He is dead. Any physical passions he may have once possessed have long since been quenched."

"Then it's not lust," Math said. "That doesn't make it better. Greed and obsession work as well. You just told me he's been sneaking into your vault for . . . Tri-Mother knows how long." He met her eyes. "You're not a person to him, Kai. You're *treasure*."

She opened her mouth, but no words came. Horror poured through the bond—thick, suffocating.

"I'm sorry," Math said quickly. "I'm an ass. I shouldn't have—" He shook his head. "I'll shut up."

"No," she said. "I am . . . it is fine. It is better that I face this now." Her hands had curled into fists. She stood so rigidly upright she was in danger of pulling a muscle.

"Regardless of his opinion, my feelings toward him are clear. I thought of him as my father. That he saw me as . . . as . . ." Her voice faltered.

"His due," Math said.

Math felt her horror gave way to indignation and then rage. He welcomed it: better anger than paralyzing grief.

"Yes," she said. "His due, which is abhorrent. I am no one's reward." She gave him a hard look, daring him to contradict her.

"Besides being gross, it implies you're meant to be saved for special occasions." Math pretended to consider. "Whereas any rational person would want your company every day." He hesitated. "Every minute. Every second."

Kai narrowed her eyes, though a faint smile tugged at her mouth. "You need not overreach to impress me. I already think the world of you."

"Ah yes. Your only flaw."

"How soon you forget I snore. Or my love of awful puns." She stepped closer, her voice softening. "Mostly, though, I would not have you speak so ill of my dearest friend."

Math's heart stuttered—but not in a good way. What did she mean by "friend"? After everything she'd endured, she was likely—painfully likely—to be wary of anything resembling a romantic overture.

Her voice softened, almost reverent. "Thinking well of you is not a flaw, Mathaiik Kaven."

"I was just joking."

"No," she said. "You were not."

Kai stepped in, curled a hand around the back of his neck, and drew him into a kiss—too brief, too charged. When she pulled back, her eyes were steady. "I would love nothing more than to spend time convincing you of your worthiness. But there is no time." She sighed and stepped away. "Sanistral will soon follow."

"He can still use the Kaliri waystation," Math said.

She grimaced. "You are right. Naturally, he lied about that as well. We must assume it still functions."

"No need to assume," Math said. "He told me outright."

Kai raised an eyebrow. "Did he?" She paused—then giggled. "Did he truly reveal his plans? Brag about everything he intends?"

"Mostly," Math said. "Could've used more detail. Maybe a map or two. But I'm not complaining."

She brought a hand to her mouth, trying—and mostly failing—to suppress laughter.

"Unfortunately," Math said, sobering, "that's the bad news. Lomar didn't work—so I have to go back to Bashan."

PRICES

The moment they stepped outside, Math saw they weren't alone. "Oltaxath?" He blinked at the Souna warriors who'd evidently never left. "What are you still doing here?"

Oltaxath glanced up from sharpening her halberd. A broad grin broke the severe planes of her face. "What, still? You only left yesterday afternoon. We planned to leave this morning." She pointed at them. "But you came back. That's what matters. I am *very* pleased."

Oltaxath's change in mood since her father's recovery was miraculous. It was as if there were a limited quantity of stern or dour expressions among the Souna. Now that Dulbach was back, he was hoarding the supply.

"And we are pleased that you are pleased," Kai told her. "But that is not why we returned."

"It should be. We'd be a better fit for you than those foolish Avansi." She tipped her head toward Math. "Not you. You're fine."

"Of course. You meant the *other* foolish Avansi." Math doubted he was hiding his amusement well.

"Yes, exactly! Wait—" Oltaxath tilted her head, bemused.

Kai wasn't in the mood for jokes. "Do you always break camp this late?" She glanced at the sun. "Wait much longer, and morning will become afternoon."

Oltaxath's eyes widened as she looked at Kai. She immediately unfastened the pin on her cloak. "Take this. You shouldn't walk around so."

Math stifled a cough. Technically, Kai was dressed, but the fabric was so thin he couldn't blame Oltaxath for thinking otherwise.

Kai ignored the offer and crossed her arms. "We are not here to discuss how I am dressed."

"We gave you good clothes," Oltaxath protested. "How have you lost them already?" She waved a hand. "The wind will go right through that. You'll catch a cold! And you!" She pointed at Math. "How will you ride in that? You'd have to bunch all that fabric at your waist to give your legs enough room. Someone give this person pants."

One man rolled his eyes skyward and muttered something under his breath. Another rider placed a consoling hand on his shoulder. He wasn't the only one bothered by Oltaxath's words.

Math leaned toward Kai. "Why are they mad about Oltaxath giving us pants? We're not taking them from someone else, are we?"

"Oh, no." Kai held back a smile. "I suspect it is the covering up they find objectionable. No doubt some of them were hoping to see you with your robe hiked to your waist." She paused. "I know I was."

"They'll have to settle for the fully clothed version."

"And will I?"

He met her eyes. "No."

"Good."

A flying pair of pants cut the moment short. One of the riders smirked as Math fumbled to catch them.

"Both!" Oltaxath amended. "Both need pants! Don't give me that look—you can daydream about them naked later." She wagged a finger at them. "Shoes will have to wait. We didn't bring extras."

"It is very kind of you, all the same," Kai said, with admirable decorum.

Math expected he'd need to change behind a blanket to guard his modesty, but once the joke wore off, the riders went back to what they were doing and left them alone. He dressed quickly, mourned the loss of his boots, and watched Kai fold her dress and tuck it into a satchel. It was fine enough to sell, should the opportunity present itself.

He tied off a coat that was slightly too large (probably accidental) over pants that were slightly too tight (definitely not) and walked back to Oltaxath. "Are you still here because you were worried about us, or because you were wondering whether it's safe to loot the tower?"

"What an accusation. I would never! The thought hadn't even crossed my mind." She paused. "Is it safe now?"

Math scratched his nose and looked away, barely stopping himself from laughing.

Kai sighed and shook her head. "It is—though perhaps not in the sense you had in mind."

"Let's start with the sense where my people stay unharmed and I leave with whatever's valuable and not nailed down. Is it safe that way?"

"Given that an evil grim lord may emerge from this tower within a few hours, I would say no," Kai said. "I would not stay, were I you."

"Besides," Math added, "I was hoping you might help us out?" Their fastest way to a major city was by horse—and the Souna controlled the horses.

Oltaxath's smile vanished. "Ah."

Math's stomach turned. "What does 'ah' mean?"

The woman turned and started walking toward the horses.

Math and Kai exchanged a look. That was it? She was just leaving?

"Oltaxath?" Math called after her, wondering if he'd have to chase her down.

He didn't.

After about twenty feet, she stopped, cracked her neck with a wince, and turned back.

"The thing is," she said, "we had a deal. It was a good deal—we both kept our ends. But if you're not joining the tribe, and you still want our help, then we need a new one." She looked vaguely apologetic.

Math cursed.

Kai narrowed her eyes. "We bargained for safe passage through your lands. We are still *in* your lands."

Oltaxath waved at their clothing—more specifically, the ornate sandals where boots should've been.

"And yet, somehow, you've journeyed to a far-off place, changed clothes, and returned without leaving that tower. Magic, I assume? Yes?" She leaned in. "Do not insult our growing friendship by pretending otherwise. I am not a fool."

"I could give you the dress I was wearing," Kai offered. "I imagine it is worth a great deal."

Oltaxath perked up—briefly. "Perhaps. But I think I have a better deal for such wonderfully talented people as yourselves."

Uh-oh.

Math scratched his jaw. "And what would this better deal be?"

Oltaxath chuckled, grinning at her people with arms raised in a *you see?* gesture. Laughter followed.

"We didn't set out to rob that metal snake you Avansi send across our land. Our arrival was"—she waved a hand—"an accident. We were chasing a monster that's been tearing up the earth, and we tracked it nearby. It's still out there and it must still be slain."

Math didn't groan out loud, but he wanted to. "This is an emergency, Oltaxath."

She stopped smiling. "So is this. It was bad enough when it was eating our horses. Now it's moved on to people. I think it is what you Avansi call a grimcock."

"Grimmock."

"Yes, that. A grimmock, the size of a large bear." She crossed her arms over the saddle. "Help us kill it, and we'll escort you wherever you're going."

Unspoken: refuse, and they'd get nothing.

Math glanced at Kai and saw she'd followed the same line of thought. He felt her frustration through the bond and gave a small nod.

"Very well," Kaiataris said. "Describe what we will be facing."

GRIMMOCK

They returned to the train tracks—specifically, the site of the Parnathi ambush.

"This is a bad year to be in the train business, apparently." Math's face twisted as he studied the carnage before them.

The train company hadn't wasted time. Judging by the scene, repair crews had come from both directions: two trains loaded with cranes, crews, and likely a mandate to clear the tracks as quickly as possible.

Noise, blood, movement, and warmth had drawn the grimmock like a lion to a wounded gazelle. This follow-up attack had caused significantly more damage than anything the Parnathi tree forces had done.

A massive sinkhole, easily a hundred feet across, had swallowed the tracks, leaving train parts scattered and broken. The twisted edges of the broken tracks jutted into the air like poorly sharpened knives.

There was blood, and signs of something massive clawing at the ground—but no bodies.

The wrecked carriages from the first attack were now on their sides, one of which shuddered with irregular thuds, while a sharp scratching noise filled the air.

"What could make such a sound?" Oltaxath asked.

It was a question immediately answered, although not by their party.

The monster lifted its head from behind the carriage. Not a plant, but a grotesque blend of reptile and mammal—the stuff of nightmares. Six wormlike stalks erupted from the middle of the creature's forehead and swiveled in their direction. A wet-looking black dot crested each tip—something not an eyeball yet functionally similar. The beast snarled as it spotted them.

It was, without question, a grimmock. Several of the horses immediately reared, for which Math could hardly blame them.

"Oh, heavens," Kai murmured.

"That thing's way bigger than a bear," Math muttered.

The carriage had hidden it only because the beast was long rather than tall. In terms of mass, it rivaled one, maybe two elephants.

What sort of animal the grimmock had originally been was a matter for debate. It had scales, mammalian legs, and claws meant for rending. Its rodent-shaped head sported the fangs of a predator—not a scavenger. Then there were those tentacle eyes. Math could not imagine any normal animal with such features.

"Back up," Math ordered sharply. "No one moves in until I say so."

"You are not in charge—"

Math turned on the Souna chief. "Have you fought a grimmock before? Because this is what I have trained to fight for my entire life."

Oltaxath paused, considered his words, and made an *after you* gesture to Math.

Math ordered the group to shift position, keeping their movements slow enough to avoid a chase response, should the monster be the sort to find that irresistible. Kai circled the group, finishing the final carvings to activate their protections.

"Only five minutes," she told Math. "Make them count." She wiped sweat from her forehead, her face paler than usual.

He felt the pull of her fatigue, a tightness in his chest that wasn't entirely his own.

Oltaxath began speaking to her people: "Staying out of its striking range is most important. Be nimble. Be fast. Never stop moving."

A horse's angry scream drew Math's attention—not because it was unusual in the tension-filled atmosphere—but because it was too far away to be part of their group. A quick scan revealed the horse in question, an upset, anxious stallion circling the periphery of the accident site.

Math pointed. "Whose horse is that?"

That wasn't a Souna horse. Even at this distance, its bulk marked it as a larger breed.

"That's not one of ours," Oltaxath protested. "We don't use those kinds of saddles."

But Idallik Knights *did*. Quick on the heels of that thought came a more horrible recognition: that he not only knew those saddles, he also knew this *specific* horse: Inquisitor, Alik Nuhzar's horse.

"Damn," Math breathed out. "They must have sent the Order out to investigate the Parnathi attack on the train."

He saw no sign of Nuhzar or any other knights. No other horses, either. The lack of partially eaten carcasses on the ground—or even torn remnants of saddles and kit—suggested the creature liked to drag its prey to another location, probably a tunnel.

Math eyed the carriage container the monster had been so persistently trying to open and took note, again, of the horse refusing to leave the area even though such bravery put his own life at risk. Inquisitor was every bit as much an asshole as his rider, but he was a very loyal asshole.

Math had a pretty good idea where Nuhzar was.

"Arrows ready!" Oltaxath called out. The group spread out as they carefully rode around the sinkhole and the train wreck to put themselves into position.

So far, the grimmock had paid little attention to them, more intent on whatever lay inside the overturned train carriage. If Math's guess was correct? An injured Idallik Knight.

"Loose!" Oltaxath called out, which seemed to be as much direction as any of the archers expected.

They began firing, while Math watched and tried to judge just how dangerous it would be to move close enough to use his borrowed halberd.

Right away, they learned the scales were considerably tougher than those of a snake. Most of the arrows bounced off, little more than annoyances.

Then someone got a lucky shot off and hit one of the eye tentacles.

The monster howled and whipped around to face the riders. It almost certainly hadn't been able to tell exactly who had fired the shot.

So instead, it attacked randomly. The monster leaped over the downed train carriage and rushed a horse and rider. There was a flash of light as the creature landed on the hunter. Math remembered the talismans Kai had created, and how they would protect against all but the most serious injuries. It didn't take a genius to realize that this qualified as "serious."

Kai's charms would be useless against the full brunt of the monster's attack.

The man tried to dodge, but the creature was absurdly fast for something the size of a house. Math winced at the screams, the cracking bones, the hot spray of blood.

One of the Souna riders called out a name, anguished.

He had to hand it to the Souna, though. Not one of them stopped moving, and none of the horses panicked.

Math had expected the creature to keep attacking the Souna. What he did not expect—what none of them would've suspected—was that the grimmock would return to the carriage and resume trying to claw it open.

Yet that was exactly what it did.

Math met Kai's incredulous gaze even from across the battlefield.

Evidently, the grimmock wouldn't be deterred from its original prey. Even as he had that thought, the creature's claws broke through the cladding on the carriage. It ripped backward, peeling back a section like it was something substantially more fragile than wood and iron.

"Kai!" Math shouted. "Can you distract it? I need to get closer."

She nodded, expression grim and unhappy, clutching a necklace around her neck. She yanked off the chain, holding it up in one hand while she stared at the monster.

Math felt the spike of determination in her like a hot wire across his ribs, followed by fear, and something else—regret? Resolve?

Meanwhile, he jumped off his horse and ran the rest of the way—or as close as he dared without provoking the grimmock into a lethal change of targets.

A white glow started around Kai's fingertips and flowed from her hand to the creature's head. It roared and reared back. Its eyestalks changed colors, first turning gray, then lighter, then the same hue as polished silver.

Math knew in an instant what she'd done—just as she had with Huraiik, she'd silvered the outsides of its eyes, rendering it completely blind. It roared, while its eyestalks thrashed.

That was probably the single most helpful thing she could've done. Unfortunately, several of the Souna must have seen the white magical light from Kai's spell, the silvering of the monster's eyes, and decided that they were unlikely to get a better opening. Two of them charged in with their halberds aimed low.

The grimmock spun, jaws gaping wide. The teeth snapped shut so fast Math felt more like he was re-creating the scene in his head later than watching it happen. The lead rider and half of their horse were simply gone, and blood sprayed over the monster's head.

With a casual, almost dismissive flick of its tail, it swatted the other rider off his horse and sent him flying several dozen feet to land with an unpleasant crunching sound. As bad as that was, the flare of light at the impact and the fact that the stricken hunter was still moving told Math the talisman had partially shielded him, possibly saving his life.

Assuming any of them got out of this alive.

SHIELD

Math focused on shifting himself magically to the entrance of the gaping hole the monster had torn in the carriage's side.

He couldn't see at first—nearly his undoing, as a blast of icy cold grazed his ear.

"Kaven? What are you . . . how . . ." Nuhzar hauled himself upright with effort. "Why are you dressed like a Souna?"

"Really? That's what you're worried about, Nuhzar? My outfit?"

Math eased down the tilted floor toward where Alik Nuhzar had strapped himself to a cargo tie-off.

Alik didn't look great. The armor had done its job, mostly—but the chest plate was gone, ripped clean off. He clutched his gathered cloak to his stomach, where a wide red-black stain had spread.

"Please tell me you're not holding in your intestines," Math said.

"Very well," Nuhzar replied. "I won't tell you." He was pale—from blood loss, maybe shock.

"Now I know you're dying. That's the second joke you've ever made." Nuhzar looked briefly bemused, which made Math swear.

Nuhzar hadn't been joking.

Math dropped to his knees beside him in the cramped space. "You closed the wound?"

"You take me for an amateur? There's internal bleeding."

"Right . . ." Math pushed Nuhzar's hand aside, pulled back the cloak, and lifted Alik's arming doublet. The Idallik Knight didn't protest, although Math couldn't tell if that was because of desperation or just how badly he was injured.

If Math had to guess, he'd say the grimmock's strike had torn off the breastplate with one claw, while a smaller claw on the same paw had opened a gash from the base of Nuhzar's rib cage to the top of his opposite hip. The wound had been closed, but it was still puffy and slick with blood, the surrounding skin bruised and swollen. Nuhzar's breathing was shallow and rapid, his skin clammy.

Closing the wound hadn't necessarily been the best choice—Nuhzar wouldn't have had time to clean it first. Even setting the internal bleeding aside, there was the looming risk of infection. Still, Math would've done the same.

The thing was . . .

The injury wasn't all that different from ones he'd healed before—with Kai, or even himself. If anything, it was less severe.

"What are you trying to do?" Nuhzar's voice was sharp, suspicious—and Math couldn't blame him. Nuhzar knew exactly what Math should be able to do magically, and this wasn't it.

"Don't worry, asshole," Math said. "If I wanted you dead, all I had to do was ride away."

"Fuck you."

Cursing was a bad sign. "I thought we'd established I'm not your type?"

Nuhzar actually laughed—then groaned in pain. "Fuck. I hate you so much."

"You do? This hasn't all been an elaborate courtship? Gods, aren't I embarrassed. Now shut up and let me fix this. We're running out of time."

As if on cue, the carriage lurched as the grimmock slammed into its side. Math forced himself to ignore their impending doom and focus on Nuhzar's injury. Nuhzar, in turn, clenched his teeth to keep from screaming.

A rending, twisting sound tore through the wreckage—coming from the wrong direction. He felt a flicker of Kai's attention through the bond, thick with warning.

Math lifted his head, only to see the carriage wall shift and open into a doorway. Kaiataris stood on the other side.

"Hurry!" she called. "The beast will realize something is amiss at any moment."

True enough. Especially if it hunted by scent, not sight—which would explain why blinding it had not worked. It was possible those stalks weren't eyes at all.

"What—?" Nuhzar protested.

"No time." Math grabbed his arm and hauled him to his feet. As he shoved Nuhzar toward Kai, he said, "He has internal bleeding. Get him to safety and hide his scent if you can. I'm going to lead the grimmock away."

He yanked the bloody cloak away from Nuhzar and wrapped it around his arm.

Math half expected Kai to yell at him, to forbid something this reckless. She did not. Her eyes narrowed as she looked at him, and she visibly swallowed, concern bleeding through their link. Then she placed a hand on Nuhzar's arm.

"If you would be so good, kind sir," Kai said to the knight, "your steed is eager for a reunion."

A terrible ripping sound tore through the other side of the carriage.

"Go!" Math shouted.

"You damn fool," Nuhzar shouted back. "You'll be killed!"

"Have greater faith in your peers," Kai murmured—and then they were gone. She had used her magic to transport them away.

She had cut it close. Math had barely registered her disappearance when the splintering gave way to the grimmock crashing through the iced-over boards Nuhzar had conjured.

Up close, the creature was no more appealing than it had been from a distance—just larger, bloodier, and more dangerous. The gore clinging to its muzzle turned Math's stomach.

Still, Nuhzar hadn't been wrong. A few weeks ago, this fight would have killed Math without question.

It might still. But at least now, he could fight back.

Math tore splintered wood from the carriage walls and shaped it into a shield just seconds before the grimmock struck. The impact hurled him out of the carriage, but the creature couldn't follow.

It slammed into the thorned shield with a shriek of pain, then thrashed—too large to squeeze through either opening. It looked like a fox that had wedged its head into a rabbit warren and couldn't back out.

The shield wouldn't hold the creature for long, but it kept clawing toward him, still mistaking him for Nuhzar.

Math scrambled to his feet. Between Kai's talisman and the shield, he was alive and mostly intact—though his arm was numb from the grimmock's blow. Distantly, the pain echoed back through Kai, muted but horribly real.

"Oltaxath!" he shouted. "Retreat, but stand ready to charge on my command!"

"Look out!" Oltaxath roared in reply.

The grimmock had given up on escaping gracefully. It tore itself free in an explosion of wood and iron, jagged pieces flying in all directions.

Math raised the shield—and noticed it had changed. The vines had thickened, woven tight with flowers and bright green leaves. It looked as fragile as a patch of dandelions, but it had already withstood the creature's fury and remained pristine.

Math waved the bloodied cloak. "Over here! Come on!"

Then he ran.

Math knew right away he wouldn't make it. The grimmock was fast—damnably fast. It would reach him before Math reached the sinkhole.

Math twisted, trying to wedge his spring-green shield between himself and the monster.

His whole body jolted as the beast slammed into him. They went over the edge together.

Math heard someone screaming and wasn't entirely sure it wasn't him. They didn't fall far—the sinkhole wasn't a canyon, just thirty feet deep at most.

Still, the drop gave Math just enough time to grasp how much trouble he was in: he was going to hit the ground with the grimmock landing on top of him unless he did something.

Math slammed into the muddy ground at the bottom of the sinkhole; above him, the grimmock jerked back as vines and branches wrapped around it like a net. The stems constricted, dragging the shrieking beast toward the lip of the hole.

It fought—Tri-Mother, it fought—tearing free from vine after vine, root after root. Claws shredded, muscles strained, but Math kept lashing it, pulling it inch by inch toward the jagged metal beams until, at last, he drove the creature onto the broken train rails.

That *still* wasn't enough to kill it.

"Now!" Math shouted, scrambling backward. "Hit it with everything you've got!"

Oltaxath's riders obeyed.

They thundered past, slashing with halberds, thrusting spears. The grimmock lunged at a rider here, a horse there, but it was facing the wrong way—its arms too short to reach.

Its tail, however, was not. It swept sideways, cracking into a horse's legs. Bone shattered; the beast and its rider flipped behind-over-head. The horse's neck broke with a sickening snap, but Math saw the rider crawling away—then out of sight.

Math scrambled back as arrows rained down. Most struck the grimmock, though only a few found real purchase.

A halberd arced over the beast, landing near Math. From the angle, he guessed the injured rider had thrown it—offering a weapon to someone who had none.

He reached for it—and nearly lost his arm as the creature swiped at him. The talisman and shield saved him, but the shield splintered, and his left arm went limp. It felt broken.

There was no time. The creature was already wrenching itself free of the impaling rails. In seconds, it would be loose—and Math would be trapped with it at the bottom of the sinkhole.

Worse, he was starting to feel the edges of magical burnout.

He feinted once, twice, then darted forward to grab the halberd and scrambled back. Bracing it under one arm, the point aimed at the creature, he resummoned the shield and readied himself for a final, desperate charge. The shield was less for his protection than to brace his broken arm.

He had no illusions about survival—but maybe, just maybe, he could drive the blade through its mouth even as it crushed him.

A voice rang out from above.

Math glanced up and saw Nuhzar at the lip of the sinkhole, still clutching his abdomen, circling Sky.

The world slowed. His bond with Kai lengthened, stretched out, a slowing but grounding pulse.

The grimmock, still thrashing and roaring, moved as if trapped in thick sap. An arrow loosed from the far side of the pit fell in the slow, impossible way that things don't fall. A drop of spittle hung in the air, drifting from the monster's lips as though through treacle instead of air.

Math had never felt anything like it. He had never cast Sky spells that high. The most advanced version—the one that heightened reflexes this intensely—was a closely guarded secret of the Swords section.

Nuhzar had just cast it on him.

"Ggggoooooo," Nuhzar shouted—his voice stretched and oddly lower-pitched.

Math went. He tightened his grip on the halberd and used a vine from the shield to steady the shaft. Then he charged, hacking and stabbing at the creature's face—cutting deep across its nose, cheek, and jaw.

Finally, he found the angle he wanted. He drove forward with all his strength, slamming the shield into the monster's head before he rammed the halberd into the roof of the creature's mouth and up, up, into its brain. Then he twisted, hard.

Math scrambled back, graceless but clear of the creature—and was rewarded with an unimpeded view of its death throes.

The grimmock screamed and thrashed, tearing itself open on the rails, the halberd, and the few thorny vines still clinging to its body. Dirt flew, thickening the air as it spasmed.

Then, with a faint whimper, it stilled. Silence fell over the field.

Math didn't move. He waited, just in case.

But it seemed truly dead.

When the hunters above began to cheer, Math waited, caught his breath, and gave himself a second to recover. When he thought it wouldn't make him burst into flames, he traded his summoned shield for a vine and used that to climb out of the miniature crater. He had to use magic—his left arm was still useless.

Oltaxath met him at the top, flanked by Kai and a still-very-injured Alik Nuhzar.

"Nicely done," Oltaxath said, giving him a nod before turning away to see to her riders.

"You are injured," Kai said. It wasn't a question; Kai cradled an uninjured arm. Despite her own lack of injury, she looked exhausted and worried. It was odd: he would've thought she'd be happy about his survival.

"So, you finally did it." Nuhzar's voice was a sandpaper whisper. "Took you long enough."

Math turned to him. "What was that?"

Nuhzar was pale, sweat beading on his brow. He desperately needed more healing. That didn't stop him from offering Math a tired, surprisingly bitter smile.

"You didn't even notice, did you?" he said. "You manifested a shield, you fool. Shields are *also* weapons."

For a moment, Math felt nothing—just shock, a wave of dizzying disorientation.

He looked down at his broken arm. He'd need healing.

He almost said Nuhzar was wrong—that the shield didn't count, that he'd only shaped wood from the train carriage. That he couldn't have finally reached that final milestone. That he couldn't become an Idallik Knight now—not after he'd finally completely given up on the idea.

Not after Kai.

Except by the end, the shield on his arm bore no resemblance to the original scraps of wood he'd started from—and he knew he could summon it again, even now. He could do it anytime.

Math had manifested his knight's weapon.

It didn't feel like a blessing, not with Kai's despair haunting the edges of his soul. Maybe Nuhzar had said something to her. She must have realized what it meant right away.

Then Nuhzar collapsed, and for a moment, Math envied him.

RECOVER

Math sat on the train tracks, waiting for the Captain of Swords to wake. He watched the Souna tend their wounded and gather their dead. They seemed as upset about the horses as the people, but satisfied with the outcome. Most of them had survived—and they'd have plenty of stories to tell.

Everything was a mess: the train tossed on its side, the earth torn and gouged, the air thick with blood, offal, and smoke. The Souna bickered in the distance, and wild birds called overhead. He wasn't sure if it was truly peaceful, or if he was simply so drained that even the mud looked as inviting as a feather mattress.

He felt hollow. Not from grief, exactly—though maybe that too—but from something more corrosive: the slow, sinking realization that he was about to make a choice he couldn't take back.

Kai stood nearby, arms crossed, black eyes flicking too often toward Nuhzar's still form on a horse blanket. "If we leave while he sleeps," she finally said, "we might save ourselves all manner of hardship."

Math rested his elbows on his knees, head in his hands. "We need his help."

He didn't say the rest aloud—that if Math returned without proof, without someone to vouch for him, the Order would bury him. One way or another.

"Ah, yes," Kai replied. "For he was of such great assistance in Cherkiss, was he not?"

He frowned. The emotions he felt from Kaiataris were even more laced with worry than when he'd fought the grimmock—anxiety, dread, a dense, ugly fear. It didn't make sense. Nuhzar wasn't a threat; he was barely alive. Maybe she feared that lingering there gave Sanistral time to catch up.

Or maybe—maybe she was thinking what he hadn't wanted to face: that returning to the Order—accepting knighthood, if they still offered it—meant severing whatever had been building between them.

"She is not wrong," Nuhzar said hoarsely. "Thank you for saving my life, but I have to ask—why would you?"

"Like I said. We need your help."

Kai made a sharp, disdainful sound in the back of her throat.

Nuhzar's expression shifted—bleak, tired. If it was meant to be a smile, it never quite arrived. "Your grim lord seems to think otherwise."

"I am no such thing!"

"She's not a grim lord, Alik."

Nuhzar raised his eyebrows. "Don't shovel shit on my gravestone. I saw her puppet the dead."

"I refuse to be categorized as part of an organization I did not even know existed," Kai snapped. "Let alone one hunted by the very order that I—"

"Kai, please," Math cut in. The last thing they needed was her revealing the origins of the Idallik Order to Nuhzar.

She turned on him with eyes full of fury, betrayal, something deeper, but stopped herself mid-breath before giving voice to those emotions. Without a word, she turned and stalked off toward Oltaxath.

He watched her go, the urge to stop her lodged like a stone in his throat. But the words choked off inside him. Guilt twisted in his gut, sharp and relentless. He was doing the right thing. The Order had to be warned. This wasn't about him—or her. It was about saving the empire.

That didn't stop it from feeling like a betrayal.

Nuhzar followed her with his eyes. "I admit, when I think of a necromancer, hot-tempered spitfire is not the image that comes to mind."

"Yeah, well . . ." Math dragged a hand through his hair. "I'm not here to talk about her. I need to talk to you about . . ." He hesitated, then gave a short, humorless laugh. "Maybe the Tri-Mother really does send trouble in threes. I need to talk to you about the tree people, the Kaliri, and a grim lord."

Nuhzar gestured toward Kai. "But you just said—"

"Not her. A real grim lord. There is one."

"Gravespit."

"No. King Sanistral of Lomar. He's one of the originals—over fourteen hundred years old. And while I suspect he'll skip invasion and go straight to godhood, he's helping the Kaliri arm themselves with some very nasty weapons."

Nuhzar stared at him like he'd started speaking in tongues.

"How do you know this?"

"He told me."

"You haven't had time to travel to Lomar and back."

"There's a portal network—older than the Age of Bone. One links Lomar and Rokasmaa. Kai sabotaged it, but there's another to Kaliri, so it's only a delay."

Nuhzar inhaled deeply. "I suppose that merits a thank-you. But that's only one calamity. You said there were three."

"Then there are the Parnathi—the Tree Queens and their followers. Have you run into Huraiik yet?"

Nuhzar gave him a flat look. "Huraiik's dead."

"You'd think so, right? But when the Queens kill someone, they can... absorb them. Memories, skills—everything. I've fought a plant version of Huraiik. Twice. And he didn't just look like him—he could manifest his sword."

"You're mistaken."

"I'm not. I've killed him *twice*. Pretty sure the second time held. But he won't be the last. They've taken down a lot of knights."

Nuhzar's expression shifted—from skepticism to nausea. "Can you prove any of this?"

"No. Of course not." Math pulled a bundle of letters from his belt pouch. "The only thing I can prove is that we have a Kaliri spy in the Order. Someone at Isofal survived the attack. Captain Qin had the first two letters. One of his killers had the last."

"Let me see those," Nuhzar said, and tried to sit up.

"Stop that. You're going to start bleeding again. You know, this is why healers growl whenever Sword section knights walk into the Halls of Mending," Math muttered, already moving to help. "Let me."

Once Nuhzar was upright, he opened the letters. His hands shook slightly, but he read them in silence. At the last one, he paused. Frowned. Circled something—probably a translation spell—and read it again, slower this time.

It might've looked like an inventory list, if not for the way his jaw locked and stayed that way.

"And you're saying Sanistral is working with the Kaliri?"

"Yeah. You found those black-powder weapons at the ambush site, right?"

Nuhzar nodded. "We did. Concerning, but not panic-worthy. They can't be that accurate. We train on how to deal with black powder."

"You're wrong," Math said flatly.

Nuhzar's eyes narrowed. "Come again?"

"Not very accurate?" Math scoffed. "They never missed. Not once. Did you think all those holes through our knights were just lucky shots?"

Nuhzar stared.

"What?"

"Math," he said, voice gone quiet and flat. "There were no bodies."

Math sat very still, pulse racing. "What do you mean, there were no bodies?"

"Do you need one of the children to spell it out?" Nuhzar said. "We found the cart. The horses. Those strange metal tubes. A lot of blood—but no human remains."

"Then how did you know I wasn't dead?"

"Circumstantial details and a hunch. Your shackle was unlocked, but there were no signs of violence. Blood pooled around the back of the cart, but none inside. Someone had tossed Qin's scrying stone into the woods. No one but a member of the Order would've thought to do that."

"The Queens were right behind us," Math said quietly. "They must have taken the bodies."

He lowered his head. He didn't know why he'd ever thought they needed to make the kills themselves. Of course they didn't. They must've been thrilled to stumble on a pile of fresh, perfectly good human corpses. No doubt they'd be meeting plant-versions of Captain Qin and the other knights soon enough.

Neither man spoke. The silence stretched—long, taut, close to snapping.

"The weapons," Math said at last. "You found them at the site. That's evidence."

"Of what, exactly?"

"That there's a grim lord helping the Kaliri. Every one of those weapons is engraved—enchanted—in the old grim lord style. It looks decorative, but it's not. And you don't have to take my word for it—we must have samples somewhere in the archives. Or, if you don't feel like waiting until we reach a cenobium . . ." He pulled a small object from his pocket and held it out. "Here. Look at this bracelet."

He kept forgetting to give it back to Kai.

Nuhzar took it and turned it over, studying the etched lines. "What does this one do?" Nuhzar asked.

"Oh. Um. It doesn't do anything now, but it used to create an illusion. That's how you might've gotten reports of Captain Qin strolling into the Sounalla train station."

"I wondered how you pulled that off."

"Point is, Sanistral's behind those enchantments. And since these weapons can only be used by mages, don't assume your standard anti-black-powder drills will cut it."

Nuhzar's brow furrowed, but he didn't interrupt.

"I saw it with my own eyes, Alik. They weren't using match cord to set off the black powder. They were using magic."

"I believe you."

"But—?"

"There is no 'but,'" Nuhzar said, dry. "Just thinking—if they're already breaking the Innalova Accords, why stop halfway?"

Math huffed. "Funny. That's what I said."

Nuhzar exhaled through his nose. "So. We've got tree people who can suborn the dead, and a grim lord who's a head of state arming our worst neighbors with enchanted weapons. That about it?"

"Not exactly," said a voice behind them.

Kai had returned. Her posture was composed, but her words came cold and sharp. "You have yet to account for the part where Sanistral must capture one of the Queens to complete a ritual that would grant him godhood. I've little doubt this business with the Kaliri is merely a distraction—meant to ensure no one who might stop him is prepared to do so."

She fixed Nuhzar with a look so pointed it felt like a blade.

Math sighed. She was still angry. Of course she was. But even as her voice turned clipped with disdain, he felt the weight beneath it. She had figured it out—not just the tactics or the stakes, but what he was planning.

Nuhzar narrowed his eyes. "How do you figure into all this? You show up at the perfect moment, and I'm supposed to believe that's coincidence?"

"Do they not teach the members of your order basic logic?" Kai snapped. "I am here because you woke the Queens. They assailed their attackers, and as a result, Math unlocked my maze out of desperation. None of that was coincidence. Nor would any person of sense claim it to be."

"The fact that Kaven just happened to know how to unlock—"

"Nope," Math said, shaking his head. "Trying to research the Queens is what led me to the solution. It wouldn't have happened otherwise."

Kai lifted her chin. "Are you satisfied we did not save your life merely to deceive you, or shall I fetch ink and parchment and draw you a diagram?"

Nuhzar squinted up at her. "What is your problem, witch?"

"Rather, I should ask—what is yours?" she retorted. "Why do you treat Mathaiik like something scraped off the bottom of one's shoe?"

"I don't need you to defend me, Kai." Math hadn't meant it to sound cold, but it landed fast and flat.

She gave no outward reaction, but tension rippled through her. Still, her voice stayed calm. "I want to know."

Math expected Nuhzar to brush her off. Instead, the knight surprised him. "Because he's a spoiled brat."

"Excuse me?" Math wasn't sure who to glare at.

"You're a spoiled brat," Nuhzar repeated, unbothered. "You've had everything handed to you. Special treatment from the moment Talu dragged you to Isofal. You're not even a knight, yet you're allowed on missions. You've stayed a novitiate years past when anyone else would've been sent to the monks. And then there's what you were doing to the children—"

"What I was doing to the children?" Never mind. He knew exactly who to glare at. "Excuse you?"

"No. Excuse *you*." Nuhzar's voice darkened. "I told Talu time after time that it didn't matter how good you were with a sword or how competently you rode or how you were so skilled at magic that the moment you finally manifested a weapon, you'd skip knight and go straight to lieutenant. I *told him* that he either needed to knight you or take you out of the field."

Nuhzar took a breath, jaw tight.

"It wasn't fair. Not to those kids, watching you vanish for days at a time. And not to you—put in charge of them, then sent on missions where you'd be forced to—"

He stopped. Looked away. Drew a slow breath.

Kai's voice sliced through the silence. "Forced to do . . . what?" She already knew. Math felt it—her dread blooming slow and sharp.

"The Order exists to kill anything classified as a grimmock," Nuhzar said.

"And if children meet that definition?" she whispered.

"I said what I said."

Her hands curled into fists. Math felt the sting of her nails biting into her palms.

"And you dare call me a monster," she breathed. Then she turned to Math, eyes dark with betrayal. "And you—!"

"Leave him alone, witch," Nuhzar said. "He refused the order. That's why he was punished."

"Talu said—" Math's mouth twisted as he searched his memory. "He always made it sound like you thought I was incompetent."

"I complain that you don't follow orders. I complain that you shouldn't be in the field. But I've never once complained that you're *incompetent*."

Math rubbed his face. "Oh."

"You never should've been sent out there—"

"You're right," he said.

Nuhzar blinked at him.

"You're right," Math repeated, softer. "I was being selfish. I didn't want to be a failure. I wanted to manifest my weapon. And most of all, I wanted to prove I hadn't been lying about what happened to my parents. So I kept pushing. Hoping I'd find something, find proof."

The words came too easily—like something long dammed-up, now spilling out.

"I'm not your confidant or your new best friend, Kaven," Nuhzar said. "I don't care why you acted that way. Only that you did." Before Math could make any rude gestures, he continued, "However, I do care that Talu's been lying to you about my reports. Has he mentioned them before?"

"All the time," Math admitted. "Never anything good."

Nuhzar scoffed. "Well. At least now I know why you're always such an asshole to me."

Math blinked. "Wait. I'm the asshole?"

"Good of you to finally admit it."

"If you weren't injured—"

"If I weren't, I'd kick your ass. Same as always."

"Gentlemen!" Kaiataris cut in, sharp and imperious. "If the two of you have concluded your juvenile posturing, perhaps we might return to the matter at hand."

Math exhaled and rubbed a hand across his brow. "I already told you, Kai. I'm going back to Bashan to make sure the Order knows what's happening."

Even saying it made something in him ache. The words felt heavier than they should.

Kai pointed at Nuhzar. "You have already told the Order. Let him explain it."

"That makes it hearsay," Math said. "I'm the one who saw everything. The one Sanistral confided in. It has to be me." He tried to offer her a reassuring smile, but it landed crooked. Hollow. "I'm not going back alone. We have evidence. And if the captain vouches for me, I'll be fine."

"You will not," she replied, voice cool but brittle. "You may be innocent of what they accuse you of, but you are not innocent of running. And innocence is no protection from dogma."

She wasn't wrong. He knew that—had thought it over, again and again.

The Order wouldn't accept secondhand testimony, not when compulsion magic used on a witness was the gold standard for proof.

It had to be him. The only other option was a woman infamous for being the villain of countless children's stories.

And if he didn't go back—if he ran now—he wouldn't just fail to stop Sanistral. He'd be giving up his only chance to clear his name. He'd never be able to stop running. And he'd never see his sister or the kids again.

But Tri-Mother, this hurt. What he was about to lose burned at his soul.

"It's his decision," Nuhzar said. "Not yours."

"Be silent," Kai hissed, eyes flashing. "I had begun to think you might not be entirely detestable."

"And I'd begun to think you might not be entirely useless," Nuhzar replied. "We can both be wrong."

"Stop it," Math said, turning to Kai. "Please. I know you're upset. But unless you have a better plan, I don't see another option." He looked down at Nuhzar. "And Alik—try not being a mule's ass for five minutes. I know you've never done it before, but it'll be character-building."

Kai drew a shuddery breath and turned away—too slow to hide her expression. Her pain radiated like heat. Math felt every inch of it, but there was no path forward that didn't end in loss.

Just for a second, he wished he'd never met her.

Math stepped toward Nuhzar. "*Don't* get up."

"Why? What are you—"

"Captain Nuhzar of Swords," Math said, his voice formal, controlled. The title landed with intent. Nuhzar's attention snapped to him, sharp and wary.

"I'm offering to return—freely and without resistance—to testify about a far greater threat to the empire. But in exchange, you'll let Kai go. You won't try to bring her in. You won't mention her."

Nuhzar shook his head slowly. "You know I can't promise that."

"Then I'll knock you out, ride off with the Souna, and you'll never see me again." As bluffs went, this one was painfully transparent, but Math hoped it gave Nuhzar the excuse he needed to cooperate with a clean conscience.

Math pressed on. "Damn it, Alik—according to plant-Huraiik, she's the only human the Queens think can stop them. Sure, that's probably because they don't know Sanistral's still around, but if you're putting your faith in him"—his mouth twisted—"that's like asking a lion to save you from a hyena. At the end of the day, you're still the meal."

Nuhzar's eyes narrowed. He studied them both, then exhaled sharply. "Fine. I won't mention Kaiataris Von. But she's still coming with us. Congratulations, witch—you're now a Souna shaman who's graciously offered to testify." His gaze shifted back to Math. "If she's that important, we don't leave her behind."

"I don't want to leave her," Math said. "But I refuse to drag her along to her death, either."

"That is not your decision," Kai said.

They both looked at her.

"It is not your decision," she repeated, quieter now. "It is mine. And he is right." She nodded toward Nuhzar. "You won't have time to find me if you need me. Nor after you've taken your vows and become a *knight*."

The air around Math felt too thin. He stared into her eyes and finally understood.

The problem wasn't Nuhzar. She didn't care about him. The problem was the Order. The vows. The system he was about to step back into. A system that would never—could never—accept her. Not as a Souna. Not as a necromancer. Certainly not as a romantic partner for one of the Order's members.

She understood the risk every bit as much as he did. This wasn't theoretical.

This was happening here, now, and this might be the last time she stood close enough to touch.

But how could she ask him to walk away now? How could she expect him to give up the one shot he had at truth, at absolution, at being seen as something more than a liar and a failure?

She had to feel it, right? That he wasn't abandoning her, that he didn't want this choice? But he wasn't sure whose despair he was feeling, whose grief.

"I rather doubt I'll be knighted after all this, Kai."

"And if you are? If they offer it—what will you do?"

The answer lodged in his throat. He didn't know. And he couldn't lie to her.

Nuhzar cut in before he had to. "Figure it out on the way," he said sharply. "Because the time for negotiations is over. You stay with us, witch—or you run. Which is it going to be?"

He gestured east, toward the railroad tracks.

Dust rose on the horizon, spreading fast.

Math didn't need to guess. He knew the signs of an Idallik travel spell. The reinforcements had arrived.

DELIBERATION

When the Souna realized the Idallik Knights were inbound, they left so fast it almost seemed like magic of their own.

Kai stayed.

Math stood there, awkward and uncertain—unsure whether he'd be arrested or attacked—feeling out of tune with his life. He didn't know who he looked more like now: a soldier, a prisoner, or a ghost of both. Not long ago, he would've come in riding on those same horses, wearing the symbol, bearing the same confidence.

And now, none of that was true.

At Nuhzar's insistence, Math helped the man to his feet to greet the knights. He stood slightly behind and to the right—this time for two reasons: first, to avoid seeming like a threat, and second, in case Nuhzar collapsed.

The knights noticed Math. Immediately, they tensed.

"It's fine," Nuhzar said. "He's in my custody."

"But Captain, isn't he—?"

Nuhzar's tone turned sharp. "He single-handedly killed that grimmock and saved my life. If he wanted to escape us, he would have left. We need a horse for him. Did you bring spares?"

The knight was taken aback for a moment, but then straightened in her saddle. "Yes, Captain, but—" Her eyes landed on Kai. "Who's this?"

Nuhzar grimaced. "Oh, right. I almost forgot." He snapped his fingers and pointed at Kai. "What's your name again?"

Kai hesitated for a brief moment, and then said, "Xiscu."

Math managed not to choke. Xiscu had been the name of Kai's horse. It meant "trouble."

"This is Xiscu. She's a local tribal shaman. I've convinced her to come back with us and give witness before the Council." He sighed. "She'll need a horse, too."

The woman bowed and left to find those spare horses.

Another knight rode forward. Math knew just from the way the woman carried herself that this was also a captain. Of course the Order would've sent one to check on Nuhzar's group when they had failed to report back. The pin on her cloak was the wheat sheaths and roads of a Captain of Fields, which meant that she was responsible for shortening the journey. Math wondered if she was from the closest cenobium, or from Bashan itself.

"Tri-Mother help us," she muttered. "What *happened* here?"

"That." Captain Nuhzar gestured toward the still-bleeding corpse of the grimmock hanging off the broken rail lines like meat on a butcher's hook. "I suspect the vibration of the machines working to fix the track caught its attention. These trains didn't crash as much as they were thrown. Unfortunately, the attack caught us off guard."

"Very skilled ambusher," Kai said, adopting the patchwork accent of someone unfamiliar with Ginren. "That monster has raided our herds for weeks. Killed anyone who came too close."

The woman frowned at Kai, although not in an unfriendly fashion. More like Kai had presented her an interesting challenge. Whatever her conclusion, the woman nodded in acknowledgment of Kai's words and then turned back to Captain Nuhzar. "What about the rest of your unit?"

Captain Nuhzar glanced toward the grimmock's body. "Eaten. As I almost was."

The other captain's eyes narrowed. It wasn't difficult to tell that she was coming to unflattering conclusions about Nuhzar's survival.

Nuhzar didn't leave off there, however. "Now we must return to Bashan as quickly as possible, because we've discovered a threat which must be reported immediately."

"What kind of threat?" the captain questioned, sparing another glance at the giant grimmock corpse.

"A grim lord."

Everyone stopped talking.

She regarded the Captain of Swords sternly. "Are you serious?"

"I have never been more serious about anything." Nuhzar didn't once glance at Math or Kai, didn't once indicate that this was anything less than absolute fact.

A strange expression came over the woman then. Math might have almost described it as excitement. She gestured to one of her people. "Bring some horses for our brothers. We ride for Bashan."

"Kudawan," Nuhzar corrected. "If you wouldn't mind. I'd prefer to clean up before we reach Bashan."

She scoffed. "Sure, and who knows? Maybe you'll be a rebel and actually let a knight of Mending tend your wounds. Frankly, I'll be surprised if you can even stay in the saddle for the trip. On that note . . ." She raised her voice: "Where's our healer? We've got a live one over here."

She was observant, at least.

Math kept his expression passive. He didn't look at Kai. He didn't betray his thoughts.

He could only pray.

Math was quiet for most of the ride back to Kudawan. The captain's movement spell was sedate, as such things went. The horses kicked up sand as they traveled, even though there was no sand to be found anywhere nearby—and hadn't been for centuries. He didn't know how to speak to anyone without risking some horrible secret or heresy slipping out.

He especially didn't know how to talk to Kai. He wasn't sure if she was avoiding him.

He suspected she was.

"The children are fine, by the way."

Math raised his head to see that Alik Nuhzar had pulled his horse up next to him. "Are they?"

Alik's left eye twitched. "I think so. The oldest boy—Jaiik?—I saw him briefly before I rode back out, chasing after you." He stared ahead across the open plain, not looking at Math. "No one was crying."

"Is that your only yardstick? Are they *crying*?"

"No," Nuhzar answered. "Of course not. I made sure none of them were injured."

Math resisted the urge to roll his eyes skyward. Still, knowing the children had survived unscathed was a relief.

And thinking about them was easier than thinking about Kai.

"You'll find out for yourself, soon enough."

Math paused. "I will?"

"They've all been moved to Bashan. Your sister, too. You'll see them when we arrive."

"That's good." Math nodded, maybe a little too firmly. "I'd like that."

But the words felt like a borrowed truth—something he was supposed to say, not something he fully believed. Something in his tone must have struck Nuhzar wrong.

"Do you want to return to the Order?"

"What kind of question is that? I'm here."

"You're here to warn our leaders about not just one, but three dire threats. That's not the same as wanting to rejoin our ranks."

Math's heartbeat picked up. "Is rejoining even an option?"

"Perhaps. If we can confirm your claim about Sanistral. If Talu's reasons for expelling you prove unjust. If your warnings about the tree people—"

"The Parnathi."

"The Parnathi. Fine. If these warnings hold water, you manifested your weapon and comported yourself with distinction. You saved an Idallik captain's life." He hesitated. "You saved my life."

Math glanced at him. "You didn't strain yourself saying that, did you?"

"Feels like I cracked a rib," Nuhzar answered, deadpan. His next breath was shallow enough to back it up. "What I'm saying is, if you prove under oath that you're not a traitor, I'll see you knighted. If you want it."

Math's throat turned dry.

It was everything he'd ever wanted—everything he'd worked for, dreamed of. "Of course I want that." The words left his mouth before he could stop them.

He wasn't lying. But it wasn't the whole truth. He no longer wanted *only* that. It had been his only goal for so long, what he'd chased after his whole life. And now he'd known this woman for less than a week and suddenly . . .

Nuhzar wasn't looking at him. Math followed his stare. Perhaps unpredictably, it ended at Kai. Math had a feeling he knew why Nuhzar might not think his claim was serious.

"It would help your testimony if you made it as an Idallik Knight, and not a novitiate," Nuhzar said, still staring at the graven wizard.

"I imagine so, yes. And Alik—" Math stopped himself. "I mean, Captain, you should know that when Sanistral was bragging about his schemes, he mentioned 'doing something' about the Idallik Knights. We're not bystanders in this. We're targets. So yes, I want to be a knight."

"Good to know." Finally, the man stopped staring at Kai and focused his attention on Math, the road, their destination. "I'll help make your case in Bashan."

With that, he nudged his horse forward, riding back toward the front of the column. Math watched him go, unease curling behind his ribs. He didn't know if he'd made the right choice.

He only knew it was made.

Alik Nuhzar continued to treat him with that gruff, hard-edged kindness Math didn't know how to accept. Never one for soft words or easy smiles, Nuhzar made sure Math had time to visit a bathing chamber, to shave, and to transform himself into something closer to what a member of the

Idallik Order ought to look like. A cheerful young novitiate—who likely had no idea Math's standing was anything but pristine—brought him clean clothing, socks, and new boots.

Yes, Nuhzar hammered on the door and shouted for him to hurry before he'd even finished dressing, but he hadn't needed to give Math the chance to clean up. He could've made him ride into Bashan looking like he'd rolled through dirt and blood. Then again, Nuhzar would've looked the same, and this gave him the excuse to see different healers before reporting to the capital. If Math tried to thank him, he was sure Nuhzar would blame it on the local captains being too soft.

Math didn't mention it.

The trip back was fast. This time, their horses all turned to fiery hues, hooves sparking against the road with every step, each strike ringing out like a hammer against a forge. The sound made conversation impossible—and for once, Math was grateful. He wasn't ready to talk to Kai. Coward that he was, he felt torn in too many directions.

They reached Bashan in record time.

Bashan was not the empire's largest city—that was Okiakosaa—but it was the seat of royal power and the birthplace of the imperial line. Great effort had been taken to preserve its elegance. Church minarets glowed in the light of the setting sun. No building rose higher than three stories, ensuring the palace walls remained visible from any point in the city. The streets were broad and paved in crushed stone that muffled carriage wheels. Flowers bloomed from window boxes and roadside verges. Gas-fed lamps lined the roads—at night, there would be few shadows left in which a thief could hide.

Chestnut, oak, linden, and willow trees shaded the streets and clustered in lush parks. Once, Math might have found that comforting. Now, the trees set him on edge.

Bashan had begun as a walled cenobium like Isofal and most others, and had set the standard by which other towns grew—first from knowledge, then from necessity. In most cities, that cenobium remained a stronghold of the Idallik Order. But not here. Here, it had become the imperial palace.

As a result, the Order's headquarters had been built separately, at the base of the hill beneath the palace's white walls.

Math wasn't immune to its beauty. He was proud to be a Rokasmaan citizen, proud of what the empire had accomplished. It wasn't perfect, but it was better than anything else he'd seen. They were a light in a world gone shadowed. He still believed that.

And yet, as they rode through the wide avenues, he saw ugly expressions on the faces of the people watching them. Resentment. Disdain. A few openly glared.

This was Bashan. The capital. The heart of the Idallik Order.

If the Order wasn't welcome here . . .

He brooded on that until they passed under the white marble gates of the Order's headquarters. After that, his thoughts were occupied by more immediate matters.

He needed to speak with Kai. He knew he did. They had too much to talk about, and Math had no idea how to articulate everything he was feeling.

Alik was probably right to think Math was a coward, though.

Instead of searching for Kai, Math went looking for his sister.

Math couldn't find his sister.

When last Captain Nuhzar had checked, she'd been assigned to Bashan Cenobium. Now, no one knew what had happened to Tanxi or the children. Some claimed she'd returned to Isofal, others that she'd moved to another cenobium—or left the Order entirely. Aside from Nuhzar, Math didn't know many of the knights here. None of them were from Isofal.

It was almost a blessing. No one recognized him—so no one was calling for his arrest, either.

The cenobium itself was overcrowded. Knights slept in corridors. Math spent the day searching for any trace of Tanxi or the children—without success. The Master of Novitiates gave him an unfriendly sniff and claimed she couldn't possibly know. The children in the Hall of Novitiates weren't any more helpful.

Math didn't know where Kai was either. Given the state of the place, he assumed they'd housed her in a nearby hotel.

That afternoon, Nuhzar found him and pulled him aside for a magically enhanced debriefing—likely to confirm he wasn't a traitor before wasting any commander's time.

His interrogators were thorough. Math had to thread a hundred needles to avoid incriminating himself. They asked about the woman in Cherkiss. He told the truth: her name was Kai, and he'd met her outside Sounalla, where he'd rescued her from one of the plant creatures. No one made the connection to the infamous necromancer. They were more interested in whether he'd slept with her.

He confessed he hadn't. Fortunately, no one thought to ask if he'd wanted to.

After a long, exhausting session, they released him. He had no idea whether or not he'd passed. He was optimistic—but also under orders not to leave the cenobium.

He was left in limbo until the Council of Commanders agreed to see him. Alik Nuhzar had no idea when that would be.

Math felt like a wildcat in a tiny cage.

He could've spent the time training—sparring, manifesting his shield, preparing to perform for the commanders. Instead, he went to the library.

The Bashan repository held more on Kaiataris than Isofal had, but still nothing from a primary source. Just fairy tales and horror stories written long after the fall of the grim lords. No surviving texts from when Kai had lived. No facts. Just myth.

Which made sense if one considered that she had slept through the entire Age of Bone.

These were stories about grim lords, not the graven wizards who had preceded them.

There were no books about those.

It had to be intentional. The grim lords would have had access to all the repositories and archives created by the graven wizards they'd usurped. It would have been simplicity itself to erase any mention of their living predecessors.

If there was one lesson that any Idallik Knight knew, it was the importance of controlling information.

On the third day, the commanders finally called for him.

JUDGMENT

The meeting felt like a strange replay of when he'd last been summoned before the captains in Isofal. The size of the room, the flickering personal lights of the attendees, the way he stood just behind and to the right of Alik Nuhzar—it was all eerily familiar.

Math scanned the assembled group before ducking his head back down in proper deference. There was one major difference, of course. The only difference that mattered. These were not captains.

The gathering here consisted solely of *commanders*. The commanders of every cenobium in the empire.

It was both terrifying and comforting. Terrifying in that their judgment would be final. Comforting in that this meant they were taking the matter seriously.

Commander Liradda rapped a staff or rod sharply against the marble flooring; Math and Nuhzar both kept their heads lowered.

Bashan's commander, Liradda, an elderly man who probably needed to circle Land spells to wear his armor, raised his voice. "We have several orders of business today. The first is a request to reinstate Mathaiik Kaven to the Order and knight him. Captain Nuhzar of Swords has claimed that Commander Talu wrongly ejected Mathaiik from the Order. That the young man has in the time since continued to act in a manner consistent with the Order's goals and beliefs and has gone above and beyond in the line of duty." He paused after that summary. "Commander Talu, what do you have to say to this?"

Math's head snapped up. Nuhzar had said he planned to get around the execution issue with a very simple solution: not mentioning it. Talu had told no one else about the order. As long as that continued to be the case, Math could simply claim ignorance. In theory, Math shouldn't know about it either.

Unfortunately, it was a plan that had hinged on Talu remaining at Isofal.

The man himself stepped forward, giving Math a kind, fond look as he did. "I would say that it's not the captain's place to question my decisions when it comes to the security of Isofal Cenobium. All evidence at the time suggested the young man was already under the control of dark forces, infected by the same curse that had taken down many of our knights. I couldn't take that risk and jeopardize my people. That said, I harbor no ill will toward the young man. Just the opposite, in fact: given how many knights at the cenobium were calling for his head, sending him to Bashan was the only way to protect him from his enemies." Commander Talu's gaze lingered on Captain Nuhzar before continuing. "I would like to know why the young captain has taken it upon himself to decide, entirely on his own authority, that Mathaiik Kaven is his responsibility."

Math's eyes drifted over toward the interrogator whose job was to check for lies. He didn't seem to be checking the commanders, though. They could say whatever they wanted.

Commander Liradda turned to Nuhzar. "Do you have a response?"

Alik Nuhzar squared his shoulders. "With all apologies to Commander Talu, I do not consider Mathaiik Kaven my responsibility. I was simply doing my duty to curb a potential risk. I was as surprised as anyone to realize that Kaven was innocent."

"But the two of you grew up together," Talu murmured, loud enough to be heard. He raised an apologetic hand. "Apologies, Commander Liradda."

The aging commander gave Talu a sharp look. "Do you have any other questions?"

"Yes," Talu said mildly. "I would also like to know how either of these two can explain the plants."

"The plants?" Commander Liradda looked between Nuhzar and Mathaiik.

"When Kaven was treated for his injuries at the site of the first attack, the healers removed a number of stems and greenery from underneath his skin. I found the same plants discarded in the maze's antechamber—*before* the attack." He raised a finger. "I must emphasize again: *before* the attack. And this in the antechamber to the same maze that Kaven just 'happened' to open later that evening. How could I be anything but suspicious?"

And the worst part was—such suspicion *did* sound reasonable.

"I beg your pardon," a woman's voice called out. "Just for clarification, are you saying that this young man is the one who discovered how to solve the Isofal maze?"

People stepped back, to the side, like the tide pulling away from the shore. In their wake, Math saw a familiar woman wearing ornate armor and a rich, imperial-blue silk cloak.

This was the regent of the empire, Imar Shovan.

It was like watching someone pull a single thread and by doing so, unravel an entire tapestry. The indignation drained from the room. Commanders shifted uncomfortably. Math heard grumbles, spoken too low to catch the exact nature of the complaint.

Talu had an expression on his face that Math had only seen from him a handful of times in his whole life: the look of a man who'd realized he'd just made a mistake.

"Yes," Talu acknowledged, "but—"

"You must admit: it's an extraordinary achievement."

Talu straightened. "Your pardon, but I'm not sure what that has to do with anything."

She waved a hand. "Oh, I'm sure you're right. This is only the first new Illuminated repository to be opened in centuries, an event of monumental importance to the general population, who are rightfully proud of Rokasmaa's dedication to maintaining the archives."

"With all respect, Your Excellency," Commander Talu said, "we aren't certain it *is* an Illuminated archive."

Math held his breath. If they started talking about Kaiataris . . .

"Not certain?" The regent tilted her head. "With the Order's popularity at the lowest it's been in recorded history?"

Several of the commanders quietly snickered. Most, however, looked like they'd just tasted something sour.

Regent Shovan smiled pleasantly. "In which case, I suppose my own real question is: Was this new repository discovered by a knight of the Idallik Order, or . . . someone else?" She didn't say the words "Kaliri spy" out loud, but they were still perfectly audible.

Math struggled to maintain an appropriately serious demeanor. If they declared that Math wasn't an Idallik, or worse, that he was a Kaliri spy, it meant acknowledging that he'd been allowed to gain access to the holiest of holy treasures. That the Idallik Order had failed to do one of its most important jobs.

That subtlety was clearly not lost on Talu, who turned to Math. "Captain Nuhzar says you've learned to manifest. Show us."

Math knew the trick of it now. He shaped the shield carefully, making sure they all saw the vines and leaves trailing from his hand into the summoned shape.

None of the commanders said a word. Math let them study it for thirty seconds and then dismissed it. "My problem," he said to Commander Liradda, "was that I kept trying to summon a sword, and my soul wanted something else—but I am not and have never been a traitor."

The interrogator standing to the side held up his white flag, signaling that no lies had been told.

To Math's utter shock, Talu smiled then. "You've wanted this for so long. Congratulations." He said to the regent, "I think we can all agree that an Idallik Knight discovered the new repository."

"Very well." The regent smiled happily, all the while her eyes never leaving Math's. "At some point soon, you must tell me how you solved the riddle—I want to hear all about it. For now, I yield the floor."

"Yes." Commander Liradda gestured to Talu with his staff of office. "Given this new information, Commander Talu, would you change your decision?"

Talu didn't hesitate. "Of course. I was obviously mistaken. Novitiate Kaven should, by all rights, be a knight of the Idallik Order."

"And Mathaiik Kaven, would it be your preference to rejoin the Order?" Commander Liradda asked Math.

Math hesitated.

Past the crowd of commanders, he could still see Regent Shovan, still staring at him. She shook her head, ever so slightly. What did that mean? Was she telling him to say no?

"Novitiate Kaven?"

Math snapped back to attention. He couldn't refuse. The regent herself had just laid the reasons he couldn't refuse, never mind that he'd need to be a member of the Order—a loyal member of the Order—if he expected them to take his story seriously.

"Yes, Commander. I wish that."

"Very well." The old man turned back to the rest of the commanders. "Shall we allow this?"

They would.

Math tried to trace the strange twisting to his stomach, somewhere between butterflies and nausea.

"Excellent. Then consider yourself returned to the Order. I'm sure Commander Talu will take care of the knighting after this meeting is over."

Math swallowed and tried to puzzle out what had just happened. He understood why he'd been returned to the Order—ultimately it had nothing to do with his guilt or innocence and everything to do with politics and public relations. Talu acted happy about it because it was the expected reaction, not because it was the truth.

Talu hadn't mentioned the execution order. Did that mean he hadn't actually written it? Or . . .

Or, did it mean that Talu knew he didn't have a good justification?

"With that matter resolved," the old man said crisply, "let's turn to the emergency that warranted this convocation."

Math tore his thoughts back to the present. He needed to pay attention to this part.

Captain Nuhzar cleared his throat. "We have discovered the identity of a grim lord, one who is in league with the Kaliri and moving against Rokasmaa and the Idallik Order."

One commander scoffed. "I hardly think a grim witch is—"

"Apologies, Commander," Nuhzar said. "But I didn't say grim witch. I said grim *lord*."

Silence.

Unsurprisingly, the regent was the first to recover.

"That's a bold claim," she said. "On what evidence are you basing it?"

"An eyewitness, ma'am," Captain Nuhzar said.

"And where is this eyewitness?"

That was Math's cue. He stepped forward and cleared his throat. "Here, ma'am. I was attempting to travel here to Bashan, but due to admittedly strange circumstances, I found myself in Lomar, a prisoner of King Sanistral." This alone caused a forbidding amount of suspicious muttering to echo around the great hall. "Sanistral tried to recruit me into a plot to lure one of the Parnathi Queens into a trap," Math said. "He intended to use her in a ritual—to steal her power.

"During that time, he also revealed he was a grim lord. And that he's been supplying weapons to the Kaliri." Math grimaced. "When I refused, he had me imprisoned. I immediately escaped and returned here."

As one, every commander turned to the interrogator, who again held up the white banner.

Math hadn't lied.

Everyone started speaking at once. It felt just like a meeting of captains.

"Silence!" the regent snapped. Regent Shovan turned back to Math, looking distinctly bemused. "I have many questions."

Math nodded. "Of course, Your Excellency. I'll answer to the best of my ability."

By the time Mathaiik stepped back out into the hallway, he was shaking. He was the only one to leave. Everyone else—including Captain Nuhzar—remained inside. While the commanders had asked many questions, some of which had been uncomfortably insightful, it was the regent who'd really made the sweat slide down the back of his neck.

At least no one had rescinded the offer of knighthood.

They'd listened to him, although that might have been more to do with the regent's presence than his story.

He was going to be knighted. This was everything he wanted.

Maybe if he repeated it enough, he'd believe it.

The commanders deliberated for another three hours. When the doors finally opened, Captain Nuhzar was the first out the door. He seemed to put as much distance as possible between him and everyone else in the room. Math's stomach twisted; that was a terrible sign. Behind Nuhzar, the commanders began barking out orders to runners. It felt like the start of a race. No one shouted out his name or signaled for his arrest, however. No one showed any interest in him at all.

Math craned his neck, searching for Commander Talu.

As much as he didn't really want to speak with the commander, Commander Liradda had been clear about who would knight him. When Math spotted him, Talu was deep in conversation with the regent. Math decided it would be best not to interrupt them.

Talu glanced over at Math, noticed him, and smiled. He seemed pleased with himself.

Cold fingers of dread crawled down Math's spine. What had happened?

Regent Shovan said, "Please see to what we've discussed. Thank you, Commander."

The smile faltered on Commander Talu's face, but only for a second. He bowed to the regent and left.

At which point, the regent turned on her heel and made straight for him.

"Mathaiik," Imar Shovan said, "just the person I was hoping to find."

"Your Excellency, I just wanted to thank you for what you said at the meeting." He cleared his throat, trying to sound composed. "You may very well have saved my life." He paused a beat. "Only—why did you shake your head at me?"

"We'll discuss your career options later. This is for you." She handed him a small, delicate-looking stone disk that reminded him of a much fancier version of the tokens the Order used for tracking.

He studied it and frowned. "Thank you, Your Excellency. I don't understand—"

"Present it at the palace. The guards will recognize it and let you inside. Your sister's anxious to see you."

Math blinked. "My sister? What—?" He cleared his throat. "May I ask what my sister's doing at the palace?"

She laughed. "Taking care of the children, of course. Which she keeps saying she hates, but I think they're growing on her." Shovan tilted her head. "Bashan Cenobium is a very cramped place at the moment, and I found the young lady and her charges pushed out into a hallway. They were quite miserable. Naturally, I offered them temporary lodging."

Math closed his mouth and swallowed. "Thank you, Your Excellency. That's very kind of you."

She waved a hand. "I don't make a habit of doing things to be kind."

He managed a thin smile. That was what worried him.

The regent tapped him on the shoulder. "Go visit. Immediately."

"I don't . . ." He slipped the stone token into a coat pocket. "I'm not allowed to leave the cenobium."

"Oh, you seem like a resourceful young man. I'm sure you can figure something out." Without waiting for him to respond, she turned around and walked away.

Math stared after her.

What.

SENTENCE

That was how Captain Nuhzar found him: staring into the distance, contemplating inscrutable motives. Math didn't notice until a hand clapped down on his shoulder—he spun, edgy and tense, instinctively ready to defend himself.

Captain Nuhzar raised an eyebrow. "Nobody's attacking you *here*, Kaven."

Math exhaled. "No. Sorry. I'm just . . . jumpy." He paused. "What did they say? No one's told me."

"I'm a captain now," Nuhzar reminded him. "You should show more respect."

Nuhzar's fingers locked around Math's arm as the captain steered him into the courtyard. "They've decided on an all-out assault. Two battalions. Over two hundred knights. We leave tomorrow and you're riding with me."

He didn't stop walking. "Tonight, we'll check the armory to make sure they can kit you out. You should get something to eat and a full night's sleep."

Math pried the man's hand off his arm. "A full-on assault on *who*?"

They couldn't possibly mean to attack Lomar. It was an entire continent away. Two battalions might overwhelm local forces, but that wasn't nearly enough to invade another country. Were they starting a war with Kaliri? Possible, but it would also be ignoring the real threat.

It had to be that or . . .

Math shook his head, dreading the answer. "Please tell me they're not attacking the Parnathi."

Nuhzar grimaced and looked away. "If I did, I'd be lying."

"Gravefucker," Math muttered, ignoring Nuhzar's disapproving look. "They have the reports. You were at two of the battles. You know how this ends."

With a lot of deaths. He wasn't a giant fan of fighting the Kaliri, but at least in that instance, the dead didn't return fighting for the other side.

Admittedly, given that the Kaliri were ultimately being led by a grim lord, maybe that was a bad example.

Nuhzar grabbed his arm again, steering him farther aside, eyes scanning for eavesdroppers. "I'm not supposed to discuss this with anyone but my lieutenant. We have our orders."

Math dropped his voice to an angry whisper. "How do the most powerful leaders in the Order look at what happened to Isofal and think they have enough information to fight that?"

When Nuhzar's temper visibly spiked, Math added, "That's not sarcasm. Did they explain themselves?"

The captain scowled. "What choice do we have? Isofal isn't the only place those monsters have attacked." He took a breath, steadying himself. "Yes, the commanders gave their reasons. They've been tracking strange incidents and disappearances. Only two Queens remain, with maybe a dozen knights—fifty people, counting civilians—under their control. Two hundred knights should be more than enough."

"Fifty?"

Nuhzar scowled. "You've picked up some bad habits gallivanting with that woman—namely, questioning orders."

"You of all people should know I've always questioned orders." Math wrinkled his nose. "How do they know it's only fifty? That number's too low."

Nuhzar raised an eyebrow. "I should think that's obvious. That's how many people are missing."

"Are they counting the dead in that number?"

Nuhzar hesitated.

"I told you what the Queens can do with corpses. I told *them*."

Nuhzar's jaw clenched. "I know."

"We didn't burn our dead, did we?"

"No one does that anymore."

"The Souna do. We should seriously consider following their lead. Because we won't be facing fifty people tomorrow," Math said grimly. "We'll be fighting everyone who died at Kegomar, Isofal, during the ambush on the road, and the train attack. I'm not even sure the bodies need to be fresh. I'm just hoping. Because if I'm wrong, then Tri-Mother help us if those Queens *find a cemetery*."

Nuhzar backed up until he hit the stone wall of the chapter house, then slowly slid to the ground. He'd never had the most expressive face, but the emotion was clear enough: despair.

"I know," Nuhzar whispered.

"Then why are we doing this?"

He shook his head, eyes glassy, unfocused. "I believe you—but they didn't."

Math recoiled. "What? What do you mean?"

"They believe the trees exist, obviously. They're dangerous grimmocks that need to be destroyed. But they think those dangerous grimmocks are under the control of one or more grim witches. Anything else is unreliable testimony witnessed while under the effects of hallucinogens."

"The spores are more than hallucinogens!"

"They leave their victims in a heightened state of suggestibility, which won't be a problem if we get to any infected knights and cure them quickly enough."

Math could've cried. "You really can't. You can cure the part that makes you see things, sure, but that isn't what makes them so dangerous."

Nuhzar frowned then. "The Queens' control doesn't go away if they're purged?"

"No! Do you really think that Rabu and Yihura wouldn't try to cure themselves?" Math clenched his fists. "What happened after I left?"

Nuhzar wouldn't meet his eyes.

"What happened?" A sharper dread prickled up Math's spine. "What did Talu say?"

He'd looked so damn smug.

Instead of answering, Nuhzar asked: "Is there anyone else who can corroborate your story about Huraiik? Another witness?"

Math sat on the cold flagstones, heedless of the chill seeping through his clothes. His tongue felt glued to his throat, but he rasped out: "Kai was there."

"So that's a no, then."

He grimaced, but didn't argue. "What did Talu say, Alik?"

"That you mean well." Nuhzar wouldn't meet his eyes. "But also, that he thinks you're relapsing."

"Relapsing from what?" A feeling of dread stole over Math.

"The trauma of what happened to your parents." Nuhzar was still talking to the darkness, voice low, still angled away from Math.

Math's breath hitched. "How is any of that new? Everyone knows my parents were killed by grimmocks. That's the whole reason Talu ordered me to go to Kegomar with you in the first place."

A pause.

"That's not what Talu told the commanders." Nuhzar exhaled slowly. "He said you killed your parents."

". . . What."

Nuhzar's voice dropped. "You manifested early, although who can say whether your powers provoked your parents' abuse or were in response to it. When they started beating you, you reached out to the plants, and your parents' death was the result."

Math gave a single, shocked exhale. "He told them *I* was a grim witch."

"He never used those words." Nuhzar sniffed. "Several of the commanders even congratulated him on your 'rehabilitation.'"

Math couldn't breathe. This couldn't be happening.

But Nuhzar wasn't done. "Talu says Huraiik is a hallucination. You feel guilty about Huraiik's death and you're angry at Talu, so your mind is creating villains to destroy. Thus: the Queens, and Sanistral being a grim lord."

"I trusted him." Math's voice cracked. "I thought he was protecting me. I thought he—" But he couldn't finish the sentence. The words shattered in his throat. His hands were shaking.

Math scrubbed his eyes with the palms of his hands, but his reality stubbornly refused to change from this utter nightmare. "And they believed *that*?"

"Which one would be easier to believe? That one of our nation's political rivals has been a grim lord all this time and we just never noticed? That an entire race of sentient, magic-using killer trees have been living in one of our forests? Or that you're a troubled young man with an overactive imagination?"

Math ground his teeth to keep from screaming.

"What about the Kaliri? What about the weapons?"

Nuhzar waved a hand dismissively. "An intriguing development, but there have been no other attacks, and they really only have your word that matters happened the way you said."

"The letters—"

"Maybe you wrote them. They were, after all, written on Isofal paper."

"A truth spell—"

"You *believe* it, Talu said. You'll pass any such test, because you believe it's the truth. So that won't work. And anyway, they're not going to war with either Kaliri or Lomar over the deaths of a few Idallik Knights, even if we had evidence."

Math laughed sourly. "I can't believe that man has managed to absolutely ruin my life this many times in less than two weeks. A few hours ago, everything was being made right. Now? It's somehow even worse than when I started."

"No one is suggesting that you be kicked out of the Order."

Math scrambled to his feet. "No, they're just suggesting that I'm *insane*. That I cannot be trusted. Damn it, Nuhzar, at least before they let me watch the novitiates. Do you really think anyone's going to let me near those children now?" Math rubbed his eyes. "How many people did we lose at Isofal?"

Nuhzar didn't answer.

"How many?" Isofal alone typically housed at least three hundred knights. Besides the people the Order had lost at Kegomar, they'd lost still more to that

Kaliri ambush. That wasn't even counting civilians, or what the Queens might have claimed in other cenobium attacks.

"More than we're bringing," Nuhzar finally answered. "If you hadn't woken Kaiataris, we would've lost everyone."

Come day after the next, two hundred knights were going to ride off in the forest and find themselves outnumbered. Not by grimmocks, although certainly the grimmocks they'd faced back in the grasslands had been proof that even a single grimmock could be lethal. No, instead they would find themselves outnumbered by people with all the skills and knowledge of Idallik Knights, *and* any people the Parnathi had taken to be trees, *and* the Queens themselves.

They weren't just going to be overwhelmed, they were going to be slaughtered.

Math hadn't even thought they were prepared to fight the Queens. His fellow knights had no clue what an immortal sorceress who had mastered wild magic could do. Math didn't even know, except he suspected it was something very close to "anything she wanted." He only knew there would be *two* of them, plus their newly grown green knights. The Idallik Order was unprepared.

"I need to make preparations," Nuhzar announced.

"I'm going to go . . ." Math said, gesturing toward the rest of the cenobium, "see if this place has a room for screaming or something."

"You do that," Nuhzar said absently, and walked off himself.

Math watched him go as he wiped at his eyes. He felt inside his coat. His hand closed around the regent's token. Before this conversation, he'd wondered if he dare use it. Now, he didn't dare waste it.

Otherwise, two hundred knights—himself included—would ride off to their deaths in the morning.

FAMILY

A scream shrill enough to shatter glass echoed across the courtyard as Mudiya and Iduan slammed into Math like twin whirlwinds. Seconds later, Satu and Taris burst outside, followed by Jaiik with Hamu in his arms, and then Yasib and Fahura, carrying Shavru and Jura. Math ignored the screaming girls and did a quick head count. Who was missing? The twins.

He spotted them under a canopy with his sister Tanxi, whispering feverishly to another girl. That was fine—they were out of the sun and not causing trouble. But . . .

Wait.

That was one child too many. Where had they picked up an extra?

Then Math swallowed as Tanxi rose and bowed to the seven-year-old before heading his way.

Oh. They hadn't picked up a stray.

That was the empress.

No wonder the hairs on his skin had been raised the whole way across the courtyard. Archers had probably been trained on him the whole time.

His more immediate concern, however, was his older sister, whose expression was darker than the woods outside Sounalla at night.

He looked down at the children. "What can I pay you to say you never saw me?"

Iduan grabbed his belt and shook it. "Where have you been!? We were worried sick about you. Hamu wouldn't stop crying!"

As if to underline the point, Jura burst into tears and Fahura started crying too. Math suspected Jaiik might have cussed him out if he wasn't holding Hamu, but an arc of electrical energy played over both boys. Math couldn't tell which of them caused it.

"There's no need for tears. Really. It's okay. I was fine," Math lied. "Now, quick, hand me a baby so Tanxi won't punch me."

Yasib obediently gave him Shavru, who immediately declared, "No! Not safe!" and slithered out of his grip like she was buttered.

"My fault for teaching her to avoid danger," Math said amiably, smiling at Tanxi. "Please remember that I am your baby brother and you love me."

She still looked ready to summon her sword—right up until he was close enough to see the tears. Then she threw her arms around him. "Like I would ever forget! You gravef—"

"Language," Math growled.

Tanxi tightened her hold, made a sobbing sound into his shoulder, then released him and shoved him back. "What happened? Why are you even here? They said you were arrested!"

Oh yeah. That.

"Some stuff happened and—"

Cries of "Tell us what happened!" rang through the courtyard. The young empress watched—and likely listened—with interest from under the awning.

"I will—I promise I'll tell all of you—" He raised an eyebrow at Jaiik. "Have you grown? How are you taller? I haven't been gone that long." Math shook his head. "What I mean is, I'll tell all of you the story, but first I need to speak to the regent. It's important."

The children—at least, the ones not crying—looked at each other, then at Tanxi, visibly confused.

Tanxi pressed her lips together. "She's not here."

He felt like a fool. "No, of course she's not here. She's probably still at the cenobium. But I need to talk to her the minute she comes back tonight."

"She won't be back tonight," said a small voice.

Empress Asali.

Math wasn't sure of the protocol. Should he bow? He felt like he should probably bow.

He bowed. "A pleasure, Your Majesty. But uh . . . what do you mean, she won't be back tonight?"

The little girl continued her sharp-eyed appraisal. "What I said. She won't be back tonight. She'll be back tomorrow." She paused. "Maybe the next day."

Math fought down panic. ". . . Where did she go?"

"You don't need to know that."

Math inhaled. "I kind of do."

She made a face and turned to Ayiad. "Are you sure about him?"

Ayiad nodded emphatically. "He's good. He really is. It wasn't his fault he had to leave—I don't care what Jaiik says."

Math gave Jaiik a sideways look. Jaiik crossed his arms and glanced away.

"Yeah, don't listen to Jaiik," Math said. "But I need to stop something bad from happening, and I can't do it without the regent's help."

The little empress gave him a look both guilty and worried before motioning everyone under the canopy. Someone had set up a sitting area with cushions and rugs, and a bright, glittering crystal floated at the highest point, casting pretty sparkles across the ground.

Math eyed the crystal suspiciously. Fahura and Mudiya both had Sun resonance, but there was no way either of them had been maintaining a spell here while crying and hugging him on the far side of the courtyard.

Tanxi was Sun resonant, too. She must have created it.

He turned his attention back to Asali, who motioned for him to sit on a pillow.

He did. The others followed, setting up a protective circle around the little girl. Clearly, in the short time they'd been here, the children had established a hierarchy—or rather, they had taken to heart that this was their empress, who they were sworn to protect.

She was not an adorable child. Her eyes were a little too close together, her nose slightly too long, and even at seven, she struck him as gangly. Her stare was sharp, intelligent, and unsettling in its intensity—a much older person trapped in a child's body.

"It's not that I don't want to tell you," Asali said, "but that I can't. According to rumors, she . . ." The empress rolled her eyes. "The gossips say she gets so sick of the Idalliks that as soon as she's done with them, she heads to a brothel or something and doesn't surface for two days."

"Oh," Math said.

"That's . . ." Tanxi shook her head. "I don't believe that. She's an Idallik Knight herself. She'd never break her vows like that."

Math raised an eyebrow at her as he started counting on his fingers.

"Never break them so openly, I mean," Tanxi said. "She seems far too smart for that."

"What's a brothel?" Iduan asked.

Math gestured in her direction. "And there we go."

"Math! Do something!" Tanxi looked more horrified than she'd been fighting creepy animated trees.

Math smiled at the eight-year-old. "Iduan, darling, we'll talk about it when you're older."

"Truthfully, Imar always checks in with her spies after meeting at the cenobium," Asali said. "It can take a couple of days, but I don't know where she goes. No one does."

. . . And Math stopped smiling.

"Now, Your Majesty," Tanxi said gently, "the leader of the entire empire doesn't just disappear for days with no way to reach her. There must be someone who can contact her."

The little empress nodded. "There is. Commander Liradda."

"Right," Math murmured. "Right."

Commander Liradda—who was going to be absolutely no help whatsoever, because he'd already signed off on this nightmare of a mission.

Math found himself wondering how much common knowledge it was that the regent always checked in with her people after these meetings. Clearly, she'd also agreed to the attack, but he couldn't help but wonder if she'd understood how soon that attack would be happening.

No. He was being paranoid. The only reason someone would have scheduled the attack while she was gone was if they wanted to make sure that she couldn't stop it.

Doubt scratched at him.

"Math," his sister whispered. "What's going on?"

He started to tell her—but as he opened his mouth, he remembered who he was talking to. She was worse than he was, in many ways. If she found out about the mission, about how completely messed up it was, she would do something.

Something foolish. She would try to take his place or claim the children needed him more than they needed her.

"It's Talu," he said instead. "He's . . ." Math pulled his hand back from patting Satu's shoulder. He couldn't bear to look at the children just then. "He's convinced the commanders that I'm insane—he said . . ." Math paused, swallowed, and tried again, his voice barely a whisper so the children wouldn't hear. "He said I killed our parents."

Tanxi said nothing at first. She just stared at him for a long, torturous span of heartbeats and then turned to the children. "I need to speak with my brother alone. Will you lot of absolute ruffians—not you, Your Majesty—promise to behave until we return?"

Math tried to retain some semblance of composure, even as he felt like he was suffocating. "Now you've done it." Math pretended to smile as he pointed a mock-stern finger at the group. "That was not an invitation to misbehave once we're back, understand?"

His instructions were met with giggles and at least one eye-roll from the older kids. Too many of the children gave him worried looks, however, to convince Math that he'd fooled them.

Tanxi grabbed his hand and pulled him through a side door—not the one the guards had led him through earlier.

The room beyond was all plush carpets, gilded tile, and the fanciest woodwork he had ever seen. Heavy silk curtains and jeweled beadwork framed archways overlooking the courtyard they had just left. Wall sconces shaped like glass tulips lit the hall with soft gaslight, glinting off an arched ceiling of gold leaf. The air smelled of incense and fresh flowers. Brass doors shimmered behind silk curtains, leading deeper into the palace.

"Wow." Math swallowed as he scanned the interior. "You could lose your feet in this carpet." He glanced down. "Feels criminal to wear shoes on it."

"Probably," Tanxi agreed. She was wearing velvet slippers. "Funny how quickly it stops feeling special. It hasn't even been a week." She fetched a bottle from a cabinet, poured something gold into a glass, and handed it to him.

He looked at the drink, then at her. "Now you're scaring me."

Tanxi didn't look great. Physically she was fine, but the look in her eyes—not fine. She chewed her nail for a moment, not meeting his gaze.

"Tanxi."

"You're not insane," she said.

"Yes, thank you. I'm aware."

"But you did kill our parents."

He couldn't breathe. Math set the glass on a side table, pushed it away.

"Math—"

"Is that what you're saying? That Talu was telling the truth?" He felt shaky, wrung out, like he was teetering on the edge of something sharp and steep. Or maybe he'd already gone over the edge and was just waiting for the inevitable body slam.

Tanxi closed her eyes briefly, took another drink. "Our parents were really kind of shitty, to be honest."

"Were they?" Math murmured. "I don't remember."

"I'm not surprised. They were unhappy when I turned out to have a gift for magic—and furious when you did. You were supposed to become a smith, like our father. I think they thought they could just, you know—" She waved a hand, scowling. "Train it out of you."

"Train it out of me?" He let out an ugly, broken laugh. "Just say they were beating me, Tan."

"Fine. They were beating you."

He closed his eyes. He understood why she'd never said anything. But still—how had she let him go so long not knowing?

"So, I guess they must have whipped me every time I used magic but even as a kid, I bet the rules went out the window the moment I fell asleep. Most people just sleepwalk. I sleepmurdered."

"Not exactly," she said, grimacing.

"You just told me—"

"You were a child. I don't think the idea of hurting our parents ever once occurred to you—no matter what they did, not even in your sleep."

He stared at her. "Wait. Make up your mind. Did I or did I not murder our parents."

"I don't think you meant to kill them, and I don't think you raised a hand against them yourself." She sipped her drink. "I've been to the house, Math. I've seen your 'woods.'"

Math couldn't speak.

"The plants weren't like that back when the Idallik Knights came to collect me. They're not normal anymore. They're . . . they're smart."

Math winced.

"*You* did that," she accused—and he had nothing to say.

"I think you were lonely and in pain, and you needed friends. So you made some."

"And they defended me." Math sighed.

"Right."

He was tempted to reach for the alcohol, but a fiercely stubborn pride stopped him. Tanxi's story explained a lot, didn't it?

"I always assumed their abuse was why you never learned to manifest a weapon. Or rather, that you figured out how when you were five—and it horrified you so much, you've done your damndest never to do it again since."

His eyes were stinging, so he wiped them. How dared they? He wanted to scream, to hit something.

There was no way to scream loud enough.

Then Math felt something tug at him. It almost felt like a question—a prickle of concern and inquiry. Kai. He was feeling Kai.

Or rather, she must've been feeling *him*.

Math inhaled slowly and tried to calm down. He sniffed, cleared his throat.

"Okay," he said. "Thank you for telling me."

"Math, it's okay to be upset."

"Good, because I am. I'm extremely upset." He pushed away from the side cabinet. "Technically, I'm not supposed to be here. I'm still confined to the cenobium. So I'd best return before someone notices I'm no longer annoyingly underfoot."

Tanxi made a face. "About that . . ."

Math stared at her, fighting down dread. This day had already been filled with far too many surprises.

"The regent was here, earlier," Tanxi explained. "Upset about something. She had that 'I have to roll up my sleeves and fix things' attitude. She did say that she'd given you a pass to come visit—and also asked that you stay until she returns."

"Stay as in 'not go back to the cenobium'?"

Tanxi huffed. "Unless you've figured out how to be in two places at the same time, that is how that works."

"I can't do that."

"What do you mean, you can't do that? The children are here, and it's not like anyone's going to miss you."

"Ouch."

She rolled her eyes. "None of the knights, I mean."

Math couldn't help but laugh. "Yeah . . . you'd be wrong about that. Also, as it happens, I'm one of those knights."

Her brow wrinkled. "What?"

"I figured out how to manifest, Tan. It's a shield, but evidently that still counts."

"What? Show me!"

He obediently complied, and when he dismissed the shield, his sister honestly looked like she was about to burst into tears. "Tri-Mother! You did it! I'm so proud of you!" She ran at him and gave him a tight hug.

A proper Idallik Knight would've scolded her about losing control over her emotions. Math just hugged her back.

When he finally pulled back, he said, "I already have orders, so I can't stay here and wait until the regent feels like coming back."

"When do you leave?"

"Tomorrow morning. I'll check back when we return."

If we return, he didn't say.

There had to be some way to stop this avalanche. If only the regent had still been there.

"Tell the hatchlings goodbye for me, okay?"

"You should tell them yourself."

He laughed, unkindly. "No, no, no. That would be a terrible idea. I'm currently holding myself together through spite and pride. If I see the kids, I'll turn into a giant, weepy mess. You're making it hard enough as it is." He gestured down the hallway with his thumb. "This way leads out, right?"

"Yeah," Tanxi said. "The guards outside will escort you."

"I'm sure they will. I love you, big sister."

"I love you, little brother." She waved him off, her voice tight.

He looked back once—just in time to see her reach for the drink she'd poured him.

Math could hardly fault her. It would've been a shame to let it go to waste.

VIGIL

Later that evening, Math lay in a bunk bed in the barracks, staring up at the wooden slats above—uncomfortably close and suffocating. He wasn't sure how many minutes had died agonizing deaths since lights out, but it felt like centuries.

He was finally going to be the knight he had always dreamed of becoming. He was twenty-two years old, he'd manifested his weapon (ten years late, but still—he'd done it, no thanks to his parents or Commander Talu), and if he followed orders, then by tomorrow morning, he was a dead man.

What would it feel like to be fully plant? Would he even notice? Maybe it would just hurt less, when his body sprouted to heal him.

How funny, to refuse King Sanistral's generous offer of becoming his "ambassador" to the Parnathi, only to end up facing the same fate. Then again, maybe he'd be immune to that too, like he was with being controlled by the spores.

Maybe he'd just die.

That was what his dream—his honor—would buy him: a preventable, foolish death. One hundred and ninety-eight knights would cheerfully ride down to the Parnassa Forest, arrogantly certain they could handle anything the world threw at them.

Exactly two of those knights—men who'd, until recently, shared only being raised by the same man, a love for their order, and a profound sense of mutual loathing—knew differently.

Alik Nuhzar had been given orders. He'd follow them, even knowing death was waiting.

He would *go*.

Tri-Mother help him, so would Math. Not because he was an honorable knight who followed orders. He was increasingly of a mind to say the orders could go fuck a grave. But he couldn't live with himself if he stayed behind, knowing what they were walking into.

Maybe he'd figure out a solution. Something.

No wonder Sanistral had let them escape. Why wouldn't the wizard confess all his sins? He'd known the truth: Math couldn't stop him.

That was when Math felt Kai's pain.

Unlike before, though, this time she was close.

He rolled out of the bunk and started dressing before he'd consciously decided to leave. Some of the other knights made protesting sounds; he ignored them. He tugged on his boots in the hallway, waiting until he was outside the barracks before summoning a light and rushing to a window overlooking the cenobium entrance.

The gates were closed at night—probably locked and guarded, given recent events. But for Math, leaving now was just as easy as it had been earlier.

He glanced out the window to the street below, shifted his position to the sidewalk, and ran to Kai.

She was less than a block away, leaning against a wall that blocked the view from the cenobium. Someone had tried to make her presentable for civilized company. She now wore a large wool cloak with a voluminous hood over a dark dress with a fine floral print. She had a hand clamped over the opposite arm, as if she was applying pressure to a wound.

Because that's what she was doing.

"What happened? Who hurt you?" Math rushed up to her and immediately started healing the cut. He was immensely relieved to see that it wasn't serious—a shallow slice that would have healed on its own, although not without scarring.

"The superior question is: Who hurt you? For you have been in the most disagreeable turmoil the entire day." She nodded toward her arm. "This served to catch your attention."

Math stared at the healed wound. "You hurt yourself."

"Should I have knocked on the front gate? I know that Captain Nuhzar told his companions that I was to be a witness, but I think it unlikely anyone would look kindly on me calling at such an hour."

Math pulled her into his arms and held her tight. He was just so relieved that she was fine. A little annoyed about how she'd signaled him to come meet her, but he couldn't really fault her for that. It was hard to argue with success.

"Math." She pushed back against his chest until she could look him in the eyes. "What *happened*?"

He glanced around. It was the middle of the night and the gas lamps he'd been so enchanted by when originally entering the city now seemed like a horrible inconvenience. He pulled her around the corner of a building, farther out of sight.

"The commanders didn't believe me," Math explained. "They let me back into the Order and agreed to knight me, but didn't believe a word I said. They think the Queens are a grim witch cabal of some kind, so they're going to send us all off to the Parnassa Forest in the morning to take care of them."

She frowned. "Define 'deal with' for me."

"As in 'destroy.' They're sending two hundred knights—"

Kai's eyes widened. "That is not enough."

"*I know*," he agreed. "But Commander Talu's convinced them that I'm insane and making up all the stuff about Sanistral, which in turn means they didn't believe me when I tried to warn them about Huraiik. Nuhzar tried to reason with them, but . . ."

The funny thing was, Math wasn't certain that it would've changed anything even if they *had* believed him. The Idallik Order didn't have the authority to start wars with sovereign nations, and it seemed highly unlikely that the regent would've signed off on that idea. From that point of view, the Order could only attack one of those groups without jeopardizing their status. Attacking the Parnathi had the added benefit of removing Sanistral's power source on the off chance that Math had been telling the truth.

Removing the Queens was a coldly pragmatic solution to the problem—assuming they could pull it off.

Kai closed her eyes for a moment, gathered herself. "I see," she finally said. "Very well. If such is the case, then we shall have to see who else's help we might enlist—"

"I'm going with them."

She blinked at him as if he'd just spoken an unfamiliar language.

"I can't—" He shook his head. "They assigned me as one of the knights heading out to confront the Queens. And I can't just . . . run away, knowing what my brothers and sisters are about to walk into tomorrow."

Kai continued staring at him.

"I'm not . . . I mean. Kai, please. Say something."

Her eyes narrowed. "How much brain matter do the commanders allow knights to have? Did yours dribble out your ears when you were knighted?"

"Kai."

She backed away from him, eyes blazing. "You shall go with them, and you shall die with them. For no reason except that apparently you have no wish to see them lonely when they're killed?"

"Kai!" He reached over and grabbed her hands. He tried, anyway. The task was made considerably more difficult because she had hers clenched into fists. "This means something to me. I have to stop this if I can. I wouldn't be able to live with myself if I just walked away. And lest you forget, they have words for what you're suggesting I do. Desertion. *Treason*."

"But you would still draw breath." If she lowered her voice, it was only because shouting in an alley in the middle of the night would likely be noticed.

"Don't be so quick to assume I'll die, Kai. Try to have a little faith."

"I have all the faith in the world in you," she said. "But I have fought the Parnathi and I know their strengths. Tomorrow, you and your knights shall walk into that forest and face enemies in the thousands . . ."

He chuckled bitterly. "They haven't killed *that* many of us, Kai."

Her eyes widened with dismay, and she unclenched her fists to grab his hands back. "Do you think that you've been fighting the *same* Huraiik each time? That there was only one of them?"

Math suddenly found it difficult to breathe. "I'm sorry, but what do you mean?"

"One slain human does not result in but one living Parnathi. I know not what they call it now. In my time, we called it clipping. From a single plant, a gardener might make many more, not by growing it from seeds, but by cutting the stems and branches into pieces, each piece to become a full plant in its own right."

He flashed back to the logging camp, to the bodies of the dead, torn apart, divided into pieces. Tri-Mother. Math hadn't thought it could get any worse.

It had just gotten worse.

When he'd told Nuhzar they'd be outnumbered, he'd been off by a factor of at least five.

"Thank you for letting me know," Math said.

She searched his eyes. "Tell me you are not going."

"I can't do that."

She stared at him for a second longer, then threw down his hands and marched away. He suspected she only turned around and came back because she was trying to avoid shouting in the street. "You are a fool, Mathaiik Kaven."

"Seems so," he agreed. "Look, Kai. I know this isn't what you wanted, but I'm going to do everything I can to come back to you. The timing might not be great, but you deserve to know how I feel—"

"No," she snapped at him.

"No?"

She looked so mad it wouldn't have surprised him if she'd thrown a punch. "Have you forgotten, in your sublime moment of despair, what happens to *me* if you die?"

Kai absolutely had thrown a punch, just not with her hands.

Math's heart lurched. "Oh, Tri-Mother, I didn't—" Math paused.

Beneath her fury, he felt something else. Guilt. Anxiety. The prickly-sharp wariness of someone sitting down at a card game and hoping no one noticed . . .

Hoping no one noticed it was a bluff.

"You won't die, will you?" Math said softly. "You figured out that the link isn't fatal. Were you going to tell me? Or were you afraid I'd abandon you if I had a choice?"

Two could throw a punch, but even Math could admit that was a low blow.

She pulled herself up, angry and furious, and unfortunately for her, reminding him very much in that moment of a remarkably angry alley cat. "It does not seem to matter, given that you are abandoning me, regardless. Do you care so little for me that you'd take the chance that I might die—"

He grabbed her hands. "Look me in the eyes and tell me you'll die if I do."

Tears began streaming down her cheeks, but the look of fury on her face lessened not even the slightest amount. "If you die," she said slowly, "I will die."

Math knew she was lying, but at the same time, she was also completely sincere.

"How dare you," she whispered. "How dare you hold your life so cheap, when to me it is more precious than all the stars! You are the *only thing* that tethers me to this world, the only person I want to share every tomorrow with. And you will steal that from me for honor and loyalty to a nation and people who care nothing for you. I am the one who cares for you!"

Her eyes were bright and red, wet with tears, as she pushed him away. "Tell me when you return, or do not tell me at all."

He had no idea how to respond to that. He didn't want to go, and yet he was going, anyway. Math saw the tears on her face and silently agreed with her earlier assessment.

He was a fool.

Since he didn't have the words, he kissed her.

Math felt her arms wrap around his neck as she kissed him back—slow and sweet and more than a little despairing. He tasted salt from her tears before she furiously backed away from him to wipe her eyes.

She began searching their surroundings, as though looking for something. She pointed toward a high wrought-iron fence in the distance. "What lies beyond that?"

"I'm not sure," Math answered honestly. "I don't know Bashan very well, and we didn't pass this way when we came to the cenobium. It's a park? There's a lot of parks in this city."

"'Twill suffice," she growled before taking his hand and pulling him after her. She walked at a surprisingly fast pace.

They quickly reached their destination, which was mostly dark because none of the gas lamps elsewhere were present here. The gate was closed and locked.

"What are we doing here?" Math asked her.

"I didn't really find the idea of making love with you in the middle of an alley especially appealing, to be honest."

Math's mouth dried up. Then he started examining the gate with renewed motivation. "Oh, I'd have done it for you," he admitted. "In the middle of the day, on a crowded street if that was what you wanted . . ." He eyed the lock—he could break it, sure, but not without half the city noticing.

"You still have enough magic to shift, right?" he asked her.

She responded by doing so, appearing on the other side of the wrought-iron fence.

"Perfect." He followed her and then they were kissing again.

Kai began tugging them down to the ground through the simple tactic of grabbing his coat and letting herself fall, then gave a startled gasp and laughed when he caught her and swung her up into his arms. "Hold on there," he said. "Let's get a little farther away from the street. There's some shadows over there that might be a building—"

Math began laughing as he realized what he was looking at.

Kai glanced around, searching for the source of the humor. "I don't understand," she said, looking up at him.

"It's not a park," he said, shaking his head. "This is a cemetery."

CEMETERY

Math summoned a small light spell—pleased when it took the shape of fireflies—and set off across the cemetery. He refused to set Kai down, mostly because he suspected she wouldn't care *where* she started undressing him. One of them had to pick an appropriate spot.

He passed by several options. All that marble looked uncomfortable.

He settled on a patch of creeping thyme hidden between a cluster of large marble crypts, bordered by rosebushes heavy with red blooms. Their scent hung thick in the air. Math set Kai down and dropped to one knee, circling a Wood spell to coax the thyme into bloom, until the whole area became a soft red carpet.

He shrugged off his coat and laid it on the ground.

"Take off your clothes," she told him fondly.

"You really liked that, didn't you, back on the train?" Math asked. "When I was naked and you weren't?"

"Truth, you were a lovely sight," Kai admitted. She reached up and pulled the pins from her hair, tossing them aside—probably into the rosebushes. "Must I tell you a second time?" Her lips quirked and her eyes sparkled.

"No, ma'am." He yanked off his clothing as quickly as possible.

Kai was slower to undress, but she was undressing. Her eyes raked over him as she did, sighing happily.

Math sat down on the coat, weight resting on his heels as he gazed up at her. "This will be new for me," he said.

She paused, her thumbs hooked into the waistband of her gathered pants. "Oh?"

"Being able to see my partner's face," Math said. "What a delightful novelty. Please. Allow me." He beckoned her closer.

She did, then made a small, wonderful sound as he slid her pants down her waist, over her thighs, and to the ground. Math didn't just hear the sound, but felt it, a ripple through their bond that was hot and breathy and not entirely hers. It felt like another kind of physical touch, low and electric. Their pleasure was mutual, *mirrored*.

His own arousal surged in response, wild and hungry, and he knew she'd felt that, too.

Her hands tangled in his hair as he kissed his way up one thigh, paused at her hip, then slid over her taut stomach. At the other hip, he started back down.

"Oh, you ass," she murmured—more amused than upset.

"I'm sorry," Math said, lifting his mouth just enough while stroking the backs of her thighs. "Did you want something? You only have to ask." He gently bit her leg.

"I want you inside me," she said.

"Eventually." Math paused, suddenly serious. "That would be okay, right? Actual, you know . . ."

"Vaginal sex?" Kai echoed, making the phrase sound far lewder than it should. "Of course, I—" She searched his face, hands coming around to cup his cheek. "Nonprocreative sex, you said. You really haven't done this before."

With eyes like hers, it was hard to tell if they were dilated—but Math could've sworn her pupils widened.

"No, too risky. Too much chance of . . . um. Oh, there's a thought. Do you have a way to stop yourself from getting pregnant?"

Kai grimaced and chewed her lip. "Oh, Math. There was never a need."

Math lightly banged his head against her thigh. In a world where conception was virtually impossible, why would you learn contraceptive magic? And with what he now knew about wild magic, he wasn't sure he trusted an improvised attempt. Not with Kai's observation that fertility rates were rising.

"Okay," he said. "I'm okay with it. I'm perfectly happy to—"

He grunted as Kai crouched, shoved him back with surprising force, then followed, straddling his waist and settling her hips against him.

He could feel—oh, Tri-Mother—he could feel her pressing against him, her slick heat rubbing against his very hard cock.

"I am not," she told him. "I am not okay with it. If this is goodbye, then let it be sweet enough to make you want to return. Nothing would please me more than to leave this night carrying our child—"

Math began kissing her again. This time, their lips met with fierce, fiery kisses that sent tingles straight from his mouth to his groin. His fingers dug into her sides, tearing off the rest of her clothing with such violent need he couldn't be sure he wasn't ripping fabric—and didn't care.

He'd meant to linger between her legs, tongue working against the folds of her sex, but the momentum left neither of them willing to pause for foreplay. Or at least, not that sort, because she seemed happy to tease him into a state of rabid animal fervor.

He felt her—naked, slick—slide over his length, pausing as the head of his cock caught at her entrance before she raised her hips and began the whole process over again. He made wild noises into her mouth as she teased, wet and deliberate, against him.

Math didn't stop her. Didn't catch her hips and push into her. Not yet. Holding back wasn't just about control anymore. If he gave in too soon, the shared rush might burn through them both—too fast, too hard. Already, he could feel the echo of her need bouncing through the bond, wrapping around his own until he couldn't tell whose pulse was whose.

He shifted to her neck, biting and sucking as her cries grew louder, more lewd. Then he cupped her ass, fingers wandering down to slide into her beautifully wet sex.

Kai let out a choking gasp of surprise. She pushed back against his finger.

He laughed and buried his face in her hair before working that finger in and out, then adding a second, then a third. She wasn't a virgin, but she wasn't large either—hurting her was the last thing he wanted. He withdrew his fingers, shifted position, and returned them to work while his other hand rubbed her clit.

She pushed up onto her arms—whether to protest or give him better access, he wasn't sure—but he took the chance to admire her now-bare breasts before craning down to capture a nipple in his mouth, flicking his tongue across the tip before sucking hard.

Kai threw back her head and cried out. Math was almost disappointed when she pulled away from his mouth to reach down and stroke the length of his cock.

"Oh fuck me," he said, although it was closer to begging.

"Such is the plan, my fair knight." She kept her hand on him, but this time it wasn't to caress but to aim, guiding his dick to her entrance and pressing down against him.

She was hot and wet and almost painfully tight, but more than that, the feel of her pressing down around him, taking him in, was sublime. It was all he could do not to roll them over and start thrusting, but he had just enough presence of mind to go slow.

He slid his hands around, one resting on her hip, the other teasing her breasts. She'd thrown her head back, eyes half-lidded, mouth open in the most delightful cries. With each motion, she took him deeper—slowly, slowly—and he wasn't sure she could fit all of him until he looked down and saw that she had.

He would never smell roses and thyme again without remembering that moment—the scent of sex and skin, her weight against him.

She quickened the pace, and he matched it, thrusting up in time with her. When she braced her hands on his chest, he caught them, lacing his fingers through hers as they both gasped, eyes locked. A soft slapping noise filled the air, rising with their cries.

Math fought not to come, which wasn't exactly easy with the most beautiful woman in the world riding him like her favorite horse. He wanted to hear her scream. He wanted this forever. He wanted it to never end.

He reached down and rubbed her clit again. That did it. She threw her head back and screamed loud enough to wake every corpse in the cemetery. She tightened around him so hard it was all he could do to keep moving. What he couldn't do was stop himself from coming. The sensation slammed into him from two sides—her pleasure rebounding through the bond just as his own surged forward. It collided inside him, overloaded and brilliant, leaving him gasping.

He hadn't—

Math paused, sweat dripping down the sides of his face. Perhaps he hadn't fully appreciated the advantages of the magical link Kai had created.

He also wasn't finished. If she wanted something to remember him by, he was damn well going to give it to her. Repeatedly.

Fortunately, he was Wood resonant. The joke about "wood" spells wasn't a joke—they were all about healing and regeneration, after all.

"Oh god, Math, seriously?" Kai murmured once she could form thoughts again—and felt him still inside her, slower now, but still rock hard.

"Do you want to stop?" He already knew the answer.

"No, no. Oh, absolutely not. Don't you dare."

So, he didn't. Not for a very long time.

Later, they lay together, wrapped in each other's arms on his coat while listening to the wind rustling the tree branches. It wasn't dawn yet, but Math knew he was running out of time.

"I'm going to talk to the Queens," he told her, kissing the top of her head. "Maybe I can make them see reason, even if I can't do that with the Order."

A tiny frown wrinkled her forehead as she pulled back far enough to look at him. "No one can talk to the Queens, Math." Concern and worry rippled through her. "You'd have to let yourself be killed and absorbed—"

"No," he told her. "I don't. I've been able to hear them from the start, Kai. I can understand them. They don't speak out loud exactly, but I swear I can understand them."

"Truly?" She sat up straighter and slapped his chest. "Why didn't you reveal that as one of your capabilities?"

"I don't know if you remember this, Kai, but there was a point where you weren't exactly sure of my loyalties. I didn't think revealing that I could mentally hear the Queens would help my case."

Her lips twisted. "Perhaps not." Then, instead of saying anything else, she pulled a necklace from around her neck and looped it around Math's. "That will aid you in sensing danger." The bracelet she'd re-enchanted on the train followed the necklace. "And this will protect you from fatal injury—"

"You need that one. That saved your life when the train crashed."

"Take it before you upset me. I will make a spectacle of myself and wake everyone in the neighborhood." Kai removed several rings before she realized that nothing she wore would fit Math's fingers. She settled on another of her larger bracelets, made to wear high enough on her arm to allow it to fit Math's wrist.

"And what does this do?"

"For your purposes: energy," Kai told him. "It can also draw and erase gravings, but you won't know how to activate that magic. The energy is easier. Pull from here instead of from the wild source and you should stave off the risk of burnout even if you exceed your limits."

Math touched the metal. It was cold to the touch, even after having been worn on Kai's arm for the entire time he'd known her.

"Thank you." Then he sighed. "I suppose we should dress."

"We don't have to," she told him. "What if we chose instead to sleep in and missed the massacre?" She let out a very put-upon sigh at the expression he gave her then. "Fine. I didn't think you'd say yes. Foolish, stubborn, beautiful man." She stood up and began peeling her clothing off the rosebushes, dressing herself.

Math paused as he noticed the look in her eyes. It matched the emotions he could feel bubbling through her. Worry, yes, but more than that, determination and defiance, uncompromising conviction. Not at all the emotions of someone who was going to light a candle in a window and wait for their knight to come home.

But he never would've fallen in love with her if she had.

"Kai." He finished pulling up his trousers and tugged on his boots.

She raised her chin. "Yes?"

"Don't let the knights notice you following us. They won't react well."

They stared at each other for a moment. Then the corner of Kai's mouth quirked. "Do you take me for an amateur? They'll never see me."

※

Math snuck back into the barracks and ran smack into Alik Nuhzar. Who'd clearly been waiting for him.

"You're up early," Math said, as if he'd done nothing at all wrong.

Captain Nuhzar squinted at him. "You smell like flowers."

"Huh," Math said. "Yeah, that would be weird, me smelling like plants. Totally unfitting, considering my manifested weapon. I went for a walk. Did you need something?"

"Did anyone see you?"

Math threw him a scathing glare.

Nuhzar frowned, but then after a moment, nodded. "Did you get any sleep?"

"Did you?" Math was willing to bet the answer was no, even if the reason was substantially different than Math's.

"No," the captain admitted.

"Right. Then I guess we're ready to do this."

RIDE

After an early breakfast, Math joined the other knights preparing to leave. As one of the few who'd encountered these monsters before and survived, he tried to share what he could—the importance of avoiding the spores, the need for those with Land or Sea resonances to form barriers to block the stabbing vines and roots.

They didn't take him seriously.

They'd heard the briefing and assumed it would be easy. If Isofal had struggled, it was just because they weren't the Idallik's best, not like the capital's knights.

Math tried to warn them, but he had to wonder how many had already started hearing the chatter. That he was "unstable" and "inventing fantasies." Idallik Knights were ruthless gossips—and their commanders were no better.

The preparations were efficient, orderly. The two commanders—one per battalion—quickly assembled their people. Math migrated toward Nuhzar, the only familiar face. If Nuhzar had looked ever-so-briefly relieved to see him, neither acknowledged it.

"I spoke to Kai last night," Math whispered.

"Later," Nuhzar said. "Not here."

Math pressed his lips together. He understood the caution, but Nuhzar needed to know what he'd discovered. "Damn it, listen. It's going to be worse than I thought. By several orders of magnitude." He nudged his borrowed horse back into line for Bashan's Captain of Fields to work his magic.

He heard Nuhzar's soft curse, but there wasn't much he could do about it. There was a strict set of procedures to be followed. Math could no more step out of line than Nuhzar could jump ahead.

Then Math heard Nuhzar say, "Do you mind? I need to speak with my lieutenant."

The rider next to Math shifted aside, letting Nuhzar take her place.

Math gaped. "What are you doing?"

"Weren't you listening? I'm speaking with my lieutenant."

Math wished he could talk to people the same way he hoped he could talk to the Queens. Then he could've shouted, *What in the name of all that's holy do you think you're doing? You can't make* me *a lieutenant—I haven't even been knighted!* without anyone else reacting.

Alas, all he could do was glare.

Before he figured out a real response, the commanders called out the order to ride. Math urged his horse into a magical canter, and they were off.

"I was surprised to see you back at the cenobium this morning," Nuhzar said as they rode, because evidently this was one of those rides where conversation was possible. "After you snuck off to see your woman, I figured you wouldn't return."

"She's not my woman and I'm not a coward."

Nuhzar gave him a sidelong look. "If you're not a coward, maybe stop lying to yourself about that first part."

"Don't you want to know what she said?"

"Do you always ask stupid questions first thing in the morning?"

Math rolled his eyes. "They don't just rip people apart out of a love of gore, *Captain*. They do it because it splits the 'seed' into more pieces they can use to grow more people."

Nuhzar scowled. "What? I don't understand—"

"Huraiik's death didn't create one plant copy of him. It made half a dozen. I was wrong: he wasn't healing. I was just running into his twins."

Math hadn't realized that Nuhzar could curse like that, and he'd seen the man's reaction to finding frogs nesting in his helmet, or that time with the snakes.

"If we talk to the commanders . . ." Math began.

"They won't call off the attack on your word today any more than they would've yesterday."

Nuhzar said nothing else for the rest of the ride.

Admittedly, it wasn't a long ride. The Parnassa Forest stretched from south of Bashan through Valmaki County and into Kaliri. Soon enough, they were dismounting. Two hundred men and women made quick work unloading horses and wagons as they set up camp.

It was too close to the forest, Math noted. Far too close.

He tried to catch Nuhzar's attention, but the captain either didn't see him or ignored him—too absorbed in talks with the commanders.

Eventually, Math was forced to interrupt. "I need to speak with my captain."

Once they'd moved a short distance away, Nuhzar said, "What?"

"Assign me as a scout," Math said. "I'll try to talk to the Queens and convince them not to attack."

Nuhzar grabbed him by his cloak and dragged him farther from camp. "Stop," he hissed. "Think carefully before telling me you can *communicate* with those monsters. Especially, don't tell me you can plan to go off alone and have a private conversation right before a battle."

"You know I won't betray you." Math yanked his cloak free.

"Do I?" Nuhzar was red-faced with indignation. "At best, you'll give away our position—no matter how well-intentioned. At worst, the Queens will ambush you and send you back as an actual plant." He paused, expression bemused, and then looked visibly embarrassed.

"Take the win, Alik," Math said matter-of-factly. "That was a good pun."

"I didn't intend it."

"And you call me a coward? Always intend your puns."

"I've never called you a coward. Also: I hate you."

"Right back at you."

Nuhzar said nothing for a long beat, then: "If we took out the Queens, would it be enough? Would the rest fall back—or even die?"

"I don't know," Math answered honestly. "Maybe? But do you really think that's going to happen?"

"I took your warning last night to heart. Yes, I think it could. Never underestimate an Idallik Knight's determination."

Something about the way Nuhzar said that . . .

Math spun and studied the expanding camp.

Why were they making camp at all? A few tents for a field hospital, maybe—but this looked large enough to supply a protracted siege. Yet he didn't see any palisades or fortifications. Just a massive command tent in the center of camp.

A steady stream of knights were unloading wagons at the entrance, and—

Math squinted, and just as quickly, felt the blood drain from his face.

They were unloading crates of bombard mines.

"How much—?" He couldn't even finish the question.

Apparently, he didn't need to. "Enough, we hope," Nuhzar said. "It'll be enough, right? Normally we'd bury the mines, but it seemed safer to keep the powder off the ground."

Math started to tell Nuhzar that he'd better make sure knights were on hand to protect the tent from lightning strikes, from hail, from elemental magics, but Nuhzar must have already thought of that. That did, however, bring up a much more horrifying issue.

"No," Math said. "You can't. The Queens are smart. You won't lure them out of hiding so easily. That tent has to look important. It has to look busy." He paused. "Which means they'll still be in there when it explodes—"

He saw the look on Nuhzar's face and knew he'd guessed correctly—and it was nothing that Nuhzar didn't already know.

"The commanders . . . the commanders agreed?" Math asked, his voice hollow.

Nuhzar's lip curled. "You were never meant to be an Idallik Knight. I knew it when you refused to kill those monsters back in Ganda."

"Children, Alik. When I refused to kill those *children* back in Ganda." Math struggled to keep his voice down, his jaw tight with the effort.

"Monsters that haven't grown up yet are still monsters. You've never been willing to make the necessary sacrifices."

"I'm perfectly willing to make *the necessary sacrifices*," Math corrected. "Key word being *necessary*." He pointed to the tent. "This isn't."

"So you've said." Nuhzar's voice dripped with contempt. It was as if the past week just hadn't happened—like he'd regressed back into the man who only ever seemed happy when trying to convince Mathaiik to quit the Order. "That doesn't change the fact that you've never had the stomach for this. I don't trust you not to do something foolish."

"Captain, what are you talking about?" Math cursed himself. He'd been too friendly, too open. He'd made the horrible, irrecoverable mistake of thinking that Nuhzar was on his side.

"I want you out of this camp, and I want it to have happened five minutes ago." Nuhzar pulled a sealed letter and a messenger token out of his belt, shoving both into Math's hands. "Take a horse and ride back to Bashan. Deliver this to Commander Liradda. Lest your curiosity get the better of you, it's a request for more bombard powder. Just in case we didn't bring enough. That way I get my supplies, and you can't make trouble."

Math stared down at the letter. It was spiral-locked and wax-sealed.

Captain Nuhzar leaned forward. "As your commanding officer, *Lieutenant*, I'm giving you a direct order."

Math was sure that if he hesitated any longer, Nuhzar would tie him to a saddle and send him off that way.

"Yes, sir." Math's jaw trembled with anger. He was struggling not to say something reckless. This felt like betrayal, and it hurt more than he would have thought possible.

It made him angrier than he'd thought possible.

He'd trusted Nuhzar, and the Tri-Mother knew how many would die as a result, all to kill creatures who likely would've left them alone if the fine people of Rokasmaa had done the same.

For a moment, Math considered disobeying, trying to reach the Queens on his own. But it would be a nightmare of dodging patrols, hoping to find the Parnathi before either side found *him*.

And that didn't guarantee the Queens would help. Math wasn't fool enough to try a stunt on his own.

But maybe he wouldn't have to. Kai was somewhere on the road—he just had to find her.

"Get that look off your face," Nuhzar snapped. "I want you out of my sight."

"Yes, sir."

Math stomped his way to the pickets and reclaimed his borrowed horse. They hadn't even unsaddled him yet.

He set off—ostensibly for Bashan, but in truth, to find Kai.

VALEDICTION

Kai was traveling much more slowly than a magically assisted battalion of Idallik Knights. That regrettably meant she was only an hour out from Bashan when Math found her, riding a (likely) stolen horse at a steady canter.

They both rode harder as they noticed each other, finally meeting at the side of the road.

"What happened?" Kai asked.

"What happened is that I dramatically overestimated the amount of brain matter shared amongst the Idallik Order's leadership," Math said bitterly. "They're planning to blow up the Queens with bombard powder, never mind that it will probably take at least half our own men with them."

"I see." Kai frowned.

Math waved the small, carefully folded letter. "Nuhzar's sending me back for more. Mostly because he doesn't trust me."

Kai's eyes narrowed as she studied the letter. Then her hand darted out and she snatched it away from him.

He gave a token protest. "Hey!"

She flipped the letter over in her hands. "I thought you said these take time to write and fold."

"They do. Although some people are faster than others—" Math stopped, frowning.

There hadn't been enough time for Nuhzar to write that back at the camp.

They'd barely been there for a half hour—enough time to unload supplies, but not enough time to do a count, report a shortage, then write, spiral-lock, and seal a letter.

Which meant Nuhzar had to have written this before the trip even started. He'd claimed that he was sending Math away to make sure he couldn't cause trouble, but Math had only given him a reason to think he would *after* they'd made camp.

"May I have that back?"

Silently, Kai handed it to him.

The letter itself was pristine. No smudges, no jitters, no hastily scribbled notations. The folds were crisp and perfect, the wax—

He pressed the wax seal with his thumbnail. The wax was cold and hard.

This letter had been folded *hours* ago.

A feeling of absolute dread came over him.

"You think it's a trick," she said.

Math pulled his knife out of his belt and slashed open the letter. He wasn't being careful. He wouldn't be able to seal it again without more effort and time than he had, but he didn't have the supplies to do a proper job of it, anyway.

He read:

Math,

I've stayed up all night thinking about what you've told me, and I see no way to save this situation that you'd find palatable.

Talu's dirty. I can't prove he's our Kaliri spy, but it's the only solution that makes sense. The damage he's already done to your reputation is unrecoverable, and he's the one who insisted you come with us today. I think he's hoping you'll be too dead to defend yourself when he blames you for all his sins. Which I think he always meant to. He didn't raise you to be his protégé.

He raised you to be his scapegoat.

If he wants you dead, I say: be dead. They'll never be able to prove you didn't die on this battlefield. This messenger token will take you anywhere in the empire, no questions asked. Use it to take you and your woman far away from here. I cannot stand the idea of going to the grave still owing you for saving my life. Now we're even.

This is my gift to you. You should know that I meant every damn word I plan to say about how you were never meant to be an Idallik Knight. It's all true.

You were meant for so much better than this, you absolute ass.

So be something better. I know you have dreams of fighting evil, but you are one man facing off against forces you cannot possibly defeat. Let the empire take care of itself. Sometimes the bravest thing you can do is survive.

Your brother-in-arms,
Alik

"No," Math whispered. He couldn't . . .

It felt like a blade between the ribs. But even the fury that surged up was drowned by something worse: the slow, sick realization that there'd never been a request for powder. That Nuhzar had correctly predicted that Math would open the letter that had, in fact, always been intended for him. Nuhzar had pushed him away on purpose—not to wound him, but to save his life.

He'd insulted Math on purpose, dressed him down until Math would be too angry to ask questions, too angry to stay in camp.

Anything to convince Math to leave and not look back.

All to get Math out of there. Because honor had been everything to that gravefucker, and he couldn't save Math's life if the plan for victory hinged on a trap where everyone died.

"What does it say?" Kai asked, her concern obvious.

"We have to hurry," Math said as he passed the opened letter to her. "Maybe we'll reach the forest in time to stop—"

Off in the distance, a booming noise rumbled and shook the air.

For a heartbeat, Math prayed it was thunder. A storm was coming—he could see it, an anvil of dark clouds massing on the horizon.

Then came the smoke—a slow bloom of black, climbing above the treetops.

It wasn't thunder.

The trap had been sprung.

AFTERMATH

If Math had done as Alik wanted, he would've fled with Kai. Arguably, it would have been the smart thing to do.

He just couldn't.

Math had to know if anyone survived. He couldn't just *leave*.

Kai didn't question him when he said he wanted to keep going. She didn't try to convince him to take a different course of action. One might argue that she could afford to be magnanimous, since no matter what they found at the campsite, the one thing Math would be unlikely to do afterward was return to Bashan Cenobium. Or any Rokasmaa cenobium, for that matter.

There were other magical orders besides the Idalliks. None of them were in the Rokasmaa Empire, of course, but it was at least theoretically possible that he might convince the others to take him more seriously.

They would break down that door when they reached it.

Math smelled the battlefield long before he saw it. It was all too similar to the logging camp but compounded by a factor of ten: more bombard powder, more blood, more offal. This time, a metallic scent lingered in the air that had been absent from the first scene. The nearby forest arguably should have been on fire and wasn't, but it was hard to tell if that was because of the rain that had clearly come down at some point, the will of the Parnathi Queens, or the efforts of various knights before they were slain.

Then they spotted the camp and Math sucked in a breath. Kai gasped.

"Those bastards did it," Math murmured.

The center of the camp was little more than a crater. Bombard shrapnel had spread in all directions when it had exploded, likely killing everyone, friend or foe, in a broad area. Where the command tent had been lay the shattered remains of a gigantic ash tree, shattered and bleeding a green liquid too thin to be sap and the wrong color for human blood.

Math didn't need to be told that this was a Parnathi Queen.

Just one, though. He saw only a few traces of the second: some broken branches, a cluster of singed leaves. He picked up a blackened acorn, stared at it for a blank, frozen moment, and then tucked it into a pouch.

"Only Oak remains," Kai said, with a surprising amount of sorrow in her voice. "Although she is the strongest of them."

Math walked his horse through the camp, caught between searching the bits and pieces for any recognizable signs of identity, and desperately hoping not to find any. The closer to the center of the camp, the less identifiable those remains proved to be, but that left plenty of knights who had been killed by vines or branches or, even more uncomfortably, magic.

This was not a victory. Part of Math wanted to return to Bashan, just to scream at the damn commanders who had so callously thrown away two hundred of their finest.

He had no way of knowing if the two commanders ostensibly in charge of this attack had also died alongside their men. He hoped they rotted for a thousand years if they hadn't.

Math couldn't find any sign of Nuhzar. No sign that he could identify as belonging to his childhood nemesis.

"Math, I found him."

Math shut his eyes in pain. Then he walked over to Kai.

She stood next to a tree of the mundane and nonanimating variety, looking at something near its base with obvious consternation while chewing on the edge of her thumb.

Math followed her sight line with his own and immediately wished he hadn't.

Yes. She'd found Alik Nuhzar.

He'd survived the initial explosion, amazingly enough, proving that above all else, he was a tough bastard to the bitter end. Unfortunately, while he had survived, most of one leg and everything from the knee down on both hadn't. No amount of first-circle Wood spells would stop the blood loss from two missing limbs.

He'd bled out while pulling himself away from the crater.

Math squatted down next to the body. "You son of a corpse," he whispered. "I'll never forgive you for this."

He knew tears were running down his face and he didn't care.

It would've been nice to have kept trading nick-of-time rescues back and forth, cussing each other out the entire time. Math had been rather looking forward to it. Maybe they would've even stopped pretending to despise each other, although Math hadn't planned on holding his breath.

He would never know.

He felt the pressure of Kai's hand on his shoulder pauldron. He touched the back of her hand gently, acknowledging the intention to comfort.

"I'm sorry, Math," Kai said. "I'm sorry for all of this, but I'm most especially sorry that we cannot stay. It's too dangerous—"

It was as though she'd finished a summoning incantation. They both raised their heads as a rapid-fire drumming sound—incredibly fast—grew louder by the second.

"That didn't take long," Math muttered. "Someone must have seen the smoke." He stood up. "They can't find you here."

"You need to leave, too—"

"I will. Go!" He reached over and channeled power into the bracelet he knew she'd graved for invisibility.

She vanished. Math exhaled at one less distraction to worry about. Given their location, he could either go into the woods, back out to the main road, or cross the river. That seemed a simple choice. He magically shifted twice: the first time to the riverbank, and the second time to the other side. He was sad to leave the horse behind, but he didn't have a choice. The horse was faster, but he was infinitely more maneuverable with his magic.

Math was pretty sure that he'd moved fast enough to clear the area before the travel spell on the reinforcements finished, which meant they were unlikely to have spotted him. Running would attract notice, but if he skipped to the right spot, he'd be hidden—

Electricity coursed through his body, excruciating and paralyzing. He fell to the rocky ground, convulsing.

Even through the suffocating pain, he was aware of being picked up by men in plate armor, and dragged back across the river.

Math was kept too weak to spellcast by using a very simple technique: any time he seemed too coherent, an Idallik Knight with a Storm resonance would shock him again. Wood's weakness was Storm: it wasn't hard to keep him too paralyzed to take action.

Even so, he was aware of certain things. The feel of the cold water on his legs as two knights dragged him across the shallow river. The noises made by the camp horses, who'd been too far away to be killed in the initial explosion, and evidently were of no particular interest to the Parnathi.

The feel of Commander Talu's gauntleted fingers on his face as the older man examined him, and then efficiently pulled free the leather straps on his breastplate, leaving Math in nothing but his arming doublet.

The fact that Talu carried one of the Kaliri long arm weapons.

Talu stepped away from Math and raised his voice. "Kaiataris! I know you're close enough to hear my voice! Show yourself."

Nothing but the mocking sound of ravens who were waiting until everyone left to begin their feasting greeted that demand.

Talu shook his head in disappointment. He lowered the weapon from where he'd had it slung over his shoulder and walked until he was around twenty feet from Math and the two knights holding him. When he spoke, it was at a volume that suggested he'd used magic to amplify his voice. "I don't know if you've had the pleasure of seeing one of these used, Lady Kaiataris. I've only recently come into possession of this one myself. It is a truly brutal weapon." Talu set the stock against his shoulder. "And if you don't show yourself by the count of three, you're going to see what I mean firsthand."

"One—" Talu aimed the weapon at Math.

"Two—" He lined up the sight.

"Stop!" Kai called out.

. . . then *boom*.

Math screamed. So did Kai.

He could never satisfactorily describe the pain, a sensation at once like being splashed in ice-cold water and dropped into a furnace. In an abstract, distant way, he knew that he'd fallen to his knees on the sharp rocks, and his knees were unlikely to be happy about that turn of events.

Math was reminded of his father's forge and ugly stories someone had told him—maybe his father, maybe someone else—about old gods who demanded their sacred weapons be quenched in human blood. This felt like how he always imagined that would feel.

"Oh dear," Talu said. "You seem to have cut that a little close, Lady Kaiataris. Unfortunate that there really is no good place to be injured by a weapon such as this, but I made sure to shoot him in the gut." He tilted his head to examine Math's back. "Looks like it might have passed right through him. Even so, he'll take a long time to die."

"Stop this!" Kaiataris yelled. "I'm surrendering. Heal him!"

"Of course," Commander Talu promised agreeably. "Once you divest yourself of every single graven object you possess."

"Don't," Math whispered.

Unfortunately, no one was paying any attention to him. He heard jewelry clinking as it was dropped into a bag, and a familiar, no-longer-comforting voice say, "Thank you, Lady Kaiataris. That was very cooperative. Sivaiik, keep our brother from dying, if you'd be so kind, but don't heal him enough to give him a chance to do something rash."

He felt hands on his stomach, after which everything faded away.

TREASON

When Math woke, he was being carried up a flight of stone steps into a building with the familiar curves of a cenobium. A wave of disassociation immediately followed, because Bashan Cenobium didn't look like the classical cenobium design. It had been built much later, after all. No, the only building in Bashan that shared that architectural style wasn't the Idallik Order's headquarters.

Also, Math absolutely recognized it, because he'd been there just the day before: this was the imperial palace.

Math pretended he was still asleep. He was unsure what struggling would have done for his situation, anyway. He felt the itchy burn of rope around his wrists and drooled around a gag someone had thrust into his mouth. Not so long ago, that would've been enough to keep him from circling spells.

That was no longer true, but he didn't think Talu realized that.

What was also true was that he was still grievously wounded. Every jostle elicited a flash of pain across his abdomen. He didn't think his odds of fighting off other Idallik Knights—if that's truly what they were—would be very good under such circumstances. At least he could feel that Kai was unharmed—upset, worried, incandescent with rage, but unharmed.

He couldn't believe Izhiik Talu had shot him. The man had practically raised him, and the gravefucker had *shot* him.

Then again, the man had stabbed Math in the metaphorical back enough times to make this the natural progression.

Quick footsteps rang out across the stone floors. "Hey, what are you—?"

That was followed by the sharp ring of metal and the slick gurgling sound of someone choking on their own blood.

Talu and his men proceeded to quickly and efficiently murder the palace guards. Math's blood quickened, even as he tried to pretend at unconsciousness. The children were somewhere inside. His *sister* was somewhere inside.

"I don't suppose it occurred to you to give them a chance to surrender," Kai commented.

"If they did, they wouldn't deserve to live, anyway," Talu replied.

"Ah yes. Impeccable logic."

"Be quiet, Lady Kaiataris, or I'll forget why I need to keep you unharmed."

And that shut down the conversation for a while. Math concentrated on healing himself and hoped that the magic was subtle enough to allow the spellcasting to go unnoticed.

Since no one commented or attempted to stop him, he assumed such was the case.

They went through the palace at an absurdly fast pace, but most of the palace guards were normal people, not Idallik Knights.

Finally, he heard large doors swinging open, and a strange man's voice asked: "What is the meaning of this?"

"Where is Her Excellency?" Commander Talu asked congenially.

"I— She's not here. I'm not sure where she is."

"Are you certain? It's important."

"No, I—" The man's denial was cut off by his own gasp, and a gurgling sound, followed seconds later by a loud thud.

Math was going to need to invent new swear words to adequately describe his new opinion of Izhiik Talu.

A second later, Math found himself dumped on the hard marble floor.

"How about you? Do you know where Her Excellency might be?" Talu's voice still sounded perfectly friendly, even though Math was certain he'd just murdered a man.

Math opened his eyes to see Commander Talu holding a dagger with a dark teal sheen in front of a terrified noblewoman. It looked like a normal dagger; Math knew it wasn't.

"Commander, she doesn't know anything." If Math had to use magic for his voice to be heard at above-whisper volumes, he wasn't telling. Across the way, he saw Kai give him a look that clearly meant to be quiet, but he refused. He knew Talu. The man would go through every single person in the building to find the regent.

"Back with us, Math?" Commander Talu smiled at him, visibly amused. "How are you feeling, my son?"

"You don't get to call me that." Math didn't spit at the man, although Tri-Mother knew he wanted to.

"Probably just as well," Talu admitted, "considering your history with parental figures."

Math swallowed a scowl before it could choke him. Talu had mentioned his parents to strike a nerve, and Math had more important things to worry about.

"As I was saying," Math continued amiably, "apparently the regent hates talking to the cenobium commanders so much that any time she's forced to do so, instead of returning to the palace afterward, she visits her favorite taverns. Possibly her favorite brothels, if you want to believe the rumors."

Commander Talu's expression turned to annoyance, then he laughed. "I can hardly blame her. Honestly, I wish I'd had the guts. But somebody here must have a way to contact her." He bent down next to Math, ignored his flinch, and helped him sit up.

Now at Math's eye level, Talu continued: "And how do you know this information, Math? You can't blame me for being a little skeptical, hmm?"

"I know this," Math said, unsuccessful at keeping the bitterness out of his voice, "because I came here yesterday. Snuck out of the cenobium to warn the regent that this morning's mission would lead half the Order into a mass grave. So believe me, I was just as frustrated as you to find her missing. And you're right. Somebody *does* know how to contact her: Commander Liradda."

"I see." Talu looked over his shoulder at one of the other knights. Math didn't recognize the man. He didn't look Kaliri, but frankly, Math didn't think they'd have sent over any spies who did. "Lieutenant, is there any chance Commander Liradda might still be . . ."

"No, sir. He's dead."

"Damn." Talu stood. "Send someone to search his body and his room. He'll have kept the means of contact close by. Perhaps we'll be able to recognize it." In a much lower register, he muttered, "I don't know why I'm surprised. That bitch has never been anything other than a nuisance for a single moment of her life."

Math huffed out a laugh. He knew he liked the regent for a reason.

"Something amusing you, son?"

He smiled up at Talu. "Just thinking that this is not how I wanted to tell the Council of Commanders 'I told you so.'" The gallows humor of it all was suffocating. "Although even I didn't expect Kaliri's invasion to be quite so . . . immediate."

Talu's expression turned annoyed. "I'm not Kaliri. This isn't an invasion."

"Is that so?"

"This," Talu said, sweeping a hand, "is a coup."

Math laughed. "Is that what they told you?"

"Math," Kai said. "Please do shut up."

Talu pointed at her while maintaining eye contact with Math. "You should listen to her. I'm told she's smart."

"You heard right." Math staggered to his feet—an action made more difficult with bound hands. A knight advanced on him, but Talu waved him away.

"It's fine. Let him stand. At the risk of insulting his dignity, there really isn't much he can do in his current condition."

"I don't know," someone said, "he seems to be doing a pretty good job of giving us all sad, puppy-dog eyes. Isn't this the one who can't manifest?"

"No, he recently had a breakthrough," Talu said in a very conversational tone of voice. He stage-whispered: "It's a shield."

That was cause for laughter all around, and for once, it made Math glad. They were dismissing him as a threat. They were underestimating him.

Talu sighed. "I really do wish you'd taken the hint and just run after you managed to escape my assassins. We might have avoided all of this. Alas, here we are. I'll do what I can to protect you, but it's a very fine line. Don't make me cross over it."

"Those were your assassins? And you wonder why I think you're working for the Kaliri?"

"Working with," Talu confessed. "I believe they call it a mutually beneficial arrangement."

"How you can think I'll believe a single word you say is astonishing. I am curious, though: Why the sudden pressing need to kill me? For that matter, why go through all the trouble to send me away? You could've killed me at any time, at your convenience."

Talu's expression turned rueful. "I should have thought it was obvious. Because of Kaiataris. You told me that you'd figured out how to solve her maze. I couldn't allow you to do that. And I sent you away for the same reason farmers always exchange hogs to slaughter in the autumn. No one wants to butcher their own pet."

"I came to you saying that we had to make sure her maze *was never opened*."

Talu gave him a skeptical look. "I've been a young man, Math. It was only a matter of time before curiosity overruled sense."

"Okay, great. You were trying to save the world from the Evil Grim Lord. That doesn't explain this." He looked around the room, took note of the cluster of nobles shuddering in a corner.

The old man sighed and dusted off his tabard. "I'm curious: Are you trying to delay me for a reason or are you just hoping I'll spell out all my plans?"

Math gave him a small, weak shrug. "It was worth an effort." He was hardly going to admit it was both. He'd hoped he might get the commander talking, *and* every second delayed was another second to heal his wound.

Talu looked mildly amused. "I'm sure. Anyway, you wouldn't understand."

The commander started to motion to someone, no doubt to some horrible instruction.

"Try me."

Talu rolled his eyes. He stopped, looked thoughtful, then returned his attention to Math.

"Very well," Talu said. "Let me explain it thus: we're taken from our homes, forced to become weapons to protect the empire regardless of our feelings on the matter. We're allowed nothing—not wives or husbands, not children, property, or wealth. And what is our thanks?" He glanced around the room, as if this were a class, and he'd just asked when the Innalova Accords were signed.

"Being spat on in the street," a knight answered.

"And then shat on," another added. There were murmurs of agreement from around the room.

"It's your duty!" one of the nobles cried.

Said noble was immediately impaled by a knight with a dripping spear in his hands.

"Oops," the knight said. "I slipped."

Talu laughed, and he wasn't the only one.

"And we're expected to smile," Talu said to Math. He was smiling, but it was a long way from being friendly. "And be grateful. So what if we took the gifts that people gave us for saving their lives? So what if we expected nobles to pay more than peasants for risking ourselves to protect them?"

"That's called corruption," Kai said.

"It's called our fucking due!" Talu snapped. "Am I really supposed to think that the nobility are somehow better when they're demonstrably not? They can't do magic. Most of them can barely *read*. Who has the Tri-Mother blessed again? Who protects the archives? It's not them!" He scowled and waved a hand. "Someone find me Shovan!" Talu visibly collected himself. "Where is Her Imperial Majesty, by the way?"

"Upstairs," a female knight supplied. "We locked her in her room with her playmates. There was another knight up there with them. She caused a bit of a problem, but it's handled."

Math clenched his teeth together at the usage of past tense. *Please, no.*

Talu's brows drew together. "Who was it?"

"Tanxi Kaven, Commander."

Math inhaled sharply, even though he'd already known it couldn't be anyone else.

A flicker of concern crossed Talu's face, and he glanced quickly at Math. "What's her condition?"

"Alive, sir. A little worse for wear, but we're keeping her unconscious." She smiled wryly. "The children seem to like her, so we've told them that if they make any trouble, we'll kill her. When she wakes up, we're going to tell her the same thing about them."

Math exhaled. At least Tanxi was alive.

"*Well done*, Lieutenant Wanimar," Commander Talu said with feeling. "Thank the Tri-Mother. Something's gone right today." He pointed to Math. "Hear that, my boy? Your sister is proving to be our most valuable hostage."

"I'm sure she'll be thrilled to hear it."

"I can well imagine her outrage." Talu's smile settled into something significantly nastier. "But more importantly, *she's* someone I can kill. Which means I can count on you to behave now, can't I? I don't want to kill Tanxi. I *like* Tanxi. Don't make me do something we'll both regret."

Math stared. Talu had said something similar before, but Math had been in too much pain to pay attention. Why couldn't Talu kill Kai? No, that wasn't the real question. It wasn't why Talu couldn't kill *Kai*. It was why he hadn't killed *Math*. He had already tried once. What had changed? Why was Math's cooperation now important?

If Talu was working with the Kaliri, keeping Kai alive made sense. The Kaliri might easily consider Kai nothing short of holy.

The Kaliri had no motivation at all for keeping *Math* alive. Unfortunately, though, Math knew one person out there who had a great deal of motivation to keep Math alive—as a hostage on Kaiataris's behavior.

Talu cleared his throat. "Say the words out loud."

"I'll behave."

Which was a lie. Math wasn't behaving at that very moment. He was just waiting for the right opportunity. Which he hoped would come soon, because now he knew something that he hadn't just a few moments earlier.

Now he knew who Talu worked for, and it wasn't the Kaliri.

Talu worked for Sanistral.

EMPIRE

Talu was still giving Math an assessing look when Lieutenant Wanimar asked, "What should we do about them, Commander?" She hooked a thumb toward the cluster of simultaneously frightened and indignant nobles.

"Oh, them," Talu said. "I'd forgotten about them. Apparently, the nobility *can* keep their mouths shut with the right incentive. I'll have to remember that in the future." The commander smirked. "Kill them."

Math looked away as the knights set to work. He couldn't watch. He wouldn't be able to stop himself from doing something foolish.

Given the noise, at least a few people tried to fight.

They didn't last long.

Math sought out Kai and found her standing close by. Her horror mirrored his.

The next five minutes were possibly the hardest and most difficult of Math's whole life.

He was still injured. The knights were practically begging him to try something. They were ready for him if he did. All Math could do was bide his time, wait for the right moment.

Sometimes the bravest thing you can do is survive.

If Alik had still been alive, Math would've called him a thousand names and kicked his ass. The last thing in the world that this felt like was bravery.

He looked up through tears to realize Kai stood beside him again, her eyes full of unspoken questions he couldn't answer.

Talu gave Math that fond, wry look again, the one that once would have made Math so pleased and now made him seethe. His examination of Kai was more speculative, and much more openly antagonistic. He headed up to the dais of the imperial throne, although he was apparently not so completely disloyal as to try sitting on it.

"Hurry this up!" Talu called to his people when they finished with their massacre. "You've had your fun. Now we have a schedule to keep."

Math felt something brush up against his arm and looked down to see Kai, face pressed against his arm as though she were tired, in the middle of crying, or both. What he felt from her, however, was nothing but anger and determination. He didn't react as he felt her fingers behind his back, following the line of his arm down toward the cuffs. Something clicked.

"Hey, get away from him!" a knight called out a second before Kai was dragged away. She did her best impression of an upset young woman, but didn't fight back.

Math banged the back of his head against the wall. So close.

Math searched faces when he could see them, armor designs when he couldn't. Most of them, he didn't recognize. One of those knights stood in the middle of the room and circled Land spells to break up the marble flooring and move aside the resulting rubble.

Gradually, an underlayer of stone was revealed.

Kai made a catlike hissing noise.

The revealed floor had been graved with a travel circle, exactly like the one they'd used in the tower to take them to Lomar. Unlike that one, however, a piece of this graving was missing, a thin wedge cut away from the pattern.

This transport gate wouldn't have shown up on the map, because it hadn't been complete.

Someone handed Commander Talu an object wrapped in fabric, which he unwrapped to reveal the missing piece. He carefully set the piece down into the empty space, fiddled with it a bit until there was a click. He stepped back from the pattern, frowning.

"I'm not sure if that worked," Commander Talu admitted. "I suppose we'll find out in a few minutes."

"I really hate being right," Math said bitterly. "I was honestly kind of hoping you really were a Kaliri spy. Better that than working for Sanistral Lomar."

Kai's anger drained away, replaced with horror.

Talu glanced at his knights to see who might be paying attention. "We have compatible goals," the commander explained.

"Whatever he has promised you," Kai said, "whatever sweet words he has whispered in your ear, I promise you that his vows are nothing but lies."

Talu shrugged. "He's never failed to deliver before—"

The pattern glowed. Math made one last effort to pull free from his bindings, but whatever Kai had done, it hadn't been enough.

The glow increased to sunspot brightness, forcing everyone to shield their eyes. When they could see again, Sanistral Lomar and a dozen of his undead soldiers stood in the throne room.

"Well done, Commander Talu," King Sanistral said. He didn't so much step off the pattern as float off.

The undead spread out immediately. One grabbed Kai. Another one pulled Math toward the center of the room.

Math caught Kai's eye and she shook her head in warning. "Don't," she mouthed silently. *Don't try anything. Don't fight.*

This still wasn't the right time. Just survive.

"Very well done," King Sanistral murmured, as his gaze lingered on Kai. He touched her cheek with a finger that looked alive. The dead guard holding her arms kept her from flinching away. "Are you ready to help?"

She scoffed. "How could you possibly think I ever would?"

King Sanistral and his guards, almost as one, stared at Math.

The implication wasn't subtle.

"If you kill him," Kai spat, "I will never aid you."

Sanistral nodded. "Understood, but you're not thinking this through. If I kill him, then you only have one way to restore him to life: by helping me. It's your decision, but wouldn't it be more reasonable to save him such excruciating agony and bow to the inevitable from the start? One way or the other, you will do as I demand." He paused before delivering the fatal blow. "After all, you love him."

Kai closed her eyes.

"Don't," Math told her. "He finishes that ritual, and we all die anyway—"

One of Talu's knights punched him in the mouth. Math tasted iron; the world flashed white. He couldn't be certain how much time passed during that flash, but people were in the same relative positions, so probably not more than a few seconds.

Kai was staring at Math with a look of infinite, inconsolable sadness, her eyes bright with tears.

"Don't do it," Math whispered.

"I'm sorry," she mouthed back, too quiet to be heard.

King Sanistral nodded firmly, as if she'd given him an answer. He gestured to Commander Talu. "Did you bring what I asked?"

"Yes, Your Majesty," Talu said. On cue, a knight came forward, carrying several large tree branches, hit by lightning or damaged in an explosion. They dripped a green fluid more like the consistency of blood than sap. The leaves resembled oaks. "The battalions we sent after the Queens destroyed Ash."

"Impressive," Sanistral said, and sounded like he meant that sincerely.

"They gave their lives to do it." Commander Talu's expression was hard to read. Math couldn't tell if he was pleased or angry at the outcome of that encounter. He motioned for the knight carrying the branches to hand them over to one of Sanistral's people. "Fortunately, we assume the Queen of Oaks survived, if injured."

Math scowled. Part of him hated how close the Idallik Council of Commanders had come to making the right call. If they *had* killed both Queens, Sanistral's plans would have been ruined.

"A few branches would not be sufficient for the ritual plans you showed me in Lomar," Kai commented. "You would need the Queen herself."

Sanistral gave Kai an indulgent smile. "You're right, my dear. But you'll find a few branches are more than sufficient for a curse. Her only chance of escaping it will be to locate these branches and destroy them. That means she'll have to come to me."

Kai's eyes narrowed. "You were never planning to gain her cooperation, were you?"

"Of course not. The Parnathi are the *competition*. Fortunately, I don't require her cooperation. She is but a single piece of a much grander design."

Commander Talu cleared his throat. "Is that all, Your Majesty?"

Math rolled his eyes. Sure, he didn't work for Sanistral. Clearly.

"Yes. It is. Excellent work, Commander. Always a pleasure to deal with a professional. The city—and the empire, for that matter—is yours."

Talu inclined his head. "Not yet. First, we'll need to repel 'a Kaliri invasion.'" He gave a knowing smile to Sanistral, who returned it. "That should be more than enough of a distraction to keep anyone from paying attention to you."

Math narrowed his eyes. So Talu had been telling the truth. It wasn't an invasion, only meant to look like one. In the aftermath, Talu could claim that the Kaliri had taken the palace, killed the regent, and conveniently murdered all of Talu's political rivals.

Depending on how Talu had arranged matters, it was possible that the Kaliri wouldn't even make an appearance.

But no. Math immediately corrected himself, thinking of the real Kaliri assassins who had tried to kill him. Talu's deal with the Kaliri was real, and he'd need real bodies to present as proof of his victory.

Sanistral gave Talu an ambivalent nod. He didn't give a damn about Talu's plans to make himself king.

"We'll be on the roof. We are not to be disturbed—unless it's by an enormous oak tree. Do allow that one through." Sanistral held out a hand to Kai. "Shall we?"

Kaiataris raised her chin even as she placed her hand in Sanistral's. She didn't look at Math. Her face betrayed nothing of the loathing that boiled within as she nodded to her former teacher. Those emotions were mixed with determination, resignation, and acceptance.

Kai would do whatever was necessary to stop the ritual. If that meant her death, so be it.

"What about the prisoners?" Commander Talu asked.

"As long as you keep them out of my way, do whatever you like."

"Sanis..." Kai warned.

"Fine," the grim lord allowed. "Please continue to see to the young man's safety. We do not wish our lady to be upset."

Talu bowed his head in acquiescence.

Sanistral studied Math—a collector examining an interesting specimen—before adding: "I wouldn't dream of telling you how to do your job, of course, but why is he still in armor?"

Talu's smile was flat. "We didn't have time to remove it."

"Ah." With that, the grim lord lost interest.

Sanistral gestured toward the front of the throne room, and pieces of marble immediately began rearranging themselves, stacking together to form a stairway leading up to a seemingly new door in the ceiling. He flicked open the doors—again without touching them. What lay beyond was, perhaps not surprisingly, another flight of stairs leading farther up.

The negligent ease with which Sanistral cast his magic could only mean one thing: at some point, probably centuries before, Sanistral had graved the walls of the Bashan repository to create a second domain.

Sanistral led Kai upstairs. The stone doors slammed shut behind them.

ESCAPE

There was a moment of silence as the doors shut. No one moved, and the only sounds were the scraping noise of bodies being dragged over marble.

Lieutenant Wanimar turned to Commander Talu. "What ritual?"

"*Now* you ask?" Math scoffed.

She glanced angrily at Math. "I'm not fool enough to question things when that . . . that . . ." She gestured toward where King Sanistral had vanished.

"Grim lord," Math said. "The noun you're looking for is *grim lord*."

A different knight paused from where they'd been dragging bodies. "Fuck. Really?"

"That's enough," Commander Talu said. "He's not a grim lord, he's just powerful."

"Don't believe Talu," Math said. "Sanistral is absolutely a grim lord. *The* original grim lord. When he finishes that ritual, it's either going to make him a god or destroy all life or both. He doesn't care: *he's already dead.*"

Commander Talu gave him a frown that might have made him quake not that long ago. "Please remember I have your sister locked away upstairs and *be quiet*." He turned his head. "Someone find me a secure room where we can put this puppy. I don't want to hear him yapping. Make sure he stays out of sunlight."

It was almost a comfort to know that Commander Talu didn't want to take the chance that Math might convince his people. It meant that these really were Idallik Knights, and not secret Kaliri.

Whatever their motivations or complaints about their treatment, they were still citizens of Rokasmaa. They were still Idallik Knights. That meant they'd grown up believing their order had been founded for the sole purpose of defeating grim lords and their minions.

More than a few of them had to be questioning what was happening.

At least, Math hoped.

Talu's knights found a secure room for Math: it was a linen closet.

Math said, "Ask yourself what's going to happen when Sanistral doesn't need you anymore. He has zero motivation to allow the Idallik Order to exist."

The knights threw him inside the closet and closed the door, plunging him into darkness.

For about three seconds.

That's how long it took him to circle a Sun spell and summon up a light. This time, it looked like a series of softly glowing mushrooms sprouting from the walls and ceiling.

"I like those," Math admitted.

He examined the room and found it stubbornly remained a linen closet. A very fancy linen closet, with a lot of beautiful fabrics embroidered with the imperial lions, but still a small room filled with shelves. He reached for one of those fine sheets, only to be reminded that his hands were still bound. Math thought the problem over for a minute. He didn't know if he could shift out of the bindings. Shifting took his clothes along with him, after all. It seemed like the same idea.

He glanced down again at the shelves. The wooden shelves.

Dead wood, but he could work with that.

He needed to find his sister and the kids, then figure out how to rescue Kai. She was fine at that moment. He felt her through the bond, miserable but whole.

He returned to contemplating the shelves. Math could manifest a shield made from plants regardless of whether any plants were in the area, but he'd also done the opposite. Math had deliberately pulled materials from the environment to reinforce his shield of vines and brambles.

Vines . . .

It turned out his ropes were also made from plant fiber, so escaping his restraints proved absurdly easy.

As he rubbed his wrists, he noticed that Kai's bracelet was missing. Had he dropped it?

No. Kai had taken it back. She hadn't been trying to untie his hands, she'd been retrieving the bracelet. Talu had forced her to remove her jewelry, and Sanistral hadn't been fool enough to give any of it back.

Math hoped she could make good use of it.

The door opened. Math spun around, shield in hand, expecting Idallik Knights.

But it wasn't the right door, and it wasn't Idallik Knights.

Members of the Idallik Order, yes, but not *knights*.

A secret doorway, hidden behind a panel, had slid open, revealing seven-year-old Empress Asali. She held a glowing ball of golden light in her hand and a pleased expression on her face. Beside her stood Jaiik and Taris. Jaiik held his lightning javelin, and Taris had her hands clenched around an inky-black spear.

They'd both manifested their weapons. He wished he'd had time to properly congratulate them.

"Come on!" Jaiik whispered while making a hurried motion for Math to follow.

Math didn't need to be told twice.

"What—" he muttered as he stepped out of the linen closet and into a small, cramped tunnel. It seemed less like a servants' tunnel than an escape route.

Empress Asali raised her chin. "Told you," she murmured to her older companions, and closed the door to the linen closet again.

Math stared at the glowing ball of light in the empress's hand. When she noticed, she blushed and looked away, but made no comment.

Tanxi hadn't created the glowing light Math had seen when he'd first met the little empress. Asali had.

The empress had a Sun resonance.

No wonder the regent hadn't minded leaving her with a bunch of Idallik novitiates. No wonder she hadn't wanted Asali left playing with the children of nobles—children guaranteed to gossip to the wrong people.

Any child with magical ability was required to enter the Order, but as the sole heir to the empire, Asali would be required to marry, to have children. One could not be both an Idallik Knight and empress of the empire.

Much as he sympathized, they had more important problems.

"Nicely done," Math told her. "Thank you. You don't know where my sister is, do you?"

"We've got her," Jaiik said. "She hasn't woken yet. They shocked her pretty hard. Come on, this way."

"No," Asali corrected. "This way." She pointed down a side tunnel.

"Right," Jaiik said. "I knew that."

Taris hit his arm.

"I did!" he protested. "Or, I would have figured it out! Eventually!"

Asali just rolled her eyes, and kept leading them down a hallway, then down a set of stairs, until Math had no idea if they were even still in the palace. They came out into an abandoned cistern, still wet, covered in moss and algae. It didn't smell nearly as bad as it should have.

This was either not the first time it had served as a hiding place or the children had been very busy, because someone had found a rough, serviceable couch and placed it on top of old, moth-eaten rugs. They partitioned off rooms with torn sheets and clotheslines. Math thought back to memories of a young girl playing fort under a table in Cherkiss and had a feeling he knew who was responsible.

One curtain was pushed aside, giving Math a clear view of Tanxi being helped into a sitting position by Iduan and Satu. He saw the other kids sitting on pillows in the area. A few of them were sleeping. Most huddled under blankets.

"We got him!" Jaiik called out, at which point Tanxi's head snapped up.

"Jaiik, Taris, you two were supposed to be in charge," Tanxi immediately scolded. "You let the empress go off with you all alone?"

While the two preteens flushed and stammered excuses, Asali calmly walked forward. "It's not their fault. I'm the only one who knew the way," she reminded Tanxi.

Taris indignantly pointed at the empress. "See?"

"No offense, big sister, but we have bigger problems."

Tanxi stilled, staring at Math. "What happened?"

"Hmm." He thought that over for a minute. "In summary? Commander Talu—"

"No," Tanxi snapped. "What *happened*?" She pointed to the front of his jazerant coat, which admittedly had a pretty sizable hole in it, front and back. Blood had dyed a significant portion of the surrounding fabric dark reddish brown.

"Right," Math said. "That."

"That, yes. Were you *stabbed*?"

"In a way? Commander Talu shot me with a Kaliri black-powder weapon. I've mostly healed it."

"Commander Talu?" Her voice was disbelieving.

Math doubted the Idallik Knights who'd knocked her unconscious had bothered explaining exactly whose orders they'd been opening.

"Yeah. Turns out the commander is a traitor who's staging a coup. He's killed just about everyone who can stop him and has invited the grim lord Sanistral into the palace. The grim lord has taken Kai prisoner and plans—"

"Who's Kai?" Iduan asked.

Math hesitated. "The girl who was asleep back in the center of the maze in Isofal."

"The girl you were with in Cherkiss?" the empress asked.

"Did you kiss her?" Mudiya asked.

Jaiik glanced over at Taris, who was watching him with narrowed eyes. The boy didn't say a word.

"That is . . . so not the point right now," Math answered. "Sanistral is—"

"Tri-Mother. You *have* kissed her." That was from Tanxi.

"Seriously. Focus, or I am going to start talking about the time I walked in on you and that girl from the Charters section. Sanistral is going to enact a ritual that will either make him a god or kill all life. Possibly both. We need to stop him, and we need to find the regent, and we need to do both things *yesterday*. And then we need to do something about Talu, and him being a traitor who may or may not have killed all the other commanders."

Tanxi's mouth had dropped open in shock, but she pulled herself together quickly. "We have you, me, and thirteen *children*." She raised a hand to Jaiik's and Taris's protests. "I don't want to hear it from either of you. You're *babies*." She turned back to Math. "How do you plan to do any of this?"

"That's a good question."

Tanxi waited.

And waited.

"And . . . ?"

"I was hoping you might have an idea."

"You need Imar," said one tiny, adorable little empress.

Math stopped pacing and went down to one knee in front of her. "Yes," he agreed. "I do need the regent. I just don't know where she is. And yesterday you said you didn't know either. Is that still true?"

She flushed, turned her head to the side, then pulled a necklace over her head with one hand and held it out, the chain dangling from her clenched fist. It was a cameo of the imperial lions, carved into shell and set in gold. "If I ever really, really, really need to find her, she's said I could use this."

Tanxi came over, too, gently taking the necklace. "Did she explain how?"

Asali frowned. "She just said that she had a necklace made from the same piece of shell."

Tanxi grinned. "She's right then. I can find her with this."

"Great!" Math said. "Then we just need to finish escaping the palace, find the regent, let her know what's going on, and see about maybe bringing in an army or two to fight off some rogue Idalliks and give Sanistral a hard time on the roof. First, though, we need to get you kids to safety."

Tanxi squinted. "And then what?"

"Then I need to find the Queen of Oaks, convince her to join forces with us against a mutual enemy, and stop a ritual that's going to destroy the world and turn the woman I love into an undead abomination."

Math didn't really think he was fooling anyone into thinking this would be easy. Or even possible. Even little Hamu looked skeptical.

"—the woman you love?" Tanxi repeated.

Figures she would home in on that part.

"If everything goes well, I'll introduce you," Math promised. "She has a terrible sense of humor: you'll love her. But first, let's get out of here."

"That's easy," Asali said. She pointed toward an old door. "That's an escape tunnel."

"Neat," Math said. "Let's go."

They chivvied all the children down the tunnel, carrying the ones too small to otherwise keep up. The mood was tense, but not nearly as bad as it could have been. Math had the sense that the children were feeling pretty good about themselves: they'd *rescued adults*. Heady stuff, for a group of kids who wanted to be heroes when they grew up.

The tunnel led up a flight of stairs and took several sharp turns before arriving at another stairway. It was marked by a distinct change in character and construction, newer than the imperial palace.

Math found himself drawing a mental map of their progress and frowned.

"Stop," he told them.

The kids did, although their eyes were full of questions.

Math crouched down in front of the empress. "Your Majesty, does this tunnel lead to the Idallik cenobium?"

Tanxi inhaled sharply.

"The top floor. But no one will be there," Empress Asali told him. "No one will expect us to be there, either."

Math smiled. "Very smart, Your Majesty." He looked at the rest of the children, each in turn. "You all need to be quiet, though."

Iduan huffed and crossed her arms. "Don't treat us like amateurs."

"I wouldn't dare," Math agreed seriously. "Come on."

The stairway ended at a small, unassuming wooden door. Math lowered the light levels on his summoned spell and stepped out into the room. One by one, he helped the children and his sister exit.

The door slammed shut and locked without Math touching it, and someone spelled a strong, bright white light. Out of the corner of his eye, he saw his sister summon her sword.

"Now, now," Commander Talu said. "We really don't have time for that."

Talu and a dozen Idallik Knights waited for them.

BETRAYAL

Math summoned his shield immediately.

Oddly, though, the knights didn't close, although perhaps that wasn't so odd considering they were facing off against two adults and thirteen children, some as young as three, one of whom was the imperial empress. If they wanted to make sure Asali wasn't harmed, a little discretion would be necessary.

A logical explanation, but it rang false. The knights weren't hanging back in the hopes of a peaceful surrender. They were *distracted*. Three of them weren't paying attention to Math or Tanxi at all, but stood by a window, curtain drawn aside to stare down at the street. There were knights covering the doors, knights watching out the other windows. One woman sat at a table, wincing as another bandaged her arm.

Math wasn't positive just how much time had passed since he last saw the man, but he really didn't think it could've been more than thirty minutes.

What on earth had happened in the last thirty minutes?

Commander Talu had aged *years*. He stared at Math with an expression carved from stone: stubborn, angry, and yet somehow also resigned.

Math had grown up around the man his whole life. He knew him, or thought he did.

He understood that expression.

Something had gone wrong, and Math didn't think it was his almost-escape.

"What *happened*?" Math asked, wary.

Talu's jaw worked against his throat. His lips were such a tight, angry line they were almost invisible. He held up a finger. "Listen."

Math did. At first, his mind refused to comprehend what he was hearing. Hard bangs, too sharply pitched to be exploding bombards, too tightly packed together to be someone hitting a barred gate with a battering ram.

But it was a sound he'd heard before. Just that morning, in fact.

Completely ignoring the danger, Math dismissed his shield and rushed to a window.

Not one of the knights made a move to stop him.

Math gazed out the window and felt his breath shudder in his chest, like the air itself was trying to retreat, hide.

Kaliri soldiers were advancing—on the palace, and on the cenobium.

More Kaliri soldiers than he could count. More than this city could withstand.

Math circled the proper spells, sharpened his vision, and confirmed his worst fears: they were, all of them, using Kaliri long arms.

Math turned and stared at his former commander.

"They told me they'd be sending thirty people to attack," Talu explained in a dull, flat voice.

"Someone decided to add some zeros to that number," Math replied. He felt sick, and he took no joy at all in being right.

Talu deserved everything that was about to happen to him, but the rest of the city didn't.

"I don't understand how they got so many people inside—"

"Weren't you listening?" Math snapped. "I told you! I told the entire Council of Commanders! I just watched you activate a dead gate portal. Are you really naive enough to think that was the only one? That Sanistral didn't have other missing pieces he gave to other agents?"

"Control yourself—" one knight chided.

"Fuck controlling yourself!" Math snapped. The last thing he wanted to hear from these damn hypocrites who ranted at, betrayed, and murdered people was that *he* needed to control himself.

"Math! Language!" Iduan chided.

Math let out a shocked laugh and tilted his head in acknowledgment of her scolding. He stopped smiling when he turned to face Talu. "I warned you," he repeated.

"The Kaliri don't have the infrastructure, the industrial capacity—"

"But Sanistral does!"

"I just couldn't imagine the Kaliri putting themselves so fully under the control of another sovereign nation." He sounded like he was in shock, still trying to rough out the shapes of his own failure.

"He's a grim lord," Math growled. "They literally worship him as one of their *gods*."

A little girl's voice interrupted everyone. "That doesn't matter."

Math turned to face Asali. "No, I suppose it doesn't."

She nodded at him, but kept her attention focused on Talu. "What are you going to do? Why are you here?"

"I need to know where the regent is," Talu said.

Empress Asali's expression turned obstinate. "No."

"You're a little girl. You don't know what needs to be—"

Math could've told the man that was the wrong tactic.

"No!" Asali said in a louder voice.

A sharp, loud sound rang out, accompanied by the sound of breaking glass. A small burst of plaster rained down dust from the ceiling. Several knights jumped back away from the windows.

They all paused, but no more shots rang out, at least not specifically at the cenobium. Maybe someone had seen a flash of armor and tried for a lucky shot. Maybe it had just been a stray lead ball.

"We can't stay here," Tanxi said. No one disagreed with her. The Kaliri were marching on the palace, but it was unlikely they'd ignore the Idallik headquarters.

Math turned back to Talu. "Why do you want the regent?"

Talu bared his teeth. "I am not a traitor, Mathaiik."

Math stared. From off to the side, Tanxi let out a single, mocking laugh.

"I would never harm the empress. I was doing this because—"

"Don't," Math interrupted. "Just don't. I am not interested in your excuses. Just answer the damn question."

Talu's jaw tightened. "There's a command structure problem."

Of course, there was.

Tanxi snorted. "What does that even *mean*?"

Math curled his lip. "It means he can't ask for aid from the other cenobiums—because he killed their commanders. The Order has no authority over the army, and anyone who had that authority at the palace is dead."

Math almost laughed. Sanistral had said the Idallik Order wouldn't be a problem.

He'd been right.

"Except for the regent," Talu said stiffly. Even saying it looked like it hurt.

"Fine," Math said. "That fits with our plans nicely. But you don't get to come with us. Once we're outside Old Town, our two groups part ways."

Talu said nothing for several seconds and then shook his head. "No."

"No?" Math raised an eyebrow.

Talu's expression turned obdurate. "No. We're not leaving. My people and I will hold them off while you get the children out."

Math paused. "You know what those weapons do."

"I'd rather meet the Tri-Mother shot from the front than the back." Talu stood, gestured for the other knights to fall in next to him. He held up his chin as he seemed to dare Math to say something. "I will not be hanged."

A better man than Math might have forgiven him then, given Talu a pardon. Maybe Talu was even expecting it.

Math said nothing. He just picked up little Jura and walked out.

PLANT

The next ten minutes involved a lot of noise, a lot of running, a lot of ducking behind buildings and down alleys.

By the time they made it to New Town, Tanxi and Math were the only adult Idallik Knights with the group. Math hadn't kept track of where he'd lost their escorts.

He didn't care. The children were safe. That was all that mattered.

The streets were a chaotic mess as people rushed about, trying to find loved ones or collect their belongings or warn their neighbors that the Kaliri were just a few blocks up the road. They played hide-and-seek for several blocks, avoiding the invaders except for the one time when a Kaliri who'd wandered off for some fun looting rounded the wrong corner. Math discovered that his shield could, in fact, stop Kaliri long arms and that such weapons were just as good at blocking Tanxi's Sun sword as anything else.

That is to say, not good at all.

Finally, they reached the address where Tanxi said the regent's matching necklace could be found. The building seemed innocuous enough. It looked like a hotel. Then he noticed several people leaving the building who seemed to be in an understandable hurry to be anywhere else. Some of them had been dressing as they ran.

"Yup," he said. "That's a brothel." He put a hand out to stop Jaiik from walking forward. "You want to watch the kids while I go—?"

"I don't think so," Tanxi told him, rolling her eyes. "*You* watch the children. I've got this." Without waiting for his response, she walked inside.

"What's a brothel, again?" Iduan asked. She had her hands crossed over her chest in her most stubborn "I want something" pose. "I'm older now. You have to tell me."

Math turned to make sure that Tanxi had already left before he turned back to the group. "It's a sex thing," he told them.

"Eww," was the universal response. Or almost universal response.

Jaiik looked like he wanted to go exploring immediately.

"You're still too young," Math told Jaiik. "Way too young."

Jaiik sighed and then shrugged. He didn't seem that upset, which only proved Math's point.

The boy was curious, not *interested*.

"It's a business," Empress Asali commented with great solemnity. "Auntie Imar says that it has to be monitored carefully, or people act weird."

"I imagine she's right," Math agreed. He tried not to be distracted, but he felt a sense of wrongness coming from Kai through their link. She felt... numb. Which scared him more than pain would have.

Math had no idea how long Sanistral's ritual would take. His gut told him he was running out of time.

Fortunately, making sure a baker's dozen of children didn't wander off or get into trouble took all his focus and attention, so he didn't have any left to brood.

A side door opened. Tanxi and a cloaked figure who pulled back her hood to reveal Imar Shovan ushered them inside. To Math's surprise, Asali didn't immediately become a sobbing mess, but held herself primly while gracing her regent with a solemn nod. She seemed surprised when Imar Shovan pulled her into a tight hug.

Then the regent stared at Math and shook her head. "I thought I told you to wait for me?" She held out a hand. "Never mind. Probably as well you didn't. Now explain everything."

They discovered that Imar Shovan was already engaged in organizing a defense of the city, because she had ears and was just as capable of hearing the loud volleys of black-powder weapons discharge as anyone else. Math and Tanxi filled the regent in on everything that happened at the palace, Talu's betrayal, and the Kaliri's betrayal in return.

The "brothel" was a cover for one of the regent's intelligence hubs. Imperial agents surrounded them. Math didn't doubt that the imperial armies were already on the move. It wouldn't be easy—not with the Kaliri having those weapons and most of the Idallik Order members in Bashan being either dead, traitors, or dead traitors—but it was possible. There was also the matter of the Idallik cenobiums outside of Bashan. Math expected to see whole swaths of Idallik Knights arriving as soon as the messages were received and magic would allow.

None of which would be in time to stop Sanistral's ritual.

"We need to find the Queen of Oaks," Math said.

Regent Shovan eyed him coolly. "And do you have any idea how to do that?"

Math nodded grimly. "Yeah, I know exactly how."

He reached into a pouch, pulled out an acorn he'd taken earlier that day, and handed it to his sister.

DIPLOMACY

The Queen of Oaks's location came as such a shock that Tanxi recast the spell three times. Each time, the answer was the same.

She was already inside the capital city.

In hindsight, Math wasn't sure why he'd been surprised. The Queens were sorceresses in their own right. They were smart, and they paid attention to their enemies. The forces who had killed the Queen of Ashes had come from Bashan.

Of course the Queen of Oaks had gone there.

If anyone had noticed a giant oak tree springing up in the middle of Brightstar Park, no one thought it a matter worth reporting. The citizens might have even thought this sudden case of surprise ancient oak was connected to the upcoming anniversary celebrations.

The hardest part had been convincing everyone else to let him go alone.

"Absolutely not," Tanxi had said. "What if something goes wrong? What if the negotiations fall through or she loses her temper?"

"If the negotiations fall through or she loses her temper, I honestly don't know how you'd help."

Tanxi summoned her sword. "Those trees still burn."

It was even tempting. Sanistral needed the Queen alive, after all. Or at least, he'd claimed such. If it turned out that he'd been lying, then they would have lost their potentially most valuable ally.

If a grim lord was the only thing the Parnathi feared, the reverse also seemed true.

"No, Tanxi. I have to do this. It can't be anyone else."

They tried to argue. Finally, Math had resorted to appealing to the regent.

Imar Shovan had simply nodded in his direction, touched him on the shoulder, and said, "Good luck."

Math went to Brightstar Park alone.

The closer he drew to the giant tree in the center, the less it looked like an oak tree. Something about it didn't feel right. The tree was also damaged in exactly the way he would've expected, given the branches that Talu had presented to the grim lord. High winds or some equivalent violent force had ripped away several branches, nowhere to be found on the nearby grounds. The damage revealed soft white tissues and odd green sap. The bark cracked with black lines, as though something corrosive was spreading inward.

Math had seen optical illusions formed from the random shapes on trees that looked like faces or old men or people trapped just under the bark. This time, it didn't seem to be an optical illusion. He felt certain the woman he saw in the tree was really there. She could move if she desired.

Something was wrong.

Her leaves were changing color, falling off, even as he watched. A darkening blight was spreading out from the site of her injury.

Sanistral had mentioned a curse.

As he stepped forward, he heard a rustling noise. He stopped. The rustling did not.

Huraiik crawled out from behind a bush.

Except this wasn't Huraiik anymore. Math could tell right away. There wasn't an ounce of recognition in his eyes as he stared at Math. He seemed feral.

More rustling. More vine people came out, crawling out onto limbs or squatting among the roots. Math recognized far too many: Captains Rabu, Yihura, Qin. No small number of Idallik Knights. One face stopped him cold—Catimus Abhigan. His features were intact, his eyes empty as he stared at Math. He was a plant-made puppet with no spark of memory and no more intelligence than a clever dog.

So, finally you have come. Far too late.

Her voice in his head was the same one he'd heard before. Her tone, though—if such a term could describe a message sent without spoken words—was much more bitter.

"I was scared," Math said. "I didn't know why you wanted to talk to me."

Nothing answered him except the chirp of birds and rustle of leaves, the startling interruptions of black-powder reports echoing through the city. Not one of the vine people—and certainly not the Queen herself—seemed to understand him.

Math sat down in front of the tree and tried sending back a message. His was admittedly a crude, awkward attempt, ugly compared to the grace of the Queen's mental prose.

You scared me. I felt threatened. I ran.

He felt her surprise. Not just surprise, but shock. That he would be afraid of her wasn't just strange; it was utterly incomprehensible. How could he possibly fear her?

Math didn't understand. He tried to communicate that. He didn't think he succeeded.

He paused to glare at her drones, bitterly resentful of the empty shells that they'd become.

I need your help, he told her.

Her answer was immediate and angry. He saw the bombard explosion, felt the searing pain of her own injury, experienced the horror of the Ash Queen's death.

The images were rapid-fire lightning, but if he had to translate them into words, into comprehensible language, the message was easy enough to understand.

Where were you when I needed yours?

Of course she was angry.

She'd watched a sister die that morning. Many of the lives in her "forest" seemed to be fugitive, disposable, but not all. Certainly not the mother trees.

I didn't understand that you were asking for help. Huraiik never explained.

Possibly because the mother trees never explained it to any of the earlier versions of plant-Huraiik. She may have thought it was too obvious to require an explanation. What other motive could she possibly have for wanting to speak with a human?

Her emotions jumbled. He saw flashes of images that made no sense.

Tri-Mother help him, this wasn't working.

Maybe if he'd come the first time Huraiik had offered, the vine man could have acted as a translator before his own memories and skills drained away. But Math hadn't, and now they didn't have the time. They didn't even have the time for the Queen to grow someone new.

Either he figured something out fast or he'd have no choice but to take Sanistral's suggestion and . . .

He didn't know how that would work. Could he join their collective, their "forest," without dying himself first? Never mind that dying didn't really fit in with his goals.

They just didn't have the *time*.

Math walked under the Queen's canopy, uncertain that she'd allow it, relieved when she did. He sat down above her roots, although he wasn't positive that she had them. She only looked like a tree.

He placed his palms against the damp earth, tried not to think about tiny spores and sprouts, little vines, growing from his hands, his arms, down into the ground. It felt too intimate.

Math felt it when he made contact.

His mind filled with colors, with smells and tastes, with sensations and experiences older than words.

PATHWAYS

Math found himself lost in a mental maze for the third time in his life. This time, it was one of his own creation.

Math's life appeared before him in disjointed flashes that moved so quickly, he could barely place the location, the event, the feelings involved before events had already moved on to the next scene. After a time, he came to realize that the scenes were not haphazard but followed branches of experience—the last time Math held a sword, followed by all the times he'd held one before that, all the way back to him as a child, holding a practice blade for the first time. How one weapon had led to many weapons, to armor, to horseback riding. The same pattern followed for every skill he'd ever known, for learning to speak, learning to read, learning to walk.

Then followed emotions: jealousy, pride, ambition, hate, anger . . . fear . . . except here, things did not follow through to the beginning. The path ended in a snarl, a tangle of impassable bramble and thorns. Love and a whole slew of more positive emotions swirled around Kai before gliding across multiple friends, the children, his sister, but eventually this, too, moved too quickly from his path.

The Queen of Oaks was tracing along the pathways of his mind as if they were roots, digging into all his thoughts and experiences, each time stopping at the unassailable tangle of his earliest memories.

Was she trying to understand humanity? If so, he wondered why she hadn't tried this with any of the others she'd absorbed.

Then he thought: maybe she had.

Again and again, they returned to the briar. Math knew what lay beyond it and he had no desire to see it, to remember it.

His opinion meant nothing.

With each dead end, Math felt her frustration grow. Math found himself detached from the experience, from the emotions involved, viewing it all as if these were a stranger's memories.

Last, she traced magic. Every spell learned, every manifestation of belief. Here, too, he felt her frustration, her annoyance at every time the Idallik Order had taught him to apply arbitrary rules to something they didn't comprehend.

And it was here, when she reached the same tangle, that she was not stopped, because it was the tangle she was tracing, and not what lay beyond it.

The whole twisted knot untangled and fell apart.

His detachment went with it.

Math remembered everything: a childhood riddled with pain and terror. He remembered parents who had been too angry and frustrated and ultimately afraid to see him as something worth protecting. He remembered beatings and so-called discipline and punishments meted out at the barest of excuses.

He remembered his only solace being the woods, the flowers that would bloom for him, the trees that would press their branches against his hair. The woods had loved him, even if his parents . . .

Even if his parents had not.

He couldn't remember what had provoked them the last time. Probably he'd never known. Just that his parents had both been too angry and too loud, animalistic in their savagery. He'd been thrown against the anvil of the forge so hard he'd broken his arm, and his mother had grabbed a hammer and—

The plants had saved him.

All his plants and more. Every plant in the garden, the roses, the jasmine in the window boxes. Trees had grown in seconds, tearing back the roof of the house and the back of his father's skull with equal ease. His mother had bled to death, impaled by foot-long rose thorns.

Math hadn't understood what was happening—except part of him had understood exactly what was happening. His parents had convinced themselves that he was a monster, a grimmock, a horror ultimately responsible for all their suffering. Maybe they hadn't planned on killing him, but the result would've been the same.

His sister was wrong. He appreciated her faith in him, her adamant belief in his innocence, but it had never been about guilt or innocence. It had been about survival. Even if Math had been too young to understand, the part of him that resonated so strongly with trees, flowers, and every other kind of green and deadly thing had understood the lesson perfectly.

That part hadn't hesitated.

The rest of him had hid under his bed, sobbing, until two days later when an Idallik Knight—a much younger Izhiik Talu, in fact—had coaxed him out and returned with him to the cenobium.

Do you understand? The Queen of Oaks almost sounded tender.

No, he told her honestly. He blinked open his eyes to find himself still sitting in the park, underneath her branches. Tears slid down his face, dripped from his chin.

They'd reached an equilibrium. They spoke each other's language with perfect comprehension.

History never repeats, but certain shapes, certain roles, certain seasons come in cycles.

I still don't understand.

She was being very patient with him. *In another cycle, you did not exist. Instead, we did.*

That seemed like an obvious statement. So obvious that he felt sure he was missing the point.

He tried to work it out. *So if I'd been born in your cycle, I would've been . . . ?*

One of us.

I'm not . . . He swallowed.

We thought it would not matter if we used the animals of this time to remake our species. What were they except flesh? Parts of us are as well, or something close.

But it does matter.

It does matter, she mournfully agreed. *The lives of this age cannot be taken whole into our forest. They do not stay. They become puppets, and we did not want puppets. We wanted our children back.*

You can't force . . . He inhaled deeply. *What did you expect? You can't force people to love you.*

He scowled to himself. She didn't understand.

Maybe she *couldn't* understand.

You, though . . . you are what we could have been. If we'd been born here, now, in this age. You would be a father of trees, instead of a mother. Awaken whole forests, give life to countless young. You might still. The plants you left behind in your sprouting place are no longer simple plants, and their intelligence does not fade.

Why . . . why me, though? Why am I like this?

Do not assign rules to children of the Green. Perhaps it was proximity to where we slumbered. Perhaps every Green cycle will contain something like us. The random seed that finds fertile soil.

Just a new variety. Pure wild luck. No doubt there would be more people like him in the years to come.

He laughed harshly, thinking of the absurdity of thinking of himself as some new strain of vegetable.

You know what grim lords are. I know you do. And there's one who is trying to . . . tie you . . . to what you call the Green. Shape you into a kind of avatar. Except it's a trap. I'm not sure exactly what kind. I only know he wants to absorb the power of wild magic—of the Green—or destroy it entirely.

He's a fool.

The danger is real.

I know it is. But you cannot remove death from life, or life from death, without destroying both. Name for me one being, one creature, one blade of grass that has not required something else to die so it might live. All that lives, kills. All that dies, gives life. We grow in soil made of corpses and decay, we return to that soil with our own deaths. This grim lord is a fool.

The certainty in her voice was comforting. It also made him fear she was underestimating the problem.

Except she wasn't done.

That does not mean he cannot do it. Fools can cause great harm.

Math grimaced. *He has some of your branches. He said he would use them to put a curse on you, so you'd have to go to him or die. And I don't know what to do.*

Yes, you do. You've known for some time.

He really couldn't hide anything from her, could he? *Is killing you really the only option?*

You don't need to kill me. I'm already dying.

Math honestly didn't know how he felt about that. Disturbed, certainly.

It didn't feel like victory.

That won't stop him, the Queen of Oaks said. *Nothing in your memories tells me that I alone must become this avatar. Sanistral himself said it didn't have to be me.* The end of a branch brushed against the top of his head.

He shuddered. *So if you die before he finishes the ritual, then he just switches targets, and if you die after, he wins.*

Yes, the Queen of Oaks agreed.

If we keep you from dying . . .

You cannot. And I am overdue.

Math turned over, sat down with his back against her tree trunk. The park was lovely, and in the distance, he could see the rest of Bashan.

Parts of the city were on fire.

I can think of one possible solution, the Queen said.

He turned his head toward her trunk. *Yes?*

I am one of the mothers. What power and nourishment I have is shared with my children, and they feed me in turn. He can give me this power, but he cannot make me keep it.

Math let his head fall back against the tree. *You think you could pass along the position to one of your children?*

No. I told you. These are not . . .

He felt her grief. Worse, he felt her loneliness. Each new mind leached of its personality and memories had torn at her like an open wound. She hadn't thought she was killing humans. She'd been trying to adopt them.

Oak had not saved her people, Kaiataris had told him. Only herself and her sisters.

Now she was full of the most bitter regret.

None of these sprouts are my children. We even tried your sprouts, but they could not find good soil.

Math shuddered. It wouldn't have been difficult for her to take human children. He forced himself not to think about it.

They all leave me, their minds falling away like leaves. None of them could handle that much power. None of them are strong enough. They would burn.

Math exhaled, remembering his own experiences in that area. *If your sisters were still alive . . .*

They are not.

I'm sorry. The grief of knowing they'd been so close to a solution tasted bitter in his mouth.

Sorrow is unnecessary. One hope remains.

As no other names had come up during their entire conversation, it wasn't difficult to connect those dots. *You can't mean me.*

You have the potential.

I'd burn too, he protested.

Not if you stood proud at the center of the forest. Not if you became my child, my heir. Not if you took my place when I am gone.

But I'm not one of your children. You said I'm not.

You could be.

He didn't understand, and then he did. All he had to do was let her in. This time, there would be no force—only consent. A willing version of what she had done to Huraiik, to all the others. Let her in and let her remake him into something inhuman, a Parnathi. A child who would not fight her, who loved her as much as she would love him.

And who she would love enough to die for.

But it would also mean . . .

Math had told himself this was about stopping Sanistral—and it was. But that wasn't the whole truth. Some foolish part of him had clung to the hope of a miracle: that he might somehow win not just the day, but a future. That if he fought hard enough, was clever enough, brave enough, the world would reward him with more than survival. That Math wouldn't have to lose Kai. That they might somehow walk away from the wreckage, hand in hand, toward something better.

But this?

There could be no happy ending here.

He wouldn't just be someone who looked human most of the time, a few wayward weeds and flowers notwithstanding. He would be a Parnathi, and every single time Kai looked at him, she'd be looking at her family's murderers.

If Math took the Queen's deal, then he'd be saving Kai at the cost of never being able to be with her. Even if she survived Sanistral, even if he stopped the ritual, at the end of it he would truly be something alien.

Not human, not even a grimmock.

If he wanted to save Kai, he would have to give her up forever.

He made his choice.

GOD

Math learned more about wild magic in the first five minutes of his existence as Oak's child than he had in all the twenty-two years before.

He couldn't blame the Idallik Order for trying to contain a wild talent—but he could never return to them, either.

For so many reasons.

Traveling back to the palace was easy. They didn't travel over the earth but under it, emerging near the palace.

The sun was setting and everything was chaos.

Sanistral had not been idle. He had reassembled another transport pattern on the roof, using it to bring in an army from Lomar to guarantee that no one could disturb the ritual.

As said army consisted entirely of the dead, they were doing a good job of it.

Fortunately for everyone, Sanistral was still bound by all the difficulties of being a graven wizard in a world where such power was dying. He could and did reanimate anyone so foolish or unlucky as to die within the boundaries of his domain in the palace, but most of the fighting was happening outside on the streets.

There, it was mostly Idallik Knights and Rokasmaa soldiers facing off against Kaliri invaders, but there were far more Kaliri wild mages than Idallik Knights. With the addition of the deadly black-powder weapons, the battle did not seem to be moving in Rokasmaa's favor.

Math had no idea if reinforcements from the other cenobiums had already arrived. He prayed to the Tri-Mother that they had not, because if such help had already come, it was also leaking blood into the streets.

With no small amount of difficulty, Math forced himself to focus on his own battles.

On Sanistral.

Finding him was easy. Sanistral wanted to be found, or rather, he wanted to be found by the Queen of Oaks.

The entire top of the palace—normally a rooftop garden—had been cleared of all plants and converted into a ritual site, with a speed that made

Math suspect such had been its original intended use. Math saw something else familiar too: all the corpses from the pyramid back in Lomar had been relocated.

Math understood their purpose now. Sanistral had his own equivalent of the Queen's forest children, except Sanistral's had been crafted from the cursed corpses of every graven wizard foolish enough to trust him.

Somewhere out in the world was a tablet graved with the gray sigils that ensured that Sanistral would continue to be mobile, continue to think, continue to function, even while dead. Sanistral wouldn't be foolish enough to carry that tablet on his person.

Kai stood next to her former mentor, looking exactly the same as when Math had last seen her. She held herself with statue stillness, but he could see no sign that Sanistral had done the same thing to her as he had to the other graven wizards. They reached a point in the ritual where Sanistral pulled power through his network of unwilling donors. While Sanistral leached his energy from them, Kai lifted her hand and gave him her own contribution.

She was helping Sanistral. Even through their bond, Math couldn't tell if she did so willingly.

Math pulled himself up onto the roof and advanced.

No one tried to stop him. No one attacked him or fired so much as a single shot in his direction.

Why would they? He looked like a giant oak tree.

He only *looked* like a giant oak tree. In truth, he was hidden behind an illusion, less a trick of the mind than a trick of light. Math knew how Sanistral liked to set up his defenses. Any attempt to magically influence Sanistral's perceptions within his domain was futile.

So Math didn't. He used his magic to shape how light reflected off Math himself.

The illusion wasn't perfect, but Math hoped that Sanistral would be too distracted by the dragon to notice that the giant tree walking into his meticulously crafted trap was not the Queen of Oaks.

The Queen of Oaks? She was the dragon.

Oak trees were beautiful, but not precisely the most mobile or appropriate creatures for a battlefield. They had both agreed that all eyes needed to be on her. Personally, Math also suspected that she wanted her last moments of existence to be glorious.

And oh, how they would be.

Dragons weren't creatures of myth to her, even if they had only existed in children's stories for all of written history. She'd grown in an age when they'd ruled the land and skies.

She made an excellent dragon.

The signs of her arboreal nature were still present if one paid attention to the way her horns were branches or the thornlike shape of her claws. Most probably only noticed that her scales were shiny and hard, shifting between brown and green, and her tail was fast enough and sharp enough to kill a dozen men with a single flick.

Sanistral saw her and began laughing.

"Beautiful!" the necromancer announced, turning to the giant tree now standing on the roof and bowing. "Truly magnificent. I cannot hope to match such splendor, but I hope you appreciate my paltry efforts, Your Majesty."

It seemed like the grim lord had fallen for their ruse, but Math's sense of triumph was short-lived.

Boxes that had been scattered around the rooftop opened. Corpses spilled out. Many corpses. Math could only guess that they numbered in the thousands.

The bodies began assembling themselves into a giant.

Careful, Math warned as the giant stepped too close to an attacking battalion, killing them instantly. It didn't crush them so much as pull the life out of them.

He couldn't help but flinch when the undead conglomerate impacted against the Queen's scaled side, but fortunately its deadly touch seemed proportional to its victim's mass. The attack left nasty blackening gouges in the Queen's scaly sides, but was incapable of killing her in a single hit.

Eventually, the damage would prove too much, but they weren't at that point yet.

The undead-body giant stepped down into the street, swinging a fist consisting of dozens of corpses intertwined with each other, and connected with the dragon's side. The Queen staggered, crashing into the wall of a nearby building and causing the front of it to collapse in a shower of broken stone and mortar dust.

The Queen reached out with a taloned hand, each claw the size of a thirty-year-old pine, and ripped the hand of the giant free, flinging it away even as the necrotic flesh blackened and withered her claws. Sadly, the giant neither bled nor was particularly inconvenienced by the attack, shifting more bodies from the dead squad of soldiers, causing a ripple through its form as new bodies displaced older ones. The hand regrew almost instantly.

Unless she could rip the thing apart faster than it could keep replacing its parts, there was no way the Queen could win this fight. And already, even after only a couple of exchanged blows, much of her exterior was rotten, wilted.

While the two behemoths fought, Math advanced on the cursed tree branches floating above a glowing spectral pattern of graven magic. He didn't do so purely because it was the expected behavior. Math needed the Queen to live for long enough for Sanistral to complete his ritual.

Sanistral smiled indulgently at the scene before turning his attention to the oak tree on the roof. "I don't believe your dragon is going to win this," he told Math, "but I acknowledge it was a far worthier effort than I expected."

It was fortunate that Math's disguise required his silence, because he didn't know if he could have kept himself from saying something nasty.

Sanistral made a gesture—no, the gesture was a distraction. He touched a bracelet on his wrist. The curse pattern turned from silver to red and the Queen screamed in agony. Fortunately, Sanistral was facing the wrong way, so he hadn't been able to see that no blow from his giant had prompted that reaction. If Sanistral kept torturing the Queen like this, however, it was only a matter of time before he realized that he had the wrong Parnathi on his roof.

Math needed to do something about that.

To anyone watching, the oak tree would have seemed to bend over in a way impossible for oak trees. A set of branches bunched together in a manner suggestive of an arm slammed down against the stone-and-plaster roof of the palace.

Sanistral was unimpressed. "Centuries of gravings protect this place. You cannot hope to damage so much as a single speck of stone."

For obvious reasons, Math didn't correct him.

A mixture of hot mud and ash bubbled up from the surface of the roof, flowing with shocking speed over the plaster surface. The mixture raced toward the marble slab that Sanistral had engraved with the Queen of Oaks's curse prior to transferring it from Lomar to Bashan.

Math had to hand it to the man: he had a keen eye for craftsmanship. The engraving was an evil, twisted, and elegant creation; smooth, sharp lines carved deep into stone.

Sanistral scoffed as he saw what Math was doing. "You cannot remove a graving by covering it, or half the enchantments on this domain would have been erased by accident centuries ago." With a contemptuous flick of his wrist, he activated some unseen graving on his person.

Fire raced across the roof of the palace and burned up Math's legs.

The only thing that saved Math was the root-and-vine scaffolding he'd grown to lift himself high enough—and make him weigh enough—to mimic the Queen's impact. The false limbs shielded him just long enough to finish his own spell.

That spell summoned a lahar of fine, hot mud that flowed into every elegant, curved line of the marble slab holding the Queen's curse. Then Math transformed all that mud into marble again. Not just any marble, but the same marble as the original block.

He knew better than to try to damage Sanistral's graved work.

Instead, he healed it.

The cursed faltered, failed.

Kaiataris watched it all, expressionless. She had never looked so much like a statue as she did just then.

The Queen let out a scream of victory just seconds before the massive ball of undead bodies, now resembling nothing so much as a sinuous, six-legged worm creature, leaped at her from a rooftop, sending them both tumbling down the street. The worm left a trail of broken bodies as everyone it touched—everyone who wasn't a very large dragon—died instantly.

The passage of that death worm probably killed more people than all the fighting previously.

As Math straightened, Sanistral scowled and said, "Enough!" He crossed over to the largest ritual circle—the one that Math knew was meant for the ascension spell. "Let us finish this," he said to Kai.

Kai nodded once at her mentor and teacher, then stared to the side, straight at Math. In theory, she didn't know it was him, but through their bond, Math felt a flicker of sorrow, threaded with quiet resolve.

Math wanted to scream for her to stop, but he couldn't.

She began the working.

Meanwhile, the Queen of Oaks leaped into the sky, unfurling wings of woven branch and frond. It wasn't enough to allow her true flight, but she could glide, banking sharply around the vast plaza in front of the palace, away from the undead abomination.

The corpse giant humped in on itself, becoming a ball with dozens of legs, and scuttled toward her even as she landed on the roofs of several buildings across the plaza. The bodies on the undead creature's "feet" grabbed sills and pipes and ledges, allowing the thing to "roll" up the side of the building.

The Queen leaned over the side and vomited forth a torrent of hot, sticky sap followed by another of sharp slivers of wood. Had the bodies of the giant creature still been alive, it would have been a devastating attack. Instead, it merely slowed the creature momentarily before it could absorb the bodies covered in sap and replace them with clean ones from deeper inside itself.

The monster heaved itself onto the roof, and the battle resumed.

Math bent over again. Sanistral saw the motion, realized that it must have meant the "Queen" intended to try the same trick a second time, and triggered a spell of his own. A silvery iridescent wall sprang up around the circle, enclosing Sanistral, Kai, and all of Sanistral's murdered peers.

The mud that Math conjured splashed against the magical barrier like floodwaters against a stone levy—loud, violent, and utterly useless. Math suspected there was very little that could penetrate that field while it was fully powered and intact.

Math also suspected that if Sanistral could have kept that field up for long periods of time, he'd have done so at the start of the fight, rather than waiting until now. This was a last line of defense, a way to buy the last few valuable seconds needed for Sanistral to finish the ritual and become a god.

Sanistral glared at Math, raised a hand, and triggered another spell.

For a brief second, Math didn't know what Sanistral had done. Then Math collapsed—still none the wiser. He didn't collapse because he was weak or injured, but because the plants underneath him had been crushed. It felt like a terrible pressure was bearing down on him, like some kind of invisible giant foot was slowly descending, trapping the air in his lungs, preventing his heart from beating. An invisible mountain was slowly crushing him.

It took everything Math possessed not to drop the illusion, but even so, he saw the form of it waver and shift in strange ways.

He's changed your gravity. The Queen of Oaks's voice sounded distant and faint. He didn't know which of them was the cause, but he didn't like it.

The Queen stripped the spell away like fog, although not without cost: her branch-like horns burned. That confused Math, because she should have been all but immune. Whether they were her children or simply her drones, the Queen still had a web of living beings spread out across a thousand acres of wilderness to quench any fires from reaching for too much wild magic, too quickly.

Math carefully pushed himself up on his root stilts. He didn't have to fake how tired he was, but it was absolutely vital that Sanistral think that even with the curse broken, the Queen of Oaks was all but dead. Too weak to defend herself against all the horrible onslaught of energy that would be released when the ritual finally caught.

Tragically, Math suspected that might still be true.

He reached the wall of energy and began smashing his fist into it like his father's hammer against the forge, each blow strengthened by magic into an earthshaking reverberation.

Sanistral glanced up at him and smirked.

"Too late."

RITUAL

The wall of energy vanished, replaced even as it fell by a giant column of scintillating light that shot up into the sky, large enough to encompass all of the palace. Math was blown backward. In the total whiteout of that light, he lost sight of Sanistral. He lost sight of Kaiataris.

Somewhere in the distance, simultaneously in his mind, Math both heard and felt the Queen of Oaks scream.

He tried to cushion the damage, save her from the fires of wild magic, but he realized too late that she was pushing him away. She had been the whole fight—throwing all of her resources into protecting him and leaving nothing for herself.

She had never planned to survive this fight, to be left with godlike power in a world without a single sister, with no family, with no people of her own. No people except for a single adopted child, whom she knew she would never really ever understand, but had decided to fiercely love.

Math fell to his knees on the roof as he felt her mind go quiet and still. The city trembled as, somewhere out in the city, the giant form of a dragon collapsed to the ground, dead. Math fought not to scream as the power that had seared through her leaped into him.

It wasn't fire, though. It felt like sunlight in his veins, at once hot and bright and powerful enough to light the whole world.

He closed his eyes, lowered his head to rest against the roof, and took a moment to mourn a mother he wished he could have known.

Then Math stood and faced Sanistral.

If the ritual had worked the way Kaiataris thought it might, then they had a problem, because although they'd kept Sanistral from becoming the all-powerful personification of both Order and Chaos, he'd still held on to Order. That was not insignificant, even assuming the current celestial alignment had left him weakened.

If they fought, they could cause inconceivable damage. So Math would have to make sure that if they did fight, it wasn't here in the city, or near any population center.

The grim lord still stood in the same place he'd been when Math had last seen him. He still looked exactly the same. Now, however, he stared at his own hand with what Math could only describe as a deeply bemused expression. He seemed to sense Math approaching, because the man murmured, "I thought it would feel different."

"Don't tell me it's not everything you wanted?" Math didn't bother hiding his contempt.

The fighting hadn't stopped, but its rhythm had changed. Wild magic burst in the distance like fireworks, pulsing like music through his blood.

Behind Sanistral, Kaiataris was still there, also standing where Math had last seen her. She looked . . .

She looked beautiful. Perfect and radiant and as cold as frozen stone. Underneath the surface, though, he felt the quiet blaze of her triumph.

In her hand, she clutched the bracelet that she'd taken back from him. As power sources went, its strength would have been insignificant for a fight like this, so why had she been using it?

That bracelet had two powers, didn't it? She'd said Math would only need the battery, because its second power, the ability to create or erase gravings, was unlikely to be any use to a wild mage.

Math glanced down at the ritual circle, still legible, if slightly melted. He had no idea how to read or understand the remarkably intricate markings.

Kai could, though. And now he saw it: she hadn't been *fueling* the ritual—she'd been rewriting it.

Math felt like laughing. He felt a surge of joy well up in him.

"Apologies, Kai. I'm a little slow, sometimes."

She inclined her head gracefully and smiled.

That smile made his heart sing, because at least she wasn't looking at him like he was a monster.

Sanistral's head snapped up. "Wait. Since when can you *talk*?"

Math dropped the illusion and had the roots and vines gently lower him to the ground. "I've always been able to talk. Many would argue I talk far too much."

Sanistral narrowed his eyes. "Who are you? And what happened to the Queen of Oaks?"

Standing behind Sanistral, Kai rolled her eyes.

"Aw, Sanis, don't you recognize me?" Math grinned impishly.

Math wasn't surprised. He probably wouldn't have recognized the plant version of Huraiik, either, if he hadn't grown up alongside the man.

"Who—Mathaiik Kaven?" Sanistral had finally made the connection. He frowned as he examined the newest and last Parnathi. "You did it? You joined the Queen's forest?" His frown deepened. "Where is she?"

"Dead."

Sanistral studied him. "She transferred her power to you."

"She did, indeed."

"Very well." Sanistral sniffed in a manner that suggested a metaphorical rolling up of his sleeves. "I've accomplished half my goals. Now I must simply deal with you."

Kaiataris's voice was even. "Sanistral, you'll do no such thing. It's over, and you are not the Avatar of Order."

The wizard turned back to her in surprise. "But the spell worked."

"Perfectly," she said as she stepped down from the ritual stone. "You made one mistake."

Sanistral's eyes narrowed. "And what would that be?"

"You left me alive," she explained. "You really should not have. I can only assume out of sentimentality, since I was willingly helping you, unlike the other, unfortunate members of our order." Kaiataris glanced at the gently writhing mass of undead wizards surrounding the stone. "That reminds me."

She didn't do anything, say anything, make any definitive motion. The cursed graven wizards stopped moving, anyway. Math knew that this time, they were finally at peace.

Math sat down on the edge of a rooftop planter that had been pushed to the side. In the distance, Kaliri weapons misfired. Closer, people gathered the wounded and the dead. There was no sign of the undead amalgam that Sanistral had created. The dragon form of the Queen of Oaks was already decaying at a decidedly unnatural rate, decomposing into a rich loamy soil, which would soon put forth bright green shoots of trees, weeds, and flowers.

Roses. He would definitely make sure there were roses.

He rested his chin on a raised knee. He'd meant to kill Sanistral, but . . .

Kai had it covered. It was her moment, anyway, considering everything that Sanistral had meant to her, versus what he'd become.

"How dare you," Sanistral sneered. He raised his hands, no doubt to trigger some graving.

Nothing happened.

Kai tilted her head to the side. "Is there a problem?"

"What did you do to my magic?" A hint of panic threaded through Sanistral's voice.

"Why would I allow you to have magic? That would be foolish of me . . . and I am *not* a fool."

The graven wizard turned grim lord gaped at her. "You usurped my ritual."

"Easily." She looked positively radiant in her serenity. "You have spent so long alone in a prison of your own making that you forgot you're not the only one who can grave." She glanced down at the pattern contemptuously. "All I had to do was add the metaphysical equivalent of a hyphen to the definition of 'recipient.' Not undead, but un-dead. And as I was the only living person connected to this side of the ritual . . ."

"How thoughtful of you," Sanistral growled, "to critique my work."

"You always said one should be magnanimous in victory."

Sanistral searched the rooftop for some last ploy, some way out of the situation. There was nothing to find. Even the ritual stone was now blank. All the gravings had vanished. Probably all the gravings in the entire palace had vanished.

Kai didn't need them.

"What will you do?" Sanistral finally said. "If you destroy me, all you'll do is prove that you're no better than me. That power is just as corrupting for you."

She raised a single, perfectly arched eyebrow. "I want to know why."

"Why?"

"Yes. Why? What reason have you for all that you've done? I do not refer to this ritual. I understand your motives in that, even if I don't agree with your methods or what you would have done with such power. I mean, why kill your fellow wizards, who trusted you. Why become a grim lord—if my suspicions are correct, the first grim lord, the one who convinced all others that this folly was rational. *Why?*"

"I didn't mean to," Sanistral admitted after an awkward pause. "I overreached, triggered enervation. I thought your plan was cowardice. That it would be better to dull the edge of the solstice's blade than go into hiding. I thought I had figured out a way. I was wrong."

Sanistral's eyes narrowed, and he swung out an arm to take in the entire city, probably the entire world. "You've seen them. They're nothing but animals, lacking all direction or wisdom, slaves to their emotions. The celestial polarities aren't a mistake, they are a test. A way of cleaning house of any race that doesn't deserve to pass. Leave them like this, and they'll destroy themselves."

"I understand," Kaiataris said gently. "One more question: Why did you keep me alive?"

"How could I destroy my greatest creation?" Sanistral said, sounding genuinely confused about the question. "I made you, and you were the only one who could ever keep up with me. You are a work of art."

"I am not a possession," Kai corrected. "And I would protest, too, that you did not create me, but I suspect you are incapable of reason on this subject, so I will simply say this: your hubris, arrogance, and megalomania have killed *millions*. You would have killed millions more. You are not capable of regret, only revision. The difference between us is that what you've done was atrocity and murder, whereas what I am doing is fixing a mistake." Kai let the hand fall, a curtain plummeting to the stage.

Sanistral dropped to the ground.

He never moved again.

Math didn't bother to check; he felt safe in assuming that the wizard was dead. For real, this time. Kai had stripped Sanistral of the magic that had kept him animate. In fact, every undead, anywhere, had just been stripped of the magic keeping them animate.

Math grinned at her. "Part of me wants to raise him from the dead just so I can watch you kill him again."

She threw him a dirty look. "I'd rather he stays where he is, thank you. The death knights were never meant to be eternal. Truthfully, he died fourteen hundred years ago." Her gaze then transformed into something softer . . . and sadder.

Oh. Right.

Math glanced at one of his hands. Distinctly green, and with a surface texture that seemed more like leaf than skin.

"It was the only way," he said, swallowing. "I had to become Parnathi. I guess this just makes my nonhuman status official."

"You're the Avatar of Chaos," she said, putting a hand to his cheek. "Of wild magic."

"Yeah."

She leaned over and whispered, *"Then you can take whatever form you desire, my love."*

Math felt a jolt of shock arc through him, from hair to toes. He laughed. "Don't I feel silly? One second." He concentrated on his hand, watched with pleasure as it shifted back to his normal brown color, with a more comfortably human skin texture.

Kai smiled at him and bounced her forefinger off the tip of his nose. "You gave yourself green eyes."

"Seemed only appropriate," Math admitted.

"I like it. You also removed your armor."

"It was starting to chafe."

She paused again, and he could feel her at the edges of his mind, filled with laughter and fierce bubbling joy no matter how even her expression looked on the outside.

"We're still linked." Kai's voice was full of wonder.

"I'm sure we could break it if we really wanted to, but—" He pulled her into his arms. "I admit I don't really want to."

Math kissed her. When they parted, Kai looked up at him. "He wasn't wrong about power, though. It is the worst sort of trap. Do you want to be a god?"

He chewed on his lip and thought it over.

"Not really?" Math frowned. "Besides seeming like a ton of work, I think I'd also be expected to let go of immediate worries and focus on the big picture. You know. All of a country, all of humanity, that sort of thing. I just want..." He swept out his arm in a more gentle mimicry of Sanistral's all-encompassing gesture, before bringing that arm in to caress Kai's cheek.

"You," he answered. "I want to be with you, and I want to raise a dozen plus one children, and I want to travel and do fun things and read *a lot* of books. So many books. And keep everyone from going insane and mutating into terrible things during the next magical solstice."

"Or dying during the one after that," Kai agreed. "I think we can manage that. We are much less likely to be worshipped as gods if no one knows that we're gods in the first place."

He started to protest that they weren't gods... and stopped.

Sanistral's ritual had worked. It had worked *perfectly*. If Math wanted, he could feel every single life form on the planet. He could change entire ecosystems, weather patterns, cause untold modifications in ways both small and profound. If he wasn't completely omnipotent, it was only because he shared the other half of that totality with Kai.

So maybe it was entirely possible—assuming one overlooked the lack of followers and tenets and anything resembling a moral system—that he might meet the definition of god. Demigod?

Ascended hero, at the very least.

So instead, he said: "You are right, as usual. So, what are you suggesting we do next, just walk downstairs, tell everyone we slew the big, evil villain, and get on with our lives?"

Kai pondered that. "Yes."

"Sure, why not? Keep things simple." He tilted his head to the side and made a face. "I'll give Commander Talu one thing: he is a survivor. He lives. *And* he's escaped."

"Has he escaped, though? Truly?" Her expression was innocent.

Math squeezed her hand. "Now that you mention it, no, I don't think he has. We'll add him to the list." He grinned. "After that... wanna fix magic?"

"Is that what we're calling it now?"

"I meant a celestial realignment of magical poles, but I like your idea better."

"I do believe if we do it right, it will make the heavens move."

He threw back his head and laughed.

ROOTS

By the time Math caught up with Izhiik Talu—no longer a commander, not officially—he was halfway to Vilsenor.

It was a smart choice. Kaliri was closer but between their betrayal of Talu and Talu's betrayal in return, odds were not good that Talu would've been welcome.

So, Vilsenor—locked in the most politely vicious of "border disputes" with Rokasmaa for the last fifty years.

He didn't make it.

Math whistled merrily as he walked into the clearing created as trees and grasses uprooted themselves and moved to the side. Only one tree remained, a juniper tree whose craggy, twisting branches now trapped a struggling Izhiik Talu in their grasp.

"Not too uncomfortable, I hope?" Math said to him. "I made sure they didn't hang you upside down. At your age, you probably would've had a stroke before I showed up."

"Math?" Talu stared at him in stunned shock. "How did you find me?"

"Is that really what matters right now?"

Only then did it seem to really occur to Talu that he might be in danger. He inhaled sharply and stopped struggling. "I never wanted to hurt you, you know. I only shot you because . . . because I knew King Sanistral would kill me if I didn't bring Kaiataris back, and even then, I made sure you didn't die! That has to mean something, doesn't it?"

Math stared at the man. He seemed older now, more worn. And he was sick. Talu didn't know it, but he had a degenerative heart condition that would kill him in a few years.

Math fixed it.

"Funny how everything you've done on my behalf has made me miserable," Math commented. "I was like a pet to you. A mascot. And if I was a little slow to train, that was fine. I still had my uses."

Talu forced a smile on his face as he strained at the branches holding him captive. "I've looked the other way for you all your life. Surely just once you can return the favor. Don't kill me!"

"Kill you?" Math smiled grimly. "Who said anything about killing you? I'm here to punish you, not *me*."

Talu sagged in relief. "Thank you. Just let me go and you'll never have to see me again."

If only that were true. It was the unfortunate side effect of what Math was now that it would be all too easy to see Talu, whenever the urge came to him.

"Not just yet," Math said. "Like I said, I am here to punish you. You hurt more people than me. You ordered the deaths of your own knights, Talu. And treason? Really?"

He swallowed visibly. "I told you, I had my reasons—"

"Would you like to hear something hilariously ironic?" Math asked.

The man closed his mouth, his expression wary.

"It goes like this: little Empress Asali is *Sun resonant*." Math waved a hand. "I think her parents must have known and that's why they left instructions to bring in another Sun-resonant person—Imar Shovan—as regent should anything happen to them. Someone had to train the next ruler of the empire, right?"

"You're joking," Talu wheezed.

"I'm not. Asali is Sun resonant and yet there is no way she was ever joining the Idallik Order, so I imagine in the next few years, we'd have seen a significant loosening of restrictions."

Talu's brows drew together, his expression trouble. "Would have seen?"

"Yeah. There's nothing gradual about this now, thanks to you. Rokasmaa disbanded the Order."

Talu's eyes closed in grief. Math understood. He hadn't celebrated either, even if the first words out of his mouth when Regent Shovan had asked how she could reward him had been: "Let me leave the Order."

The Order had raised him, broken him, and saved him by accident. Losing it felt like failure, like shame, but it had been rotten to the core: there'd been no saving it.

"Can you blame them?" Math asked. "It's the poorest-kept secret in the empire that an Idallik assassinated the old emperor and empress, and then you attempt a coup? And do it so disastrously that it results in the capital being invaded for the first time in centuries?" He continued, speaking right over Talu's attempt to interrupt him. "And don't give me that story about how you just wanted recognition. You wanted power. Power and wealth and your hand either on or behind the throne. Bad timing, old man." Math ordered the tree to lower Talu to the ground and release him, which it did.

Talu couldn't hide his surprise. "That's it? Your idea of punishment was a lecture?"

Math raised both eyebrows. "Are you complaining?"

"No, no, I—I'm just grateful."

"Don't be," Math said, his smile cold. "Because as it happens, no. Your punishment isn't just a lecture. It's a curse."

"—what?"

"A curse. You know, like in children's stories. Honestly, Sanistral gave me the idea. So here it is: nothing you do for your own advantage will ever succeed. If the truth would gain you admiration, no one will believe you. If a lie would gain you power, it will be as transparent as glass. Money will slip through your fingers, valuables will crumble to dust. No one will listen to your orders, no one will respect your wisdom. You have won yourself an ill wind that will affect you and you alone for as long as you live—and you're going to live for a very long time. *I will make sure of it.*"

Talu's eyes were wide, and his mouth dropped open in horror. Then—not unexpectedly—he gathered himself up. "You can't do that. No one is powerful enough to cast such a curse."

Technically, Talu wasn't wrong. It had taken Math *and* Kai to cook up this little gem.

Math just smiled. "If you'd like to test it, keep heading to Vilsenor and tell the soldiers at the first posting that you're requesting asylum." Math paused. "Actually, don't do that. You don't want to spend time in a Vilsenor prison at your age."

Talu's mouth quirked. "I have to hand it to you, my boy. You have learned to talk a good game, but I don't think—" He paused and stared at his hand, which was held out in a familiar pose, a pantomime that only made sense if one imagined Talu holding out a weapon.

For the first time since he'd been released from the juniper tree's embrace, true fear returned to Izhiik Talu's eyes.

"As a woman I admire said recently: Why would I leave you with your magic? That would be foolish, and I am not a fool. You can't cast spells anymore. You never will again." Math made a shooing motion with his hands. "Now be off with you. You've wandered into Souna territory and you are not Souna. You don't want them to find you here."

Talu's fear transformed into horror. He turned and ran.

The Souna would leave Talu alone. Math had already seen to it.

"I still would have killed him," Kai said as she became visible next to him.

Math took her hand and smiled.

"I know," he told her fondly, "but I'm not as nice as you."

ACKNOWLEDGMENTS

Bringing a novel into the world is never a solitary endeavor, and I am deeply grateful to the many hands and hearts who helped shape this one.

To my brilliant editorial team—**Stephanie Stein** and **Julianna Kim**—thank you for your insight, precision, and unwavering belief in this book. Your guidance was instrumental in honing the story to its finest edge. I'd also like to thank my copy editor, **Christina MacDonald**. Please let my terrible grammar be our little secret.

To **Katie Klimowicz**, whose jacket design so beautifully captured the spirit of the novel—thank you for giving the book an unforgettable first impression.

To **Rafal Gibek**, **Dakota Griffin**, and **Jacqueline Huber-Rodriguez**—thank you for shepherding this book through production with grace, clarity, and care.

To **Isa Caban**, for your thoughtful marketing efforts, and to **Sarah Weeks**, for your work in spreading the word—I am ever grateful.

To the leadership at Tor—**Claire Eddy**, **Will Hinton**, **Lucille Rettino**, and **Devi Pillai**—thank you for your support and vision throughout this journey.

And on a personal note, my deepest thanks to **Chris Lotts**, my incredible agent, for championing this book and helping me get here. Your faith means the world to me.

Most of all, thank you to my husband, **Mike**, for your unwavering love, encouragement, and belief in me. You are my greatest supporter.

ABOUT THE AUTHOR

Twice-nominated Astounding Award finalist Jenn Lyons lives in Atlanta, Georgia, with her husband, a rebellious cait sìth and a nearly infinite number of opinions on everything from Sumerian mythology to the proper way to make a martini. After thirty years as a graphic artist, art director and video game producer (in that order), Lyons now happily splits her time between game development and novel writing. Her geek roots run deep, beginning with first edition Dungeons & Dragons in grade school and continuing today with an ever-evolving roster of hobbies – recent obsessions include pyrography, stenography and medieval occult manuscripts.

jennlyons.com

@JennLyonsAuthor
@JennLyons

Discover *The Sky on Fire*, a dragon heist adventure full of magic, high stakes and revenge

'A spectacular and sexy fantasy heist story'
Freya Marske

'*The Sky on Fire*'s wily world-building is deeply enjoyable, and its plot races like wildfire atop wit and banter'
Kate Elliott